PRAISE FOR JEFF BUICK
AND *BLOODLINE*!

"Buick has created an intense, gut-twisting thriller with his brilliant debut. With characters modeled from real-life headlines, he gives the book depth and a life of its own."
—*The Best Reviews*

"*Bloodline* is an action-packed thriller...[that] starts faster than a racing car in a straightaway and never slows down. Jeff Buick is a writer with a great future ahead of him."
—Harriet Klausner

BREAK-IN

The intruder scanned the hard drive for Wes Connors's client's files. They were grouped together in a folder in Microsoft Word. Each client had a profile, including their address, phone number and why they had sought out the services of a private investigator. Most were local clients but a handful were from out of state. Attached to the client profile was an accounting sheet with detailed expense reports, billable hours and dates. The intruder switched his approach when he saw that Connors kept exact dates on when he worked for each client. He searched the client files for any customers with August 2005 dates. The search produced three names. He perused each of the files and sent them to the printer. Then he closed each file, shut down the computer and shifted his attention to the filing cabinets.

They were locked but it took him seconds to pick the lock and slide them open, one drawer at a time. He flipped through the files, looking for hard copy on the three clients Wes Connors had been working for during August. He found a single file for each client. Receipts were neatly filed in the folders and when he opened the third one he knew he'd hit pay dirt. Gordon Buchanan's file had a Visa receipt for an electronic ticket to Richmond dated August 31, just five days prior. And Connors had been in Richmond, poking into something that had ruffled some big feathers. The man replaced the files exactly as he had found them and quietly left the office, locking it behind him.

When he was on the street, two blocks away at his car, he made a phone call from his cell. "I think I've found what you want," he said.

Other *Leisure* books by Jeff Buick:

BLOODLINE

LETHAL DOSE

JEFF BUICK

LEISURE BOOKS NEW YORK CITY

To Ron and Nancy Buick

*My parents, who gave me
so much more than just life.*

A LEISURE BOOK®

September 2005

Published by

Dorchester Publishing Co., Inc.
200 Madison Avenue
New York, NY 10016

ISBN 0-8439-5578-3

The name "Leisure Books" and the stylized "L" with design are trademarks of Dorchester Publishing Co., Inc.

Printed in the United States of America.

Visit us on the web at www.dorchesterpub.com.

Special thanks to George Hunter, PhD

Department of Pharmacology
University of Edmonton

If the technical stuff is correct,
George gets the credit.
If it's wrong, the mistake is all mine.

1

A little bit of fear is a good thing.

The thought passed through Gordon Buchanan's mind as he gazed into the smoke from the approaching forest fire. The April sun was a hazy red ball, diffused and weakened by the floating ash. Six miles and closing quickly. Inside twenty-four hours, the flames would be licking at his timber concessions. Destroying the forest and costing him millions of dollars. No upside to the fire. None at all. And in forty-eight hours, it would be threatening his sawmill.

He glanced away from the incoming carnage as a voice, almost obscured by static, came over his two-way radio. One of the mill hands asking for him.

"This is Gordon," he said into the transmitter. "Go ahead."

"The forestry guys are here, Gordon. They want to speak with you."

"I'll be there in twenty minutes," he replied, and returned the walkie-talkie to his belt. The air was thick with smoke and ash, and his throat burned with each word he spoke and each breath he sucked in. He hailed a rugged-looking logger working the trunk of a sixty-foot Ponderosa pine with his chain saw and

1

pointed in the general direction of the sawmill. The man nodded, and Gordon jumped in his truck and steered onto the bumpy trail leading back to the mill.

Gordon Buchanan was in his domain—the forest. His father had worked with timber, and after his father had passed away at an early age, Gordon had followed on, building the business into a thriving sawmill. At forty-four, Buchanan was a self-made multimillionaire who preferred faded jeans and denim shirts to business casual. The leather on his steel-toed work boots was cracked and peeling. He wore no jewelry and seldom carried more than fifty dollars in his pocket. His face always had a tinge of red, either from the summer sun or the blustery winter winds that howled through the Montana forests. His face was well proportioned, with a long, sloping nose, bushy eyebrows framing intelligent brown eyes, and a high forehead with a full head of dark hair swept back in a permanent wave. At six-two and a hundred and ninety-five pounds, he was lean and powerful, something most women found attractive. That he was rich didn't hurt his appeal either. But to date, no woman had managed to get him in front of a justice of the peace, despite many trying. For good reason: Gordon Buchanan liked being single.

The sawmill materialized through the trees as he took the last sweeping turn and entered the log yard. To the north were stacks of felled pine, their limbs removed and ready for a trip through the planer. Almost five million in rough timber. To the south of the mill were hundreds of pallets of finished precision end-trim studs, another eight million in product ready for market. And between the raw and processed wood stood a thirty-million-dollar mill. He glanced again to the sky, darkened with acrid smoke, and wondered if this was the time he would lose it all.

Fires had threatened his mills in the past, burning one of his smaller ones to the ground, but he had never had so much at stake as now. This mill was different, larger and more sophisticated. The equipment was new, fast, and very expensive. The building itself had cost over three million just for the frame. Count in the timber on either side of the operation and he was looking at well over forty million in losses if the fire could not be stopped. He wasn't sure he could recover from that.

The main administration building was attached to the east side of the mill, and he parked close to the door. Three forestry trucks were already occupying spots near the office. His brother Billy's truck was there as well. He entered the office to exactly the scene he expected. Six forestry officers, Billy, and his mill foreman were huddled over a huge table in the center of the room. They looked up from the map as the door slammed shut.

"Hello, Gordon," one of the forest rangers said. He was mid-fifties, with wisps of gray tracing abstract lines through his black hair. His face was worn from too much exposure to the sun and wind—too many days in the vast Montana wilderness. He was the oldest of the group and their leader.

"Sam," Gordon said, outstretching his hand. Sam Bennett was the top dog in the Beaverhead-Deerlodge National Forest Department, and a friend for more than twenty years. Both men ended up working in the forestry industry, one saving them and the other cutting them. But it was Gordon's commitment to responsible logging that kept the men best friends. Sam Bennett knew that if the timber concessions were granted to someone other than Gordon, his days would be filled with monitoring the areas slated for clear cut. Theirs was a symbiotic relationship that had survived many years, both bad and good.

"What's the situation?" Gordon asked. "How close is the fire?"

"About five and a half to six miles. It's moving quicker than we thought," Sam said, looking back to the map. He pointed to a series of closely spaced isometric lines, indicating a sharp ridge. "We thought the fire would veer once it hit Sheep Mountain, but it circled the peak and kept coming. The pines are dry, Gordon. Not enough snow, and hot spring temperatures."

"That and the damn pine beetles. Water-starved pines don't produce pitch, and that leaves them at the mercy of the pine beetles. We've got thousands of dead Ponderosa pines out there, and they make good firewood." Gordon glanced down at the forestry map. "If it's broached Sheep Mountain, that leaves one natural firebreak between it and the mill. Canyon Creek."

Sam nodded. "Other than the creek, it's all dry timber. Crazy that everything's so dry before the end of April, but it goes with having no snow last winter."

"It's a tinderbox out there, all right. And there's nothing to stop that fire from coming right at us," Gordon said quietly. He rubbed his temples gently, fished a toothpick from his pocket, and clenched it between his teeth. "What's the weather forecast?"

"Dry for a couple of days, but there's a low-pressure front moving in from southern Canada. The guys in meteorology are saying there's a good chance of rain when it hits. First couple of days should see heavy rains, tapering off to a drizzle."

"Two days until we get rain," Gordon said, staring at the map. "That's going to be cutting it pretty damn close."

Bennett looked grim. "Too close. I had my crew run the numbers using the current wind speed and direction, and extrapolating the fire's progress since it started. It doesn't look good."

"How not good?" Gordon asked.

One of the technicians, a black man in his mid-twenties with close-cropped hair and a stack of papers in front of him, answered. "Given that the variables don't change, and the fire continues its progress unabated, you've got between forty and fifty hours." Lewis Carling was Sam's second in command, meticulous in his work, and more knowledgeable about forest fires than anyone in the forestry service in the northern states or southern Canada. "Without the rain, the fire will reach the mill."

Gordon was silent. Everything he'd worked for all his life was on the line. He was insured, but only to seventeen million, the max his insurer would cover. The shortfall, some twenty-five million, would be a total loss. It would wipe him out. Pattengail Creek was too far west to provide a break, and Trapped Creek was south, almost at the mill. Too dangerous letting the fire get that close before trying to stop it. That left Canyon Creek, a rough slash through the virgin forest. Extremely rugged country and totally impenetrable by land.

"Billy," he said, turning to his brother. "Could you get a crew on the south edge of Canyon Creek, down in this area?" he asked, his finger stabbing at the map.

Billy Buchanan was thoughtful. He was a large man, almost six-three, with an athletic frame and chiseled features. His face was sunburned from the early-spring heat wave, highlighting his rugged features and accentuating his blue eyes. "We could cut a firebreak at the creek, but the only way in is by chopper. I'd need at least fifteen men with chain saws. The break for the creek is already sixty to eighty feet wide. If we can extend that by another thirty feet, we could stop the fire from jumping."

Gordon looked to the young technician. "What do you think, Lewis?"

"What height are the trees on the north side of the river?"

"Fifty feet, tops."

Lewis checked the wind speed and slowly nodded. "If Billy can widen the break to just over a hundred feet, we might stop it." He looked directly into Gordon's eyes. "I say *might*, Gordon. There's no 'for sure' here."

Again, Gordon was silent. Everyone in the room looked to him for direction. This was Gordon's timber, his mill, and his decision. Dropping men in to hand-slash a firebreak was not without its risks. Chain saws were dangerous, the terrain rugged and unforgiving. A misplaced foothold or a felled tree snagging and kicking back could injure or kill a man in a split second. Dropping a crew into an unreachable region and keeping them supplied with food and water as they worked was going to be difficult. The logistics were completely against it.

But this was not just his livelihood on the line, it was half the town as well. Without the mill, two hundred jobs would be lost and the town would suffer immeasurably. Businesses would close and families would be forced to move away. The small town of Divide would probably not survive, and the damage to Butte would be significant.

"Well, I've always said that there's nothing more useless than burnt timber." He glanced about the room at the men waiting for his decision. "Let's do it," he said to Billy, running his hands through his thick brown hair. "Let's get a crew in there and try to save the mill."

Billy Buchanan grinned. "You got it, Gordon." He grabbed a phone from the desk and dialed.

2

Canyon Creek slashed a jagged and dangerous line through the thick blanket of Ponderosa pines. The bank on the north side of the creek was almost vertical, a sheer rock wall with few outcroppings running parallel to the fast-flowing water. This was the side from which the fire was approaching. The slope on the opposing side was gentler, about sixty degrees, but still a good test even for an experienced climber. The gorge ran for almost six miles, and access in from either end was through dense bush, thick with thorns. With the exception of a foolhardy few, this section of Canyon Creek was seldom visited.

Billy Buchanan had ventured into the gorge twice over the past six years, both times to estimate the timber potential on the southern edge. Both times he had found the outing dangerous. His past experiences stayed fresh in his memory as he expedited supplies for the crew. Time was scarce, and once the men were in, they wouldn't be coming out until the trees were cleared. He checked the lists on the table in front of him for adequate supplies of food, water, fuel, tents, generators, and chain saws, complete with spare parts. Once he was satisfied the crew would be properly outfitted, he signed off on the list.

The process of acquiring the gear and moving it to the helicopters began. He took one last glance at the map before he rolled it up.

Once dropped into the chasm by chopper, his crew's job would be to hand-slash an additional thirty feet to create an eighty-foot-wide firebreak. This would entail removing almost every tree from the southern edge of the water to the start of the incline that defined the river bank. Billy had two pumps being dropped in six hours after the team, to spray down the recently cut timber and the underbrush. In theory, the idea was to stop the fire when it hit the cliffs on the northern side and not allow the flames to advance up the other bank. With the creek bed devoid of fuel for the fire, the line should hold, deflecting the fire east and west and containing its advance.

In theory, anyway.

Billy rolled up the map and slipped an elastic on to keep it from unraveling. It was a forestry map, 1 to 50,000 scale, and showed every cut line, service road, and goat path that crisscrossed through the forest. Like an American Express card to a logger: Don't leave home without it. At two o'clock, he found his crew suited up and ready. Chris Stevens, his lead hand for the task, approached him as he slipped on a pair of steel-toed work boots.

"The guys are champin' at the bit, Billy," he said. "They want to get cutting before dark." Chris Stevens was a graduate student in forestry, working on his master's in conservation. He was mid-twenties, athletic, and well liked by everyone at the mill. Billy had decided on Chris for lead hand over any one of the three foremen who were heading into the gorge, mostly to keep from ruffling any feathers. So far, it seemed to be working.

"Yeah, I know. I've got lights and a generator coming in before sundown, but it'll be a lot slower once we lose the natural light. The chopper's ready, so let's get it loaded. Pick seven men to come with me. You wait for the second trip."

"Eight men max for each trip?" Chris asked, nodding his head at the company's Bell 412 helicopter, sitting on the far side of the clearing.

"That baby can usually manage fifteen, but we're taking in a lot of gear with us on each trip, so that cuts the number down to eight or nine."

"That's only two trips to get the entire crew in, Billy. That's not bad." He headed over to the group of men waiting for the go-ahead, and as he pointed at them, the men moved quickly to where the chopper was sitting, its blades just starting to turn. They loaded gear as they entered, and within a couple of minutes, the Bell 412 was airborne and moving over the treetops toward Canyon Creek.

Gordon Buchanan pulled up in his truck, killed the engine, and jumped out. "Everything okay, Chris?" he asked, moving toward his brother at his usual fast gait.

"No problem, Gordon. Billy just left with the first crew. Chopper will be back soon to pick up the rest of us."

Gordon hung around the clearing, checking the piles of gear stacked near the tree line. He ticked off a checklist, concentrating on the fuel and food. At this point, any downtime could spell disaster. The crews, working toward each other from each end of the target zone, had to get firebreak cut inside forty hours or not bother. It was going to be tight. The thumping of the chopper's rotors cut through the afternoon air, and once the wheels hit the ground the crew was ferrying supplies aboard. Gordon shouted a few words of encouragement to Chris and his men as they boarded the craft, watched it depart, then headed back to the main office.

The fate of the mill was in their hands.

Billy wiped the sweat from his brow and lowered his aching body onto one of the many stumps dotting the south side of the creek. Thirty hours and the two crews were within earshot of each other. They would have the firebreak cut inside the deadline with no problem. And there was good news from the weather forecasters. The winds were abating and rain was on the horizon. The fire was slowing, and if the rain fell, it would stall the flames in their tracks. He took a long draft of cold water and replaced the bottle on his hip.

"Billy?" It was Chris on the walkie-talkie.

"Go ahead, Chris."

"We're moving our pump forward another two hundred yards. We've soaked the hell out of the first thousand yards of underbrush. Even if a few burning spars come crashing down the slope, I don't think anything will ignite."

"Excellent work, Chris."

"We've got this thing beat, Billy," he said. There was pride at a job well done in his voice.

"I think you're right. Gordon called about an hour ago. The fire's at least twelve hours from reaching us. It's slowing."

"We'll reach each other in less than eight," he said. "We've got another load of logs ready to go. Send the chopper over when you're done with it."

"Roger that," Billy said. He signed off and looked over to where the helicopter was hovering over a horizontal stack of logs, preparing to lift them out of the gorge and fly them back to the mill. Leaving the cut trees on the ground was senseless, as the fire could ignite them almost as easily lying prone on the ground as when they were upright. The logger on the ground gave the thumbs-up, and the pilot took the machine straight up until the logs cleared the surrounding treetops, then angled off toward the mill. Billy started back toward where his crew was cutting, some hundred feet distant.

In the sea of cut trees, a solitary stump stuck up three or four feet higher than the rest. Billy knew that additional height might cause problems for the crew lifting the logs out of the ravine. He picked his way through the wet underbrush and, once he reached it, threw his feller pants on the ground next to the stump. The thick material was designed to protect his legs, but it was one simple cut, like ten thousand before, and he wanted to get back to the crew. He pulled the cord on the chain saw and it barked to life. He set the blade against the stump and pulled the trigger with his index finger.

The saw was loose in his right hand, the thirty-inch blade tight to the wood and perpendicular to his left leg. The second the clutch kicked in and the blade began to spin, the teeth kicked off the bark and·flew back into his leg. Billy's immediate reaction was to release the clutch, but he wasn't quick enough. The blade slashed into his flesh, tearing into the muscle and tendons just below his knee. He screamed with pain as the blade embedded in his bone and stopped. He dropped to the ground, blood flowing freely from the wound.

Within seconds the entire crew was around him, two men ripping open a first-aid kit and Chris on the walkie-talkie to the mill, calling for the chopper. It took about thirty seconds for Chris to get Gordon.

"How bad is it?" Gordon asked, taking the walkie-talkie from the front-office employee who had answered the call.

"He's cut right to the bone. We've taken the blade out and I've got a couple of guys working on the bleeding. It looks pretty bad, Gordon."

"The chopper's dumping that load of logs in the yard. It'll be airborne again inside two minutes. Six to seven minutes out once it's in the air."

Chris did the math. Less than ten minutes for the helicopter to arrive, another couple to load Billy, and a fifteen-minute ride to the hospital. Under half an hour. "He'll be okay if the blade didn't hit an artery."

"Is the blood spurting?" Gordon asked, knowing that a severed artery pumped blood like a crimped garden hose.

Chris looked at the cut. The blood was flowing quickly, but not spurting. "No, but he's bleeding badly."

"Get a tourniquet on it," Gordon said, relieved. "It's not great, but it'll stop the flow. I'll call it in to the hospital and have them get some blood ready."

"The guys are getting one in place, Gordon. I'll keep this line open."

Gordon turned to the employee who had initially taken the call. "Get the emergency ward at the hospital on the line. Tell them they've got an emergency coming in and they'll need A-positive blood." He returned to the walkie-talkie. "Is the tourniquet on yet?"

"Just pulling it tight, Gordon."

Gordon could hear voices, indecipherable but panicked. "What's going on, Chris?"

A few moments of background noise. Chris said, "They can't get it to stop, it's pouring out. The cut is too close to the knee to get the tourniquet tight."

Gordon fought the panic in his chest. "Christ, you've got to stop the bleeding."

"We're trying," Chris yelled back. There was desperation in his voice. There was more background noise, raised voices, men shouting. Chris's voice came over the air, but he wasn't talking to Gordon. "Pull it tighter, for Christ's sake," he screamed. "Keep him conscious! Don't let him pass out."

"Chris," Gordon said. "Chris!"

More noise, pandemonium as the men, well trained in first aid, fought to stop the bleeding. Gordon slammed the walkie-talkie on the table and ran from the room, shattering the glass in the door as he banged through it and into the late-afternoon sun. He sprinted to the helicopter, which had just finished dropping a load of logs, and jumped in beside the pilot. Seconds later they rose above the trees and banked toward Canyon Creek. He glanced at his watch. *Hang on, Billy, we're coming.*

The clearing materialized as they crested the treetops next to the creek, and Gordon could immediately see the swath of forest the two crews had cleared over the past thirty hours. He pointed at the group of men huddled over Billy and the pilot nodded, gently setting the craft down only fifteen yards from the group. Gordon leapt from the open door and weaved through the sea of tree trunks. The odor of pine sap was strong in his nostrils. He reached the group and knelt down at his brother's side.

The wound was still bleeding. The loggers had secured the tourniquet immediately below the knee joint and cinched it tight. But although the flow was slowed, the blood was not coagulating. And Billy had already lost too much blood to lose any more. Gordon pointed to the chopper, then he and three other men hoisted Billy's unconscious body into the air and staggered through the stumps to the waiting craft. They slid Billy in the back, and once he was in beside him, Gordon gave the pilot the thumbs-up. They were airborne in seconds.

Gordon turned his attention to his brother's leg. The wound was gaping, but not as severe as he had imagined. The tourniquet was well placed and tight, but it was the refusal of Billy's blood to coagulate that was the problem. Gordon slipped Billy's wrist into his hand and felt for a pulse. Almost nonexistent. He looked down at his brother's face, white as fresh-fallen Montana snow. He looked at the blood pooling and felt tears welling up in his eyes. Billy had lost too much blood. They were still at least twelve minutes to the hospital, plus time to get him from the chopper to emergency. There wasn't time. And then he realized.

He was watching his brother die.

Gordon cradled Billy's head in his arms and felt the tears let loose. They spilled down his cheeks onto his brother's face. He gently brushed them off as he felt Billy's body stiffen, then go limp. He brushed Billy's hair back from his forehead. His body was still warm.

"Oh God, Billy," he said softly. "Oh my God, what have you done?"

3

Billy Buchanan's house was small but impeccably kept. Billy was the younger brother and had never reached the financial independence Gordon had achieved, but that didn't stop him from taking immense pride in his modest abode in an upper-end neighborhood. He had often told Gordon that buying the smallest house on the street was the best financial decision he had ever made. The property value had shot up, mostly because of the larger houses lining the street. Billy had been very proud of that.

Gordon entered the house just after noon on the day after Billy's funeral with a key his brother had given him some years earlier. As he turned the key in the lock, it struck him: He'd never had to use the key before. Billy had always been at home when he'd visited. He pushed open the door and was greeted by the faint scent of fresh strawberries. He removed his shoes and raincoat and glanced outside at the drizzle that had saved his sawmill, then closed the door.

The blinds were drawn, and Gordon moved through the house pulling back the shades and opening a couple of windows to get some air flowing. The house was a three-bedroom bungalow, with a country kitchen and a living room. There was no formal dining area, which Billy preferred, calling a dining room a total waste of usable space. Gordon returned to the living room and paused, scanning the multitude of framed photos on the wall abutting the kitchen. Many of the pictures were of Gordon and Billy fishing, hunting, at the mill, enjoying a cold beer together. Gordon stood motionless for a few minutes, remembering the weather and their conversation at the time when each picture was snapped. His eyes were moist, but his hands never moved from his sides to wipe away the tears.

A noise at the front door jerked him back to the present and he turned to see Sheriff Boyle framed in the doorway. Boyle was a large man with a prominent beer belly and jowls that moved every time he spoke. He was nearing retirement, and his eyes spoke of too many years seeing the downside of humanity. His uniform was clean and freshly pressed. The lawman removed his hat as he entered. "Hello, Arnie," Gordon said. "Thanks for coming down."

Boyle looked uncomfortable. "Not a problem." He was quiet for a minute. "I'm so sorry, Gordon. I know how close you and Billy were."

Gordon managed a hint of a smile. "Yeah, thanks. We *were* close, weren't we?"

"You sure were," Boyle said, relaxing a bit. "Not everyone gets to be so close to another person. You were lucky."

Gordon walked over to the sheriff and placed his hand on the man's shoulder. "I know this is tough for you too, Arnie. Don't think I don't know. I really appreciate your coming out today."

Boyle nodded. "Where do you want to start?"

Gordon shrugged. "You're the cop. You know what to do. I'm okay if you tell me how we should do this."

"Well, usually we look around, take a few pictures, and make some notes before we disturb anything. Once that's done, you can collect valuables and keepsakes, bankbooks, stuff like that. Best if you take it with you so nothing goes missing. We should keep an eye out in case Billy had a will."

"That sounds good, Arnie. You have a camera?"

The sheriff produced a tiny digital camera in a leather pouch. "We're high-tech now," he said as he started snapping shots of the various rooms. He concentrated on the areas of the house where Billy had left personal belongings: paper, mail, keys, and such.

Gordon followed him, sorting through kitchen drawers and then Billy's bedroom. There was little of any value aside from some cash and a couple of gold chains. His brother had been a caring man with simple tastes, and searching through his belongings was no adrenaline surge. The bathroom was last, and Gordon poked through his shaving cream, razor, toothbrush, and deodorant, then opened the medicine cabinet. There were only two items: a tube of Polysporin and a bottle of prescription pills. Gordon picked up the pills and studied the label. Triaxcion. He'd never heard of it. He replaced the pill bottle and shut the cabinet. He stared at his reflection in the mirror for a moment, opened the cabinet again, and removed the pills. He twisted the cap until the arrows lined up and flipped the cap back. The bottle was about half full of green pills. A quick shake of his wrist and a few pills spilled into his palm. He looked at them thoughtfully.

"Arnie," he called out. "You ever heard of a drug called Triax-cion?"

The sheriff appeared at the bathroom door and stared at the pills in Gordon's palm. "Can't say I have," he replied. "What does it say on the bottle?"

"Take one tablet twice a day with food. Avoid direct sunlight."

"Which doctor prescribed them?"

Gordon scanned the bottom of the label. "Dr. Hastings. You know him?"

"Yeah. He's in Butte, on West Granite Street. Been around for a few years now. Good guy."

"Good guy or good doctor?" Gordon asked, tipping his hand so the pills slid back into the bottle. He snapped the lid in place.

"Bit of both," the sheriff said. "My wife's sister goes to him. She likes him."

Gordon nodded. He pocketed the pills. "Probably nothing, Arnie, but I never knew Billy to take pills. Think I'll find out what they're for."

"Yeah, good idea."

Arnie Boyle left about one o'clock, clutching his digital camera. Gordon spent another two hours in the house, going through the fridge and removing anything that might spoil, shifting Billy's laundry from the washer to the dryer and running the clothes through a cycle, and checking the latest entries in his bother's checkbook. It was just after three o'clock when he finished for the day and locked the house behind him. As he slid into the front seat of his car, he felt the pill bottle in his pocket. He pulled it out, eyed the front label, and checked his watch. He still had time to drive to the doctor's office before closing. He started the BMW and slipped it into gear.

Hastings's office was less than twenty minutes from Billy's house. Gordon pulled up in front of the pale stucco two-story building at exactly three-thirty. An elegantly crafted sign hung next to the main door, black lettering on a white background. There were a handful of names followed by their M.D. designations, with Alex Hastings third from the top. His office was on the second floor with a north-facing view of the ravine that snaked in an east-west direction behind the building. He found the office, modern with comfortable leather chairs for the waiting patients. Gordon approached the mid-fifties receptionist and dug the pill bottle from his pocket.

"Good afternoon. I'm Gordon Buchanan, Billy Buchanan's brother."

The receptionist's smile faded and a look of genuine sorrow slid over her features. "Oh, Mr. Buchanan, I'm so sorry."

Gordon forced a grim smile. "So am I," he said. He set the pill bottle on the woman's desk. "I found this prescription in Billy's medicine cabinet and I'd like to know why the doctor prescribed it."

She glanced at the bottle. "Mr. Buchanan, before I can even

let the doctor know you're here, I need to see some identification. We can only speak to immediate family on such matters."

"Of course," Gordon said, producing his driver's license. She studied the name and picture, and he replaced it in his wallet. "Dr. Hastings did prescribe this, didn't he?"

She nodded. "Yes. I remember Billy very well, Mr. Buchanan. He was such a nice man, so polite and always smiling."

"Do you know what the medication is for?"

"Yes, but I'd rather you talk to Dr. Hastings about that. I'll slide you in next, between patients. The doctor is pretty well on schedule and can afford a few minutes, given what happened."

"Thank you," Gordon said, taking a seat. The wait was short, perhaps five minutes, before he was shown into the doctor's office. The furnishings were rough-hewn pine with coarse berber carpet; the walls were covered with degrees. A couple of minutes later, Alex Hastings entered and closed the door behind him.

He was younger than Gordon had envisioned, just into his thirties with a full head of unruly red hair and the white, freckly complexion that usually accompanied this hair color. He offered his hand. "I'm Alex Hastings," he said, his voice surprisingly deep for his thin frame.

"Gordon Buchanan. Thanks for meeting with me, Doctor."

Hastings sat in the chair next to Gordon and said, "Call me Alex, please. My deepest sympathies to you and your family, Mr. Buchanan."

"Thank you. I'm fine with Gordon."

"I understand you found one of my prescriptions in Billy's house."

Gordon handed over the pill bottle. "Triaxcion. Why did you prescribe it? Billy wasn't one to take pills."

"No, he wasn't. But this was different. Triaxcion is an anti-balding drug, and your brother was very self-conscious of his hair loss. I counseled him for a few months on this problem, and he tried a variety of shampoos and creams before I finally gave in and issued the prescription."

"It was his idea to take pills for this?" Gordon asked, perplexed. His brother had always been adamant about not taking medication.

Hastings nodded. "I can understand your surprise. Billy was antimeds. He refused antibiotics on a couple of occasions, and when I recommended a more holistic approach, he jumped at it. He wasn't one to take pills for no reason." The doctor stopped for a moment and ran his hand through his thick locks. "But the whole balding thing was really getting him down. In his mind, it was a grave problem. Enough to alter his thinking on drugs to the point where he was insistent I write the prescription."

"Why Triaxcion?" Gordon asked.

"The pharmaceutical company that developed and markets Triaxcion is pretty slick. Their television ads target men with hair loss, and as the boomers age, it's becoming a huge market, almost bottomless. The money Veritas is making off this drug is sinful."

"Veritas? What's Veritas?"

"Veritas Pharmaceutical, the manufacturer. They're a medium-size pharmaceutical company out of Richmond, Virginia, and Triaxcion is an enormous cash cow for them."

"Does it work?" Gordon asked, fingering the bottle and reading his brother's name again, as he had done twenty or thirty times since finding the pills.

Hastings shrugged. "The FDA approved it, and for them to approve any drug it has to have passed Phase III clinical trials."

"What's a Phase III clinical trial?" Gordon asked.

"It's the third tier of a system that starts with Phase I. Phase I trials are small, maybe twenty to fifty people who are closely monitored to see what kind of side effects there are and how much can be taken before the drug becomes toxic to the system."

"Sounds dangerous—like they should be using rats, not people."

"Oh, by the time the drug enters a Phase I trial, they've got a pretty good idea that it's reasonably safe. It's already undergone a lot of testing in the labs. The rats have already had their doses."

"Then what?"

"Phase II trials are conducted on people with the disease. Half the test group, usually a few hundred, is given the drug, the other half a placebo. They're testing the effectiveness of the drug more than anything in this phase." He took a sip of water and continued. "Phase III trials are the real test. They concentrate on long-term effectiveness and side effects. Once the drug passes Phase III trials, the company can apply for a New Drug Application, or NDA as they call it."

"Then the drug's on the market?"

"If the FDA approves, yes." Hastings returned to Gordon's original question. "So does Triaxcion work? I can't say exactly how effective it is, but I suspect there's some benefit."

Gordon nodded. "Is there any downside to it?"

"Every drug has side effects, Gordon. Veritas acknowledges the user may suffer upset stomach, and because Triaxcion targets conversion of testosterone to dihydrotestosterone, there could be changes in sexual performance. They don't say for better or worse, just that desire and performance may change."

Gordon looked skeptical. "I'm sure if it enhanced sexual prowess, they'd mention it. Viagra doesn't have any problem advertising that."

Hastings nodded. He glanced at his watch. "I have patients, Gordon. I should get back to them."

Gordon stood and offered his hand. "Thanks, Alex. I appreciate your time."

"Not a problem. Call me if you need any more information."

Gordon stopped in the doorway to the office. "Anything in Billy's file that would indicate he was a hemophiliac?"

"Nothing," Hastings replied immediately. "I checked through his file thoroughly when I was informed of his death."

Gordon took the stairs to the main floor and sat in the driver's seat of the BMW, going back over the meeting in his mind. Billy had no history of being a bleeder, and this certainly wasn't the first time he had cut himself and needed stitches.

But this time had been different. Very different. Billy had died. And that didn't make sense. The only variable that had changed in his life was that he was taking medication daily to prevent his hair loss. If the FDA had approved the drug, how could it be dangerous?

But try as he might, Gordon couldn't shake the feeling that something wasn't right.

4

BioTech Five is one of seven research buildings in the Virginia BioTechnology Park in Richmond, Virginia. One block north of the Coliseum, it's tucked between a group of horseshoe-shaped buildings to the east and south, and BioTech Three to the west. The entire third floor, almost twelve thousand square feet, is dedicated to the corporate offices of Veritas Pharmaceutical. The office of Bruce Andrews, CEO of the company, occupies the southeast corner, with a partial view of the Coliseum and City Hall. But the view was the last thing on Andrews's mind this particular Wednesday morning. He sat with his back to the window, peering at his computer screen.

An imposing man, over six feet four, Bruce Andrews had the body of a pro linebacker—for a good reason. For two years he was one, playing for the Pittsburgh Steelers, crushing opponents into the natural turf and enjoying every minute of it. He was selected to the Pro Bowl in his sophomore year, but one of his own teammates was flattened by a running back and fell back, landing on Andrews's knee and tearing the anterior cruciate ligament. A professional sporting career was erased in a few seconds of agonizing pain. The upside was that Andrews had a 3.8 GPA in the sciences even as he was playing college ball at Stanford. He took his degree and entered the pharmaceutical business as a researcher.

Andrews was a good catch. He was bright, well-connected, and extroverted. His face was well proportioned, with a prominent chin and inquiring eyes. He had an easy smile, which disarmed most people within a few seconds of meeting him. And in the research industry, where most of the staff are graduates of college chess and glee clubs, a physically attractive employee with good social skills was worth his weight in platinum, not gold.

Looking at the career offers on the table, Marcon was his first choice, and when they offered him a position in R&D working at the new one-hundred-million-dollar research facility bordering Harvard Medical School, he had to control his shaking hand as he signed the contract. Four years later, he reluctantly closed the door behind him as he left for Frezin, one of Marcon's top rivals and another of the Big Pharma companies. Frezin's offer was too generous to turn down: his own research group, an excellent salary, bonuses for meeting or exceeding expectations in Phase I and Phase II trials, and totally flexible office hours.

He excelled at Frezin, clearing the way for two new cholesterol drugs, one of which found a spot on the crowded shelves of America's pharmacies and generated almost six hundred million in sales before the patent expired and the generics jumped in. His success in the research labs led to a high-level management position, at which he immediately excelled. He reworked the Frezin mindset on R&D, modeling it after what he had seen at Marcon.

It worked. It worked very well. Frezin passed Marcon on the Standard & Poor's 500 Index and the bellwether Domini 400 Social Index, putting Frezin in the enviable position of being the new benchmark in pharmaceutical research and development. His salary went through the roof, and his bonuses eclipsed his wages. He had found his niche and was enjoying huge personal success, despite the public's dislike and distrust of the pharmaceutical giants. Bruce Andrews often looked back on the day that 260-pound lineman crushed his knee as a great day in his life.

But even with all the perks and the money, he was, in his own mind, still a lowly vice president. He coveted the top position, but after a few years he realized that he was not moving in that direction. The upper echelons of Frezin were powerful and connected, and he was not one of the chosen. He realized that if he were to ever achieve the position of CEO, it would entail moving to a competitor. He found a heavyweight headhunter and the search to find a company that needed a CEO was under way.

Veritas Pharmaceutical was not a major player in the industry, but neither was it a lightweight. Four drugs with household names were under patent, and three more were in the pipeline. Wall Street was behind Veritas and investor confidence was high. What they lacked was vision. And when the board of directors interviewed Bruce Andrews, they knew they had found their visionary.

Andrews's agent drafted a ten-year contract, collected a huge finder's fee, and disappeared back where he came from. Andrews planted himself in the corner office and took stock of his new empire. The company had annual sales of six hundred million, which Andrews considered low, considering the company had four drugs still under patent on the market. Their R&D budget was $162 million, marketing $73 million, and administration $12 million. Legal fees and payments on class-action suits ran to almost $200 million, courtesy of an FDA recall on Haldion, a drug that was designed to reduce blood pressure but actually caused heart palpitations. Not heart attacks or death, at least not that had been proven—simply palpitations. Veritas had pulled the drug from the market, but the damage was done. The ambulance chasers were all over it, and tort suits kept appearing, even seven years after the negative reports had chased Haldion from the shelves.

Andrews rearranged the financing within his first three

months as CEO. R&D remained constant at just under $170 million, but marketing shot up to $240 million. He brought in a team of image consultants and lawyers, and focused on stopping the bleeding from the class-action suits on Haldion. The first tort action against Veritas after he took the helm was from a medium-size law firm in Kansas. Andrews unleashed his new legal team on the unsuspecting lawyers and let them know that the free ride was over. Every legal action against Veritas as a result of a client suffering from the side effects of Haldion would be vigorously challenged in court. No more cash.

The majority of claims against Haldion had already been initiated and settlements reached, and his company was now fighting an attack by hundreds of small law firms with one or two clients. The power of numbers was lost now that the large tort suits had been dealt with, and the image spin doctors sent a clear message to the press. Sue Veritas and you've got a fight. The Kansas lawyers took one look at their return on the suit and dropped the case. One by one the lawsuits disappeared as legal firms across the country realized they would have to face Veritas in court. The bleeding was stemmed. Two hundred million dollars a year in savings. Investors liked what they saw, and Veritas's stock shot up.

The new image that Veritas and its market-savvy consultants began pumping out to the public was that they were a modern-day Marcon, taking over where the pharmaceutical giant had once stood. They were sympathetic to the little guy and committed to bringing down the price of drugs, especially for seniors and those on fixed incomes. Andrews coaxed his legal hound dogs to get creative and find new ways of extending patent lives on three of the company's existing drugs. When they did, by patenting the metabolite synthesized by the drugs once in the patient's body, it guaranteed Veritas over seven hundred million in income for another three years.

Wall Street noticed. A new and aggressive Marcon had been born, and investors lined up like lemmings to grab chunks of

Veritas before it punctured another hole in the ozone layer. Veritas surged into the Fortune 500 list, and Bruce Andrews's face was plastered on the covers of *Financial Times, Forbes*, and *Time*. Life at Veritas was perfect. Except for one small detail.

Everything about Veritas was a lie.

Haldion *did* cause palpitations, and those palpitations sometimes led to cardiac arrest, which in turn occasionally led to the morgue. The claims against Veritas, while now ineffective, were often legitimate. And while the image Veritas portrayed to the public was one of a corporation that cared, people were dying because of the drug. And that wasn't the only FDA-approved drug with problems. Triaxcion was a disaster looking for a home. The antibalding drug, which halted the conversion of testosterone to dihydrotestosterone, also caused clotting factors to fail in some people with A-positive blood. So far, the image experts had held their fingers in the proverbial dike, but the waters were threatening to overflow the dam itself. And now, as Andrews sat at his keyboard, he knew they had a problem inside the company.

Being a cautious man, he had covertly asked one of his programming staff to insert a packet sniffer into the company software. It ran a constant stream of cross-correlations and nonlinear filters, looking for any employee who accessed the confidential research files on any drugs, whether FDA approved or in Phase IV or later development. Andrews wanted to know who the whistle-blowers were before they had time to type up a demand letter. And now he had one.

Albert Rousseau. One of the research rats working in their statin department on the latest cholesterol drugs. His computer had accessed a number of restricted files over the past few weeks. On each occasion, he had inserted a few lines of code in his search engine, spoofing the detection software to other terminals belonging to other employees. But the sniffer was one byte smarter than Rousseau. Because it was nonlinear, it recognized patterns otherwise untraceable. And the one thing Andrews was certain of was that Albert Rousseau was positioning himself to deliver a pay-or-suffer letter to Veritas. That was something that Bruce Andrews could not allow to happen.

He picked up his phone and dialed a number from memory. It was time for Albert Rousseau to take a vacation.

A permanent one.

5

Evan Ziegler hit the mute button on the television remote and gave his wife a quizzical look. She was standing at the end of the couch with her hand cupped over the mouthpiece on the cordless telephone. She did not look happy.

"It's that East Coast client," she said quietly. "Remember, Ben's birthday is tomorrow." She handed him the phone and disappeared into the kitchen. The sounds of pots banging and dishes rattling followed.

"Good evening, sir," Evan said in a cheerful voice. "What can I do for you?"

"Hello, Evan, I hope I didn't interrupt anything." The caller didn't wait for a reply, just kept talking. "We've got a situation here, and I hope you can free up a few days. We've just brought on a new division in Richmond, and they need their new copiers immediately."

"I'd rather not leave today if possible. It's my son's nineteenth birthday tomorrow. I could fly out after his party."

"Tomorrow night is fine, Evan. When can I give you the details on the order?"

"I'll make a quick trip back to the office. Be there in an hour. I'll call you once I'm there."

"Fine. I'll talk to you then. And thanks, Evan."

Evan clicked the talk button and the phone died. He hoisted himself off the couch and joined his wife in the kitchen. "I've got to make a quick trip to the office to go over a new order, but I don't have to fly out until tomorrow night. After Ben's party."

Louise Ziegler smiled, released a relieved smile, and gave her husband a hug. "He's a nice man, Evan. You're lucky to have clients like him."

He returned the smile and the hug, staring into her eyes from only a few inches away. His wife was aging, almost forty, but she still looked great. Her hair was deep brown and hung to her shoulders; she refused to cut it short, thinking that to do so was admitting middle age had set in. Her eyes were deep brown, with tiny wrinkles ebbing out from the edges and disappearing under her hair. Her skin was olive and her lips thin, but just right for the contours of her face. He kissed her, pushed off, and headed down the hall to his son's room.

Ben Ziegler hadn't moved an inch in the last couple of hours. In fact, he hadn't moved in almost three years. Not since the day he had dived into the pond at Shilling Creek without checking first for submerged rocks. He grinned as Evan entered the room, one of the few movements his damaged spinal cord allowed.

"Hi, Dad," he said. "What's up?"

"Nothing much, just came in to say hi. I'm surprised you're still inside on such a nice spring day."

"Didn't much feel like going out," his son quipped back. "Couldn't decide what to wear."

Evan sat on the bed next to the wheelchair. He ran his hands through his son's hair, gently massaging the scalp under the thick thatch of dark brown locks. The top of Ben's head was the one spot he still had feeling, and he loved it when someone, especially his father, touched him there.

"I've got to head into the office for a while, Ben," he said, kissing his son on the top of his head. "See you later."

"Sure, Dad," Ben said, grinning. "Remember, it's my birthday tomorrow."

"Yeah, son, I know. I'm here for you."

He left the room, his teeth clenched and the tears ready to flow. His son, his only child, paralyzed. He fought back the tears, but they still came. His wife, knowing how he hated her to see him cry, kept her eyes on the cutting board as he walked through the kitchen to the garage door. He brushed the tears from his eyes as he backed the Audi out and shifted into first gear. He wound out the first two gears, then eased off the gas. His neighbors didn't complain, but he knew they watched his driving with narrow eyes. He slowed at the corner stop sign, his emotions slowly coming under control.

Ben Ziegler had been the brightest light in a good marriage. Always a star athlete and top of his class in all the required subjects, Ben was touted as the one who would carve new paths in the business world. He was never without his patented smirk, a look that said he knew something no one else knew. Teachers adored him, classmates respected him, and the telephone was constantly ringing, girls giggling as they asked for him.

Until the accident.

Evan steered through the evening traffic, the Denver freeways their usual jam of vehicles. It was Wednesday, but that hardly mattered anymore. The streets were always busy; too many people, all in a rush. He glanced in the rearview mirror and looked into his own eyes. They were a delicate shade of blue, not deep or cold, but soft and understanding. His brown hair was receding slightly, but the high forehead suited him. And what hair was left was thick and wavy. He wore it slightly over his ears, but not what would be considered long. His face was chalky white from the long winter months, but a tinge of sunburn showed on his cheeks, the result of mowing the grass the day before.

A nondescript office condo appeared on the north side of the freeway and he took the off-ramp, reducing his speed and steering hard right at the first access road. The entrance to the

30

parking lot was three short blocks down, and he pulled in, the only car in the lot. He switched off the ignition, slipped out of the car, and unlocked the door immediately under a sign displaying a couple of large photocopiers. The printing between the two pictures read *Mile High Copiers.* He locked the door behind him and slid behind the desk in the first office on the right. A picture of Ben in his high school jersey hung on the wall, and Evan felt the sadness again as his eyes swept over it.

An office phone with buttons for numerous lines sat on the desk, but he unlocked one of the desk drawers and lifted out a second phone. Its cord was attached to a black box about six inches square: a scrambling device. Evan dialed a long-distance number and leaned back in the soft leather chair, waiting for the voice he knew would answer.

"Are you on the secure phone?" The voice belonged to Bruce Andrews.

"Yes. What can I do for you?"

"I have a problem, Evan. One I need handled quite quickly."

"Where can I pick up the package?"

"The Commonwealth Park Suites Hotel, in Richmond. It's at the front desk under Brent Saunders."

"Anything else?"

"Just that this person poses a very real threat to the direction I want our research to go. And if that happens . . ."

Evan's voice was terse. "I read in the newspaper that you were scaling back on your biotech division—that your investment into brain chips was waning."

"Don't believe everything you read, Evan." Andrews's voice had gone cold. "Just get to Richmond and take care of my problem. Let me worry about getting your son out of that wheelchair."

"You do that," Evan said as the line went dead. He replaced the phone in its cradle, returned it to the drawer, and locked the handle. A solitary copier sat in the corner of his office: an old relic just for display. He walked across the carpet, opened the front access panel, and pulled on a colored handle. The copier's guts slid out on a metal track. He reached in behind the array of gears and lenses and pulled on the toner tray. Inside was a package, wrapped in thick cling wrap. He set it on top of the copier and peeled open the wrapping. Inside were a passport, two credit cards, a driver's license, and a large bundle of cash. He checked the identification, all of which displayed his picture and a different name, for expiry dates. Then he pocketed the ID and two thousand dollars. He phoned in a reservation on United Airlines from Denver to Richmond, departing Denver at 10:23 P.M. the next day, locked the outer office door, and headed home. Only for a brief moment did he wonder one thing.

What had this person done that they now had to die?

6

Albert Rousseau clicked on an icon resembling a laboratory beaker and sixteen file folders appeared on his computer monitor. He moved the cursor to one titled "MM-1076" and clicked on it. A series of chemical formulae unraveled on the screen. He scrolled through the first ten pages, right-clicked on the mouse, and sent the entire file to a Sony MicroVault, a portable storage unit plugged into the USB port. The transfer took a few milliseconds. He slipped the drive out of the port and secured it in his front pocket. Then he deleted the file on his computer, switched off the lights in his office, and locked the door.

It was still early to be leaving the office, and the elevators were almost empty. He nodded to a couple of people he vaguely knew, exited the building, and made his way to his assigned parking spot. His freshly washed Ford Mustang gleamed in the evening light. A quick twist of the key in the ignition and he was moving.

Rousseau lightly touched his shirt pocket, reassuring himself that the evidence was still there. He had a very secure location for it at his house in his safe. No one knew about it. He'd had a contractor come in and build the safe into a place that no one would think to look. He grinned, crooked teeth showing through thin, pale lips. What a bunch of dumbasses. He had enough proof to sink the company if they didn't play ball with him and cough up some money.

Serious money.

Not a million. Not two or three, but ten or twenty. He hadn't decided yet. But they were going to pay. And when they did, he'd be living life large in the Caribbean or Europe. He ran his hands over his cheek, feeling the acne he'd lived with all his life. That would be gone, and his teeth would be straight and capped. He'd have all the women he'd always dreamed of. Money could perform miracles—he'd be living proof of that.

He touched the storage device again like it was a winning lottery ticket. But unlike sheer luck in a lottery, he'd worked for this. He'd noticed small things in the clinical trials for Triaxcion, errors that somehow had been overlooked by the other researchers and eventually by the FDA. He suspected someone inside the Food and Drug Administration was on the take, as the problems with the drug were too serious to be swept under some convenient carpet. No matter, he still had enough to fry the company's top management—enough to lever a few million from the corporate coffers, then head overseas.

He pulled up in front of his town house on Cooley Avenue, a red brick building with black trim around the door and windows, and switched off the ignition. One week more and he'd be gone. No more lonely nights watching the Devils play hockey or reruns of *Seinfeld* on television. He had definitive proof that Triaxcion was dangerous, that it prohibited coagulants in human blood from bonding. And by searching the Internet with key words, he had clippings from six newspapers with stories of people with no history of hemophilia bleeding to death. Six deaths. And one of them, that Buchanan guy in Butte, Montana, had died just last week.

Perfect.

Christ, he was the keeper of the key to the Holy Grail of pharmaceutical lawsuits.

He grinned again as he slid out of the Mustang and slammed

the driver's door. Maybe he'd hit them up for twenty-five million. Recent memories are always the sharpest, and that Buchanan fellow had died at just the right time.

Such luck.

7

A gentle mist settled on Mirror Lake, hovering three or four feet above the water. A solitary loon burst through the covering and glided inches above the murky cloud, trailing wisps of mist in its wing vortex. The bird reached the shoreline and banked sharply skyward, barely clearing the hemlocks bordering the lake. Jennifer Pearce watched until the loon disappeared behind the trees then glanced back over the soupy cloud blanketing the water.

The sun had yet to rise, the Porcupine Mountains still shrouded in the lingering shadows of the spent night. The spring air was cool, and as she exhaled, her breath sent short bursts of steam into the mountain air. The sound of approaching footsteps drifted to her and she turned to see who else was up before dawn. A man in his early fifties, tanned and dressed entirely in Eddie Bauer, nodded to her as he reached the lake's edge. He leaned over and dipped his finger in the water.

"It's cold," he said with a hint of irritation in his voice. "Everything about this place is cold."

"It's not the Caribbean, Mel," Jennifer said. "It's Michigan and it's the last week of April. Get used to it."

"I don't like cold weather," he said, standing next to her and looking out over the lake. He was quiet for a minute. "I should have brought my camera. This is really beautiful."

Jennifer didn't speak. She didn't like Mel Lun, just tolerated him for the doors he could and sometimes would open for her. Lun was a sycophant of the highest degree, with his perfect nose up so many Marcon assholes she was surprised to see him walk around without someone attached to his face. Lun was a regional director for Marcon Pharmaceuticals, and to some degree held the purse strings for her research money. Not directly—even with his Harvard degree he didn't have that level of clout with the pharmaceutical giant. But he had the ear of those who controlled the money, and that made him a valuable ally.

"You made an excellent presentation yesterday," Mel said, squinting slightly as the sun finally crested one of the eastern ridges. "They were impressed."

"It's important, Mel," she said quietly. "I believe in what I'm doing. This goes far beyond the funding. It means quality of life to a lot of people." She kept her gaze focused on the lake. The last thing she wanted Mel Lun to see was even the slightest hint of vulnerability. That could be taken as a sign of weakness, and that was not a trait to exhibit this week.

One week of every year, top Marcon executives and their department heads dropped off the corporate map to a remote retreat and made the decisions that would dictate which direction the company's research and development would follow for the next twelve months. To the top executives it was an opportunity to meet with their key research scientists outside the lab environment. To the team leaders, each one with up to fifty lab technicians under them, it was crucial to whether their projects were funded or dismantled. Jennifer Pearce was no exception.

Her group was twenty-two highly trained researchers, intent on finding a drug to halt or eliminate Alzheimer's. Their research was through Phase I and well into Phase II, which meant that the drug was already undergoing clinical trials on humans. And if Phase II results were good, the chances of having an FDA-approved drug were also good. And with the right drug for the right disease, that could translate to a billion dollars for the company. Big risks also meant big money.

"They made their decision, Jennifer," he said, rubbing his hands together briskly, then returning them to his jacket pockets.

"And . . ." she said after he was silent for a few seconds. The short bursts of steam had stopped, and she realized she was holding her breath.

"They decided to fund Jenkins."

She spun to face him now, anger flashing in her eyes. "You think this is a game, Mel? You tell me I made a good presentation, knowing they decided against funding my research. Do you enjoy hurting people, Mel? Is that it?"

He shrugged. "I didn't make the decision, Jen, they did. Take your case to them."

"I did," she fired back at him. "Yesterday, in my 'excellent' presentation." She felt the tears welling up and secretly cursed herself for being so emotional. This was business, and emotions had no place here. She stared into his cold eyes. "The difference between my research and Ray Jenkins's is that mine will save lives. His will wipe a few wrinkles off some aging faces."

"Wrinkles are big business, Jen, you know that. The boomers can't get their credit cards out fast enough when what they're buying will strip off some of the years. And they've got the money."

"Money," she said. "It's all about money. Always money."

He snickered and shook his head slightly. "Look at you. Talk about a hypocrite. If the board had decided to fund your research, you'd be ecstatic. Because you got the money. When you say that it's all about money, keep in mind you're as guilty as anyone else."

"But I want it for the right reasons, Mel."

Jennifer Pearce turned from the lake where the morning sun was burning off the mist and strode back toward the parking lot. Her hands were clenched in fists, and she could feel her teeth grinding as her jaw tightened. The tears spilled down her cheeks, but she didn't brush them away. The rented Taurus sat in the parking lot, one of only two cars at this early hour. She glanced at Lun's rental, wondering how he knew where to find her. It was a passing thought; she didn't really care. She slid behind the wheel and gunned the engine, slamming the transmission into drive and spinning gravel across the driver's side of the other car as she careened out of the lot.

Eight years.

She wiped the tears now, so she could see the twists and turns in the road as it descended from the top of the ridge toward Lake Superior. Eight years of her life with Marcon Pharmaceuticals, and this was where it was to end. Her research usurped by another group whose focus was on esthetics, not disease. She couldn't believe Marcon had stooped to the levels of the other Big Pharma giants. The one reason she had brought her box of pens and her Ph.D. to Marcon was their commitment to discovering and developing new drugs that targeted disease. Under Roy Vagelos, the company's CEO from 1985 to 1996, Marcon was the industry trendsetter in R&D. The company encouraged individual thinking that fostered new ideas and looked to lighting paths seldom traveled. It was the one by which all the Big Pharma companies set their benchmarks. Edward Pittman, the pharmaceutical analyst for the big money pension funds, used Marcon as a barometer for what was happening in the industry.

Marcon was the cornerstone of excellence. And that was why she had hung her shingle at Marcon rather than the hundred-odd other companies that had wooed her when she exited MIT with the ink still fresh on her doctorate. That, and the promises.

Her own research team, almost unlimited funding, the chance to set her own agenda; the offer was too good to turn down. And although her Phase I tests had gone well, her Phase II tests were average at best. Now they were pulling the rug out from under her.

The tears returned when she thought of the failed marriage and two other disastrous relationships, ruined by her reluc-

Jeff Buick

tance to commit one hundred percent to anything or anyone outside the lab. She smashed her fist on the steering wheel, remembering the sadness in her husband's eyes as he walked out the front door for the last time. She had let him go, choosing her career over his love. The road blurred as the tears flowed freely now. She accelerated into a curve and then hammered on the brakes as she realized she wasn't going to make it. The rear end of the Taurus fishtailed and slammed into a gnarled basswood. The car threatened to veer into the trees for a second, then regained its grip on the road and came back under control. She slowed and sucked in a few deep breaths, aware of how close she had been to serious injury or death. Her hands were shaking, but she didn't stop. There was one man who deserved a piece of her mind—and he was going to get it.

She reached Peterson's Cottages on the distant edge of Ontonagon and pulled the battered rental up in front of Cedar Lodge, the largest of the guest cabins. She adjusted the rearview mirror so she could see her reflection. Her eyes, usually so clear and bright with sparkling hazel irises, were bloodshot. Framing her eyes were naturally thin, dark eyebrows. Her forehead, nose, and cheeks flowed flawlessly to her full lips, and when she smiled her teeth were white with few imperfections despite her never having had braces as a child. Her shoulder-length auburn hair was windblown but fell into place with a few flicks of her fingertips. She stared at her reflection for a few moments, taking in the toll of the last eight years.

She had been thirty when she first arrived at Marcon. Thirty and in demand by both pharmaceutical companies and a long line of single men. Her hair was longer then, past her shoulders, and her face leaner with no laugh lines. Her eyes were intelligent, and although she was strikingly attractive, they told the observer that this woman was no waitress at the local pub. She dressed well and carried herself with absolute confidence, something that scared some men and intrigued others. To say that she had been an interesting addition to the Marcon research was a gross understatement. Jennifer Pearce had been the primary topic at many lunch tables and over many a Budweiser at the bars near the research facility. But that was eight years ago, and this was now.

She opened the door and headed for the cabin without checking the damage on the rental. She knocked on the rough wood and waited. A half minute later, a tall man in his mid-sixties opened the door. He was dressed in a track suit and there was little fat on his frame. His hair was silver and his gaze steady and powerful. He didn't smile when he saw her. He stepped aside, and she entered the rustic cabin. The aroma of freshly baked scones tinged the air.

She wasted no words. "What's going to happen to my team?" she asked.

Sheldon Zachery, CEO of Marcon Pharmaceuticals, closed the door behind her, his face taking on a grim look. "It will be dismantled. We'll try and find places for all your staff on other teams."

"Then I quit, Sheldon," she said. "Effective immediately."

Zachery was thoughtful for a moment. "I wish you'd take some time, Jennifer, rethink things. You've invested a lot in Marcon and we've invested a lot in you."

"I've given you the last eight years of my life," she said, her voice rising. "In retrospect, I should have spent more time with my husband. Maybe I'd have kids, something to show I had a life once. My decision is final. I'm leaving."

"You can't take the research with you, Jennifer. It's proprietary. It stays with us."

She leaned close to one of the most influential and powerful men in the global pharmaceutical market. "What I have in my head stays there, Sheldon. That, I take with me. And it's far more valuable than what's on the discs in the lab."

Zachery's eyes narrowed. "What are you saying, Jennifer?"

"You figure it out, Sheldon. You're the CEO. You're the one with all the answers."

"If you run to a competitor and deliver them proprietary goods, we'll sue," he said. "We'll shut you and your new company down in record time."

She smiled, even white teeth showing beneath her rekindled

Jeff Buick

eyes. "Take your best shot, Sheldon, because what you've got in a court of law is squat. You've got Phase I and Phase II tests, but you don't have a billion-dollar drug. Not by a long shot. That is going elsewhere, courtesy of your stupidity."

His face took on color. "Are you threatening me?"

"You can take the truth as you wish, Sheldon. I know where I want to go with my research. You don't. No one else does. For the past few months I've been biding my time, waiting to see whether Marcon would back a new approach to fighting Alzheimer's. Now I know. Looks like keeping my trump card close to my chest was a good idea."

"Maybe if you'd brought it out," he said, "we would have seen things differently. Maybe the funding would have gone your way."

"I doubt it," she said. "I don't think you understand. Marcon doesn't think like it did when Vagelos was at the helm." She turned to the door and opened it. A gust of cool spring air rushed in. "Have HR send my final check to my house. And don't forget the vacation pay. You can keep whatever personal stuff is on my desk."

She jumped into the Taurus and jammed it into gear. What a disaster. But in the back of her mind, she had suspected Zachery might hedge on her funding. Her group's approach to the Alzheimer's quandary was not novel, but more of the same, targeting the beta amyloid protein that was known to force healthy tissue aside and invade key spaces in the brain. But what Zachery and the other Marcon brass didn't know was that she had isolated a new chemical in the sequence, one unknown and unnoticed in the hundreds of thousands of previous screened molecules by all the big pharmaceutical companies.

She had the key. She just had to prove it in clinical trials. And that knowledge was going with her when she left Marcon.

8

Evan Ziegler deplaned in Richmond, cursing the rain. It was the last day of April, but there was no warmth to the heavy mist. Just a gray day that chilled the bones and made driving ugly. He navigated the rental car through the sodden streets, past a group of school kids on their way home from classes, splashing in puddles and laughing when one of them slipped and fell, soaking his pants. Evan cracked a smile as a memory of Ben, drenched from a sudden downpour, came to mind. The smile faded as quickly as it had materialized.

He found the Commonwealth Park Suites Hotel easily enough and collected the package from the front-desk clerk. He sat in one of the wingback chairs in the oblong lobby and slowly opened the sealed flap. He tilted the envelope and the contents spilled onto his lap. There were three pages and a small plastic envelope with three tiny bags inside. He slipped the plastic envelope into his pocket and perused the written material. The cover page had a picture of his target and a brief bio. Albert Rousseau. Ziegler had pictured him as a geek, and he wasn't far off. The man's skin was pockmarked and fresh acne was scarring the few remaining smooth patches. Under the unruly mess of hair was a pasty complexion and bad teeth. Albert was never going to make the cover of *GQ*.

The address was on Cooley Avenue, in Carytown, a trendy section of Richmond just off the Fan District, and Evan found a Starbucks on the way. He picked up a latte and set the car's radio to a classic rock station as he sipped on the drink. It was a few minutes after four o'clock when he pulled up in front of Rousseau's town house. He found a parking spot halfway down the block and walked around to the rear of the dwelling. Each of the units had a small yard with a wood deck and a gas light. He counted the units from the corner and let himself into Rousseau's yard. A neighbor three doors down glanced over, but Evan knew the look: Nothing was registering. He wouldn't even remember that someone had entered the yard, let alone what that person looked like.

The back door had two locks, one on the handset and the other a deadbolt. Evan picked the lower one and tried the door. It opened. He grinned at the stupidity of having an expensive deadbolt on an outer door and not using it. He closed the door quietly behind him, listening for any sound that would indicate the house was protected by an alarm. Nothing.

He was in the galley-style kitchen, dated but clean. He glanced at the stove and noticed the gas burners. Excellent. A quick tour through the town house assured him that no one was home and that he was in the right place, then he got to work. The stove pulled away from the wall with a minimum of effort, and he hopped into the narrow space between the stove and the wall. The flexible gas line to the stove was old, probably twenty years. He smiled at that; this was getting easier all the time. Grasping the line with both hands, he bent it back and forth, weakening the line at one of the joints. It took the better part of fifteen minutes before the line cracked and the unmistakable odor of natural gas stung his nostrils. He immediately placed a small piece of clear tape over the break. The smell lingered for a moment, then dissipated through the house. He jumped up on the counter, then dropped to the floor and pushed the stove back in place.

Now it was time to wait.

Albert Rousseau counted the number of days until he would be fabulously wealthy. Twenty-three. He grinned and shut down the operating system on his office computer. He wanted to be home by seven in case it was a *Seinfeld* he hadn't seen, although the chances of that were just about zero. He put the Mustang through its paces on the drive home, thinking about what kind of car he would buy with the money. He didn't even worry about whether Veritas would pay for the information he had stashed in his town house on that tiny disc. They would pay.

Oh, my God, would they pay.

He found a parking space almost directly in front of his unit. Another sign the gods were smiling on him. He unlocked the door and pushed it open, a handful of mail in his right hand. He swung around and closed the door with his left. For a split second he was face-to-face with another man. A stranger. A stranger in his house. He reacted, but it was far too late for that.

Evan grabbed him by the hair and spun him 180 degrees, pulling him back all in the same motion. Evan's forearm closed over Albert's windpipe and instantly cut off the air supply. Albert tried to grab the assailant's arm but found both his arms trapped against his body. His attacker had immobilized both arms by pinning them behind his back. He tried to scream, but there was no air. He fought to find some way to breathe, but the arms that held him were like vises. Panicked and seething with adrenaline, he mustered every ounce of strength and lashed out with almost superhuman strength. He felt the pressure on his windpipe slip a fraction as he managed to turn slightly, but the grip on his arms tightened and only a tiny gulp of air got through. The room went fuzzy, then gray, then black. His body stopped fighting and the pressure subsided. He willed his muscles to move, but there was no response. Then, as the last neurons in his brain stopped firing, he realized he was already dead and that his brain had taken longer to die than his body. He had a strange thought as his brain shut down; how long did the brain continue to function after the guillotine came down?

Evan let the lifeless body drop gently to the floor. The last thing he needed was bruises anywhere on the corpse; they might be noticed in the autopsy. He had been very careful not to squeeze the windpipe so hard as to crush it, a useful trick he had picked up during his tenure with Team Six. He had picked up a lot of useful information while with the Navy SEALs, most of which dealt with killing people. It was proving to be most valuable.

He carried the body into the kitchen so there would be no drag marks on the floor and propped it against the stove. He retrieved the plastic pouch from his pocket and carefully opened it by cutting a slit down one side. Inside were three smaller plastic bags, the combined contents weighing no more than one ounce. Another cut in one of the tiny bags and the odor of sulfuric acid wafted up and stung his nose. The other two contained potassium chlorate and methenamine. He mixed the three chemicals together and gently set them on the counter. They were a ticking time bomb now. He had less than ten minutes before the mixture would ignite. But he didn't need ten minutes of gas in the house or the entire block would disappear. Three minutes tops. He had a few minutes to kill before he removed the piece of tape from the gas line.

Rousseau's ID card was attached to his shirt pocket, and Evan glanced at it. Something wasn't right. He cradled it in his right hand and read the inscription: *Clearance level 6 . . . Statin Group.* He held the photo ID for a few moments, then let it drop back against the dead man's shirt. Statins. That wasn't right. Statins were cholesterol drugs. Bruce Andrews had sanctioned Albert Rousseau because he was threatening the BioTech research into brain chips.

Or so Andrews had said.

Evan recoiled from the body and almost toppled over one of

the kitchen chairs as he staggered backward. Jesus Christ. What was going on? How could Rousseau be a threat to the brain chip program if he worked on cholesterol drugs? That didn't make any sense. The two weren't even in the same building. Evan knew the corporate structure of Veritas well, and he was positive the statin research group was in BioTech Five, along with the corporate offices. Brain chip development was in one of the satellite parks in White Oak, a biotechnology park in Henrico County, miles from the Richmond research park.

Evan checked his watch. Shit, he had to get moving or the trigger was going to ignite before the house had a chance to fill with gas. He grabbed the kitchen chair that had fallen over and tucked it back under the table, then hopped up on the counter and slid his arm down behind the stove. He felt the tape with his fingers and pulled. The unmistakable odor of natural gas immediately filled the room. He set the trigger device on the back of the stove, picked up the plastic bag and left through the back door, locking it behind him. There were no neighbors about, and he walked briskly down the back lane and around the corner to his car. He checked his watch again, quickly started the car, and pulled away from the curb. He was less than a block away when the town house exploded.

The explosion blew out the back of the unit and all the front windows on the main floor. The side walls held, which was good as it limited collateral damage. Flying bricks, jagged shards of glass, and splintered wood rained down on the town houses backing onto the target. Dogs were barking, children screaming, and adults yelling as Evan rounded the corner and the carnage disappeared from his view. He would read about it in tomorrow's newspaper, but the explosion had gone off almost exactly as he had hoped and he doubted there would be any casualties except for Albert Rousseau.

But that didn't mean no innocent people had been killed.

Evan pulled over at the first coffee shop he passed and ordered an extra-large latte. He sat by the window and watched the rain splatter in the puddles. Albert Rousseau was a lab rat

Jeff Buick

from BioTech Five, not a key player in the brain chip department, as Andrews had said.

How many of the four people he had killed for Andrews were legitimate threats to the program that could give his son back feeling in his body? One? Two? None? He drained the last of his coffee and returned to the rental with one thought on his mind:

Get face-to-face with Bruce Andrews and ask the question. Why is he killing these people?

9

Elsie Hughes stuffed her groceries in the plastic bag, wondering who had come up with the bright idea of charging three cents per bag. As if they didn't make enough money off the food she had to buy every few days. She smiled at the clerk as she left; it wasn't his fault.

The Texas sun was hot, the mercury pushing ninety-two, as she exited the store. It took less than a minute to load the bags in her trunk and return the cart to the small corral and retrieve her quarter. She plopped into the front seat and checked her watch. She could stop by the bank if she hurried; the kids wouldn't be out of school for another eight minutes. Her paycheck sat on the passenger's seat, and she ripped off the stub showing her deductions as she waited for a traffic light. Fleetwood Mac played softly on her radio, and she twisted the knob slightly to the right. Stevie Nicks's quivering voice shot shivers down her spine. The light changed and she hit the gas, singing along with Stevie.

Her bank was two blocks north of the supermarket and on the way to the kids' school. She pulled into the parking lot and lucked out with a spot right by the ATM. There was no line, and she took the open machine on the far left. Deposit envelopes were tucked in a slot next to the machine, and she pulled one out, slipped her check in, and licked the flap. It tasted tart, but she swallowed the glue residue and tucked the check in the opening. She glanced at the account balance and grimaced slightly. Why was money so hard to earn and so easy to spend? She returned to her car and dropped the slip of paper into the console between the two front seats. The dashboard clock read 3:15, the exact time her kids were released from classes. She swung out onto the road from the parking lot and gunned the car. She'd make it in time.

The taste from the envelope lingered on her tongue, and she scraped the top side against her upper teeth. First the grocery store charging three cents for plastic bags, now foul-tasting glue on the envelopes.

Why were the simple things getting complicated?

10

The law firm of Stevens and Hilbrecht was tucked away on the second floor of one of the old historical buildings on Harrison Street. On the side of the building was a prominent ghost sign in white paint on red brick, promoting the long-defunct Bronx Lounge. Parking was in a secluded lot behind the building, and Gordon left his BMW in the stall closest to the alley and entered through the rear door. A musty smell tickled his nostrils and he sneezed a couple of times. It happened every time he visited his lawyer.

The stairs were wooden and creaked slightly under his weight. He reached the second-floor landing and veered right, down the hall and into Christine Stevens's office. Her receptionist and paralegal, Belinda, was manning the scarred wooden desk and smiled as he entered.

"Hi, Gordon," she said cheerfully. "Christine said to send you right in when you arrived."

"Thanks, Belinda." He tried to force a smile, but he couldn't seem to force his lips to make the journey. He strode down the hall and into the second office on the left. A mid-thirties woman sat in the pewter and tanned-leather chair behind the desk, a pair of reading glasses perched on the end of her nose. She was diminutive, no more than five-four, with a slender figure that probably fit into a size two, three at best. Her hair was dark brown with a few lingering streaks of color she'd tried months back and realized she didn't like. Her face was chalk white and bony, and her teeth were too big for her mouth when she smiled. But this Friday morning, she wasn't smiling. She pointed to one of the chairs facing her desk, and Gordon sat. The chairs were more tanned leather on pewter frames and decidedly uncomfortable. They melded with the rest of the room, which was sparsely decorated with spindly halogen lamps and cold metal sculptures.

"I've been on the phone for fifteen hours on this file, Gordon," she said. Christine Stevens charged by the hour and didn't make idle conversation. "And I don't have very good news."

Gordon was stone-faced. "Just tell me what you found."

Christine Stevens focused on some papers on her desk. "Veritas Pharmaceutical is a medium-size company if you compare it to the Big Pharma companies, but that doesn't mean it's small potatoes."

"Big Pharma?" Gordon asked.

"Marcon, Frezin, GlasoKlan—the big guys in researching and marketing new drugs. They're collectively referred to as Big Pharma. I don't think it's meant as a term of endearment. These are the guys who spend up to eight hundred million to bring a new drug to the market. Their research and marketing budgets are in the ozone. We're talking big-time here, Gordon. Anyway, Veritas is a few billion short of fitting in with the big boys."

"Okay," Gordon said. "What did you find out about Triaxcion?"

She flipped over a few pages. "Not the best drug on the market. There have been some rumblings over the past couple of years that Triaxcion might cause peripheric tissues to mutate slightly, rendering A-positive blood incapable of coagulating."

Gordon stared at her. "What?" he finally said. "What are you saying?"

"Billy was A positive, Gordon. And when he slashed himself with the chain saw, he bled to death because his blood wouldn't clot. And Billy was taking Triaxcion for his hair loss. It doesn't take a rocket scientist to put two and two together."

"That drug caused Billy's death?" Gordon said quietly.

Stevens leaned back in her chair. "I can't say that with total conviction, Gordon. If you were to ask me if I thought Triaxcion was responsible for Billy dying, I would say yes. But proving it in a court of law won't be so easy. I've spoken with twelve other lawyers who have clients with family members they suspect have died as a result of Triaxcion, but none of them feel they have what is necessary to go to court."

"Each one of them has a body, Christine," Gordon said tersely. "What more do they need?"

"Definitive proof. Veritas isn't going to lie down and die on this, Gordon. This drug is worth hundreds of millions of dollars to these guys. They have a legal department that rivals Microsoft. Forty-two lawyers, three times that many paralegals, and an investigative budget in the tens of millions. They're going to protect their patent and their legal right to keep the FDA approval until someone can prove beyond any doubt that the drug can be fatal. And we don't have that proof."

"Billy wasn't a bleeder, Christine. When we were kids, he used to get cut all the time. His blood always clotted. Something caused things to change, and the only variable is Triaxcion. I say that's definitive proof."

She shook her head. "If you're going to initiate a class-action tort suit against a major pharmaceutical company, you'd better have the evidence and the money to back it up."

"We have both," Gordon said.

"No," Christine said slowly, "you don't. You have a few million dollars, Gordon. Maybe twenty or thirty tops. If we're going after Veritas, we'll have to bring in another firm, a major player, with at least twenty lawyers on retainer. You'll have a fight that will last years and eat up every dollar you've ever earned. You'll lose the mill, spend more time in court than at home, and in the end, probably lose. And you'll lose because they have the connections—inside the FDA and on the Hill in D.C. You'll lose because you're angry at what happened, but they're ruthless. You're a decent person, Gordon, and these guys eat decent people for breakfast. You'll lose because sometimes life just isn't fair."

Gordon was silent. He stared at her with tired eyes. "And this is one of those times," he finally said.

She nodded. "I can take the case, Gordon. I can bring in medical and pharmaceutical experts and have them testify. I can build a solid legal team and fight a good fight. I can bring public awareness to the drug's side effects. But I can't win, Gordon. I know that going in."

"Then what do I do, Christine?" he asked. "Just accept the fact that these people killed my brother and get on with my life?" She didn't answer. "How can I do that, Christine?"

She shrugged. "I don't know, Gordon. But I do know this. Billy wouldn't have wanted you to destroy yourself over this. It was his mistake with the chain saw that caused the accident. And he chose to take the drug to stop his hair loss. There are always choices in life, Gordon, and your brother made a couple of bad ones. Don't get me wrong, I'm on your side. But if you want to pursue this, it's against my advice."

"There's no other lawyer ready to file a litigation claim against Veritas?" he asked.

She shook her head. "As I said, I've managed to dig up twelve other lawyers looking at Veritas, but none of them are willing to serve papers. And every one of those twelve firms is considerably larger than this one."

"How did you find them?" Gordon asked. "The other deaths?"

"Sometimes lawyers file paperwork with their respective jurisdictions when they have a client who may have a litigation claim. It's precautionary, that's all. It doesn't mean they have to proceed, but just filing gives them the option to pursue an action against the drug's manufacturer at some point in the future."

"Can I have the names?" Gordon asked.

Christine didn't waver for a moment with her response. "The

information is privileged, Gordon. It's not in the public domain until they begin proceedings. These families would get pretty upset if someone showed up asking questions. Imagine how you'd feel."

"If a stranger showed up on my door and told me someone they loved had died as a result of Triaxcion, it would give me hope. It would let me know I'm not alone."

She shook her head. "I can't do it, Gordon. I could get disbarred."

He ran his fingers through his hair, then pulled a toothpick from his pocket and peeled off the protective cover. "Where do we go from here?"

"Wherever you want. But keep in mind that I'm strongly opposed to starting any legal action against these guys."

"All right. Leave it with me. Let me think about it." He stood up and offered his hand. "I'll get back to you in two weeks, around the end of May."

She nodded and walked him to the door. "This could consume you if you let it, Gordon," she said, her voice softer now. Like a friend would tell another friend not to do something stupid.

"Yeah, I understand. It's a big decision."

The sun was just touching the tips of the trees on the westerly foothills as he exited the legal office. He slowly walked across the parking lot, fingering the keys to his car. Even with his wealth, he was powerless against this corporation. They were killing people and they knew it. But the dollar signs outweighed the rights of the poor bastards with A-positive blood who were losing their hair. What were thirteen dead when profits ran into the hundreds of millions? What did it matter if every one of those dead people had families who loved and cherished them? Who missed them?

He set his hand on the roof of his car and stared at the darkening sky. He had to decide which way to go. Indirectly, someone at Veritas had murdered his brother. Yet pursuing them would probably destroy him. For a split second he wished he'd never found the pill bottle; that the police had cleaned out

Jeff Buick

Billy's medicine cabinet and thrown the damn thing in the garbage. But that hadn't happened. He knew, and now he needed to decide. He felt sick to his stomach, because he knew one thing for certain.

He was facing a lose-lose situation.

11

BioTech Five was a busy place for a Friday, even busier than usual with the aftermath of Bruce Andrews's press release the previous day. The reporters were gone, but the activity levels were exaggerated, employees moving briskly about with purpose, fueled by the positive quarterly report on earnings. The company was on a high, and everyone was looking to its CEO as the driving force behind the surge. It was an image Bruce Andrews did little to dispel.

He was in at six, and by nine had made rounds through four of the on-site labs, shaking hands and thanking his staff for their efforts. At nine-fifteen he was back in his office, checking e-mail and waiting for his nine-thirty appointment. He glanced at the lone file on his polished desk and opened it, although he already knew what was inside.

Jennifer Pearce, research scientist with impeccable educational credentials and a proven track record for team management. A Marcon star who, for some reason, had become disillusioned with the pharmaceutical giant and put herself on the market. Her attractive face stared back at him from the cover page, her eyes conveying intelligence and self-confidence. Her hair was cut just above her shoulders, streaked with differing tones of blond and well styled. Her face was lean and her slender, toned neck and shoulders indicated the gym was part of her regular regimen. He liked what he saw.

At precisely nine-thirty, there was a soft knock on his door and his executive assistant ushered Jennifer Pearce into his office. She moved across the expanse of carpet to his desk with confident strides and offered her hand, her eyes locked on his.

"Good morning, Dr. Pearce," he said, accepting her hand. He was shocked at the strength in her grip but masked his reaction.

"Mr. Andrews," she replied.

"That sounds pretty formal," Andrews said, pointing to one of the wingback chairs facing his desk. "If first names are okay with you, I'm Bruce."

"First names are fine, thank you," she said, sitting and crossing her legs. She wore a sage-colored pantsuit with a finely knit crew-neck sweater. With the exception of two small diamond-stud earrings, she wore no jewelry.

"It's a little crazy around here this morning," he said. "We had a news conference and posted our quarterly profits yesterday. Things went very well."

"I saw the highlights on the late business report," she replied. "Veritas seems to be riding a wave right now."

"One that we've worked for," Andrews said with an easy smile. He glanced at her file, which sat open on his desk. "You spent eight years at Marcon, in their Alzheimer's research division," he said, getting right to business. She nodded. "Who did you report to?"

"Allan Connors, one of the regional vice presidents," she replied. "Sometimes directly to Sheldon Zachery."

"I know Allan," Andrews said. "He's a pretty good guy. Knows his stuff from a technical stance."

"Very good with the research end of things," she agreed.

They bandied a string of names back and forth for a few minutes, and Jennifer was impressed with Andrews's knowledge of who was where and what they were working on. The man had his finger on the pulse of the pharmaceutical industry. She liked the man's easy manner and quick smile; he was sincere and likable. His knowledge of Alzheimer's research was impressive from both a technical and management viewpoint. And to Jennifer, that was a key factor. Where Marcon had failed was in their lack of vision. They professed to still be the industry benchmark for R&D, but the upper management was decimating the teams working in the research trenches. And ultimately, that had cost Marcon. She had left and taken a potentially huge idea with her.

"We would have you in our Alzheimer's group, of course," Andrews was saying. "In fact, what I had envisioned was a second team with you heading it up."

Jennifer leaned forward slightly. Even with her credentials and experience, it was highly unlikely she would immediately land a team leader position with a new company. "What sort of resources would I have at my disposal?" she asked.

"Ten to twelve researchers with a minimum master's degree and at least two doctorates in the group. Seven assistant researchers with undergrad degrees and proper maintenance staff for your equipment. Your admin lab would be here, on the second floor of BioTech Five, with an additional six thousand square feet at our facility in White Oak. Most of your time would be spent here."

"What is White Oak?" she asked.

"The Virginia BioTechnology Research Park at White Oak is a satellite park to this one. There just isn't enough space in downtown Richmond for all the new high-tech industry, so in 2001 Henrico County and Virginia's Science Park struck an agreement to set aside over two thousand acres for development. Hewlett-Packard and White Oak Semiconductor are just two companies with major R&D facilities at White Oak, and with that sort of muscle going into the new facility, we saw the park as an ideal alternative to the high prices we pay for space here. So we purchased two hundred and eighty thousand square feet of space when it first opened. Turned out to be a great investment; we could sell it now for triple what we paid for it. The only downside is that it's about forty minutes when traffic is moving. Considerably longer when I-64 is jammed up."

She nodded. "And what salary would you be offering?"

"I had initially asked the board to clear an offer of two-fifty a year plus bonuses, but I revamped that yesterday, partly because we've had such a good first quarter."

She waited a few seconds. "And what would the other part be?"

He looked confused for a second. "How's that?"

"You said *partly* because of your earnings. That would indicate there's another aspect."

He smiled. "Yes, there is, Jennifer. The other part is simple. I want you at Veritas. I'm no fool. You are going to have a stack of offers to choose from once you've made your rounds of available employers, and I want you to pick us. That's why I had the board okay an initial offer of three hundred and sixty thousand a year, plus bonuses."

"What are the bonuses based on?" she asked, her mouth suddenly very dry.

"Timely Phase I and Phase II trials. We can sell a new drug in the pipeline to Wall Street once we have good Phase II results, and that buoys investor confidence. Even if we're still five years from putting a new Alzheimer's drug on the shelves, you'll have earned every cent we're paying you and your team in increased stock prices."

"You sound confident I can deliver," she said.

He shifted slightly in his chair, leaned his elbows on his desk, and steepled his fingers. "I have a lot of respect for anyone coming over from Marcon. Especially a team leader with eight years under her belt. Who knows what insights you've managed to garner over that eight years."

Jennifer leaned back in her chair. This was the one constant in every interview she had had in the last two weeks. What was she bringing with her from Marcon? Did she have something that could translate to a fast-track Phase II trial? To date, her interviewer's tactics in broaching the subject had varied from aggressive to mouselike. She liked Andrews's approach—subtle, but on the table.

"I have some ideas that may seem a little out of the box," she responded. "Would it bother you if my team were to investigate a new approach to the beta amyloid buildup?"

Andrews didn't give anything away with his body language. "Not if the approach was well grounded. That's how new drugs are discovered, Jennifer. By researchers thinking outside the box."

She was thoughtful for a moment. "Should I assume that you're offering me a position, Bruce?"

He nodded. "Yes. The salary I mentioned and six weeks holidays. Plus you'll need to relocate to Richmond. We'll cover all costs of your move, including the sale of your house."

"All right," she said. "I'll give your offer serious consideration. I'd like to take about a week to make my decision. By, say, May twentieth. Does that work for you?"

"Absolutely," Andrews said, rising from behind his desk and extending his hand. They shook, and he gave her a business card. "My direct line is on the card if you need to speak further."

"Thanks," she said.

Jennifer left BioTech Five feeling upbeat. She liked the building, the company, and she liked Bruce Andrews. And what he was offering was exactly what she was looking for: her own team, autonomy to move her research the direction she wanted, and excellent money. She knew Richmond a bit, having visited a few times, and she liked the city. It was vibrant and progressive, with a thriving theater scene. She would be leaving New Jersey and a lot of very good friends, but with six weeks holidays, she could visit home whenever she felt the urge. And with three-sixty plus bonuses, money wouldn't be an issue.

She reached her rental car at the same time she reached a decision.

She was moving to Richmond.

12

BioTech Five was in its nightly hibernation, the tardiest lab techs gone for the weekend for over an hour. Hallways were dimly lit with emergency lighting and faint night-lights cast eerie shadows through the laboratories. Armed security guards sat chatting at the front doors, making their rounds on the top of each hour. A lone light burned in Bruce Andrews's corner office.

Andrews's exterior door opened quietly, then closed. A solitary figure, dressed entirely in black, crossed the carpet with stealth. The CEO felt another presence and turned away from his laptop. His visitor sat on the edge of the desk, a silenced pistol in hand.

"What the hell?" Andrews said, leaping from his chair.

"Sit down," the man said, leaning forward into the glow from the computer monitor.

"Evan Ziegler," Andrews said, an audible sigh escaping as he recognized his hired killer. "What's with the theatrics? And what the hell are you doing here?"

"I've got a couple of questions, Bruce," Evan said, the gun horizontal and unwavering.

"Evan, it's incredibly dangerous for you to come here."

"Dangerous for whom?" Evan asked. "I don't see how coming here could be dangerous for me. Maybe for breaking and entering, but who's going to press charges?"

Andrews sat and folded his arms on his chest. "What do you want, Evan?"

"I want some answers, Bruce. Like why do you have me killing people in your statin department? Perhaps you can explain to me how cholesterol drugs are tied in with brain chips."

"You're talking about Albert Rousseau," Andrews said, his mind racing through his options. Trying to take Evan Ziegler by force was totally out of the question. The man was a killing machine, with or without the gun. Lying to him would only infuriate the man, and he already looked extremely pissed off. But telling him the truth wasn't a good idea either. "Rousseau was getting ready to release information to the press unless we paid him off."

"What sort of information?"

"Highly classified, Evan," Andrews said, piecing together his train of thought as he went. "Rousseau was a researcher working on one of our cholesterol drugs, but he also had access to confidential computer systems outside his department. Someone was hacking into the highly secure files in our brain chip lab, and we traced it back to Rousseau's computer. Once we suspected it was Rousseau, we attached a sniffer pack to his office and home computers and monitored both of them for over a month. There was no doubt in our minds that Albert Rousseau was preparing to either blackmail us or go to the press."

"With what, Bruce? What are you hiding?"

Good question, Andrews thought. He didn't have a clue. He was ad-libbing his way through this mess. Ziegler had caught him flat-footed. "Evan, we are moving through the exploratory stages of the brain chip development at an extreme pace. We are bypassing federal guidelines that insist we spend a certain amount of time on each of the Phase I tests. If we were to comply with the government regulations, it would add months,

Jeff Buick

maybe years, to the development of a brain chip that will give your son upper-body movement. I'm pushing the envelope, Evan. And I'm sticking my neck out for Ben."

The gun barrel angled down toward the carpet. "How did Rousseau get this information? I mean, if the systems are so secure."

Andrews was relaxing now, knowing that he had disarmed the situation. "Come on, Evan, the guy was a computer programmer and a research scientist with master's degrees in computers and microbiology. He was no dummy. Once he saw how we were circumventing the federal laws, he saw an opportunity. Whether he was going to go to the police or blackmail us, I have no idea. But we saw it coming and brought you in to stop him."

"You keep saying *we*. Who is the *we?*"

"That is none of your business, Evan," Andrews said, now taking control of the conversation. "And what's with the gun? You going to shoot me?"

Evan glanced at the silenced pistol. "No, of course not. It was in case I ran into some of the guards."

"Then put it away," Andrews said curtly. "And don't shoot any of my security guards on the way out."

"I've got another question, Bruce," Ziegler said, slipping the pistol under his sweater. "How many more people do I have to kill for you? When we first spoke, I thought this would entail removing one of two people, but this is getting ridiculous. I've killed four people in cold blood. That's not what the American government trained me to do. That's not what I want to do with my life."

"I pay you well to remove obstacles, Evan," Andrews retorted.

"I don't do it for the money," Evan replied, knowing that his quality of life and his copier business in Denver had profited greatly from the cash Andrews forwarded to him after each hit. "I just want Ben out of that chair."

Andrews nodded and leaned forward. "That's why I approached you, Evan. The SEALs gave you certain skills that I need, and I have what it will take to get your son walking again. I would never have asked you to help me if Ben didn't desperately need the technology Veritas is developing. I knew when I embarked on the brain chip program that I would face heavy opposition, that there would be people who would do anything to stop it. Some people feel a moral obligation to oppose it; others want to stop it for economic reasons. It's a drain on our finances, Evan. It reduces research in other sectors. Scientists don't like watching their funding go somewhere else. They're funny that way. And sometimes they react much differently than an ordinary person with a normal IQ would. And when those threats become real, I call you."

"How much longer, Bruce?" Evan asked in a hushed tone.

Andrews shrugged. "We're close to beginning Phase I trials on humans. Perhaps another year, maybe two. I will make sure Ben's application to be in the first test group is approved."

Evan Ziegler was quiet, reflecting on Andrews's words. One year, maybe two. Ben would be twenty or twenty-one. And if the brain chip did stimulate the neural pathways as Andrews had promised, Ben would almost certainly regain movement in the upper portion of his body, possibly in the legs as well. His spinal cord was not so severely damaged that the amplified signals wouldn't make it through. And once those synapses were functioning again, he would walk. Christ, his son would be cured. A normal life, not one as a thinking vegetable, locked in a prison on wheels. Ben would be back.

"That's encouraging, Bruce," Evan said. "One or two years. That's very encouraging."

Andrews smiled, reached out, and set his hand gently on Evan's shoulder. "Yes, Evan, it's incredible. We just have to keep things on track."

"Right," Evan said. He stood slowly, then walked to the door. "I'll talk to you later, Bruce."

"Okay, Evan. Your money will be in Denver in a couple of days. I'll call down to the guards and tell them you're on your way out. They won't bother you."

Jeff Buick

Evan waved his hand nonchalantly and closed the office door behind him. He didn't like Bruce Andrews, and he certainly didn't trust him. But the man was a necessary evil. No other company was pressing forward in brain chip technology as quickly as Veritas. They were the leader, and he would do what he could to ensure they stayed on target.

Even if it meant killing people.

The door closed behind Evan Ziegler and Bruce Andrews's face darkened. Ziegler's statement that he had brought the gun with him in case he ran into a security guard was a total crock of shit. Andrews knew his hired killer had brought the gun with every intention of either forcing some sort of a confession from him or killing him. Which meant Ziegler was quickly becoming a liability. And liabilities were dangerous. Especially when they were capable of walking and talking.

But was killing Ziegler the right course of action? He had the resources in place to remove the man if he desired, but Ziegler was defused for the time being, and was still an asset in some ways.

Things were getting complicated. He was starting to feel like one of those jugglers spinning plates on dowels. And if he got too many plates spinning, they would all crash. He had to settle things down, get a grip on things. And fast. At some point, the press would sniff out the subtle signs that the brain chip division was being terminated. There was no money in helping the one-in-a-million cases out there. And that's exactly what Ben Ziegler was, one in a million. The prognosis for most paraplegics or quadriplegics was hopeless, their spinal cords damaged beyond repair. Ben Ziegler and others like him were the lucky ones. The ones who could actually walk again if enough was invested to see the technology come to fruition. But Veritas was not going to be the company that invested two or three hundred million dollars to reap a few million in rewards. No charity cases here. No orphan drugs—that was for Marcon and the other do-gooders. But that left him with a problem. A very real problem.

If Evan Ziegler somehow learned that the brain chip program was slowly being dismantled, the man would explode. And when a former Navy SEAL exploded, people were sure to die. And Bruce Andrews harbored no doubts that he would be first on Ziegler's list. The man was a time bomb.

He picked up the phone and dialed a number. A man answered. "It's me," Andrews said. "I had a visit from someone tonight, and I need you to put surveillance on him."

"Who?" the voice asked.

"Evan Ziegler."

"I told you bringing him in was a bad idea," the man said. "We never needed him. I could have taken care of everything he did." He sounded irritated.

"What I do not need right now is someone telling me 'I told you so,'" Andrews said. "Just get someone on him. If he books a flight to Richmond without my invitation, kill him. I don't want him near me again."

"Why don't we just take him out now?"

"No, not yet. He may prove to be useful."

"You're playing with fire," the man said, much more than just irritated now. "He's going to fuck things up, Bruce. Mark my words."

"Just get someone to tail him and submit reports. Leave him alone for now. I'll let you know when I want him killed."

"You do that." The line went dead.

"Asshole," Andrews said to the dial tone. He switched off his computer and locked his office for the evening. The guards smiled and told him to have a good night. He smiled back, all the while wanting to beat the stupid grins off their faces. He was beginning to feel the stress. Maybe he had stretched things too thin. Maybe the plates were beginning to crash.

He reached his Cadillac and sat behind the wheel, breathing deeply and reminding himself of the resources he had in place. He had not reached this position in life without risk. The only difference now was that the risk was coming at him from numerous fronts. All he had to do was weather the turbulence. Four or five months, six tops, and the corrections would be in place. It was going to be a rough ride, but he could weather it.

As he started his car, he noticed something. He was smiling. And somehow that made him feel better.

13

Doug Hughes twisted the handset on his front door and pushed, all in the same motion. The handle didn't turn, and he almost smacked his face into the door. He tried the handle again. Locked. He rang the doorbell and waited. Nothing. It was just after five on Monday—no reason for Elsie to be out with the kids. He dug in his pocket, fished out a key, and opened the door. The house was quiet.

"Hello," he said, a slight lilt to his voice. "Honey? You home?"

Silence.

A small, scarred wooden table sat in the foyer, and he dropped his keys on it. The day's mail, usually stacked neatly and waiting for him, was nowhere in sight. He opened the front door and checked the mailbox. It was full. He closed the front door and set the mail on the table next to his keys. Something wasn't right. Unless the kids had some sort of sports or after-school activity, Elsie was always home when he arrived from work, and tonight was no different from any other: The train had dropped him at the station precisely when it did every night. He was positive their calendar was clear. And where were the kids? He slipped off his shoes, calling again for his wife and kids.

Silence. Not a sound.

His wife had been under the weather for the last week, quite sick actually, but if she was heading out to the doctor's office, she would have called. He stopped at the garage door and peeked in. Her vehicle was parked next to his. He felt his heart beating faster and a steely taste in his mouth. Panic. He moved quickly through the house now, checking each room as he went. The main-floor family room was clean and quiet, the television and audio system both turned off. The kitchen was exactly as he had left it, the glass from his morning fruit shake still in the sink. He ran up the open staircase to the upper floor, glancing in the kids' rooms as he moved down the hall. Nothing. Everything clean and quiet. He grasped the handle to the master bedroom and turned. The knob rotated easily and the door swung in a couple of inches.

"Elsie," he said quietly as he entered the room. The bed was ruffled and he could see the outline of his wife under the covers. He took a deep breath and exhaled. She was sleeping. Probably had a neighbor or one of her friends pick up the kids so she could sleep off whatever bug she was fighting. He walked across the room, his stocking feet making no sound on the thick nylon carpet. He reached the edge of the bed and folded the covers back.

And then he screamed.

Doug Hughes screamed again and again as he staggered back from the bed, knocking over the night table and spilling a full glass of water. Staring at him with bloated eyes, one popped completely out of its socket, was a dead person. His wife's face was a strange shade of purple, her lips almost black. A thick, vile liquid was oozing from her mouth onto the sheets. Her mouth was set in a horrific grimace, as though her last breath had been in total agony. A pungent odor drifted to him and he vomited onto the carpet. It was an odor he had never smelled before. It was the odor of death.

LETHAL DOSE

He grasped the phone with unsteady hands and dialed 911. "My wife is dead," he said when the operator came on. "My wife is dead. Oh my God, my wife is dead."

He dropped the phone on the floor, then fainted.

14

"What killed her?" Gil Jacoby asked. Elsie Hughes's death, although not a homicide, had been assigned to his department and he'd drawn the short straw. No one in homicide wanted to deal with any infectious-disease death, let alone one this ugly.

Katie Wood, the chief medical examiner for Austin, Texas, snapped off her protective gloves and deposited them in the biohazard trash just outside the autopsy room. She shook her head as she removed her plastic hair net. "I'm not sure, but I know what it looks like and I hope I'm wrong."

Jacoby was suddenly awake. The tone of the ME's voice was not good. "What?" he asked.

"You'll have to wait a few minutes," she said. "I've got to shower." She left the detective standing in the anteroom, wondering what had just happened. He was even more concerned when another employee showed up a few minutes later in full protective gear and removed the trash can that contained the gloves and hair net. Another person, dressed from head to toe in rubber and plastic, placed a strip of yellow tape across the door to the autopsy room. Neither spoke to him.

"What's going on?" he asked when Wood returned. Her short dark hair was still wet.

She pointed to another room abutting the examining room and they entered, shutting the door behind them. "This is serious," she said, pouring two coffees and offering one to the homicide detective. "Right from the start I suspected this was something different, dangerous. The symptoms the victim exhibited were synonymous with some sort of hemorrhagic fever. Pharyngitis, conjunctivitis, and bleeding from openings in her body."

"Whoa, talk English, Doc. What did you just say?"

"Her throat was inflamed, as were the mucous membranes in and about her eyes. That's what forced her eyeball out of its socket."

"Okay, but what makes this so dangerous?"

"Ever heard of Ebola?" she asked, sipping her coffee.

Jacoby instantly went white. "Of course. But that only happens in Africa. And it's spread by animals."

Wood raised an eyebrow. "Very good, Detective. Ebola's not the only virus that causes hemorrhagic fever. There's one more: Marburg. They're both filoviruses, and they're both very dangerous and very communicable. Once I suspected I may have a filovirus, I stopped normal autopsy procedure, cut out a slice of infected tissue, and magnified the sample on our electron microscope. The viral particles are about fourteen thousand nanometers long and encased in lipids. The only reason I know it's not Ebola is that the particles are over a hundred and sixty nanometers in diameter, twice that of the Ebola virus. And I'm pretty sure they're not Marburg, either."

"Then if the virus isn't Ebola or Marburg, it isn't a filovirus," Jacoby said hopefully.

"I can't say for sure that it is or it isn't," she said. "But we'll know soon enough. Can you find out for me if the victim has been in Africa recently?"

"Of course. I'll call her husband." He started to stand up, but the ME put her hand on his arm.

Jeff Buick

"Use your cell phone, Detective, because neither you nor I are going anywhere until we find out if we've been infected."

Jacoby slowly sat down. "How does that happen?" he asked after a few seconds.

"An hour from now, this place is going to look like something from one of those plague movies. Everyone in protective suits, washing every square millimeter of this place down with the strongest industrial cleaners on the market. They'll bring the necessary equipment with them to run an immunohistochemical procedure once they've fixed a skin biopsy with formalin. It's a pretty definitive test. And if whatever killed her turns out to be a filovirus, we've got a real problem."

"What's that?"

"This facility is rated Biosafety Level Two. Somehow they'll have to get her body to the U.S. Army Medical Research Institute of Infectious Diseases in Fort Detrick, Maryland. It's the only Biosafety Level Four facility in the country."

"Holy shit," Jacoby said. "What about us?"

The ME looked grim. "That's a good question, Detective. A very good question indeed."

15

BioTech Five was a three-level maze, filled with lab rats in white coats scurrying from office to office, notes in hand. It took Jennifer Pearce almost fifteen minutes to find her assigned lab. Everything looked similar: banks of windows, long desks covered with beakers, and small offices, most stuffed with paper overflowing from desks, bookshelves, and filing cabinets. When she finally found her space, she was greeted in a reception area by a woman in her mid- to late twenties.

"Are you Dr. Pearce?" she asked, her voice encumbered with a touch of accent.

"Yes," she replied, trying to place the accent. "And you are?"

"Kenga. Kenga Bakcsi. I'm the executive administrator for your group." She stood and held out a hand. "Welcome to Veritas."

"Thanks," Jennifer said, shaking the woman's hand. She noticed the manicured nails and tasteful bracelet. "Your accent is different. Australian?"

Kenga shook her head. "Not even close. Transylvanian."

Jennifer did a double take on the woman. She was average height with off-blond hair, soft eyes, and cheeks angling down to a chin just a shade too small for her face. She was an attractive young woman with a warm smile and an almost shy demeanor. "You're kidding," Jennifer said. "Transylvania. I've never met anyone from Transylvania."

"Yeah, home of Count Dracula and his friends. Lots of them about. Vampires, of course." Her eyes turned mischievous. "Actually, Transylvania is part of Romania now, so you don't hear it referred to by its original name too often. But enough of that. Your staff is waiting to meet you."

Kenga led Jennifer down a short hall, bare of any pictures or plaques. Jennifer smoothed her light green pantsuit with her hands and ran her fingers through her hair as she walked. She didn't mind meeting new people or even speaking in public, but she knew there would be some tension in the room. Twenty-some people all waiting to meet their new boss. For all they knew, she could be Ms. Ogre with a pocket full of pink slips. They reached the end of the hall and entered a casual boardroom. A long table with enough chairs for all the staff centered the room, while a collection of whiteboards covered the walls. Most were filled with writing and chemical formulas. She immediately recognized some of the work. It was specific to the beta-amyloid approach to Alzheimer's. This was obviously their meeting room, where the team brainstormed new ideas. She liked that—it indicated there was good communication within the group.

The chairs were mostly filled, every eye on her as she entered. She scanned the room quickly, assessing her staff. Most were in their late twenties to early forties. They were dressed in everything imaginable, from the standard white lab coat to ripped blue jeans. She liked that as well. Stifling creativity was a problem in the industry, and lax dress codes indicated an easygoing atmosphere, conducive to independent thinking. She stood at the head of the table.

"Good morning. I'm Jennifer Pearce. Not Dr. Pearce. Not Ms. Pearce. Just Jennifer. And the first thing I'd like to say is that no one in this room is going to lose their job or be transferred." She could almost hear the collective sigh of relief as she continued. "But that said, things are going to change. I have some ideas

I've brought with me from Marcon, and I'd like to incorporate them in how we do things. If you guys are okay with change, we'll get along wonderfully."

Ten minutes later, she thanked them for their attention and left the room with Kenga. Her assistant had a smile on her face.

"That was good," she said as they walked. "Our previous team leader was a tyrant. He had no people skills. Not a good choice to head up an entire division." She pointed to an office on the left, a window office considerably larger than the rest. "This is yours."

Jennifer was tempted to ask what had happened to her predecessor but kept the question to herself. She entered the office and glanced about. It was spacious for a researcher's office, about twenty feet long by fifteen feet wide. The entire twenty feet bordering the exterior was windows. The blinds were up, and she walked to one of the windows and looked out. The view was good, similar to Bruce Andrews's, except one floor lower. She could see the edge of the Coliseum and a portion of Abady Festival Park. The walls were clear, ready for her degrees and diplomas, her teak desk clean and highly polished. A Pentium computer was tucked under the desk and a laptop sat in the work area. The interior wall was all bookshelves, mostly filled with medical and pharmaceutical texts. She glanced at the titles, glad that she wouldn't have to lug all her books from home.

"What do you think?" Kenga asked.

Jennifer sat in the high-backed chair and smiled. She set the mouse in the center of its pad and placed a pen at a forty-five-degree angle next to the mouse pad. "I like it, Kenga. I like it a lot."

"Would you like some coffee?"

Jennifer gave her a gentle admonishing look. "Kenga, if I want coffee, I'll get it. Your job is to administer this group, not get me coffee or doughnuts."

It was Kenga's turn to smile. "I think this is going to work out just fine," she said.

Jennifer nodded. "Me too."

16

It was a perfect day, sun beating down on the city and the harbor, the mercury stuck at eighty-five. A wisp of wind came in off the ocean, cooling the sunbathers a touch but not enough to send anyone packing from the beaches to the parking lot. No one was complaining: This was San Diego in mid-July. Life was perfect.

Jimmy Gamble worked the counter at the post office in Grossmont Center, just east of San Diego State University. He enjoyed dealing with people and found the job rewarding—or as rewarding as working for the U.S. Postal Service can be. He arrived for work on Thursday, covering the ten-to-six shift, his favorite. Early mornings were for birds looking for worms, not for people who enjoyed a few cups of coffee before working the postage meter. He pinned on his name tag and stepped up to the counter.

Something on the floor near the cash register caught his eye. A prepackaged book of ten stamps was lying on the floor. He took a couple of steps, stooped over, and picked it up. He glanced back at the wall, where hundreds of similar packages hung in neat rows and columns. *Now, how the hell did that get*

there? He shrugged, brushed off the dust, and slipped the rene-
gade package onto the most accessible peg, then returned to
his counter and opened for the day.

The sixth customer in his line asked for a package of ten
stamps for mailing a standard letter, and Jimmy pulled the
package off the wall and set it on the counter. The man also
had two small packages: one for Phoenix, the other for Boston.

"That will be twenty-three dollars and sixteen cents," Jimmy
said, printing a receipt and making change.

"Thank you," the man said.

"You're welcome, Mr. English," Jimmy said, reading the name
off the return address on one of the packages.

The man did a double take at the sound of his name, and
Jimmy pointed at the return address. English smiled at the ex-
tra initiative the postal employee had taken and returned to the
July sunshine. The smile was still on his face as he climbed be-
hind the wheel of his Cadillac and steered for Maderas Golf
Club.

It was a perfect day for golf. What the hell, it was a perfect day.

17

The lighting in BioTech Five was muted, almost nonexistent. Jennifer Pearce slipped off her reading glasses, set them on the stack of printouts she was studying, and rubbed her eyes. The clock in the bottom right corner of her monitor read 11:15. She moved the cursor to the start icon and shut down her computer. Enough was enough. Working until almost midnight was stupid. And after three months of working for Veritas, she had her team functioning exactly as she wanted. There was no reason to work so late. She closed her office door, locked it behind her, and took the elevator down to the main foyer.

"Good night, Art," she said to the graveyard security guard.

He brightened as she passed his desk. "Good night, Dr. Pearce. Take care driving home."

"Thanks," she said, and smiled as she passed through the doors into the muggy August air. She liked talking with the night watchman at Veritas, and she had a suspicion that he quite liked her. For a rent-a-cop, he was an interesting fellow, always with a story to tell about something or other. It was too late tonight to hang around for whatever the flavor of the day was. She'd find out tomorrow or the day after.

It was still hot for pushing midnight. Richmond was in a mini heat wave, typical for the last week of August, and there was no relief when the sun dropped out of sight at night. The mercury hovered near one hundred and the humidity was rotten. Clothes here were always wet and clammy, and that was something she wasn't accustomed to. Her mind started to wander as she crossed the parking lot and she let it go. In seconds, she was a Russian ballerina, a product of the prestigious Moscow Ballet, defecting to the West. The night was dark, no moon, and she moved stealthily, keeping to the shadows. A solitary car was parked in the lot, her ticket to freedom. The Americans had been begging her to come across since 1978, and now was the time. Her parents were both dead at the hands of the KGB, and there was no reason to linger in Moscow any longer. Things were getting dangerous.

She approached the car slowly, glancing at the bushes and wondering why her contact had parked so close to a possible hiding place for Soviet spies. She thought of turning and running, but she had come too far. Tonight was the night. Tonight was freedom. She reached the car and tried the handle. It was locked. She felt the panic rising, tasted fear in her mouth. She readied herself to run or fight, whatever would save her life.

Then she was back. At her car with her keys in hand. She pressed the key fob and the park lights blinked twice as the door locks opened. She slid in behind the wheel and took a couple of deep breaths before starting the car and backing out.

Jennifer Pearce had spent a substantial part of her life in denial. Denial of her reality. Her childhood had been an unhappy one, left alone to cook and clean while her parents doted on her younger brother. Her only escape had been to enter a fantasy world, where she was someone special, not Cinderella before the ball. Trips to school in the snow were long treks through hostile blizzards in the wilds of Canada, where hungry polar bears and wolverines tracked her, ready to pounce. Washing and drying the dishes after supper each night was using the suds to uncover secret codes on the bottom of the plates. Her imagination had no limit. And even as she matured, she still let herself enter that fantasy world on occasion. It was harmless and sometimes quite entertaining.

The streets were empty and driving was easy. This was one aspect of working late she really liked. The drive home was enjoyable. It gave her time to think. Tonight, her mind went back over the last three months at Veritas. She had restructured her team after about two months and, with a full month now under her belt, she felt she'd made some good decisions. Three of her staff had risen to the challenge and they were now her key people. And last week, when she finally shared her thoughts on the beta-amyloid chemical sequence, all three had stared at her like she was a nutcase from the local loony bin. Four hours later, after she had filled every chalkboard in the conference room with scribbles and formulas, they were somewhere between speechless and blathering idiots.

"Do you really think it's possible?" Dawn Sergeant, a specialist in cellular microbiology, had asked. "It's a totally new approach to the problem."

She referred back to the chalkboard. "The key is here," Jennifer said. "When this protein, tau, is altered, the neural structural support system is compromised. Once that happens, the amyloid precursor protein is subject to being cut, first by this enzyme, beta-secretase, then by gamma-secretase. The result is fragmentation of the amyloid precursor protein, which forms toxic plaques, causing healthy neurons to die. Then the neurotransmitters, especially acetylcholine, are reduced and the damage to the brain is irreversible. My approach to the problem is here," she said, poking at the board, "by altering the beta-amyloid sequence. It's never been tried before."

"Impressive," Dawn said.

"And to answer your question, yes, I think it will work. We just have to iron out the problems. Now, it's getting late . . ."

The group broke up, most of her researchers leaving in groups of twos or threes, discussing the new approach to a disease that affected over four million Americans. Jennifer headed for Kenga Bakcsi's house to visit her cat. It was Wednesday, and she had promised Kenga she would check on the little fellow at least twice a week while her coworker was on holidays. She hadn't been over since Sunday.

She cut off on Broad Street and headed for Shockoe Slip and the Mayo Bridge. She had to check the cat's litter box and make sure there was still water in his dish. No better time than now, when the traffic was next to nil. She crossed the James River, followed Hull to Sixth, then east to Everett. She pulled onto Everett Street and slowed, trolling for a parking space. She found one a half-block up the street from Kenga's condo, parallel-parked, and jogged back. She let herself in with the key and switched on a light.

"Hello, cat," she said as he poked his head out to see who was home. She couldn't remember his name, and simply called him "cat." "Could you really care less if I showed up? I doubt it. Just give you some food and water, and leave. Cats. How the hell did you guys end up so different from dogs?"

Jennifer picked up the mail that had accumulated on the floor under the slot in the front door and wandered into the house, glancing about and satisfying herself that all was in order. She set the mail on the kitchen table and refilled the cat's water dish. A quick trip to the litter box to scoop out a few little logs and she was ready to leave. Then it hit her.

What if she focused on somatostatin and corticotrophin to help as communication vehicles between damaged cells? She needed to access the Veritas mainframe and make a note for herself so she would remember this brain flash.

Jennifer powered up Kenga's computer and logged onto Veritas's database. Since each computer that was authorized to access the mainframe required its own code, Jennifer knew her password wouldn't work on Kenga's computer. Not a problem. As the team leader, she had access to all the codes. She signed in to her home computer, pulled the file, and found Kenga's password. Mischief. She logged off, then entered the Veritas site by typing "mischief" when prompted. She was in.

An hour later, she closed the research file and leaned back in the chair. Now it was late, but that had been very productive time. Tomorrow, she would follow up on the ideas she had typed into the system. She logged off the Veritas site and moved the cursor across to power down the system, then stopped. A small icon shaped like an ankh caught her eye. It was tucked into one corner, almost obscured by a word processing file. She double-clicked on it and a file opened on the screen. Inside was a complex chemical formula. She scrolled through the remainder of the file, wondering why Kenga Bakcsi had this formula on her home computer. It was filled with links to other sites, all internal to Veritas and all dealing with a drug called Triaxcion. One of the sites answered her question. The formula resisted the modification of testosterone into dihydrotestosterone. The drug was touted as an alternative to hair loss in middle-aged males. Probably a big seller, she thought, still wondering why it was on Kenga's computer. She was scrolling down to sign out when she saw a text file buried among the numbers. She opened it.

Inside was a name and an address: Gordon Buchanan, Butte, Montana. There was no phone number. She tucked her hair behind her ears, stared at the name for a minute, shrugged, and closed the file. She powered down the computer, stroked the cat a couple of times, and headed home.

Her new digs were in the Fan District, an expensive and trendy area just west of Richmond's city center. She was on Plum Street, on the eastern edge of the Fan and one full block off Cary Street. One block to excellent dining and some of the best shopping in Richmond. Coincidence? Not a chance.

The town house–style home was almost everything she liked mixed with a few things she hated. But her realtor had insisted you never get ten out of ten with a resale house. To start with, it was old, turn-of-the-century. That she did not like. Jennifer preferred new, with no sod and sticks for trees, and a bathtub that had never seen a naked bottom. But the previous owners had done extensive renovations to the house, including all new drywall, windows, doors, an off-white kitchen, and new fixtures in all three bathrooms. This she did like. Her ebony baby grand sat next to the massive bay window in the living room. She turned on one muted light and sat on the bench. Her fingers glided over the keys, Enya gently filling the room. She played "Watermark" and "Only If . . . ," then "By Heart," one of her favorite Jim Brickman pieces. The room, with its soft tan and black striped sofa and love seat, and pewter and glass tables, resonated quietly with the last notes as she drew her fingers back from the keyboard. She used the remote to turn on the stereo and found a Yanni CD on her multidisc system. She filled a diffuser with vanilla scent, lit the tea candle, and lay quietly in the darkness.

Gordon Buchanan. The name kept drifting back to her. Why would Kenga have his name inside a file she had pilfered from Veritas? And why the Triaxcion file? What was going on? She lay on the couch for three or four songs, then dragged herself vertical and switched off the stereo.

Six-thirty tomorrow morning was going to come awfully early.

18

Ian Goett, Jennifer's immediate supervisor at Veritas, poked his head in her office. "Got a minute?" he asked. The look on his face was serious.

"Sure," Jennifer said, dropping her pen and waving at one of the chairs facing her desk.

Goett closed the door, moved the stack of computer printouts from the chair to the floor, and sat. "Kenga Bakcsi is dead," he said.

Jennifer froze. Kenga was on vacation. How could this be? What were the chances of someone dying while tanning on a beach in the Caribbean? She took a moment to collect her thoughts. "What happened?"

Goett cleared his throat. "She was on some sort of rain forest tour on Saint Lucia when the vehicle she was in went over a cliff. That's all we know right now."

"When did it happen?"

"Two days ago, on August twenty-third. The island authorities contacted her family and they passed along our number. I took the call from the investigator assigned to her case."

"And that's all they said, just that she went over a cliff?"

"Basically, yes. She was staying in the capital city of Castries and arranged for a driver to show her the island. They were deep in the jungle when he lost control and the cab slid off the road into a deep gorge. She was killed instantly."

"Driver killed too?" Jennifer asked.

Goett looked taken aback at the question. "No, he managed to jump out."

Jennifer nodded, just a slight motion of her head. Her mind was racing. Kenga had classified information on her home computer; information that dealt with a drug in a totally separate division. She had technical data that would see her fired immediately if the brass at Veritas knew she was poking around in secure computer files. And now she was dead. That thought slammed her mind against a brick wall. She was being paranoid. It was simply her imagination drawing a connection between Kenga's death and the information on her home computer. Veritas had nothing to do with this tragedy.

"Thanks for letting me know, Ian," she said to her supervisor. "I'll break it to the staff. Any idea when her body will be back in the States?"

"Not at present. In fact, her entire family still lives in Romania. They may want her body shipped back home for the funeral. I'll find out and let you know."

"Okay."

She watched Ian Goett leave, and her mind kicked into gear again. Was it really such a stretch to think Veritas could be involved in the woman's death? Veritas was a multibillion-dollar company that protected its secrets fiercely, as did every pharmaceutical giant. The chemical formulas, like the one on Kenga's computer, were public knowledge, but the process by which the company produced the drugs was its bread and butter. And that process was also on the computer's hard drive. A process that Veritas would protect with a vengeance. Hundreds of millions of dollars went into research, and marketing the formula and the process, and it would be natural for a company to protect so valuable an asset. Then she shook her head and said aloud, so she could hear her own voice, "This is crazy thinking. This is your imagination. Companies don't murder their staff for having classified information on their home computers. Kenga went on a vacation and died when the car she was in went over a cliff."

The words sounded hollow in the confines of her office—forced, even. And she realized that the right side of her brain was not going to let go of this easily. She ran her hands through her hair and glanced at the clock on her desk. Three o'clock. She would wait until four to bring the staff together and break the news to them. They would be free to go anytime after they found out. There was going to be a lot of tears and disbelief. Kenga was a well-liked person in the office, and many of her staff had worked with her for a number of years. This was not going to be easy.

Jennifer watched the last of her staff leave. One was a junior research assistant who'd been best of friends with Kenga, and he was in no condition to drive. Jennifer ordered him a cab and gave the driver her Visa number to cover the fare. She shook her head in disbelief as she locked her office. Kenga was gone. The woman had been the lifeblood of the office, always smiling and organizing their silly little outings to the local pub or bowling alley. She fostered a real community spirit among her coworkers, and Jennifer knew it would be impossible to replace her. She felt a strange sense of depression wash over her as she left the building and started her car.

She checked her watch. Almost five o'clock. She couldn't have picked a worse time to drive over to White Oak. I-64 was a mess. A semi with a full load of live chickens had jackknifed and spilled its load across the westbound lanes. Some of the crates had split open, and the road was littered with dead chickens. Live chickens were running around in no particular direction. The eastbound lanes were clear, but the rubberneckers were in fine form, slowing traffic to a crawl so they could have a good look at the carnage. It was after seven when she passed the Richmond airport and the traffic thinned out. She reached the intersection of I-295 and I-64 and took the off-ramp, watching her speed as she drove the last half-mile to the research park. The cops loved to check their radar guns along this stretch.

She reached the entrance to the park, identified by a slab of white stone with a large green *W* etched in it. Underneath, just in case the visitor didn't know what the *W* stood for, was "White Oak Technology Park." Technology Boulevard was still busy, mostly with vehicles exiting the park. A good number of the research staff worked flex hours and preferred to come in late and leave long after rush hour had run its course. Jennifer pulled in at the second set of buildings on her right and parked in the third lot, next to a grove of mature hickory. The building housing Veritas's office space was a sleek two-story silver structure with neatly trimmed lawns and a bank of windows framing the foyer. She walked through the storm door and swiped her card. The interior door opened automatically and the guard at the front desk smiled as she passed.

"Good evening, Dr. Pearce," he said.

"Hi," she said, returning the smile. At first, she had wondered how the guards knew everyone's name, but after a while she noticed that a new line scrolled across their screen every time someone entering the building swiped his or her identity card. Technology in a technology park—go figure.

Veritas shared the building with the software development division of another corporation. The Veritas offices and labs were to the right of the main entrance, and she used her card to open the steel fire door that automatically closed at six o'clock every weekday. Once she was through the outer security door, there was a short section of hall, perhaps twenty feet, then another set of doors. A security camera registered every person who swiped their access card through the card reader. The doors were steel, with rectangular glass windows, but Jennifer suspected that this particular glass was virtually indestructible. She smiled at the camera, ran her card through the reader, and moved into the secret world of Veritas Pharmaceutical, White Oak Division.

Most of the Veritas labs were relegated to White Oak, for two reasons. The first was cost. Square footage at White Oak cost the company less than half what they paid for their space at BioTech Five. Second was security. Security in the new complex, built two years earlier, was vastly superior to that in Richmond's older buildings. There were no back entrances or windows to smash for easy entry or exit. The glass in every exterior window was bulletproof, and every exit was monitored with a closed-circuit camera and an alarm. All the systems reported back to a central location that was constantly monitored. Secrets were easy to keep at White Oak.

Jennifer walked the length of the off-white sterile hallway and past scores of blue doors to the first of three crossroads. She turned right and walked into a construction zone. Three midsized HEPA filtration units and a pile of other boxes were sitting in the hallway outside the entrance to the brain chip department. The HEPA units were high-end systems designed to keep even the tiniest airborne particles from entering or leaving a sterile lab environment. She suspected that the intricate design of the brain chips required the air to be totally purified. She glanced in the open door as she passed. Rows of sophisticated machines were in the process of being moved. A researcher in a lab coat was involved in a heated discussion with one of the moving men. He was Chinese, slim with thick black hair and a long oval face. She recalled seeing him in the halls a couple of times, but they had never stopped to talk. His picture was on one of the staff memos, and it occurred to her that he was a department head, but she couldn't remember which one. She continued down the hall, blue doors flashing by on both sides. At least her department was not in flux, she thought as she reached the doorway that gave access to the Alzheimer's department. She had enough on her plate right now without her labs undergoing renovations. She swiped her card and entered the lab.

Veritas's Alzheimer's lab at White Oak was state of the art. Seven different and distinct labs were functioning as one, with each division having their own thrust at the problem. She had structured the labs that way, and the results to date were exceptional. Her staff members were in healthy competition with one another, approaching the disease from different directions but ultimately all with the same goal: to develop a drug to cripple the debilitating disease.

"Dr. Pearce," a young woman said as she entered. "Thank goodness you're here. Team Three is getting some really strange results. They want you to have a look."

"Sure," she said, slipping on a lab coat and entering the lab.

Two hours later she removed the coat, washed her hands, and left the building. The wonky results were a direct result of improper lab procedures. The samples had become contaminated, and it was the contaminants that had reacted to the enzyme. They had identified the guilty party and she had spoken with him—quietly, off to the side. There was no reason to go off the deep end—she just had to make sure it didn't happen again.

As she reached her car, her mind went back to the thoughts of Kenga crashing over the cliff in the car, the driver somehow escaping. Things that didn't add up. And things that were not subsiding into the far reaches of her memory. She couldn't shake the idea that there was more to Kenga's death than a simple automobile accident. Maybe she would take a detour on the way home and visit Kenga's house.

Another look on Kenga's home computer would dispel these crazy thoughts.

19

Kenga's condo was dark as Jennifer pulled up in front. She switched off the car ignition and fingered the keys for a minute, wondering if she really wanted to know what was on the dead woman's computer. What if these crazy suspicions she had were true? What then? If Veritas was killing its employees to keep them quiet, what could she do about it? And if they were, wouldn't that put her next in the line of fire?

Jennifer sucked in a couple of deep breaths. What were the chances her suspicions would play out? Marginal to nil. She found Kenga's key and held it tight between her thumb and index finger. As she exited the car, she glanced furtively up and down the street. Parked cars, a couple walking hand-in-hand, lights on in most of the houses. Nothing sinister. She walked quickly to the front door and let herself in. The cat poked his head out, saw it was her, and came over to rub against her leg.

"Oh, you poor thing," she said, crouching and gently stroking the animal. "Your master isn't coming home. You're a nice cat— someone will want you."

She straightened and walked directly to the bedroom Kenga had converted to a home office. She approached the desk and stopped. The computer was not as she had left it. Every time she left the office or shut down her home computer, she centered the mouse on the pad and laid a pen across the mouse pad at a forty-five-degree angle. It was a quirk of hers, but now she was glad she had done it. The pen was not on the mouse pad but beside it, on the desk. Someone had been in the house since her last visit on Wednesday.

She turned her attention to Kenga's house. Was the intruder still somewhere inside? The house suddenly seemed darker, more sinister. She snapped on lights as she moved from room to room, checking the closets and under beds. A broom shifted when she yanked the door to the utility closet open, and she let out a short scream. She replaced the broom, feeling silly. The back door to the house was locked, all windows were closed, and the basement, which was unfinished, was empty. She returned to the small office, still on edge but confident no one else was in the house.

She powered up the computer and searched for the file with the Triaxcion data in it. Nothing. It was gone. She closed her eyes and let herself drift. One reason Jennifer Pearce was such a valuable researcher was her ability to envision chemical reactions without using paper or a computer screen. It was like playing a game of chess in her mind, without moving any of the pieces. She scrolled down slowly, line by line, her mind computing the formula, adjusting the molecules as the drug would once inside a human body. Finally, her brain overloaded and refused to store any more information. She squeezed her eyelids even tighter and let herself drift.

Triaxcion targeted testosterone, of that she was sure. It prohibited the conversion of the male hormone to dihydrotestosterone, enlarging the hair follicles in the subcutaneous layer of skin. This in turn kept the hair follicle intact and producing new growth. But, in her opinion, the chemical reaction inside the body would not be limited to the conversion process. This process involved the liver, as what she was looking at required the medicine to be broken down by liver enzymes. Furthermore, the dihydrotestosterone, once metabolized, immediately bound to albumin. But what would happen to the small percentage of DHT left unbound and wandering about the body? She wasn't sure.

She was preparing to sign off when she remembered the file she had found embedded in the Triaxcion file. What was the name? She used her memory to replay opening the file. Slowly, the letters came into focus and she saw the name. Gordon Buchanan, Butte, Montana. She signed on to the Internet and keyed in a search for Butte Montana Buchanan. There were thousands of hits, but only one found all three keywords. There was an article in the *Montana Standard* with the name Buchanan, and she went to the paper's Web site and opened it.

BUTTE—Tragedy struck the Twin Pines Sawmill on April 20, 2005, when Billy Buchanan died of injuries incurred while cutting a firebreak with a chain saw. According to witnesses, Buchanan was cutting a stump when the saw kicked back and sliced into his leg. Medically trained mill staff were on the scene and attended to Buchanan, but were unable to stop the bleeding. A helicopter, only minutes from the gorge where the accident occurred, rushed Buchanan to the hospital but he died en route.

The victim's brother, Gordon Buchanan, is the owner of Twin Pines, and one of the primary employers in the Butte area. He was unavailable for comment.

The article went on to give some history on both brothers and their contributions to the local economy. Both men were apparently highly respected by everyone they interviewed. Gordon was painted as a highly successful businessman with strong ties to the community through his philanthropic gestures. Jennifer sent the page to Kenga's printer and sat back in the chair.

From all appearances, someone had signed on to Kenga's computer within the last twenty-four hours. But that was highly improbable. Kenga's family was in Transylvania, and none of

the other staff at Veritas had a key to her house—at least none
that Jennifer knew about. And surely Kenga would have mentioned it if she had given another person a key. Two people
both showing up at the same time and neither knowing the
other had a key would be heart attack material. But considering that the Triaxcion file was missing, it didn't take her Ph.D. to
figure out who had been in the house.

Someone from Veritas.

But why? What in that file was so damaging to Veritas that
they would break in and remove it from Kenga's computer? Triaxcion was an FDA-approved drug, which meant the medication had passed Phase III trials and met regulatory standards.
The chemical formula, which Veritas kept under lock and key,
was patented and couldn't be replicated by any of the generics. So even if another company managed to steal the formula,
they couldn't bring it to market without making substantial
changes or fighting Veritas in a court of law. No, that angle
didn't make any sense.

She lifted the papers off the printer and reread the article on
Billy Buchanan's death. What was the connection? Had Triaxcion somehow contributed to Buchanan's death? And how did
Kenga figure into all this? She wasn't involved with Triaxcion
other than as an employee of the company manufacturing it.
Which meant that Kenga would have access to the Veritas
mainframe. And with a little ingenuity, she could probably
download everything Veritas had on Triaxcion and pass it
along to a third party.

Gordon Buchanan.

She glanced again at the address. Butte, Montana. If she remembered her geography classes, Montana was one of the
northern states, tucked up against Canada. Maybe visiting Gordon Buchanan was the thing to do. If there was a connection
between Kenga and Buchanan, maybe she could figure out
what, if anything, was going on.

Crazy thinking again. She shook her head at the total absurdity of it all. Her imagination was taking over, controlling her cog-

nitive thoughts. She was wide awake and lucid, but thinking of taking a cross-country flight to talk to a man who'd probably look at her like she had two heads. Gordon Buchanan had probably never heard of Veritas or Triaxcion. He was a sawmill owner whose brother had recently died in a tragic accident. There was nothing to connect Gordon Buchanan to Veritas.

Except the fact that Buchanan's name had shown up on Kenga's home computer. How was that possible? It was highly unlikely that Kenga had just picked a name at random and stored it in a secure file. Gordon Buchanan's name was stored on her system for a reason. And now Kenga was dead, killed when her driver missed a curve on a windy road through the St. Lucia rain forest. And the driver had survived. How did *that* happen? The driver would have been at the wheel, struggling to regain control of his vehicle. If he had enough time to jump out of the car, he had enough time to react to the curve and keep from crashing into the ravine. No, something was wrong. When a car went over a cliff, everyone went over, not just the passenger. And add in that this passenger had a classified chemical process worth hundreds of millions of dollars to her employer on her computer, and the waters were getting very murky indeed.

Jennifer stared at the mouse and the pen. Someone had visited Kenga's house inside the last twenty-four hours and removed a solitary file from her computer. As much as she kept telling herself that this was simply her imagination, the evidence was pointing a different direction. It was pointing to Veritas. And right now, the way to find out if there was any basis to this insane line of thinking was to meet with Gordon Buchanan.

As she switched off the computer and replaced the mouse and pen on the pad, she made a decision. This weekend was open—nothing pressing at the office, no friends to visit.

She was going to Butte.

20

Gordon Buchanan took the back stairwell to the second floor, the wooden stairs groaning under his weight as he navigated them two at a time. He swept past Belinda who was on the phone setting an appointment for one of the firm's lawyers, and strode into Christine Stevens's office. He closed the door behind him in a single motion, causing the door to bang shut. Christine looked up from the brief on her desk.

"Good afternoon, Gordon," she said. She slid her reading glasses off her nose and set them on the brief.

Buchanan didn't sit but paced back and forth as he spoke. "I'm not satisfied with where things are going, Christine," he said. His voice was strong, his words clipped. "I want some action. It's been four months since Billy died and we haven't made any progress. These bastards at Veritas are treating us like a bothersome fly, just brushing us off. That's not good enough."

Stevens's voice was equally curt. "What do you want me to do? There's a certain legal protocol to follow. I can't just go charging into their corporate offices and demand they pull Tri-axcion off the market, then issue you a formal apology and a big check. Motions have to be filed and responded to. This takes time."

"You've had time, Christine," he said. "I'm not kidding. I want to move this to the next level. You've had this on your desk for almost four months. Billy died in April, and it's August—September in another week."

"How, Gordon? How do I move this to the next level? We have no definitive proof that Triaxcion causes clotting factors to fail in people with A-positive blood. We have suspicions, but that's all."

"That's a load of shit and you know it. This drug is dangerous. It killed Billy and it's killed at least eleven other people we know about."

"There's no solid proof," Christine said, leaning on her desk and raising her voice. "And without proof, we'll get killed in a court of law. Not one of the other lawyers representing clients who have died as a result of Triaxcion has filed for litigation. We just don't have a winnable case."

"So they get away with it?" he asked, his face taking on color.

His lawyer relaxed a bit, leaned back in her chair. "I told you from the start that these tort cases are difficult. They don't happen overnight, and no matter what we do, Billy is not coming back. The best I can do, and I stress it's the best, is that we get Triaxcion pulled off the market. You're not going to get any personal satisfaction out of this, Gordon. No one from Veritas is going to end up in jail."

"Maybe. Maybe not."

Christine was immediately struck by her client's tone of voice. "What does *that* mean, Gordon?"

Gordon stopped pacing and placed his hands on her desk, leaning over so he was only a couple of feet from her. "I took the liberty of hiring a private investigator. He managed to dig up a woman, a Veritas employee, who agreed to work with me, collecting information from the company's classified files."

"You did what?" Stevens said, aghast. "That's illegal."

"I don't care. I told you, I want answers."

"I don't want to know what they found. If they've stolen classified information from the company, I could get in serious trouble if you tell me."

"Okay, Christine. If you can't help me, I'll have to take another approach. Outside the legal avenues available."

"Again, Gordon, I don't want to hear this."

He withdrew from her desk and walked slowly toward the door. With his hand on the doorknob, he turned back to face her. "The woman who agreed to help me . . ." He opened the door and stood half in the hall, half in her office. He locked eyes with his lawyer.

"She's dead," he said, then left.

21

The mood in the room was somber.

The room in question was an office on the fifth floor of L'Enfant Plaza, the head office of the Department of Homeland Security in Washington, D.C. Four men in suits sat on one side of the conference table, one woman and one man in lab coats on the other. The four men were handpicked from their agencies, the best merger of science and field experience from the Central Intelligence Agency, the National Security Agency, the FBI, and the Department of Homeland Security. All four had file folders and glasses of water in front of them.

"What are we dealing with?" one of the suits asked. He was a wiry man, only five-ten and one-seventy, but his voice carried unmistakable authority. His close-cropped hair was graying slightly, the only indication he was over fifty. His name was J. D. Rothery, Under Secretary of the Department of Homeland Security, Science, and Technology. Appointed by the president to one of the top posts inside the agency, Rothery took his job seriously. A small plaque sat on his desk: *Country comes first. Family comes second.* His wife had it made for him. He took it as a compliment.

LETHAL DOSE

The man in the lab coat responded. He was Dr. Edward Henning, biological warfare specialist for the U.S. Army, on special assignment to DHS. Twenty-three years with the military, with postings in Iraq and Afghanistan to ferret out biological weapons, had made his name a household word around most mess halls. He was the first African-American with a Ph.D. to join the armed forces, and his tenacity and knowledge had paved the way for many more. "We've confirmed the two cases were caused by the same virus," he said, consulting his folder. "The first victim was Elsie Hughes in Austin, Texas: female, age thirty-seven, employed in the accounting profession. She contracted the virus through licking a contaminated envelope at her local bank on May twelfth. She died four days later.

"The second victim was Robert English: male, forty-six years of age, resident of San Diego, California. He was a self-employed computer programmer. The virus was found on postage stamps in his home office. One stamp was missing from the package of ten. We can't be as sure of the exact date when English was infected, but we suspect on or about the seventh of July. He died on the tenth."

"What about the virus?" Rothery asked tersely.

"It's a virus that causes a hemorrhagic fever. To date, there are only two known hemorrhagic viruses, the most well known being Ebola. The other is Marburg. This one is neither."

"So we're dealing with an entirely new virus. And a deadly one."

Henning took a sip of water and a deep breath. "Deadly is a gross understatement, Mr. Under Secretary," he said. "This virus, if let loose inside our borders on any significant scale, would be absolutely catastrophic. It is communicable, terminal, and we do not have a cure."

"Where the hell did this virus come from?" Rothery asked.

Henning shrugged. "No idea. I've checked with every government facility from Fort Detrick to Plum Island, but no one has been working on developing a new strain of hemorrhagic virus. This didn't come from any of our labs."

"Have we got ourselves another anthrax-type situation here?" he asked.

"I have no idea who is behind this, sir, just what kind of virus it is."

Rothery turned to the man beside him. "Jim, what's your take on this?"

Jim Allenby, Special Agent in Charge for the FBI out of the Washington, D.C., office, consulted his file. He was a lifer with the Bureau, six years from full pension. His face, like his body, was still lean, but taking on the vestiges of age: Small jowls were forming and the skin under his chin was sagging slightly. But his mind was as sharp as or sharper than when he had first joined the Bureau as a young recruit, wet behind the ears. His hair was graying, and age lines were forming on his forehead and at the edges of his intense blue eyes. "When we had Elsie Hughes's body shipped to Fort Detrick," he said, "we suspected we had some sort of hemorrhagic virus. We traced her movements for the week preceding her death and found the envelope in the recycling trash at the bank. We forwarded that envelope ahead to Dr. Henning after it had been initially screened at Fort Detrick. We took the same procedure with the stamps we found in Mr. English's house. The two attacks, being so separate from each other with respect to geography and method of contamination, lead us to suspect some sort of conspiracy."

"Terrorists?"

"It's a definite possibility, Mr. Under Secretary. They could be testing the proverbial waters to see if there's any collateral damage or if only the primary infected target dies. They may want to know how many strikes are necessary to infect our population before unleashing the main attack. Or they may be willing to play a game of terror by paralysis. If the news were to seep out that items we take for granted, like stamps, could be infected, panic would be sure to follow. And with that panic will come a huge blow to how efficiently we run the country. It could easily outstrip the anthrax scare of 2003."

"So where did this virus come from? How is it possible that a new hemorrhagic virus just suddenly shows up? How was it created?" Rothery asked the pathologist.

"You're sure you want an answer to that? It's pretty technical."

"Try me."

"I suspect that some group has developed it by mutating Ebola or Marburg," Henning answered. "But that said, the manner in which this virus binds to the host cell is quite different from Ebola or Marburg. We've isolated a unique set of proteins on the outer viral membrane, which we think are targeting chemokine receptors for the bonding process. But how it enters the host cell is a complete mystery at this point. Once it's inside the victim, at the human cellular level, it uncoats and its nucleic acid undergoes transcription into mRNAs. Genome replication follows, which is standard, except we suspect it's a DNA virus that uses only the de novo pathway and somehow does not require the salvage pathway." He stopped for a moment to let the string of technical jargon sink in, then addressed Rothery's question. "So how was it created? We're not sure. There's still a lot about the virus we don't understand."

Rothery rubbed his forehead. "Why? Why would they bother to create a new virus? Why not just use Ebola?"

"Ebola is unpredictable and incredibly dangerous. I'm running tests on the virus we found in Hughes and English to see if whoever mutated this thing mellowed it a bit, but that's not overnight work. It's going to take a lot of tests to find out those differences."

"What extent of damage could this cause if the wrong people are controlling it? Give me an educated guess, Dr. Henning," Rothery said.

He was pensive, choosing his words carefully. "If I was in their shoes and my intentions were to unleash a virus on the United States, I'd want one that was controllable until I released it. After that, maximum destruction. Easily spread through contact, possibly even aerosol contamination. I'd look for a fast-acting bug with ugly symptoms and no known cure. And so far, from what I've seen, they've got check marks next to most of those.

And if they have enough of the virus and the manpower to spread it quickly when they actually start, I'd say we could see deaths numbering into the hundreds of thousands, possibly millions. And very quickly—within days, not weeks."

"Jesus Christ," Rothery snapped. He turned to his FBI counterpart. "Jim, what have you guys got on any groups acting inside our borders that may have this technology and the facilities necessary to develop and store the virus?"

Allenby glanced quickly at his files. "A handful of possibilities, J. D. I'll get entire dossiers on each one to your department by end of work today. We'll be approaching this problem with total interdepartmental cooperation. Anything you need, just ask."

Rothery nodded his approval. "Thanks, Jim. What's going on outside our borders, Craig?"

Craig Simms, Deputy Director of the Central Intelligence Agency, had been quiet, assimilating information. He was a thoughtful, academic man with intelligent gray eyes and a full head of silver hair that matched his eyes perfectly. He was a veteran of the espionage community, and his knowledge of terrorist cells operating worldwide was renowned. He shifted his gaze to the people at the table as he spoke, ignoring the thick file he had brought with him to the meeting.

"We have identified twenty-seven possible locations in nine countries where there is what we consider to be the right mixture of personnel and facilities. There are thousands of buildings that could be used to create and breed this virus, but only a few molecular biologists that would have the expertise and hate the United States enough to actually do it. We've spent the last few weeks tracking these experts and we know where most of them are. Getting into some of these labs will be easy; others will be next to impossible, but we're ready to begin covert ops if necessary. Seventeen of the labs are in countries where our operatives can move about in relative anonymity, but the other ten are in very hostile territory. At present, we're using satellites to watch every vehicle that leaves these labs and we're trying to intercept them whenever possible. We've had some success, but to date we haven't found anything that resembles this virus."

"What about the seventeen labs you could gain access to?" Rothery asked. "Have you done anything about that yet?"

"You mean have we sent in operatives to terminate operations?"

"Yes."

"No. We suspect at least twelve of these labs are al-Qaeda, and we've been monitoring them, trying to identify al-Qaeda members as they come and go. It's working very well. We'd rather not go busting down their doors and lose the information trail we've spent months, sometimes years, putting in place."

"But if you had to . . ."

"If we had to, we would cooperate, Mr. Under Secretary," Simms said evenly. "But let's try to keep that avenue as a last resort. Identifying al-Qaeda operatives is our top priority right now, and I'd hate to lose what we've worked so hard to put in place."

Rothery nodded and pursed his lips. "I understand, Craig," he said. "Let's let the status quo remain intact for now. I'll let you know if we need to shut down those labs."

"Thank you."

"Tony, what does the National Security Agency think about all this?"

Tony Warner, the youngest of the four and just into his thirties, shook his head. He had *GQ* looks, and his jet-black hair, which he wore just touching his shoulders, swung back and forth with the motion of his head. "We don't know what to think at this time. Our people at NSA are analysts, and we need time and data before jumping out on a limb."

Rothery nodded and glanced about the room. "Anything else?" he asked, closing his folder. No one spoke. "Then let's get working on this, gentlemen. I want whatever group is behind this shut down." He locked eyes with each person individually.

"Shut down or dead," he said. "Either is fine with me."

22

Twin Pines Sawmill was tucked into a dense stretch of forest about twenty-two miles south of Butte. Signage was good and the main road into the mill was paved and well maintained. The rugged foothills of the Beaverhead Mountains framed the smokestacks that rose above the trees and quietly released thin trails of white smoke against the crisp blue sky. Aside from a low droning sound and the occasional high pitch of a saw slicing into cut timber, the woods were quiet.

Jennifer Pearce parked in one of the assigned visitors' spots near the front door and stared at the sawmill. What was she doing here? It had taken her seven hours of flights and connections to arrive in Butte, and another hour to rent the car and drive to the mill. It was five o'clock Saturday afternoon and she was tired, irritated with airlines and airports, and apprehensive about meeting Gordon Buchanan. She ran a comb through her hair and stepped from the car into the warm Montana sun. It felt good on her skin.

The front-end offices of Twin Pines were modern and bright, the walls painted sage with ocher trim, the floors gleaming hardwood. Four maple desks with flatscreen monitors and dedicated laser printers dotted the office. Only one of the desks was occupied, and the young woman stopped typing on her keyboard as Jennifer entered.

"Good afternoon," she said pleasantly. "Can I help you?"

"I'd like to see Gordon Buchanan," she replied, ready for the usual runaround when you ask to see the top dog. It didn't happen.

"Let me find him for you," she said, reaching for a two-way radio. "Mike?" she said, depressing the talk button. A voice came back over the air in a second or two. "Do you know where Gordon is?"

"At the planer." The voice was clear and resonated through the almost empty room.

"Thanks, Mike," she said, and set the radio back on the desk. "I'll show you where the planer is, but I can't take you personally. It's Saturday and I'm the only admin staff in." She rose from her desk and walked to a window overlooking the main mill. She pointed to one of the larger buildings. "Go in the north entrance and just ask someone. They'll know where Gordon is. And here, you'll need these." She handed Jennifer a hard hat and a visitor's pass.

Jennifer signed the guest book, thanked the woman, and headed across the lumber yard to the building the woman had singled out. When she had dressed in the morning, it was with a sawmill in mind, and she wore snug jeans, running shoes, and a button-up-the-front cotton shirt. The mill hands seemed to appreciate her choice, and most of them stopped what they were doing to watch her as she made her way between the pallets of trimmed lumber. She locked eyes with one of the men, and he smiled and tipped his hard hat. She returned the gesture, which elicited an even wider grin. She reached the planer building and entered, asking the first man she saw if he knew where Gordon Buchanan was.

"Sure," he replied, giving her a quick glance, then focusing on her face. "He's over here."

She followed him through the building, which housed a series of large machines where raw lumber was being sliced into thinner strips. It was noisy inside the building, but not to the point of displeasure. The smell of wood sap and freshly cut timber was strong, and the fine sawdust floating in the air tickled the inside of her nostrils. She sneezed a couple of times, and the man leading the way said, "Bless you," both times. They reached a machine that was quiet, the massive saw blades sitting idle. Her guide pointed at the ground under the machine.

"That's Gordon," he said, then turned and headed back to work.

A pair of legs stuck out from under the machine, blue jeans ending in cowboy boots. She was still staring at them when the owner slid out from under the machine, his eyes focused on hers. Buchanan had stripped off his shirt to loosen the saw blades so they could be removed and sharpened.

Jennifer took note of the man's physical condition. His upper body was well developed and his waist was trim, abs showing. He smiled as he rocked himself into a sitting position, then up on his feet. He wiped his hand on a flannel rag and extended his hand.

"Gordon Buchanan," he said. His voice was deep and strong and fit the environment perfectly.

"Jennifer Pearce."

He slipped on a shirt that had been draped over one of the levers sticking up from the machine's control panel, buttoned it, and tucked the tails into his jeans. "Now, Ms. Pearce, it's not often I get visitors who look as good as you in a hard hat. What would you be doing at a sawmill in the middle of the Montana forest?"

"I wanted to speak with you, Mr. Buchanan."

"Nobody calls me Mr. Buchanan. Gordon is fine." He smiled.

"All right. I think we need to talk, Gordon." She returned the smile, the thought dragging through her head that this was one very self-assured and quite handsome man.

"About what?" he asked, motioning toward a door leading to the afternoon sunshine.

She waited until they were outside to respond. She slipped

off her hard hat and held it in her hand. "I work for Veritas Pharmaceutical." The moment she uttered the words, she saw Buchanan's face and eyes harden and his body language shift to the defensive.

His voice was different when he spoke, almost threatening. "Why are you here?" he asked, leaning on a tubular steel railing outside the planer building.

She faced him, the afternoon sun in her eyes. His face was in the shadows, but she could see his eyes, and they were focused on her, unblinking and cold. "I've been with Veritas for about three months now, in the Alzheimer's research group. Actually, I head up the group. Kenga Bakcsi worked for me. She was my office administrator."

Gordon was silent. He crossed his arms on his chest. "What does this have to do with me?"

"I was taking care of Kenga's cat while she was on vacation. When I was feeding the cat, I thought of something that might be important to my research. I logged on to Kenga's home computer and typed the information into a file. As I was signing off, I saw a file that contained restricted information—a file that if the brass at Veritas knew was on her computer would have gotten her fired. I glanced through it. And I found your name."

"What was in the file?" Gordon asked.

This was the moment Jennifer had been dreading: the point at which she would either tell Gordon what she had seen or keep the data close to her chest. She had flown all day to get here, and she knew that his brother had died and she strongly suspected he was looking at Veritas for answers. The chances were good that Buchanan already knew what was in that file. She made her decision.

"The file contained both the formula and the process for manufacturing Triaxcion, an antibalding drug commonly prescribed to middle-aged men. A drug that had been prescribed to your late brother, Billy."

"I'm still not sure how this interests me, Ms. Pearce."

At least he was using her name. She pushed on. "A couple of days ago, I got some bad news. Kenga Bakcsi was killed while vacationing on a Caribbean island. I kind of put two and two together."

"And what did you come up with?" Gordon asked.

"That you think Billy's death is somehow tied to Veritas Pharmaceutical," she said. He didn't respond, and she continued. "Kenga couldn't possibly have accessed that information on Triaxcion by accident. She had that formula on her computer for a reason. And *your* name. Why would she store the name of a sawmill owner from Montana inside a secure, stolen file? But when I read about your brother dying, I knew I had the connection."

"That Triaxcion killed my brother."

"Somehow, yes. At least, you think it did."

"That's very interesting, Ms. Pearce. And if any of this were true, what would happen? Why are you here?"

"Kenga's dead, Mr. Buchanan. And I think her death may be suspicious."

"So you're concerned that someone in your company found out Kenga was stealing classified information for me and they had her killed."

It sounded crazy when put that way, so matter-of-fact. "Yes, something like that."

"So you're accusing your own employer of killing its employees. That's quite a serious accusation, Ms. Pearce."

As much as she tried, she couldn't read the man. She felt he was prodding her, knowing all along exactly what she was telling him but never opening the door, not even a crack. "I flew out from Richmond, Virginia, specifically to meet with you, Mr. Buchanan. That speaks to how serious I think this is."

"All right, let's assume some glimmer of all this is true. A dead woman on St. Lucia, my brother's death tied to Triaxcion. What then? Where do we go from here?"

"You've probably already tried the legal channels, where the biggest and most prestigious firm in your hometown sends Veritas a series of threatening letters and they swat at you like you're an insignificant insect," she said. There was something in his eyes that told her she had hit a nerve, and she continued. "It's pretty typical. The drugs that are released on the markets often have side effects. Listen to the television advertisements. Half the talking is the announcer telling you not to take the pill if you have high blood pressure, diabetes, are subject to skin rashes, are or could be pregnant, blah, blah, blah. There are risks associated with taking prescription drugs. And with risks come reactions to the drug and accidents the research company did not foresee. Suddenly, there are seriously injured or dead people looking for justice.

"So their lawyers begin to circle the castle. But the guys inside the castle are smart, powerful, and flush with cash. The corporation's lawyers fill the moat, pull up the drawbridge, and fortify the walls with a hundred high-priced lawyers. Then they tell you to come and get them. Most legal firms won't touch a major pharmaceutical company unless they've got a serious tort case. Even then, there are no guarantees. So if Billy's death is tied in to Triaxcion, it's natural that you're going to want answers. Just as I want answers about what happened to Kenga. But answers and retribution are slow coming, if ever."

"And how would we find those answers, Ms. Pearce?" Gordon asked, leaning forward. The waning light ebbed onto his face and she could see an incredible inner strength in his eyes.

"You could have a source inside the company," she said.

"According to you, I already had one. She's dead now. Remember?"

Jennifer didn't take the sarcasm well. "I came to you," she snapped. "I'm offering you assistance. Being facetious is not necessary."

"Why would you offer me anything, Ms. Pearce?" he asked, backing off, his voice softer. "You don't know me from a hole in the ground, yet here you are, asking me if I want your help nailing your employer to the wall. Can you see how I may be a little skeptical?"

"Why would I want to help you?" she asked, and he nodded, unfolding his arms and dropping them to his sides. "Because I liked Kenga. She was a really nice woman, with a life that no one had the right to take. If they murdered her, then they should pay."

"I see," Gordon said quietly.

"And," Jennifer added, "because I'm scared. I don't want to work for a company that kills its employees. I don't feel safe quitting, not after seeing what I saw on Kenga's computer. And I know that someone from the company came back to Kenga's computer and removed the Triaxcion file. The file that had your name in it, Mr. Buchanan. I didn't know where else to go. I thought of asking the local police for help, but that would be insanely stupid. If the police were to begin nosing around, whoever killed Kenga would be looking for a piece of paper somewhere in the precinct report with a name on it. And eventually they would find it. Then I'd be in the same condition Kenga is—on a cold slab in some morgue."

"There are other avenues of help available, Ms. Pearce," Gordon said. "Both the FBI and the FDA would probably take an interest. The CIA as well, as Kenga's death happened outside the country's borders."

"Same reason," she said. "I'm sure the FBI could protect me much better than the local police, but what about my life? I'm a pharmaceutical researcher with a great career. And if I went up against these guys, I could never work in my chosen field again. I don't want to end up in a witness protection program for the rest of my life. And that's the best-case scenario."

"So you came to Butte to meet with Billy Buchanan's brother."

"Yes. I came to Butte to talk with you."

They were both silent for a minute. Gordon pointed to the main administration building and they started walking slowly toward it. The sun was peeking through the treetops and the woods had come alive with chirping birds. The air was fresh and felt good in her lungs. An occasional machine whirred for a bit, then stopped, but other than the birds, it was quiet.

"It's really beautiful here," she said as they walked.

"I enjoy it," Gordon said, his cowboy boots kicking up puffs of dirt. "Logging and working sawmills has been my life." He glanced over at her. "It's been a good life."

"I can imagine. I read the article on your brother that was in the Butte paper after his death. He was quite the guy. Everyone liked him."

"Yeah, Billy was a great guy. I miss him."

They reached the edge of the parking lot, and Jennifer pointed to her rental. They walked across the cooling pavement and she got in the car. She dug in the small travel bag she'd brought with her and extracted a business card. She handed it to him, and he took a few seconds to look it over. He tucked it in one of his jean pockets.

"Well, thanks for meeting with me," she said, offering her hand.

He shook it. "Thanks for coming. It was an interesting story."

"Give me a call if you think we could help each other," she said, starting the car and putting it in gear.

"I'll do that," he said.

"And Gordon," she said as he moved back from the car so she could pull away. "I never said Kenga died on St. Lucia. Just mentioned it was a Caribbean island."

She left him standing in the parking lot, a thoughtful look on his face.

23

The closest charter service that featured either Lear or Gulfstream jets was in Helena. When Gordon Buchanan wanted to get somewhere fast, he didn't rely on United—he chartered a private jet. He called the company and booked a Lear 31A to fly him to St. Lucia, then called the Twin Pines helicopter pilot at home. He apologized for calling late on Saturday and asking the pilot to work on Sunday, but stressed how important it was that he be in Helena by eight in the morning. His pilot agreed to come in without telling Gordon he would just as soon be flying as sitting in church. It wouldn't have mattered—Buchanan would have appreciated it anyway.

Sunday, August 28, dawned cool and rain threatened. Both men were a bit early, and at ten minutes before the hour, the chopper lifted off and, after forty minutes of choppy flying, deposited Gordon on the tarmac in Helena. The Lear was waiting, the fee for the two-day trip already preauthorized on Gordon's Visa card. Once the plane was airborne and en route to Miami, Gordon opened his files on Veritas and withdrew the folder on Jennifer Pearce.

Hers was a thin file, with her being such a recent hire. His investigator had pulled a brief work history covering her time at Marcon, and he started there. She was a brilliant woman, of that there was no doubt. She held a Ph.D. in microbiology and had been instrumental in bringing two midlevel drugs to market before shifting over to head up the Alzheimer's division. And Gordon knew that Alzheimer's was an arm of the corporate structure that every pharmaceutical giant looked to for a huge breakthrough drug. A pill to combat Alzheimer's was a multibillion-dollar pill. And being offered the lead position was definitive proof that Marcon was enamored with its rising star. Yet three years later, that star had somehow tarnished. Nothing in the file indicated why.

But she had moved over to Veritas three months earlier, assuming the same coveted position with the rival company. Gordon glanced out the window at the passing clouds and wondered what tucked-away secrets Jennifer Pearce had brought with her to Veritas. At three-sixty plus bonuses a year, she was too well paid to have come across empty-headed. Gordon suspected Bruce Andrews had made a good choice when he offered her the position. But without knowing Jennifer personally, how could Andrews have been so sure?

And therein lay the problem. Did Bruce Andrews and Jennifer Pearce know each other prior to her starting work at Veritas? If the answer was yes, then chances were good that Pearce was another Andrews toady. If no, then maybe she was someone he could trust. The answer to that question was weighing on him.

He scanned down the page detailing her short tenure at Veritas. She was telling the truth about Kenga Bakcsi working in her department. She was Kenga's direct boss. His investigator had not been able to ascertain whether their relationship went beyond the office to friends, but Jennifer's story about tending to Kenga's cat seemed plausible. In fact, there was nothing about Jennifer Pearce that did not seem plausible. He stared out the window and tried to put himself in her position. She was the new gal on the block in an increasingly alien environment. She suspected her employer might be responsible for the death of one of her staff. How disconcerting must that be? It would scare the crap out of most people, have them running for the door. But Jennifer Pearce did not run. She was doing the same thing he would do: assimilating information. She was making no decisions until all the facts were on the table, then she would make a rational choice. But what were her options? Remain at Veritas, bury her head, and hope the ax didn't strike her? Unlikely: She wasn't an ostrich. Involve the police while continuing to work at Veritas? Dangerous; very dangerous. Quit, walk away, and develop a severe case of amnesia? Again, dangerous if someone at Veritas was killing people to keep them quiet. Or search out someone to help her?

Gordon knew he was beginning to believe her. Time to play the devil's advocate. Someone inside Veritas had been alerted by their legal team that Gordon Buchanan in Butte, Montana, was considering legal action against the company. They recruit a new hire, Jennifer Pearce, to visit Buchanan and find out the validity of his claim. He grinned at the absurdity of it. Jennifer Pearce was a Ph.D. researcher with a proven track record in the pharmaceutical industry, making extremely good money, with no history of being anything except what she claimed to be. She started at almost the same time Billy died, and at that time Veritas had no idea their product was responsible for Billy's death. And if they were to send someone across the country to visit, the last thing a company spy would do is accuse her employer of killing its employees.

Gordon made his decision. Jennifer Pearce was the real thing.

He had an ally.

24

The Lear 31A touched down at George F. L. Charles Airport in Castries, St. Lucia's largest and most modern city, and taxied to a private hangar. The Castries airport serviced mostly private jets and cargo, while international travel came in through Hewanorra on the south tip of the island, close to the world-famous Pitons. Gordon waited until Customs had come and gone, lazily poking their heads into the fuselage to see who had arrived, before deplaning. The sun was intense, even late in the afternoon, and he lounged in the shade next to the hangar, waiting for his ride to show. Ten minutes later, an older silver van pulled up a few feet away. The driver glanced over at him and waved. Gordon opened the door and slid in the front seat. The upholstery was worn but clean.

"Christopher," he said, shaking the man's hand. "Good to see you, my friend."

"Gordon Buchanan," the man said in lilting English. "Welcome back to St. Lucia, mon." He was native Lucian, with roots easily traced back to when the slave traders had populated the Caribbean with Africans, torn from their homes and families on a distant continent. He was a large man, over six feet, and

117

had a perpetual smile, his teeth punctuated with gold fillings. A pair of sunglasses was perched on the top of his head, and he was dressed in blue jeans and a crisp white shirt. "What brings my favorite country singer to our beautiful island?"

Gordon grimaced. Christopher had talked him into singing a country song at a local karaoke bar one night and had never let him live it down. He was good at cutting and processing trees, but not so good carrying a tune. "What new bands have you found lately?" Gordon asked as the van started moving slowly along the runway toward Vigie Beach. Christopher was the local promoter for musicians from all over the Caribbean and often brought new talent to St. Lucia. There was no place on the island that Christopher could escape to without someone shaking his hand and asking what was happening.

"He's not a musician, but I've got a good one, my friend. There's a boxer on the island who could be Olympic caliber. I'm bringing in some carded boxers from other islands and putting on a few matches. Sold out, every one of them, mon."

"Excellent," Gordon said. "Listen, Christopher, I need a favor. I'm only here for a day or two, and it's sort of on business."

"I'm your man," Christopher said.

"Can you get your hands on a police report for me?"

His guide looked puzzled. "A police report? What's going on, Gordon?"

"There was an accident last week. A tourist died when her cab went over a cliff. You hear anything about that?"

"It was in the papers," Christopher said. "She a friend of yours?"

Gordon shrugged. "Let's just say I'm interested."

"Okay, I can get you the report. But let's not visit the police station ourselves. That's not a good place to be. I'll have someone deliver it. Where are you staying?"

"Caribbees," Gordon replied. "I phoned from the plane and they had a room."

"I'm sure they did," Christopher said, steering off the runway and heading onto Vigie Peninsula. Caribbees Hotel was set into a hill near the lighthouse, with stunning views of Castries Harbor and the ocean. Vacancies were rare at the hotel, but when Gordon Buchanan flew in, things changed.

Gordon had a long history with a few of the Caribbean Islands, but especially with St. Lucia. He had been traveling to the Caribbean for years, scuba diving and spending time in the sun. Gordon had a creed he lived by, which was to always leave whatever place you visit a little better for having been there. And twelve years ago, when he first met Christopher, he had asked what was a problem on the island—a problem that dealt with people. Christopher had answered immediately: domestic violence. The stuff that happened between husband and wife behind closed doors. And there was nowhere for these women to go when threatened. Gordon had changed all that.

He returned to the United States, made some calls, had his bank wire some money to the West Indies Bank in Castries, and flew back to the island. He bought a large house in need of work, hired contractors to refurbish it, then donated it to the city. There were sixteen rooms, a fully functional kitchen, three family rooms with televisions and PlayStations, and a full-time guard on the front door. Now the women had a safe place to go, at least for the short term. His generosity had been the talk of the island for months. The island government tried to honor him by naming a street after him, but he respectfully turned them down, preferring to keep a low profile.

But that didn't mean people forgot. They didn't. And now when Gordon needed something, it became available. Like a room in a popular hotel.

Christopher pulled up in front of Caribbees and grinned. "I'll see you tomorrow morning. Nine o'clock?"

"Nine o'clock is fine. Don't forget the police report."

Christopher gave him a pained look and stomped on the gas. Gordon checked in and thanked the manager for finding him such an excellent room on such short notice. The balcony wrapped around the corner of the hotel, with a view of the Caribbean to the west and a sweeping vista of Castries and its harbor to the south. He ate dinner in one of the on-site restaurants and retired early. By nine on Sunday morning, he was sitting outside the lobby waiting for Christopher. At precisely the top of the hour, the driver/promoter pulled up, a huge grin on his face.

"What are you looking so smug about?" Gordon asked as he slid into the front passenger's seat.

Christopher held up a tan-colored file folder. "Your police report," he said.

"You're good," Gordon said, smiling as he took the report. "What's in here?"

"You want me to tell you or you want to read about it?"

"Why don't you fill me in while I read?"

"Okay, boss. Your friend was taking a tour of the island near the Edmond Forest Reserve down near Soufrière. They had passed through a twisty part of the road we call The Gap, just south of Piton Canarie. They went off the road on the Enbas Saut Trail. It's really steep and slippery there."

"Let's go have a look," Gordon said, his eyes glued on the police file. "A picture paints a whole lotta words."

Christopher nodded and shoved the car into gear. He navigated the tight streets of the island capital, flashing by brightly painted houses and small children with white, toothy smiles. Shacks with corrugated metal roofs bordered the road and un-neutered dogs lounged in the shade or strolled next to the drainage ditches, irritated at best by the traffic rushing past inches from their scrawny bodies. Bridge Street began to rise as Christopher reached the southern edge of Castries, and he geared down for the uphill series of switchbacks that dominated the road between the capital city and Soufrière. Gordon knew the road well, and he watched the city tenements slowly dissipate and lush fields of banana and mango rise from the jungle clearings. The road, a two-lane goat path that Gordon swore was the training ground for New York cabbies, weaved its way through steep Lucian valleys. Occasionally, as he glanced out the right side of the van, he caught a quick glimpse of the ocean, far below them with tiny whitecaps as the waves approached shore. As they drove south, the Pitons came into view.

Petit Piton and Gros Piton were the primary memories most tourists took home from St. Lucia. Towering above the adjacent jungle-clad hills, the cone-shaped volcanic rocks graced the cover of almost every St. Lucia publication. Gordon took a passing interest in them as the road turned inland and the jungle thickened. The interior of St. Lucia is in places a true rain forest, and the best example is in the Edmond Forest Reserve. They followed the West Coast Road to St. Jacques Road, then headed due east into the forest. The road was thinner now, at times almost impassible by a single vehicle. Encountering another car driving the opposite direction was scary in many places, as someone had to back up. They reached The Gap without incident, and Christopher drove three kilometers onto the Enbas Saut Trail and stopped. Ahead of them was a switchback, the road dropping off into an abyss. There was no guardrail.

"This is the place," Christopher said. "I read the police report after I picked it up last night. I know this corner. Lots of people go over this cliff. They should put up a concrete barrier or something. It would save lives."

Gordon stepped from the van into the jungle heat and humidity. There had been no rain over the past twenty-four hours, but the dirt surface was slick with moisture just from the mist settling out from the surrounding air. Gordon had read the police report on the drive up and knew that the vehicle in which Kenga had been the passenger had been traveling toward the switchback from the opposite direction. He walked up to the corner and glanced up the hill. A hundred feet farther, there was another sharp corner the vehicle would have had to navigate prior to reaching the switchback. That severely limited the speed at which the driver would have been approaching this curve. That and the fact that he should know the road would suggest he had been traveling extremely slowly. Yet the police report stated that the vehicle had left the road at an estimated thirty kilometers an hour.

He glanced over at Christopher. "No one in their right mind would attempt this corner at thirty kilometers an hour. Not even in a Ferrari with dry roads."

"Is that what the police report says?" Christopher asked. "Thirty kilometers an hour?"

Gordon nodded. "Seems excessive."

"Seems stupid."

Gordon walked to the edge and looked over. It was an almost sheer drop, punctuated by ridges jutting out from the wall. The first ridge was about forty feet down and stuck out six or seven feet. It was covered with trees and shrubs, their roots clinging to the rocky outcrop. Gordon stared at the foliage for a few minutes, then motioned Christopher to join him.

"See that tree?" he said, pointing to a palm angling out from the wall. "It has a huge gash in it, almost at the roots."

"I see it," Christopher said. "And a couple of shrubs are broken as well."

Gordon looked back up the road. "Imagine a vehicle coming down this road at thirty kilometers an hour. It goes over the edge but somehow manages to hit the tree next to its roots. How is that possible? The trajectory of the vehicle would send it flying out into open space, not tumbling over the edge. A vehicle moving at that speed would probably clear that tree, or at best shear it off near the fronds. But not this. This is all wrong."

"Maybe the car did clear the tree. Maybe that's an old cut mark on the bark."

"You know that's not true, Christopher. In this heat, that mark will be overgrown in another week. No, that's where her vehicle hit. Which means it was just barely moving when it went over."

"Pushed?" Christopher asked.

"Pushed," Gordon said, gazing out over the St. Lucia rain forest canopy. "Which would explain why the driver wasn't in the vehicle when it went over the cliff." He brushed his hair back off his forehead and slipped a toothpick from his pocket and between his teeth. "I think someone murdered Kenga Bakcsi."

25

The estate was invisible from the main road, obscured by a border of thirty-foot butternut and black birch, trees indigenous to the central Virginia area. Numerous flower and shrub beds ran parallel to the highway asphalt and offered a warm touch, almost inviting. But the wrought-iron gate and eight-foot fence told a different story. So did the guard dog signs posted every hundred feet on the fence. Bruce Andrews took the issue of home security very seriously.

Inside the gates was a true country estate. The drive was long and winding, through groves of trees, trimmed grass fields punctuated with equestrian hurdles and numerous ponds, some complete with ducks and geese lazing on the still, summer waters. The main house was set almost in the center of the forty-six-acre package. Its facade was two-story, Southern plantation style, with Ionic pillars on volutes. A wide second-floor balcony ran the length of the house with four separate sets of French doors opening to it. The mixture of Grecian columnar architecture and Palladian-style house worked beautifully, and off-white shutters framed all the windows.

Bruce Andrews was perusing a copy of the *Financial Times*

on the rear deck. He often wondered if the land he viewed from where he sat was that which Grant and Beauregard had fought over during the siege of Petersburg in 1864. Many a brave man on both sides of the skirmish had died on this quiet tract of land south of the Appomattox. Occasionally, he wished that time would slip and he could see the historic battle first-hand: trench warfare in its infancy, breastworks shielding the soldiers as they reloaded their Springfield muskets. But the field remained quiet, and it appeared that he was destined to replay the siege in theory only.

He sipped on freshly squeezed Florida orange juice and scanned the article the *Financial Times* had written on his company. When he finished, he set the magazine on the table and smiled. They had taken the bait and swallowed it whole. And that was all he needed. With such a glowing review by one of the premier financial publications, it would be months before anyone took another serious look at Veritas's books. And by that time, the danger of his house of cards collapsing would be history. The smile just didn't want to leave his face. He had done it. He had taken a huge risk and succeeded.

Haldion, the FDA recall that had threatened to empty the company's coffers, was behind them. The lawsuits were finished, the cash flow stemmed. Triaxcion, Veritas's antibalding drug, could hurt them, but with the new projections, they could now weather a full-blown tort suit. That had yet to materialize, but the possibility was ever-present and real. The most active legal challenge they had to date on Triaxcion was from some irritating ambulance chaser in Butte, Montana. Christine Stevens kept threatening a substantial tort action unless Veritas admitted Triaxcion was responsible for altering blood chemistry in A-positive men and women. They hadn't mentioned anything financial yet, and when pushed to name a figure that would see them disappear quietly, she had insisted that this issue was not financial. Her client simply wanted them to admit that their drug was dangerous.

"Yeah," Andrews said to himself as he finished his morning coffee. "Like you'd just let the whole thing go if we admit fault.

You bastards would be on us like hyenas on a rotting carcass if we publicly said we made a mistake." Not a chance in hell that was happening.

He glanced again at the *Financial Times.* What a coup. He had manipulated the interviewer in such a way that she had seen exactly what he wanted her to see, and arrived at precisely the conclusions he had wanted arrived at. With the Enron scandal still a glaring reminder of where creative accounting can lead, he had chosen his words carefully. Veritas did not have the wide array of offshore subsidiaries Enron had when falsifying its economic performance, but they had other, more discreet methods of reporting higher-than-truth incomes for the year. There was nothing as simple as shifting day-to-day expenses into the investment column. Andrews had different methods that used government tax credits, very difficult to discern even with a forensic audit.

But he had an up-and-coming problem: Evan Ziegler. The man was going to discover that Veritas was shutting down its brain chip operations. The future of spinal cord injuries was now moving in a new direction, courtesy of the researchers at Duke University Medical Center. Fat cells, harvested through liposuction, were now being transformed into stem cells that could be used to repair spinal injuries. That cut through a lot of red tape—no ethical issues with using embryonic stem cells. And there were lots of available fat cells, which eliminated the painful procedure of cutting into bone to harvest them. This ability to create neurons from fat cells had essentially doomed the future of brain chips, which looked to generate new electrical synapses in the spinal cord.

And once Ziegler knew he had been used, he would become very dangerous very quickly. The man was a trained killer, an ex-SEAL who wouldn't think twice about coming after whoever set him up. Andrews knew that that someone was him.

No level of security would stop Ziegler. Armed bodyguards, the walled and gated estate with patrol dogs, a pistol under his pillow—everything would be useless once Ziegler was unleashed. So the trick was to take care of Evan Ziegler before he found out. Too bad, Andrews thought. Evan was an excellent assassin. He was organized and efficient. His downside was a stubborn streak of human kindness the army had been unable to snuff out. The same goodness he showed to his wheelchair-bound son was the one weakness that would eventually be his downfall. Andrews had some ideas for removing Ziegler, but nothing was imperative yet. No need for panic. Wait for the right moment, the right opportunity.

Patience.

It had served him well over the years, and Bruce Andrews had a feeling that it was the key to dealing with Evan Ziegler. The cordless phone rang. He plucked it off the table and punched the talk button.

"Hello," he said, knowing who it would be. This was a private line, and only one person dialed this number.

"How are things?" the voice asked.

"Okay. Just thinking about our potential problem in Denver."

"Yes. That's going to be an interesting one when it arises."

"Interesting for sure. Why did you call?"

"I've been monitoring a situation you have in Richmond."

"What sort of situation?" Andrews asked. This man did not call on this secure and scrambled line unless the issue was serious.

"Kenga Bakcsi, the employee of yours who recently died while she was on vacation—someone signed onto the main-frame from her house while she was in St. Lucia."

"When?" Andrews asked, his eyes narrowing.

"Wednesday, August twenty-fourth, just before midnight."

"It's Tuesday morning. Why am I just finding out about this now?"

"I needed time to react, to see what files they'd accessed. Damage control, so to speak."

"What were they looking for?" Andrews asked.

"Kenga Bakcsi had a secure file with a chemical formula on her home computer. Triaxcion. That was the file the person opened."

"Anything else?" Andrews asked, his mind racing. Who had been in Kenga's house? And why?

"There was a text file with a name and address in it. Gordon Buchanan, Butte, Montana. You know him?"

"I've heard the name through our legal department. Buchanan's brother died of something-or-other and he's got a lawyer looking into a possible litigation. Nothing yet."

"But why would Buchanan's name be on Kenga's computer?" the voice asked.

"I don't know. Unless Kenga was feeding Buchanan the information she was stealing from the company computers."

"That would explain things."

Like why we had to kill her, Andrews thought. "This Buchanan guy—what have you got on him?"

"Not much yet. Some hick from Montana who runs a sawmill near Butte. I'll get more on him as fast as I can without raising any eyebrows."

"You do that," Andrews said. "And get back to Kenga's place and get that file off her computer."

"Already done. The file was removed on Thursday and the computer's hard drive adjusted, so there's no history of that file ever existing."

Andrews stared across the vast expanse of trimmed grass to the Blue Ridge Mountains in the distant west. He loved this view, especially in summer when the trees were in full foliage and the skies were lazy blue. He loved sitting on his deck enjoying the million-dollar view from his multimillion-dollar house. And he didn't want that to change. "What level of threat does Gordon Buchanan pose to us?"

"In my opinion, minimal to nonexistent. He's a two-bit ambulance chaser who talked one of your employees into getting him some classified information from the mainframe. He'll fuss around with things a bit, try to light a fire under his lawyer's ass, then go away. Buchanan is no threat."

"All right. But keep tabs on him from your end. I'll have our legal department monitor things in Richmond."

The line went dead. Bruce Andrews hit the talk button and dropped the phone on the table. Life was never simple, especially when you headed up a major firm like Veritas. It was even more complicated when you played outside the rules. Killing Kenga Bakcsi was not high on his to-do list, but it had become a necessity. They knew she was selling information to someone but were unable to ascertain who. He had begun to suspect the Justice Department or the Securities and Exchange Commission, so finding out it was some nobody from backwoods Montana was a good thing. Gordon Buchanan was a pest who would either quietly go away or quietly go missing somewhere in the woods.

The choice was his.

26

The Seattle-based offices of Connors and Company were small and poorly lit. Little sunshine filtered through the north-facing window, which opened onto a narrow alleyway that abutted the older brick building housing the investigative firm and a handful of other small businesses. There were two sconce lights, neither of which had a bulb, and a solitary overhead light with two sixty-watt bulbs. But the dim working environment suited Wes Connors perfectly. He seldom made it into the office in the morning without a hangover, but as long as his coffee machine and computer were working, he didn't care about anything else.

Connors drained his first coffee quickly and poured a second, sipping it as the Advil and caffeine kicked in. He hooked his laptop computer to the printer, opened a file, and hit the print button. Six pages rolled off the HP LaserJet 4P. The printing was slightly faded and he made a quick memo on a Post-it note to pick up a new cartridge. One thing Connors had learned early in his tenure as a private investigator was that the reports handed to the clients were all they saw, and they had better be professional-looking. He never let his toner get to dangerously low levels.

Wes Connors was thirty-eight and totally disillusioned with life. He had never been a good-looking man, always on the outside looking in when attractive women were deciding who in the bar to go home with that night. His face was oblong, with droopy eyes and thick lips under a bulbous nose, now stained bright red with tiny capillaries. He tried to hide his features with ball caps and by growing his hair long, but the only way he really looked any better was after ten or fifteen beers. So he drank. He drank a lot. It didn't help; he still went home alone night after night.

But where he was unsuccessful with women, he did much better with his investigative business. There were always married men and women who wanted to know what their partners were up to when they were at work. Marital infidelity was a godsend. It paid the bills, kept him driving reasonably new vehicles, and even covered the cost of an occasional hooker. But this client was different. His work was interesting and it paid very well. Someone at Veritas Pharmaceutical had pissed his client off big-time. And Gordon Buchanan was not a man he would ever want to piss off. He was like a cornered wolverine, intelligent and dangerous.

Buchanan had come to him just after his brother Billy had died back in April, a referral from another satisfied customer. Buchanan was sure Billy's death had something to do with the medication Veritas had manufactured. He had hired Connors and Company to scratch the surface at Veritas and see what was underneath.

Connors had pulled the company's financials for the past ten years, concentrating on the long-term projections and goals. The bottom line looked good, but Veritas had not brought one new drug to market for some time now. And that hurt. Without revenues from a new patented formula and with patents expiring on two of their previous blockbusters, the company should be stretched tight. But it wasn't. They were flush with cash and tangible assets, including owning the facilities in White Oak Technology Park, where eleven different divisions had labs and offices. Connors was no financial whiz, but something wasn't adding up.

Then there was the premature death of Haldion, off the market for causing heart palpitations. The litigation against Veritas had stopped when Bruce Andrews had taken the corporate helm, but that didn't increase revenues. Three new drugs were in the pipeline, one for reducing blood pressure, one some sort of antiviral medication, and the other a cholesterol drug. But nothing concrete yet. They were touting the arrival of Dr. Jennifer Pearce, a Ph.D. with eight years of Alzheimer's experience at Marcon. According to Bruce Andrews, she was the woman with the answers to the Alzheimer's puzzle, although he was tempering his words with kid gloves, careful not to ruffle Marcon's feathers too much. The last thing Veritas needed right now was to give Marcon any excuse to tie up Pearce's hands in legal red tape by claiming proprietary information had shifted companies when she moved. So far, so good. Marcon was sitting on its hands and watching.

The one brilliant piece of maneuvering by Andrews since he took the reins was patenting the metabolite synthesized by the drugs inside the human patient. He was facing a legal challenge on that issue, but in the interim, if everything remained as it was, Veritas was looking to pocket almost seven hundred million over a three-year period. But a company that required a billion dollars a year just to keep its doors open needed more than that. It needed a new drug.

In addition to monitoring the company financially, Wes Connors had been watching its personnel. The company's medical provider was an easy target, and he had his solitary associate, Jack Ramy, a computer specialist who worked for him part-time, hack in and stash a few lines of code that relayed all new claims directly to Connors and Company's computer. The very computer that sat on his desk. There had been quite a few hits, but the one that Gordon Buchanan had been interested in was the death of Kenga Bakcsi in St. Lucia. He wondered why but didn't press. Buchanan was the kind of guy who held his cards close to his chest.

But now he had ferreted out another death. Back on April 30, Albert Rousseau, an employee working in the cholesterol division, had died in a natural-gas explosion. The file had been suspended pending cause of death assigned by the local coroner. Since there was very little left of Rousseau, the paperwork had been slow coming. The gas company had a vested interest in the findings and was pressing for the investigator to determine that Rousseau cut the gas line and then sparked the explosion himself. Suicide relieved them from a lot of legal responsibility. The insurance company was pressing for the same conclusion. They didn't get it. The final finding by the ME's office and the police and fire investigators was a faulty valve on the stove. That left the gas company open to a lawsuit, the insurance company was on the hook for the book value on his policy, and the municipality could finally assign a company to come in and clean up the mess left by the explosion.

Since the file had been in a pending state since he'd begun his investigation, it had been transparent to his computer program. But now, with a decision on the books, Albert Rousseau's death was visible. And that was news for Gordon Buchanan. That was a good thing. For the money Buchanan was paying him, Connors began to get jittery if he went a few days without finding something to report. He liked the steady income and he liked the work. It beat following a cheating husband to the local motel. He straightened the pages he had taken from the printer and lifted the phone. He dialed his client's cell, and when Gordon picked up, he introduced himself.

"Anything new?" Gordon asked.

"Maybe. There was an employee killed in a natural gas explosion back on April thirtieth." He gave Gordon the details and explained the delay in relaying the information. "They determined the explosion to be an accident, a faulty valve on the stove."

"A faulty valve on a gas stove," Gordon said slowly. "Now, how often does that happen?"

"Not often," Wes Connors replied.

"No, Wes, not often at all." He was quiet for a minute. "Let's try something. Can you spend a few days in Richmond canvassing the local real estate offices and high-end car dealerships to see if Albert Rousseau was in the market to upgrade? Use your imagination—think of places where he might have gone if he thought a large payday was on the horizon."

"Sure, Gordon," Connors said. "There'll be travel costs and a per diem expense as well. You okay with that?"

"That will be fine, Wes." There was a moment of silence, then Gordon added, "There are a lot of people who work for Veritas dying lately. I wonder why."

"You think something's up?" Wes asked.

"I'm not sure what I'm thinking. Just continue to monitor the company through their health care provider and find out whatever you can on Albert Rousseau. I don't care how you get the information, just get it. Expense what you have to."

"Not a problem. I'll be in Richmond sometime tomorrow."

"Keep your cell phone on."

"Of course."

The line went dead and Wes Connors replaced the handset in its cradle very slowly. Gordon Buchanan was digging for something. His client was leaning toward his brother's death being far more than just an isolated incident. Buchanan was favoring some sort of conspiracy. And that was just fine with Wes Connors. Christ, how often did a small-time private investigator get to go up against a company like Veritas? Never. This was like Erin Brockovich and that PG&E thing. One in a million.

And to top it off, he was getting paid damn well for his time.

27

It was 10:24 A.M. on Wednesday, August 31, when Jim Allenby took the call. It was patched through directly from the Department of Homeland Security to his office in the J. Edgar Hoover FBI Building on Pennsylvania Avenue. It was not a pleasant call.

"We've got a real problem, Jim," J. D. Rothery said tersely. "The virus has reappeared. And this time we've got more than one infected person."

"How many and where?" Allenby asked, holding his pen over a small pad of paper on his desk.

"Miami. An entire family is sick. Mother, father, and two kids. Only one death so far, but we don't think any of them are going to make it."

"Shit," Allenby said under his breath. This was going to be difficult to keep under wraps. And if the media found out . . . "What do you need from us?"

"Get down to Miami and liaise with the local authorities. You can have jurisdiction if you want. It may look better with the FBI involved rather than DHS. We'll stay in the background."

"Okay. Where are the victims right now?"

"The three still alive are in their home." He recited an address. "The father's body is already en route to Fort Detrick for autopsy."

"Who's in charge at present?"

"Local cops, but they don't know what's going on. Let's try to keep it that way."

"This is going to be difficult, J. D.," Allenby said. "Christ, an entire family."

"I know, Jim, but do your best. And keep me in the loop."

Jim Allenby hung up, then dialed again. He requested a company jet on standby at Reagan within the hour, then called the Miami field office. Arthur Wren, Special Agent in Charge, took the call. Allenby and Wren went back twenty years, and he was glad he was dealing with a veteran agent on this one.

"How are things in science, or counterterrorism, or whatever it is you do?" Wren asked. He was a likable man in his late fifties who had been decorated twice for bravery. Both medals were under a bunch of socks in his underwear drawer, and his office walls were covered with pictures of his grandchildren.

"They've got me stuck right in the middle," Allenby said. "Anything relating to science or drugs and I'm the guy they call. That'll teach me to pick a career with the Bureau after getting a science degree." His tone shifted as he moved to the reason for the call. "We've got a problem, Arthur, and it's in your backyard."

"What's up?"

"Local cops are all over an incident in Olympia Heights, but we're going to be taking jurisdiction on this one. And quick."

"It came through on the scanners about twenty minutes ago. How do you know about it?"

"Let's just say I'm in the loop on this one. I'm leaving D.C. immediately and flying down, but I want you to personally take charge until I get there. And Arthur, don't let anyone in that house without full protective gear. I'm talking lethal virus here. Very scary stuff."

"Holy shit. What's going on?"

"You control the scene and I'll tell you when I get to Miami. Just keep the press away if possible. DHS will be around, but

135

they're going to stay in the background. When the victims die, the bodies will be wrapped and moved to Fort Detrick. DHS will handle that."

"Department of Homeland Security? What's going on, Jim? Have we got an act of terrorism on our hands?"

"I'll fill you in when I get there. The longer I spend on the phone with you, the longer it'll take for me to get to Miami."

"Okay, Jim. I'll take care of things on this end."

"Thanks." Allenby hung up, clipped his cell phone on his belt, grabbed his briefcase, and moved quickly to the elevator. A car was waiting on parking level one, and he slid into the backseat. The driver already knew they were heading for Reagan and was en route within seconds. Jim Allenby made a few calls, ensuring he had the right resources, both people and equipment, in place. By the time they reached Reagan, the cell phone was back on his hip, his emergency team in place or on their way to Miami.

Jim Allenby's position in the Bureau was unique. He was the only special agent in charge who didn't report directly to one directorate. He floated between the Counterterrorism Division and the directorate for Criminal Investigations. His knowledge of drugs, diseases, pharmaceuticals, and research techniques made him a specialist with skills that worked for both divisions of the FBI. And he was a favorite of DHS as well, especially when they had a virus or a bacterial strain on the loose. This wasn't the first time J. D. Rothery had requested that Allenby coordinate a response to a viral threat. But by the looks of things, this one was the most serious.

Allenby boarded the Gulfstream and settled in for the flight. The fax machine beeped three minutes after they were airborne and he ripped the page off once the transmittal was complete. A full dossier on the stricken family was included, plus their movements for the past week, courtesy of Miami Dade police. It took all of eight seconds for Allenby's gaze to land on one line and stay there. The entire family had eaten at TGIF, a family restaurant chain with franchises across the country, four days ago. The time frame worked, as did the locale. His suspicions ran to either the food or the cutlery as the method of delivering the virus. Since only one table of diners were sick, his best guess was that someone had replaced the cutlery with tainted forks and spoons, which the family used to eat their dinner. That would account for how the virus was ingested and why all four of them were sick, but no one else. He placed a call to his counterparts in Miami and advised them to quarantine the restaurant immediately. Confiscate every knife, fork, and spoon, and identify the booth the family had sat in. Check it for any traces of the virus.

It was a long shot. The virus had probably been planted four days ago, and every piece of cutlery would have been put through the commercial dishwashers on site, probably killing any remaining virus. That was good and bad. Good in that the virus, once dead, would be unable to infect additional people. Bad in that without proof they would never be one hundred percent sure TGIF was the source. He glanced at the pictures of the family that had come through with the fax. A nice-looking family, probably of Cuban descent, the boy about twelve and wearing a Florida Marlins ball cap. The girl was younger, with a beautiful smile. He shook his head at the waste.

The Gulfstream landed at Miami International and a government-issue Crown Victoria whisked him off the tarmac and onto the freeway system. Traffic was reasonable for two in the afternoon, and the trip to the district of Olympia Heights took twelve minutes. He grimaced as they pulled onto the street. Numerous police cars, a few nondescript Bureau vehicles, and four television crews were present. Add in every nosy neighbor for a square mile and the place was as busy as the Orange Bowl on game day. He cursed silently as the car pulled up to the barrier. The driver showed his creds and they proceeded through.

Arthur Wren came out to meet him. "Believe it or not, this situation is controlled," he said before Allenby could say a word.

The SAC out of Washington glanced about. "How's that, Arthur? It looks kind of busy."

"The father is someone in the Cuban community. He's big in the local church and ran for political office last municipal election. It's hitting the fan, Jim."

"Yeah, it's in my dossier," Allenby said. "What's the status of the victims?"

"Three dead, fourth won't last another hour."

"The bodies?"

"Two already bagged and en route to Fort Detrick. We're holding the third body until the last family member dies so we can send them down together."

"What spin are you putting on this?"

"That they contracted a strain of bacteria at the restaurant four days ago. The press is going to put two and two together and figure out that the quarantine on TGIF is related, so we gave it to them. No sense appearing uncooperative."

"Anybody asking why the Bureau is involved?"

"No serious questions yet. They'll clue in sometime soon. Miami Dade is all over the place right now, so that keeps the camera crews busy filming the local cops. We're trying to stay in the background."

"Who's here from DHS?"

"One guy, one woman." He motioned with his head without pointing. "That's them over there." An average-looking couple, dressed in summer clothes and watching the event from just outside the yellow tape, nodded back at him when he made eye contact.

"Everyone going inside that house protected?" Jim Allenby asked.

"Fully suited. Portable HEPA filters. They're okay."

Jim Allenby stood and watched the scene unfold. This was going to be a public relations nightmare. It was containable as long as they kept to the infectious-bacteria story and assured the public the source had been located and destroyed. That meant getting the press on side, and that was his job. He created the new strain of bacteria in his head, gave it a cellular structure and an antidote, then headed across the street to the nearest camera crew. He was good at this stuff, but one thing gnawed in the back of his mind.

What would happen the next time the terrorists unleashed the virus?

28

Jennifer Pearce glanced at the clock. It was after ten Tuesday evening, and she wasn't expecting anyone. There was a second knock on the front door, and she walked through her living room to the foyer. She stuck one eye up to the peephole. It was dark out, but she recognized Gordon Buchanan's face in the shadows. She opened the door, feeling bewildered.

"Hello, Gordon," she said, moving aside so he could enter. "Now, this is a surprise. Never in a million years would I have expected you to be standing on my doorstep."

He gave her a grin of sorts. "If this isn't okay, I'll leave and call you tomorrow."

"No, no, come on in," she said, closing the door behind him. She waved at the front room. "Have a seat. You want some coffee or tea or something?"

"Water would be nice," he said, sitting on the love seat next to the baby grand. "What a beautiful piano."

"Thanks. You play?" Jennifer asked as she disappeared into the kitchen. She reappeared a half minute later with two glasses of water.

"No. Always wanted to start but never found the time. Wish I had."

She handed him the water. "So what brings a logger to Richmond? No trees left in Montana?"

He laughed. Her easygoing nature had taken any edge off the situation. "I've done a lot of thinking since Saturday. In fact, I've done more than just think. I took a trip to St. Lucia and had a look about."

"Kenga?" she asked, sitting on the sofa a few feet distant, facing him.

Gordon nodded. "I know a few people on the island, and I got one of them to pull the police file. He drove me to the crash site, and I had a look around." He sipped his water. "I'm not a forensic investigator, but if I had to guess, I'd say that the car Kenga was in when she went over the cliff was pushed." He explained to her the series of switchbacks and tight corners at and close to the crash scene, and the gash he had noticed in the tree. "Another week and that evidence will be covered over with moss and lichens."

"So whoever murdered her is going to get away with it," she said bitterly.

He shrugged. "I doubt if the Lucian police will do anything, if that's what you mean. But maybe there's something we can do."

She tilted her head slightly and looked at the man, this time staring into his eyes and seeing inside him. She saw pain and anger tempered with patience and cunning. And she saw an inner strength. Buchanan had lost his brother, and he saw Veritas as the responsible party. Instead of sitting back and complaining, he was going on the offensive. Her type of guy.

"What would that be?" she asked.

Gordon held up the water glass. "This isn't cutting it," he said. "If that offer for coffee is still on, I'll try some."

"Sure," she said. "Come on in the kitchen."

They talked about her new house, Gordon complimenting her on the wooden plank flooring, which she disliked, and asking why anyone would have a white kitchen, which she liked.

As the coffee perked, he asked about restaurants, the Richmond theater scene, and what driving was like in the city. When they were each settled in at the kitchen table with a hot, fresh mug of coffee, he took some time to explain things to her.

"I suspected right from minute one that the antibalding drug had altered Billy's body chemistry somehow. Both of us have suffered cuts over the years, it's just part of working with saws, and he'd never had a problem with his blood clotting before. Things like that don't just change overnight.

"The only variable was Triaxcion. So I went to a local law firm and had them dig into what legal avenues were open to us. What we found pointed to the possibility that Veritas could be responsible for Billy's death."

"What did you find?" Jennifer asked, cupping her coffee mug, the warmth comfortable on her palms.

"There are a few other people out there who have had a family member die and have retained legal counsel. All of them are looking at possible tort suits against Veritas."

"But none have been filed yet. Why is that?"

"No definitive proof. My lawyer pushed pretty hard but couldn't get any sort of positive response from Veritas. In fact, they were adamant that if we filed, they would defend Triaxcion to the Supreme Court if necessary. My lawyer, Christine, advised me that Veritas could wear me down financially, destroy me unless there was some sort of massive tort action taken against them. And that doesn't look like it's going to happen."

"So it would have been David against Goliath, except this David would have been overrun with lawyers."

He nodded. "I'm not one to run from a fight, but I'm not one to start a scrap that I don't stand a chance of winning. So as the picture began to come into focus and I realized the legal route wasn't going to work, I changed my approach."

"You talked Kenga into getting you information on Veritas," she said.

He hesitated. Then he swallowed. "In one way, I suppose I'm responsible for her death. But I never thought Veritas would go to such lengths to protect themselves."

Jennifer shook her head vigorously. "You are not responsible for her death," she said. "If the company discovered she was passing privileged information to a third party, they should have fired her and had her charged criminally. Killing her was not a normal reaction."

"I would never have asked her if I'd known this would happen," Gordon said, his eyes wet. "She was a nice kid."

"How did you meet her?" Jennifer asked.

"Her parents are still in Romania, and her dad has a Web site he uses to post family stuff on. When I was searching the Web, looking for hits on Veritas, the search engine found a hit on his site. He mentioned his daughter was in America working for Veritas Pharmaceutical. I used the information on the Web site to locate her, talked to her a few times, then offered her money to get what she could on Triaxcion." His eyes teared up again. "Christ, I never thought they'd kill her."

Jennifer moved across to the love seat and sat beside him, her hands on his arm. "It's okay, Gordon. What happened isn't your fault." They sat in silence for a minute or two.

"Thanks," he said. He took a deep breath, exhaled, and continued. "I had an inside source with Kenga, but I wanted more. So I hired a private investigator to dig into Veritas. Among other things, he found some questionable accounting practices."

"Veritas is in trouble financially?" she asked.

"I'm not sure. But they've stretched themselves pretty thin. Haldion was their first FDA recall, and the tort suits drained a lot of money out of the corporate coffers. Triaxcion was looking like it was going to follow suit, and that's probably why they decided to defend it so vigorously. Stop the bleeding before it starts. A successful tort suit could have cost them in excess of five hundred million dollars. That's money Veritas doesn't have right now."

"What about the new drugs in the pipeline?" Jennifer asked. "Veritas is close to getting FDA approval on three new chemicals."

"One for reducing blood pressure, one an antiviral, the other for cholesterol. But not one of the three is there yet. From what I saw, they're stuck in Phase III trials."

"But if any one of those drugs is approved, the money will be flowing again. These aren't orphan drugs we're talking about here."

Gordon looked confused. "What are orphan drugs?"

"Sometimes a major pharmaceutical company will develop a drug that works against a serious affliction that only affects a few people. Without the numbers to generate the sales once the drug is FDA approved and on the market, there's no upside to manufacturing it other than some R&D credits. Orphan drugs are very much a goodwill gesture by the company."

"No, they are certainly not orphan drugs."

"What else did your PI uncover?" she asked.

"Another dead Veritas employee. Albert Rousseau. He died back in late April when his gas stove exploded."

"You think Veritas had something to do with it?"

Gordon finished his coffee and set the mug on the kitchen table. "What are the chances of a gas explosion? Natural gas is about the safest form of energy on the market. These things just don't happen every day. If I had to guess, I'd say the explosion was planned. The private investigator I hired is on his way to Richmond to see if Rousseau was planning any big purchases or trips."

"You think he was blackmailing someone at Veritas?"

"No idea. But it's suspicious, his dying like that."

Jennifer finished her coffee and poured both of them another cup. "It's decaf," she said, pouring a touch of cream into her mug. She offered him the cream and he topped off his coffee.

"This isn't my life, Jennifer," Gordon said. She looked confused, and he said, "People dying and corporations killing their employees. I'm completely out of my element here. I'm comfortable in a flannel shirt with a chain saw in my hand. This is so alien to me. I don't know what to do."

"You seem to have done pretty good so far," she said. "You found the pills, talked to the doctor, brought in legal counsel first and then a private investigator. And when that wasn't working, you searched out Kenga. You've certainly adapted to this whole mess quite well."

His face wore a dejected look. "But we have nothing. Veritas is probably guilty of some horrific things, but we can't prove it. So far, they're winning."

"So far," she said. "You look tired. I've got a guest bedroom set up. Want to spend the night?"

He shook his head. "No, thanks. It's not proper. I'll get a hotel room. In fact, I've already got one. Left all my bags there before I came over."

She nodded, knowing he had just told her the first lie of the night. "Okay, if you insist."

"I do," he said, rising from the kitchen chair. They walked through the living room, and he stopped. "Would you do me one favor?"

"Sure," she said.

"Play for me. Just one or two songs. I love the piano."

"Of course," Jennifer said, a little taken aback by the request. It had come out of left field. "Just relax on the couch and get comfortable."

Gordon stretched out on the sofa, his legs overhanging the armrest. Jennifer sat at the bench and the gentle sounds of Enya spilled through the darkened room. Every key she touched was as it should be, and her cadence was perfect. He felt the notes blurring together into a silky wall of sound. His thoughts drifted to the woman at the piano, and how she had taken the incentive to search him out and speak with him about Kenga. She was a well-educated, intelligent woman, and he admired her strength of character. Perhaps together they could give Veritas a run for its money.

The notes washed over him, and his breathing became more and more rhythmic.

29

J. D. Rothery chaired the meeting in his office in L'Enfant Plaza. The office was six hundred square feet with thick wall-to-wall carpet, a large redwood desk, and a sitting area with three leather couches and two overstuffed armchairs. Two walls were solid windows and the other two richly paneled with bookcases and original canvases. Present were Craig Simms, Deputy Director of the CIA, and Tony Warner, Director of Intelligence Analysis with the National Security Agency. Jim Allenby arrived as the meeting started. He had just flown in from Miami on a Bureau Gulfstream.

"Jim, you're back from the crime scene. What have you got for us?" Rothery asked.

"Some good news mixed with a whole lot of bad. All four members of one Cuban-American family are dead. There's no doubt we're dealing with the same hemorrhagic virus we had in Austin and San Diego. Source of contamination was a TGIF restaurant in Miami. The restaurant is under quarantine, but we suspect the terrorists planted a set of infected silverware and the Chavez family was the unlucky party. The dishes have all been through a commercial washing machine with temperatures on some of the cycles that will kill the virus."

"No chance of the virus spreading?" J. D. asked.

"At the restaurant, we suspect not. At the house, we're hopeful. These people lived inside that house for four days since they ingested the virus, and there are levels of contamination in the home. But our experts think they've got it contained."

"So what's the good news?" Simms asked.

"At first, we thought we were going to have a media circus on this one," Allenby replied. "The father, Enrico Chavez, was a bit of a public figure in the Cuban community, having run for municipal office. But the press hasn't suggested his murder was politically motivated, and we're fine with them taking that stance. And it turns out there's no immediate family in the United States. All relatives are still in Cuba. And without immediate family banging on the door and demanding autopsy results and answers to questions, this might blow over quicker than we thought. We don't have to answer to anyone who isn't directly related to the Chavez family. So we can deflect the questions, and as long as no one on our end does anything stupid, we should be able to hunker down until this blows over."

"The bodies are at Fort Detrick?" J. D. Rothery asked.

"Yes. Dr. Henning flew down yesterday afternoon. We expect a report back sometime this afternoon."

"Who is he forwarding the report to?" Simms asked.

"I've requested copies go out simultaneously to all four agencies," Allenby said. This was political maneuvering at its best: Keep everyone in the loop at the same time. "Henning estimated he would have the results of his autopsies by four this afternoon, so you should have reports on your desks by six, six-thirty at the latest."

Simms nodded his approval. "Thanks, Jim."

"What does the president have to say, Tony?" Rothery asked the NSA agent.

"He wants to be kept up to date on every detail," Tony Warner replied. "I briefed him this morning on the situation, and he's

147

very concerned. The connection between Austin, San Diego, and now Miami is more than just troublesome. The White House is viewing this as a definite terrorist threat, and the fact that they can disseminate this virus whenever and wherever they want has the president looking seriously at upgrading the terror alert status from yellow to orange."

"Probably a bad idea," Craig Simms said. "If the media sees the government moving to a higher alert status, they're going to question why. We'll end up answering a lot more questions, and someone somewhere is going to piece this thing together. And when that happens, we'll have a lot of panicked people on our hands."

"The scary thing is that these guys have got the virus in the first place," Tony Warner said. "We've been monitoring a lot of activity over the past few years, and we never saw anything like this coming. I'd like to know where they got it."

"I've got to agree with Tony," Simms said. "CIA has kept a close watch on this sort of thing. We know the scientists who've got the know-how to create these things, and this has totally blindsided us."

"Okay," Rothery said, cutting Simms off. "We don't know where it came from. I agree that's not a good thing, but focusing on the idea that this couldn't have happened isn't going to get us anywhere. It did happen and it's still happening. We've got a rogue virus on the loose and in the hands of some group that's ready to use it against us." He looked back to Simms. "Craig, what about the labs you've been watching—any unusual activity since last Friday?"

"No. We've coordinated better satellite coverage with Tony," he nodded toward the NSA man, "but nothing we're seeing is out of the ordinary. The traffic in and out of the labs is about the same as we've been seeing for the last couple of months."

Rothery was silent for a minute. The look on his face conveyed the seriousness of the situation. He looked at each man, locking eyes for a few seconds, then said, "One more incident with this virus and we are moving on those labs, Craig. I'm sorry if we blow the lid off your surveillance, but this is getting damned serious. We need to know where this bug is coming from and who has it."

Simms nodded. "I'll put a contingency plan in place to take out the al-Qaeda operatives we've identified at the same time we raid the labs. We'll find an upside to this somewhere, J. D."

"Thanks, Craig," Rothery said. His eyes scanned the room again. "Gentlemen, we have a potential crisis here and we have to chop it off at the knees. So far, what I've seen from every person in this room is absolute cooperation between agencies, and that's exactly what we need right now. Know this: Each of you has the full cooperation of the Department of Homeland Security. There is no request you can make of us right now that we will not do everything humanly possible to respond to. My line is open twenty-four seven to each man in this room. And when we merge the resources of the CIA, FBI, NSA, and DHS, there is nothing we cannot do. We *will* find the source of this virus, and we *will* eliminate it."

He stood up to indicate that the meeting was adjourned. He turned to Jim Allenby. "Jim, excellent work keeping the lid on the Miami thing."

Allenby nodded and filed out with the rest of the men. They split up and left individually in dark cars with tinted windows. Allenby glanced about as he drove onto the street from the parking garage. He knew the sight of these four men together on a Thursday afternoon would create a media storm that would be difficult to extinguish. Top operatives of the country's premier spy and investigative agencies didn't get together for coffee and donuts. They met in times of crises. And right now there was no spin the Department of Homeland Security could put on this that was positive.

Rothery waited for an hour after his visitors left before calling his driver and departing the office. He sat in the backseat of his chauffeur-driven Lincoln, watching the procession of D.C. monuments slide past. Washington was a beautiful city, especially in the summer when the trees and shrubs were in full foliage. They slowed for traffic, and the J. Edgar Hoover Building caught his attention. He personally thought they should rename that structure. They continued on Pennsylvania, past the White House, and then over the Potomac on the Theodore Roosevelt Bridge. Roosevelt's monument seemed to shimmer in the afternoon sun, surrounded by the nature and wildlife the twenty-sixth president had so dearly loved. The island with all its boardwalks and trails disappeared as they increased speed and headed up the George Washington Memorial Parkway toward McLean.

The car slipped into his driveway, and he dismissed his driver after requesting a six-thirty pickup the next morning. He walked the last few yards to his home, a low-slung ranch-style brick house surrounded by mature hickory. He opened the front door and heard the television from the back of the house. His daughter, Marissa, eighteen and registered to start her first year of college at Harvard next week, peeked out from the family room.

"Hi, Dad," she said, smiling. She was an attractive young woman, with her mother's finer features and his tenacity. Boys had been calling constantly since she was thirteen, but so far she'd been very choosy and had dated only a handful of eligible men. She met him halfway down the hall and gave him a big hug. "How was work?"

"Interesting," he said. "What's got you in such a good mood?"

"I'm going to college in six days," she said. "Why *wouldn't* I be in a good mood?"

"No more parents for a while."

"None. And tons of keg parties and visitors popping into the dorms at all hours of the night. I mean, that's what *you* did when *you* were in Harvard, right?" She grinned and let him go. "Mom called to say dinner will be late. They teed off late today and she won't be home until seven or so."

"Okay," Rothery said, watching her head downstairs to her space. She liked to be upstairs when he and his wife were not home, but the minute they arrived she headed to the basement

GET UP TO 4 FREE BOOKS!

You can have the best fiction delivered to your door for less than what you'd pay in a bookstore or online—only $4.25 a book! Sign up for our book clubs today, and we'll send you **FREE* BOOKS** just for trying it out...**with no obligation to buy, ever!**

LEISURE HORROR BOOK CLUB

With more award-winning horror authors than any other publisher, it's easy to see why CNN.com says "Leisure Books has been leading the way in paperback horror novels." Your shipments will include authors such as RICHARD LAYMON, DOUGLAS CLEGG, JACK KETCHUM, MARY ANN MITCHELL, and many more.

LEISURE THRILLER BOOK CLUB

If you love fast-paced page-turners, you won't want to miss any of the books in Leisure's thriller line. Filled with gripping tension and edge-of-your-seat excitement, these titles feature everything from psychological suspense to legal thrillers to police procedurals and more!

As a book club member you also receive the following special benefits:

- **30% OFF** all orders through our website & telecenter!
- **Exclusive access** to special discounts!
- **Convenient** home delivery **and 10 days to return any books you don't want to keep.**

There is no minimum number of books to buy, and you may cancel membership at any time. See back to sign up!

*Please include $2.00 for shipping and handling.

YES! ☐

Sign me up for the Leisure Horror Book Club and send my TWO FREE BOOKS! If I choose to stay in the club, I will pay only $8.50* each month, a savings of $5.48!

YES! ☐

Sign me up for the Leisure Thriller Book Club and send my TWO FREE BOOKS! If I choose to stay in the club, I will pay only $8.50* each month, a savings of $5.48!

NAME: _____

ADDRESS: _____

_____

TELEPHONE: _____

E-MAIL: _____

☐ **I WANT TO PAY BY CREDIT CARD.**

☐ VISA   ☐ MasterCard   ☐ DISCOVER

ACCOUNT #: _____

EXPIRATION DATE: _____

SIGNATURE: _____

Send this card along with $2.00 shipping & handling for each club you wish to join, to:

Horror/Thriller Book Clubs
20 Academy Street
Norwalk, CT 06850-4032

Or fax (must include credit card information!) to: 610.995.9274.
You can also sign up online at www.dorchesterpub.com.

*Plus $2.00 for shipping. Offer open to residents of the U.S. and Canada only.
Canadian residents please call 1.800.481.9191 for pricing information.
If under 18, a parent or guardian must sign. Terms, prices and conditions subject to change. Subscription subject
to acceptance. Dorchester Publishing reserves the right to reject any order or cancel any subscription.

JOIN NOW!

and her fully accessorized bedroom. The chief of DHS walked through his house to the private backyard. He sat on the interlocking stone patio and put his feet up on the glass table. The trees swayed in the breeze and the barely audible gurgle of the distant garden fountain tickled his ears. He closed his eyes, the rigors of the office slowly dissipating into the warm evening air. The sound of the patio doors opening caused him to turn slightly and see who was there. It was Marissa.

"Dad, what do you think this is?" she asked. She came closer, gesturing at the side of her head.

He sat up and looked at his daughter. Her eyes were red, tiny veins almost obscuring the white. The color of her skin wasn't right: It was gray and mottled with dark patches. A trickle of blood ran between her nose and her upper lip. She wiped at her ear and her hand came away stained red. More blood. Rothery jumped from his chair and stared. Dark fluid was forming at the edges of her mouth, and as quickly as she wiped it away, more of the dark, viscous fluid appeared.

"I don't feel very well, Dad," she said, falling forward. He caught her and almost dropped her on the stones, she was so hot. Burning up.

"Oh God," Rothery screamed. He had seen the pictures of the victims in Austin and San Diego. He knew exactly what he was looking at. Hemorrhagic fever. The virus. He let his daughter slip to the ground and grabbed for the telephone. He hit the talk button and dialed his office. No answer. He dialed Jim Allenby. Voice mail. He hung up and dialed 911.

"Emergency," the voice said.

"I need an ambulance," he said. He recited his address.

"Yeah, you and everyone else," the dispatcher said. "You think you're the only one with the virus. Think again, buddy."

He jerked awake, sweat running down his face and staining his shirt. His heart was beating faster than he had ever felt it, and his breath was coming in short gasps. Marissa stood in front of him with a scared look on her face.

"Dad," she said. "Wake up. You were having a nightmare." She was fine, her skin nicely tanned, her face and mouth showing concern but healthy. "Are you okay?"

He took a couple of deep breaths. "Yes, Marissa, I'm fine. Thanks for waking me. Must have had too much coffee today." His breathing was returning to normal.

"Okay," his daughter said hesitantly. "Call me if you need anything."

"Yeah, sure, honey."

She reentered the house and closed the door behind her. A nightmare. She had called it a nightmare. *Was that it?* he asked himself. *Was it a nightmare?*

Or was it a premonition?

30

"She's all-wheel drive," the salesman said as he approached the potential customer. "Three-point-six-liter rear-mounted engine, 320 horsepower, and 0 to 62 miles per hour in five seconds."

Wes Connors whistled. He lightly stroked the sleek silver-gray sports car, the metal cool to his touch. "It's beautiful." He continued to walk slowly around the vehicle, taking in the elegance of its design.

"This color is Arctic Silver Metallic, one of the most popular in the Carrera 4S series. And this baby has the Tiptronic transmission. It's a five-speed automatic with a couple of manual gearshift controls." He leaned over the door of the convertible and pointed to the steering wheel. "And if you brake really hard, the transmission automatically downshifts to help stop the car."

"How much?" Connors asked. "As it sits."

"Ninety-three thousand two hundred."

"Ouch." Wes shook his head. "Too rich for me. I'll have to look at something else."

The salesman waved his arms at the showroom. "They're all Porsches." He extended his hand. "Jack Fraser."

"Wes Connors." They shook, and Wes said, "A friend of mine referred your dealership."

"Who would that be?" Fraser asked.

"Albert Rousseau. You know him?"

A startled look swept across Fraser's face. "Albert? Yeah, I know Albert. That's the exact model he was looking at. But you must have talked with him some time ago."

Wes nodded and gave Fraser a grim look. "Yeah, just before he died. He was excited about getting a Porsche and told me if I was ever looking to come here."

Fraser shook his head. "God-awful thing, that. Getting blown up in your own house. And it happened two days after he put a ten-grand deposit on the Carrera. He said this beast was going to look so good in his driveway in Carmel."

"Carmel? California?"

Fraser gave Connors a questioning look. "You didn't know he was moving to California?"

"No idea," Connors said, laughing. "But that's typical Albert. He'd probably move without telling anyone, then invite his friends over for the housewarming party. Do you know if he'd already found a place out there?"

"He told me he'd made an offer on a house just off the ocean. Said he couldn't afford one right on the water."

"He could if he wanted, just didn't want to pay the price."

"So what car *is* in your price range, Wes?" Fraser said, leading the private investigator away from the flagship vehicle.

Twenty minutes later, Wes Connors thanked Fraser for his time, hopped in his rental, and pulled out into the Richmond traffic. He was halfway down the block when his cell phone connected to Gordon's. He relayed the information from the dealership to his client.

"So he had a deposit on a top-end Porsche and was looking at property in Carmel. Rousseau had either just collected a good chunk of cash or he was expecting some in the near future."

"It would appear so."

"Wes, get out to Carmel and find out what property he was

looking at, and when the closing date was on the purchase. And good work."

"Thanks. I'll get on it right away."

Connors clicked his phone shut and grinned. Some days, he really loved this private investigator stuff.

"He was a friend of Albert Rousseau's?" the manager asked, scanning the card Connors had given Jack Fraser. There was no company name, just Connor's name sans title, and a Seattle address and phone number.

"Told me Rousseau had referred him. Bit of a flake, I think. He did the squid when I tried to get him out for a test drive." "The squid" was auto-industry shorthand for a buyer who raises his or her hands and waves them about when they don't want to do something, usually take the car for a drive or make an offer. "Anyway, you said once that if anyone came in mentioning Albert Rousseau, you wanted to know."

"Thanks, Jack," the manager said. He waited until Fraser was out of his office, then looked up a number and dialed. "Bruce Andrews, please," he said when the receptionist answered. She took his name and asked him to hold. A few moments later, Andrews's voice came over the line.

"Mr. Andrews, I don't know if you remember me, but this is Stan Reichle over at Motorsports Porsche. You mentioned that if anyone came asking about Albert Rousseau, you wanted to know."

"Of course I remember you, Stan. I called you because we had given Albert a cash bonus and we were concerned that the IRS would find out and try to get the taxes out of his estate. What's the reason for the call?"

"Someone came by today looking at cars. Told the salesman Albert had referred him. My sales rep didn't think this guy was legit."

"So what did he want?" Andrews asked.

"No idea. But he left his card. He's from Seattle. Name is Wes Connors." He recited the address and phone number off the card. "Strange. No business name on the card."

"Well, it doesn't sound like the IRS, but you never know. Thanks for calling. In fact, your timing is perfect. We need to pick up a couple of cars and one of those new SUVs for employee bonuses. I'll send down one of my management team to pick them out. Should they ask for you when they stop by?"

"That would be fine, Mr. Andrews. Thanks."

"Thank you," Andrews said, replacing the phone in the cradle.

Bruce Andrews stared at the phone. What the hell was going on? He had figured the Albert Rousseau issue to be a dead one. Why was someone asking questions about Rousseau almost four months after his death? This was exactly the last thing he needed on his plate right now.

He picked up his phone and dialed a number from memory. The voice he knew would answer said hello. He explained what had happened at the car dealership and recited Wes Connors's name and address.

"Do you want me to look into it?" the voice asked.

"Yes. I want to know who this Connors guy is and why he's poking around. Rousseau is history. Bad history. I don't need anyone digging into this."

"I'll take care of it." The line went dead.

The CEO of Veritas Pharmaceutical rose from his desk and stood by the bank of windows, looking across downtown Richmond. He stared at the Coliseum a few blocks south. The structure had always reminded him of an alien spacecraft anchored to a matching landing pad. It was the venue where Elvis played to four sellout crowds and the same arena in which Richmond City Council, in all their infinite wisdom, had voted to prohibit the Grateful Dead from performing. Frank Zappa, yes, the Grateful Dead, no. God, life was strange.

It was the small stuff that could hurt you, Andrews thought as he released the Coliseum from his gaze and scanned across the city. Sometimes the best-laid plans were tripped up by the most inconsequential things. Trivial idiosyncrasies that came back to bite you in the ass when you were least expecting it. Albert Rousseau was a prime example. His death had been ruled an accident, the insurance company had agreed to that and had paid, and the city had released an order to allow reconstruction of the town-house unit destroyed by the explosion. But out of nowhere somebody from Seattle comes sniffing around, asking questions about a murdered man.

He didn't like this. He didn't like this at all.

31

Gordon was out in the field working the feller-buncher, a machine designed to topple the timber and strip the branches, when a message from his receptionist came through on his two-way radio. There was a call waiting that could be transferred to his cell phone. He distanced himself from the machine, with its noisy grinders and hydraulics, and found a quiet spot of forest. He used the radio to ask his receptionist to put the call through. Jennifer Pearce's voice came across the line.

"Thanks again for letting me sleep on your couch the other day," he said, relaxing back into a Ponderosa pine. The bark tickled his back, and he liked the feeling.

"I hardly let you," she said. "Two songs and you were out cold. I just covered you up with a blanket. Did anyone ever tell you that you snore?"

"Yeah," he said sheepishly. "I've been told. How are things at work?"

"Difficult to concentrate. Can't keep my mind on task. I keep wondering what's really going on around here. And everyone is still depressed over what happened to Kenga. This isn't a great place to be right now."

"How's the research coming along?"

She brightened. "That end of things is good. We've found a molecule that will bond to the membrane component. It's a significant step in the right direction. About half my staff is at a different facility at White Oak Technology Park, and they're concentrating on the new molecule. It's a pain in the butt running between the two locations, but right now the progress is worth it. So work in itself is good." She glanced about her office, the desk piled high with pharmaceutical and medical texts. Science magazines and periodicals filled with dissertations were stacked on the chairs usually reserved for visitors. She was onto something, and the research materials were taking over her office.

"I'm glad," he said. "I know you take your research work seriously."

"It saves lives, Gordon," she said. "Or improves quality of life, all depending."

"I wish everyone at Veritas had the same ethics you have, Jennifer," Gordon said, staring at the sky and feeling a warm sensation in his eyes. "Billy would be out here with me, cutting trees and bitching about the beer at the pub being warm."

"You miss him," she said. Her voice was soft and understanding. "That's natural, Gordon."

"Yeah, I guess." He lowered his line of vision to the forest and drank in the warmth of green and brown, framed by the brilliant blue sky. Moss clung to the sides of rotting stumps and tiny wildflowers peeked out from cracks in the mulch covering the forest floor. Birds chirped nearby and a squirrel squawked at him, irritated he'd chosen that particular tree to rest against. God, he loved the forest. And then it struck him. Jennifer Pearce didn't have a reason to call. They had been talking for a couple of minutes about nothing in particular. She had just called to talk.

He closed his eyes and envisioned her face and her body. She was a strikingly beautiful woman, with soft eyes that spoke of a caring and loving nature. Her smile was warm and real, and her passion for the truth unmistakable. For a moment, he was close to her and could smell the faint caress of perfume she wore on her neck. Her hair was soft in his hands, and he slipped his arms around her shoulders and pulled her closer.

"Gordon? Gordon, are you still there?"

"Yeah, I'm here," Gordon said, suddenly feeling like a schoolboy caught staring at the prettiest girl in class. "I must have missed what you said. Sorry."

"That's okay. I was just asking if you were thinking of coming back down to Richmond soon."

Reality was back. "I guess that depends on what happens with Veritas. Right now I'm just waiting to hear back from Wes Connors. He's in Carmel, digging up the real estate company that represented Albert Rousseau on his purchase."

"Why is that important?" she asked.

"Albert would need the cash to close the deal. The possession date on the real estate deal will tell us where Albert was in the process of blackmailing Veritas—if in fact that's what he was doing."

"You're pretty well convinced he was," she said.

"Yeah, I am. I think someone at Veritas had him killed because he was threatening to go public with damaging information."

"Well, the Richmond police don't agree with you. His death has been officially ruled accidental. The city has just issued a permit for the contractors to start work on his town house. Four months with yellow tape around a bombed-out building. If I were his neighbors, I'd be pretty damned upset."

Gordon was thoughtful. "Albert's town house is still intact? The same as it was when he died?"

"I think so. There was a lot of talk about who was responsible for what. The insurance company and the gas company weren't agreeing on things."

"Go figure," Gordon said. "Nobody wants to admit fault."

"Something like that." There was a voice in the background, and Jennifer said, "Sorry, Gordon, I've got to go. Small problem to take care of."

"Okay. Can I call you at home? Later, maybe?"

"Sure," she said. She sounded happy at the suggestion. "I'd like that."

Gordon closed his cell phone and sat in silence. Jennifer Pearce. He had noticed her looks the moment he had pulled himself out from under the planer machine on her visit to the mill, but he hadn't let his thoughts drift toward her as a woman he may be attracted to, not until today's phone call. Was she interested in him? She'd asked if he was planning to visit Richmond again soon. And his suggestion that he call her later had met with a very positive response. Then again, maybe someone was in her office and she had to be polite. Who knew?

A wisp of a breeze rustled through the pines and he felt a touch of sadness lift from his heart. For the first time since Billy died all those months ago, he sensed happiness creeping back into his life. It was Jennifer Pearce. In some way, her presence in his life reassured him that things would get better, that laughter and love would return. There was a goodness in her heart that was reaching out to him, drawing him close to her. Yes, that was it. He felt closer to her than any other person in his life. She was physically distant, across the breadth of the continent, and they had never touched other than to shake hands, but he instinctively knew she was drawing him in to her. And he made a decision. He would not push her away, as he had done with so many other women in his life. He would let Jennifer Pearce get to know him. He would let her get close. If that was what she wanted.

And he hoped it was.

"What is it, Robert?" Jennifer asked. Robert Blakely, one of her junior researchers, was hanging halfway in her office, trying to get her attention.

"They need you at White Oak," he said. "Josh sounded real excited when he called. You were on the phone."

"I'll call over," she said, reaching for the phone she had just hung up.

"Nobody will answer. They're all in the lab. They've got some promising results on that new molecule they're testing."

161

"Okay," she said, "I'll drive over." Her research assistant disappeared, and she glanced again at her computer screen. She had been slowly scrolling through her accounting files while talking with Gordon, and she didn't like what she saw. Everyday expenses for her research group were being shuffled over into the R&D column. That would qualify those expenses for government research tax credits. It was impossible for her to tell whether Veritas was actually claiming those tax credits or not, but the accounting practices she was looking at would allow for that to happen. And that would not only be unethical, it would be illegal.

She sat back and thought about the potential implications this kind of accounting could have on a company the size of Veritas. If they were redirecting even thirty percent of their expenses into research and claiming the tax credits, that would amount to over three hundred million dollars a year. And three hundred million a year in the asset column rather than the debit column netted six hundred million in profits that was nonexistent. Shades of Enron, she thought.

She closed the file and locked out her computer. She would talk to someone about it at some point, but right now she had to get over to White Oak.

32

The office of Wes Connors, Private Investigator, was locked, but
it took the man less than five seconds to line up the tumblers in
the deadbolt and jimmy the lock. He slipped inside the darkened office, adjusted his night-vision goggles, and switched
them on. The room took on an eerie green glow.

There was a desk, three filing cabinets, and a scratched coffee table sitting in front of an old couch. A computer monitor
sat on the desk, and the intruder immediately moved to the
computer and turned it on. He adjusted the light level on the
monitor so it wouldn't blind him, pulled out each desk drawer,
and searched through them as the computer booted up. There
was little of value in the drawers, just pens and pencils, paper
clips, scissors, and other office staples. The bottom drawer had
a few files, but they were filled with receipts, neatly labeled for
filing with the IRS. The computer finished powering up, and the
man turned his attention there.

He scanned the hard drive for Wes Connors's clients' files.
They were grouped together in a folder in Microsoft Word. Each
client had a profile, including their address, phone number,
and why they had sought out the services of a private investiga-

tor. Most were local clients, but a handful were from out of state. Attached to the client profile was an accounting sheet with detailed expense reports, billable hours, and dates. The intruder switched his approach when he saw that Connors kept exact dates on when he worked for each client. He searched the client files for any customers with August 2005 dates. The search produced three names. He perused each of the files and sent them to the printer. Then he closed each file, shut down the computer, and shifted his attention to the filing cabinets.

They were locked, but it took him seconds to pick the lock and slide them open, one drawer at a time. He flipped through the files, looking for hard copy on the three clients Wes Connors had been working for during August. He found a single file for each client. Receipts were neatly filed in the folders, and when he opened the third one he knew he'd hit pay dirt. Gordon Buchanan's file had a Visa receipt for an electronic ticket to Richmond dated August 31, just five days prior. And Connors had been in Richmond, poking into something that had ruffled some big feathers. The man replaced the files exactly as he had found them and quietly left the office, locking it behind him.

When he was on the street, two blocks away at his car, he made a phone call from his cell. "I think I've found what you want," he said.

"And?" the voice asked.

"Wes Connors was hired by Gordon Buchanan. There's a receipt for a plane ticket, dated five days ago, in Buchanan's file."

"Anything else?"

"The only other things in that file were Buchanan's particulars and a brief write-up on his brother's death. There was mention of a pharmaceutical company—Veritas, I think."

"Thanks."

The man closed his phone and slid out of the misty evening into his car, dry and comfortable. The rain picked up in intensity almost immediately, and he was glad to be inside. He started the car and pulled away from the curb, wondering why it had been so important to check out Wes Connors's office that evening. But when the orders came from as far up the food chain as they had, you didn't ask why, you just did what they asked. He called his wife as the downpour started and told her he was on his way home. When it was raining, she usually fixed him hot chocolate, even during the summer. He liked that.

The line went dead in his hand and he set the phone on the desk. The information from Seattle was interesting but not unexpected. Since his last discussion with Bruce Andrews, he had made some discreet inquiries about Gordon Buchanan, and what he had found was quite interesting.

Buchanan was a self-made man in the logging industry, a tough business in which to excel. He ran a sawmill just outside Divide, Montana, lived in Butte, and preferred the tranquillity of the northern forests to the congestion of any major cities. He had played hockey during his youth, achieving reasonable success with a triple-A junior club before an injury took him out of serious contention for a coveted spot in the NHL. One of his mills had burned to the ground, but he'd taken the insurance money, about twenty cents on the dollar, and rebuilt. The man was not a quitter. That was not good. Buchanan was intent on nailing Veritas for his brother's death, and his prodding was proving to be a nuisance, disruptive even. He called Bruce Andrews's private line.

"About Gordon Buchanan," he said when Andrews answered. "My guy found a receipt for a recent plane ticket to Richmond in his file in Wes Connors's office."

Andrews's voice was thoughtful. "Gordon Buchanan. This guy is like the Energizer Bunny. He just doesn't stop."

"He's becoming a pest."

"We have to send him a message," Andrews said. "I think I'll have someone waiting when Wes Connors arrives back in Seattle. Maybe Buchanan will get the idea I'm not to be trifled with."

"Why not just remove Buchanan? He seems to be the quar-

Jeff Buick

terback. Connors is just a PI he hired to check out Albert Rousseau."

"Because if Buchanan disappears or dies violently, eyes are going to be looking at Veritas. It's no secret that he was trying everything in his power to get some sort of admission out of us that Triaxcion was responsible for his brother's death. I'd rather just send him a message."

"Okay. Do you want me to take care of it?"

"No, it's okay. I've got someone close by," Andrews said.

"All right. Let me know if there's anything you need."

"I'll tell you what I need. I need this whole thing to stay on track."

"That's what this is all about."

"I'll talk to you later. Don't call unless it's important." Andrews hung up.

The man on the other end of the phone also hung up. He reassured himself that things were fine. When Wes Connors disappeared, Gordon Buchanan would surely understand he was battling against an unstoppable tide. One man could not derail the machine that Bruce Andrews had built at Veritas. Right now, it was just a matter of getting that simple concept through to Buchanan.

Buchanan could not win.

33

United Flight 5641 touched down at Byrd Field, as Richmond International Airport is commonly referred to by the locals, twenty minutes late. Strong headwinds out of Denver, the pilot had told the passengers. Gordon Buchanan didn't care. Twenty minutes one way or the other was of no consequence. He wasn't meeting Jennifer Pearce for dinner until six-thirty, and it wasn't even four in the afternoon. He hailed a cab and sat in the front seat with the driver, a mid-fifties leftover from the hippie days.

"Where to?" he asked. His hair was almost entirely gray, and very long, past his shoulders. He was clean shaven, but his eyes were glazed over and he looked like he needed a shower to wake up. That struck Gordon as odd, given the time of day.

"The nearest Starbucks," Gordon said. "I'll buy you a coffee."

That brightened the driver a touch. "That's great, man. I just came on, and I'm kinda still getting my brain around all the traffic."

"Great," Gordon said. "Starbucks. Get me there and we'll pour a couple of venti lattes in you. That ought to get your brain going."

"There's one nearby," he said, pulling out into traffic and cutting off a delivery truck. They saluted each other and the ride was on.

Gordon stared out the side window, his mind on Jennifer Pearce. Three days ago, on Monday, he had spoken with her and she'd asked if he planned on returning to Richmond in the near future. He hadn't thought of it. Not until she had called. Then two separate things had stirred him to action. First off, he got the feeling she wanted to see him again, and that was something he decided he wanted as well. Second, he wanted to see Albert Rousseau's burned-out town house. He didn't know why, it was just something that was gnawing at him. Rousseau's town house had been off-limits for four months while the insurance companies fought to release themselves from any obligation to pay. Funny, he thought, how quickly they took their premiums but how slowly they paid out on a claim. But the end result of the battle was that Albert Rousseau's condo had remained untouched for the duration. And maybe, just maybe, that was a good thing.

They pulled up to the Starbucks, and for his driver Gordon ordered the largest, strongest coffee on the menu. For himself, he ordered a small dark roast with a touch of cream. He watched the man wake up a little bit with every sip of the life-sustaining liquid. By the time he drained the last of the coffee from the cup, his driver was alive and animated.

"My name's Bud," he said. "Damned nice of you to visit Richmond."

"Gordon."

"Okay, Gordon, I'm on my game now. Where to?"

Gordon checked his watch. "I need to be at Amici Ristorante at six-thirty to meet someone."

"Amici? I know Amici. Best northern Italian food in Richmond. Carey Street. Better have a reservation, my friend."

"I imagine my date took care of that. What can we do in the interim? We've got a couple of hours to spare."

"What can we do?" Bud said, giving Gordon the *you've-got-*

two-heads look. "You're in Richmond, man. The heart of Civil War country. This is where Robert E. Lee took over command of Virginia's army and held the city for four years against the Union. Man, this place is the breadbasket of American Civil War history."

"And you're my guide?"

"You buy the coffee and pay the meter, and you get the best guide Richmond has to offer. I'm an original, Gordon. Born and raised. You're in my backyard now."

Armed with a second venti dark roast, Bud was unstoppable. "Main Street," he announced as they arrived on the eastern edge of downtown Richmond. "Picture this. Benedict Arnold, the son-of-a-bitch traitor, marching down this very street with a bunch of British soldiers in tow, burning down the tobacco warehouses. And tobacco in those days was like cash in the bank." He pointed as they passed Old Stone House, the oldest building in Richmond, dating back to 1736. "That's part of the Edgar Allan Poe Museum. Weird stuff in there, man. Weird guy. This is Shockoe Bottom, best nightlife in the city. Just rocks, man."

"What's that?" Gordon asked, nodding at a grand old building on the north side of the road.

"Main Street Station, and the Seventeenth Avenue Farmer's Market in back of it. Main Street Station was the Virginia Department of Health until about two years ago, when they renovated it and put in a bunch of new shops. Now there's all kinds of excellent stuff in there. Just excellent. And check this out: Shockoe Slip. Cobblestone streets and great shopping, if you like poking through little stores. Very eclectic."

Two hours and another venti dark roast later, Bud dropped Gordon in front of a yellow building with a terra-cotta awning that stretched over the sidewalk patio. A tasteful sign indicating they had arrived at Amici Ristorante was fastened to the acrylic stucco. Gordon paid the amount on the meter and handed Bud an extra hundred for the tour. The driver showed his appreciation by leaping from the cab, running to the passenger door, and opening it.

"Usually only do that for little old ladies," he said, grinning. "Thanks. That was fun."

"Yeah," Gordon agreed, shaking the man's hand. "It was. Nice city. I like Richmond."

He entered the restaurant and spied Jennifer Pearce at a table near the fireplace. He joined her, ordered a beer, and settled in. The restaurant was elegant, but with a homey feeling thrown in. The walls were deep ocher, the chairs polished ebony, and crisp white linen cloths covered the tables. A Josh Groban CD, *Closer*, played on the sound system, his throaty voice adding to the ambience.

"Do you always make decisions just like that?" Jennifer asked, snapping her fingers.

"You mean coming to Richmond?" he asked, and she nodded. "Sure. I wanted to see Albert Rousseau's place before the contractors started work on it. Probably nothing there, but Rousseau's a big piece of the puzzle, one untapped so far."

"What about Kenga? There might be something at her place."

Gordon shook his head. "Kenga forwarded everything she had to me before she left for Saint Lucia. I have all the technical data on Triaxcion, but that doesn't really get me anywhere. It's proving the drug is dangerous that's key. When she got back from Saint Lucia, Kenga was going to start searching through the technical files to see if she could find evidence that the researchers working on that drug knew that people with A-positive blood would have negative reactions."

"So what do you expect to find at Rousseau's place? It's been exposed to the elements for four months."

He shrugged. "No idea. It's just a part of the puzzle. Oh, there's something else. My private investigator found the real estate agent Albert Rousseau was dealing with on the Carmel property. Purchase price was nine hundred and fifty thousand dollars, closing date was set for the end of September."

"So Rousseau expected a large payday fairly soon."

"Exactly. He died on the last day of April with very little money in the bank. The deposits on the Porsche and the Carmel property even left one of his accounts in overdraft. According to the real estate agent, the contract required an additional deposit of fifty thousand dollars on or before July fifteenth. The remainder of the purchase price was due about mid-September. And Rousseau told the agent he didn't need a mortgage on the house."

"So he was expecting at least a million dollars from some source over the course of the summer."

Gordon nodded. "And where does an average Joe get a million dollars on short notice?"

"Veritas," Jennifer said quietly. "Christ, Gordon. These people, whoever they are, are killing anyone who gets in their way."

"Well, let's think about who *they* could be. Usually, people don't kill other people without a reason. And more often than not, that reason is money. So you have to ask, who stands to benefit from Veritas's continued success as a company?"

"That's easy," she answered. "Anyone who owns large chunks of company stock and the top company executives."

"And who owns big chunks of Veritas stock?" Gordon asked. Jennifer shrugged. "Not counting the top brass at Veritas, there's not one individual who stands out as a shareholder. Mutual fund companies and pension funds are the big stakeholders. And no one inside those companies is going to kill to keep Veritas healthy."

"So that leaves the top execs."

"Exactly."

A waiter arrived at the table with bread and menus, explained the evening specials, and disappeared.

"Bruce Andrews is the top dog. He'd stand to gain the most."

Gordon finished his beer. "He certainly would. The information is public, so I checked into exactly how much stock the top executives at Veritas own. Bruce Andrews is way out front with six million shares of common stock and another three million in options."

"Six million shares?" she said. "It's trading at thirty-one dollars. Jesus, that's a lot of money."

"It's not just the shares," Gordon said. "It's the options. He has the option to purchase another three million shares at seventeen dollars. The options expire in three months, on December fifteenth. Any downward fluctuation in the stock price is bad news, both for the common shares and the options. An upward surge would be very beneficial."

Jennifer was silent. She sipped on her drink, then said, "So I was hired by a murderer?"

"Maybe," Gordon said. "We don't know for sure. We have no proof."

The waiter reappeared, and Jennifer ordered the Vitello al Porcini. Gordon opted for the Buffalo con Fonduta Tartufata. They ordered one more drink each and sat in silence for a minute after the server had left.

"What do we do?" Jennifer asked. "What do I do? How did I get involved with something like this?"

Gordon gave her a weak smile. "There was no way you could have known. Think of it like Tom Cruise in *The Firm*. They made him a great offer and it seemed like such a good law firm to work for."

"This isn't a movie, Gordon. This is really happening. I'm working for a company that kills anyone who stands in their way."

Gordon pursed his lips and swallowed. "All right, then, let's do this. We try to find something we can go to the authorities with, some sort of evidence that Andrews or whoever is guilty of murder. Then we let the police take care of things."

"And in the interim?" she asked.

"We try to stay alive," he said, a grim look on his face.

She shook her head in disbelief. In the past few months, her life had taken an unimaginable direction, and there seemed no end to the depth of deceit someone was willing to stoop to in order to hide whatever it was they were attempting to achieve. She pasted a wry smile on her face and said to Gordon, "Veritas is Latin. Do you know what the translation is?"

"No."

"Truth," she said. Neither of them smiled.

34

Wes Connors arrived in Seattle to a light mist. *Typical crappy weather,* he thought as he retrieved his Taurus from the long-term parking lot at Sea-Tac International. It was late, almost midnight on Thursday, but he drove to his office. He wanted to total Gordon Buchanan's invoice and send it as an e-mail so Buchanan's office staff would have it the next morning. With all the travel expenses, plus his daily rate, this bill was getting up there. He wasn't worried about Buchanan honoring the bill, he just wanted the money in his account sooner than later.

Parking was easy at this time of night, and he took the stairs to the second floor, unlocking his office door and switching on the light. Nothing happened. He flipped the switch a couple of times, cursing himself for letting so many bulbs burn out that when the last one crapped out there was nothing but darkness. He moved across the open space to his desk and touched the power button on his computer. A soft glow from the monitor washed light on his face and threw a dim illumination about the room. His eyes picked up the form on the couch a split second before his brain processed the image. His right hand moved instinctively toward the top desk drawer. He yanked it open and reached in for the gun.

It was gone.

His breathing was coming quick now. He swiveled slightly in his chair and said, "Who's there?"

The figure didn't move. "Wes Connors?" was all he said.

"Who are you and what do you want?"

"Put your hands on your desk and keep them there."

Connors complied. "I don't have any money here. This is just my office. Any cash I have is either at home or in the bank."

"I don't want your money."

Connors stared at the figure, camouflaged by the shadows and lack of light. He didn't recognize the voice, but it could be a pissed-off husband from one of his marital surveillances. Some dumbass he'd caught with a young bimbo in a hotel room, their cars parked out front in plain sight, the blinds not properly closed. Maybe he'd shot them with his 35-mm through the shades, maybe a few nights of finding the two cars together, license plates front and center. Who knew how he'd nailed the guy, but that was probably it.

"Look, buddy, whatever happened with your marriage or your life, it's not my fault. If I caught you doing something and your wife was paying me, then it's just business. You okay with that?"

"I don't cheat on my wife," the man said, leaning forward slightly. "Never have, never will."

Connors could see the man's face now: Caucasian, about forty with slightly receding brown hair. He didn't recognize him. This was not someone he'd followed and photographed. He never forgot one of those faces. Sometimes they wanted to beat the crap out of him for catching them, and he wanted the upper hand in such a situation. That meant remembering who these guys were. And if this guy wasn't some jerk who let his dick do the thinking for him, who was he?

"What do you want?" Connors asked. He was sweating now, his armpits and forehead wet with perspiration.

"I want you to stop screwing up my kid's chance at having a normal life."

"What?" Connors said. "Man, you got the wrong guy. I've never done anything in my life to hurt a child."

"You ever heard of Veritas Pharmaceutical?"

Christ, where is this going? His mind whirred through the possibilities. Albert Rousseau had worked for Veritas, but none of the information he had provided to Gordon Buchanan on Rousseau was going to affect some kid. Somehow this guy had things all wrong. He made a decision.

"I was hired to look into the death of one of their employees."

"Who?"

"Albert Rousseau."

"Bullshit."

The comment was not at all what Wes Connors expected. He stared at the man. "It's not bullshit, it's the truth. Somebody hired me to find out if Rousseau was expecting a payoff of some sort. I don't know the why or what of the whole thing, just that Rousseau had recently looked at an expensive car and some prime real estate."

"That's it?" the man asked, leaning forward even farther. The unmistakable outline of a silenced pistol was clearly visible.

"That's it," Connors said.

"That's enough," the man said, pulling the trigger. The first bullet caught Connors in the throat, the second in the head as he slumped forward. They were 9-mm slugs with hollow points, designed to cause maximum damage on exiting the victim. What were two small holes in the front of Connors's neck and forehead were six-inch gaping holes in the rear. The second bullet stopped his forward progress and threw him back, brains and blood spattering the wall and carpet. He crashed to the floor, dead instantly.

Evan Ziegler rose and stood over the man. It had played out exactly as Bruce Andrews had said it would. Connors was trying to discredit Veritas by pinning Rousseau's murder on someone inside the company. And a scandal of that magnitude would surely result in all research work grinding to a halt. With the Phase I trials for the brain chips slated to begin in less than two months, way ahead of schedule, that would spell disaster. And his son Ben was at the top of the list for one of the experimental chips. No goddamn way some piece of crap like this was going to keep his boy in that wheelchair.

He unscrewed the silencer and replaced the pistol in his shoulder holster. One more glance at the corpse and he was gone, wiping the door handle clean of all fingerprints on his way out. It was late, and he encountered no one on his way out of the building or on the street as he walked to his car. He put the windshield wipers on intermittent and pulled away from the curb with one thought on his mind.

Two more months until the tests were to begin. Ben was almost out of the chair.

35

"Gentlemen, we have a real problem this time," J. D. Rothery said. He paced the carpeted floor of his office while he spoke. Present were Jim Allenby, Tony Warner, and Craig Simms. The task force against America's latest terrorist threat was assembled and listening as the head of the scientific arm of the Department of Homeland Security brought them up to date on the latest viral outbreak.

"A group of Boy Scouts was having a picnic in Franklin Park in Boston. Five of them are sick. We've isolated the cause of the infection to the Pepsi cans they were drinking from. Five of the nine boys drank Pepsi, and they're the ones contaminated. We quarantined the remainder of the cans and found traces of the virus on the metal rim next to the pop-up tab. Plus someone had written a message on the inside of the cardboard case."

"What was the message?" Warner asked.

"*A small mouse can cause great damage if let loose in the elephant's tent*. Right now, we have no idea what the hell that's supposed to mean."

"Where did the Pepsi come from?" Allenby asked.

"One of the parents bought it at a corner store close to their home in Roxbury. It's a suburb just south of Boston, and most of the kids in the Scout troop live there."

"What's the status of the kids? How bad are they?"

"All five are going to die, probably sometime today. They ingested the pop five days ago, on September fourth. But we've got problems with their families this time. Two of the kids have infected their parents, and one sibling is showing symptoms. The press is all over this. Two of the kids were admitted to the hospital, so we've got our work cut out for us just trying to contain the virus from spreading."

"Any signs the virus is loose in the hospital?" Warner asked. The NSA man was working on his computer, calculating the collateral damage.

"Not yet," Rothery said, "but we're monitoring the situation hour by hour."

Warner hit a button and glanced up. "If two kids are in the hospital for two full days, they encountered six shifts, each with three nurses and attendants in direct contact. If the two days hit on the end of a workweek for the staff, then we have thirty-six health care professionals at risk. And they would have been in close contact to at least three or four people in triage and emergency.

"Then there are the cloths and towels from the kid's rooms. They've been mixed in with the laundry from other wards. And at least a couple of workers would have been in contact with the dirty sheets and towels before they went in for sterilization. All told, the peripheral contact, just in the hospital alone, is over fifty people. And each of those individuals has now had time to go home, kiss their spouse, share a fork over a piece of pie, hug their kids, and sneeze on the clerk at the 7-Eleven. Let's assume each of the fifty has been in close contact with six other people. That's three hundred. And the more time that passes, the more cases of intimate contact those three hundred will have with others."

"We've got to get this contained, and fast," Rothery said. He turned to Allenby. "What resources can the FBI contribute, Jim?"

"Whatever you need. We can free up an agent or two from field offices across the country. That would give us up to two hundred agents we could place in Boston within twelve hours. Each of our agents is well trained in this exact scenario—they know how to interview the victims and potential victims, and how to trace the disease as it moves through the population."

"Do it," Rothery said. He turned to Tony Warner. "Tony, get your people over at Crypto-City to map out every possible route the virus could travel. I want to be proactive on this, not reactive. Let's cut it off before it gets into the general population."

"I'll have mock-up scenarios to Jim inside six hours," he said.

"Craig," J.D. said, turning to the CIA director. "You know what I need. It's time."

Craig Simms nodded, just a slight movement but enough to acknowledge that years of clandestine operations were about to go up in smoke. "All of them?" he asked.

"Every lab you know that's actively producing toxins at this time. No exceptions. Even the ones in hostile territory if you can get SEAL units in place quickly enough."

"We anticipated it may come to this and we've called in a few favors. Mossad and MI6 are both ready to assist with the raids. The British have one SBS unit and two SAS units they can free up immediately. We'll use those for the raids on the Eastern European countries. The Israelis are anxious to shut down the labs operating in Egypt and Libya. I think we have enough SEAL and Delta Force teams to hit the rest. I'll know in a few hours."

Rothery stopped pacing and said, "I'm sorry it came to this, Craig, but we've got to stop this in its tracks. And finding out where this virus is coming from is number one. Getting a cure is a close second." He looked at Tony Warner. "You were talking with Dr. Henning on this yesterday, Tony. What did he have to say about a possible antiserum against the virus?"

"His take on it was that this virus, although hemorrhagic like Ebola, is different enough that there may be the possibility of finding something to combat it. One of the keys is in the actual diameter of the virus itself. It's double the size of Ebola, so genome replication is completely different. He thinks that some sort of viral protein, processed on the intracellular level, might stop the virus from attaching to the host cell."

"What the hell does that mean?" Rothery asked.

Warner looked perturbed at Rothery's lack of technical expertise but explained. "We have to treat the patient once they have the virus, J. D. And the best possibility we have to stop the virus from spreading inside the body is to keep it from attaching to host cells. If the virus can't attach, it's finished."

"Okay, I get what you're doing." Rothery was thoughtful. "We have a lot of scientists in the government sector we can draw on for answers, but we're missing an entire slice of the academic community." He focused on Jim Allenby. "What about the pharmaceutical companies? Could we give them a hypothetical and see if they have an answer?"

Allenby thought about the impact of revealing the virus to the public sector for a minute, then said, "It's a possibility. If Marcon or Frezin or one of the big guys has something in the pipeline, it'd be lax of us not to exploit that technology. But every company we ask for help would have to sign a nondisclosure agreement. We don't need this getting out to the general public."

"I don't know how much longer we can keep it under wraps, Jim. This Boston incident isn't going away anytime soon." Rothery's voice had an edge to it, that of a man ready to explode.

No one spoke for a minute, each one alone in the silence with his own thoughts. The attack on America with a deadly virus was now a definite reality, one that the media would be all over. And they would be relentless. They would find the connections between Austin, San Diego, Miami, and Boston, and once they did, CNN and the rest of the networks would have their top story for some time to come. And each man in the room realized that stopping the virus from reaching an epidemic had to come from within that room. The power of the country's four largest law-enforcement and espionage communities sat waiting for their directions. And if those directions were wrong, the results could be catastrophic. But if they were right . . .

Rothery broke the silence. "Jim, get your agents to Boston and contain that situation. Craig, shut down the labs. Tony, ensure all our government scientists are working on this, and bring in the pharmaceutical companies that have the resources and are willing to work under a gag order."

He took one more look at each of the men. "This is it, gentlemen. We are on the edge of losing control of this thing. We need results. And we need them now."

36

The listing agent on Albert Rousseau's condo arrived at the property at precisely six minutes after ten o'clock. Her being late irritated Gordon, but when she slid out of her Mercedes, Gordon mellowed a bit. She was attractive and smartly dressed in a dark pantsuit, black heels, and a white blouse cut close to the neck. Her dark hair was cut just off her shoulders and suited her tanned face. She wore an apologetic smile as she greeted him.

"I'm Arlene," she said, offering out her hand. Her grip was firm, and she locked eyes with him as they shook. "Sorry I'm late. I got held up at another property."

Gordon shook her hand. "Not a problem. Can we see the property?" he asked, nodding toward the burned-out shell.

She glanced over at the wreckage. "Sure. We don't even need to open the lockbox on this one. Being there's no front door." Gordon chuckled at the remark, and she continued. "I just got this listing from the insurance company a week ago," she said. "I don't know much about it, other than there was some sort of explosion and they wanted it priced at $145,900. Lowest-priced property in the area, for obvious reasons."

"What kind of structural damage was done in the explosion?" he asked.

She flipped through the file, stopping at a sheet covered with figures. "There is an engineering report here," she said. "I'm not an expert on these things, but from what I can see, the major damage is to the rear of the building and the second-level floor, or first-level ceiling, depending on how you want to look at it. The front of the condo didn't fare too well either, as you can see. The floor joists are badly damaged and need to be repaired. And the city has placed a caveat on the title that whoever buys the place has to have an engineer stamp the renovations before new flooring or drywall can be installed. They want to know the structural repairs have been done properly before they'll let you cover anything up."

"Okay," Gordon said. "Can we look through what's left of the place?"

She looked down at her high heels, then at the wreckage. "I wasn't thinking," she said. "I should have worn different clothes. I'm not sure I can walk around in there with you. Would you mind if I waited out here? I can answer any questions you have after you've finished looking about."

"Probably a good idea," Gordon said. In fact, as he strode up the front walk, it struck him that this was a very good thing. With no realtor at his side, he would be able to look about freely. And that was why he was here.

He entered what had been Albert Rousseau's home through the front entrance, now just a hole in the brick exterior. Immediately upon entering the house, Gordon was struck by the extent of the damage. The explosion had blown outward from the stove, and pieces of metal and glass were embedded in what was left of the walls. The foyer was defined only by the difference in floor coverings, with ceramic tile in the entranceway and hardwood in the living room. He carefully picked his way through the remains of the living room and into the kitchen. The cabinets were almost entirely gone: Just a maple pantry in one corner remained. The sink was hanging by the drainpipe and the water lines jutted out from the walls at crazy angles.

The ends of the brass lines were shredded and water damage was everywhere. Gordon knew that some of the damage came from water pouring out of the broken lines and the remainder from the firemen pouring water onto the ensuing fire. The floor felt soggy, and he was careful where he stepped.

He spent a few minutes in the kitchen, thinking about how the scene could have played out. The damage was so extensive that there must have been quite a buildup of gas prior to the explosion. Was Albert Rousseau already dead when the stove exploded? Quite likely. Dead or unconscious. At any rate, if he was anywhere near the stove, there was probably little left of the man's body after the gas ignited. He continued through the house, checking out the second floor for any sign of a wall safe. But there was no place in the unit where the wall thickness was sufficient to accommodate a safe of any size. Gordon returned to the main floor, then continued on into the basement.

It was dark and, with the electricity off, impossible to see anything. He gave himself a small pat on the back for thinking ahead and bringing a pocket flashlight. He pulled it out and flipped the switch. A narrow beam of light illuminated the concrete foundation. The basement was unfinished, but what was once an open storage space was now a garbage heap of broken wood and soggy drywall. It felt dank and smelled of rotting wood and mold.

Gordon picked his way through the mess toward the corner where the electrical service entered. Under the electrical panel were the rusting remains of a washer and dryer. Near the appliances the floor was not so deep in crud, and he kicked away some of the garbage until he could see the concrete. The hot-water tank was a few feet from the washer and dryer, almost in the corner. Gordon gave it a quick glance. The gas line was still attached, but the gas would have long since been shut off. The water lines were intact as well, and there was a floor drain a couple of feet from the base of the tank. He looked back to the washer and dryer. The basement floor appeared to slope ever so slightly away from the hot-water tank toward the washer.

That didn't make sense. The floor drain should be at the lowest point in the concrete floor, so that any overflow water would drain out to the city services. And the floor was dry, which meant that the water had drained somewhere. Gordon looked back at the floor drain next to the hot-water tank. It was definitely higher than the floor level in front of the washer and dryer. He kicked away the sludge and garbage from in front of the washing machine. About five feet from the front of the machine, and at a low point in the concrete, was a second floor drain. Something wasn't right.

Gordon pulled the metal lid off the drain and peered in with the flashlight. Water, about six inches below the concrete. That was about right. He moved back to the first drain he had spotted, next to the hot-water tank, and pulled the cover off. He shone the light in. Nothing. Just what appeared to be a small piece of tight-fitting wood about three inches down. He pushed on the wood, but it didn't move. Holding the flashlight in his teeth, he shone the beam directly into the hole and worked the wood with his fingers. It moved. He kept pushing on it until one edge lifted slightly. He got his finger under the uplifted edge and pulled. The piece of wood popped out. Underneath, now exposed to the light, was the top of a floor safe.

"I'll be damned," Gordon said under his breath. He tried the handle, but the safe was locked. He spun the dial and it rotated easily to his touch. It was still working. All he needed was the combination. He read the manufacturer's name and model number off the safe and committed it to memory, then replaced the wood and the grate. He returned to the main floor and back into the sunshine. The realtor was waiting for him.

"Well?" she asked as he walked across the street to where she was leaning against her Mercedes.

"There's a lot of structural damage," Gordon said. "It would take at least two hundred thousand to get that place livable." He pointed to the units on either side. "What do they sell for when they're in normal condition?"

"About three hundred thousand, give or take. It depends

185

whether they've had any renovations. The top price anything on this block has sold for is three-thirty, and it was totally redone."

Gordon nodded. "Even if I could get this at one-thirty, by the time I put two hundred into it, I'd just get my money back. No upside for the renovation."

"Not if it cost you two hundred to fix it," she said. "That might be a bit high."

"I'd rather be high than low," Gordon said. "Sorry, but I don't think it works for me."

"That's okay," she said, smiling. "Thanks for not making me trudge through that place with you."

Gordon returned to his rental car and waved as she pulled away. He sat in the car for a few minutes, thinking about how to approach this situation. He needed to get back into the condo, but this time with either the combination to the safe or something that would open it. And since Albert Rousseau was long since gone, that eliminated the possibility of using a combination to open the safe. So it would have to be force. Now all he needed to know was how.

One thing was for certain. He was going to get into that safe.

37

They met two hours before dawn on Saturday, September 10, in Slivenec, a suburb to the south and west of Prague. Anders Ljent, the lead CIA operative for the Prague region, flashed the light twice and the van pulled into the small, well-concealed courtyard behind the two-story brick house. Six men emptied from the van and moved quickly to the stairs leading to the basement. Anders joined them in the underground room after closing and locking the outer gate.

"Anders Ljent," he said, shaking hands with the man who appeared to be in charge. "CIA station chief for Prague."

"Lieutenant Chris Phelps," the man responded. He made a slight motion with his head to the five serious-looking men immediately behind him. "My guys. Navy SEALs, Team Six."

Ljent gave them a perfunctory nod and then spread a map of Prague and surrounding area on the table. "We're here," he said, pointing to the bottom left corner, "and our target is here." He moved his finger to the center of the map, just east of the Vltava River. "The lab is on the second floor of a three-story brick house, facing south on Ostrovni Purkynova. It's the third house

187

from the corner, so you have neighbors on both sides to contend with."

"What sort of opposition should we expect?" Phelps asked. He was young, as were all the SEALs, mid- to late twenties. All had short-cropped hair, intense eyes, and grim looks etched on their faces. They were dressed in street clothes, but all wore Kevlar vests beneath their shirts.

"We've been watching this lab for about four months now. We're positive it's al-Qaeda, as we've identified at least three men of Arab descent on the wanted list, entering and exiting. At this time of the morning, you can expect four to six armed defenders and at least one lab worker. The shift change seems to be about nine o'clock, about two hours after sunrise. We should be gone before that happens, or this will spill out into the street."

"We'll be long gone," Phelps assured him. "How do we get in?"

"Front door is best," Ljent said. "There is a rear entrance, but when they open the door we can see the locks, and if they've got them all in place, that door is almost impenetrable. They've left the front door pretty much the same as all the rest on the street, probably to keep appearances normal. You've got a couple of locks, including a good deadbolt, but nothing that should keep you out for too long."

"What about the lab?"

"As I said, on the second floor. They've got a series of filters of some sort, and the exhaust vents to the rear. We saw them bring in a filter system recently, and it looked like a HEPA filtration unit. So whatever they're cooking in that lab, it's not nice. I'd try to avoid gunfire inside the lab itself, Lieutenant. For your own safety."

"We'll keep that in mind," Phelps said. "Anything else?"

"I don't think so."

"Are you driving us?"

"Yes."

"Okay, here's how it goes down. You stop on the street immediately in front of the building and give us fifteen to thirty seconds to assess entry. When we exit the vehicle, pull around the corner and wait in a position so you can be back to pick us up within fifteen seconds of receiving our signal." He handed Ljent a two-way radio. "The message is simple: Come and get us."

Ljent adjusted the squelch and tested the equipment. It worked fine. "I'll be ready."

They left the CIA safe house at 5:35 A.M. and made good time into the city on the Strakonicka Expressway. As he turned onto Legii Bridge, Ljent opened the window to the rear of the van and said, "At the end of the bridge, I'll make a right, then a left. Your target will be the third house from the corner on the left side of the vehicle." He reached the end of the bridge and made the first turn. This was the oldest part of Prague and the streets were narrow and bumpy, bordered on both sides by three- and four-story stone and brick buildings. Cars lined both sides of the street; passage was easy for one vehicle, tight for two. Ljent made the second turn and slowed. He stopped in front of the third house. "Red door," he said quietly.

Five seconds passed, then ten, then the locks on the front door literally disappeared in a shower of splinters. Two seconds later, Ljent saw the men streak from the rear of the van into the building, their silenced rifles held in front of them and still smoking. In less than fifteen seconds from the first bullet hitting the wood abutting the locks, the team was inside and the outer door closed. Other than the damage to the door, the street appeared normal for six in the morning. Ljent pulled ahead, circled the block, and got into position to pick them up.

Lieutenant Phelps motioned in three different directions as they entered the house, and his team quickly split into three groups of two. He moved directly ahead to the staircase, taking the risers three at a time. A second team followed him, destined for the third floor, and two SEALs remained on the first floor, moving room to room, looking for anything living. Phelps hugged the wall on the second floor as his third team brushed by and continued up the stairs. Then he pointed to his companion to take the front of the house; he would take the rear. They split and moved into the rooms off the main hallway.

As Phelps moved into the first room on the right, two men in jeans and T-shirts opened fire with automatic weapons. Bullets chewed into the door frame, and the noise was deafening. Whatever stealth they had hoped to achieve was now gone, and the clock was ticking on a short fuse until the police arrived and cut off their escape route. Phelps leaped back from the door, dropped to the ground, thrust the barrel of his weapon around the doorjamb, and pulled the trigger, spraying the room with automatic fire. He heard grunts and the familiar sound of air escaping from punctured lungs. He rolled across the opening to the room, his eyes seeing one man down, the other still standing. He fired as he rolled and saw the second man take three direct hits in the chest. Blood gushed from the wounds. No Kevlar.

He jumped to his feet and entered the room. It was some sort of a coffee room with a card table and a microwave oven. A couple of couches faced a television, which was switched off. Other than the two bodies, there was no one in the room. Phelps ran the length of the hall to the rear of the house and kicked in the door.

Two slugs hit him in the center of his chest as he flew into the room. The impact knocked him back a few feet and winded him, but he didn't lose his footing. The assailant was directly in front of him, a pistol leveled at his chest. He instinctively fired, the slugs from his M16A2 slamming into the man and knocking him back into a bench covered with lab equipment. He crashed over it, his finger tightening on the trigger as he died. One errant shot smashed into the wall just to the right of Phelps's head, missing by less than an inch. Phelps sucked in the deepest breath he could and called his team.

"All clear, second rear," he said into his microphone.

"All clear, main front."

"All clear, rear third."

"One bad guy, main rear."

Phelps could hear the gunfire from the main floor. He had

two men on that floor, and that was enough. He needed his science expert and he needed him fast.

"Joey," he said. "Where are you?"

"Third, on my way down, LT," came the response. A few seconds later, Joe Jameus burst into the room. "I'm on it, LT," he said, swinging his rifle onto his back and assessing the mass of lab equipment in front of him. A small fridge sat off to one side, and he made a beeline for it. Inside against one side were a number of vials, all filled with a white powder. A glass canister containing what appeared to be large beans sat against the other side. Jameus snatched one of the vials, popped open the container with the beans, shook a few into a plastic bag, and resealed the container. He glanced at the system of beakers and test tubes, the centrifuge, and nodded.

"We're done, LT."

"Then let's get the hell out of here," Phelps said, calling to his men on the microphone. Extraction time. He called Anders Ljent. "Fifteen seconds," he said, moving full speed for the front door. Above and below him, his men were on the move. The gunfire on the main level had stopped, and as Phelps came down the main staircase he saw both his men waiting. They had been successful in taking out the last defender. Behind him, two more SEALs came flying down the stairs. They met at the front door just as Ljent pulled up. They piled into the rear of the van, the sounds of police sirens now very audible and very close. They pulled onto Narodni, the main access to the bridge, just as the first police car entered Ostrovni Purkynova from the far end. The sounds of the sirens diminished as they put distance between themselves and the target.

"Good job, gentlemen," he said. "What was our opposition?"

"Two on the main floor, LT."

"Three on the third."

"And three on the second," Phelps said. "Eight bad guys, nobody injured. Excellent job."

One of his men pointed at Phelps's chest. "Good thing you had your vest on, LT."

"Yeah," he said. "Forgot to shoot him before he shot me."

There were a few chuckles, and Phelps turned to Joey Jameus. "What have we got, Joey?"

Jameus held up the beans he had taken from the fridge. "Castor beans." Then he pulled the vial of powder from his front pocket. "And unless I'm totally out to lunch, we have ricin."

"Ricin," Phelps said. "That shit's pretty deadly, isn't it?"

"Absolutely. Ricin inhibits protein synthesis in the body. If you inhale this stuff, you can suffer pulmonary edema and asphyxiation. Inject it and you get kidney and liver necrosis. Either can result in death."

"So we just shut down a seriously dangerous lab," Phelps said.

"Sure did, LT," Joey said, tucking the ricin back into his pocket.

"Excellent," Phelps said. "Let's just hope it was what they were looking for."

38

"I think I might have found a way to get into that floor safe in the basement at Albert Rousseau's town house," Gordon said, accepting the beers from the bartender and setting one in front of Jennifer Pearce.

"How? You said it's embedded in the cement and you don't have the combination," she said, pouring the beer into a glass and taking a sip. They were in Richmond's hottest sports bar, Out of Bounds. The old Chicago brick building, with its huge green-and-white-striped awning, eighteen televisions, and live bands, was infamous for drawing big crowds when big games were on. It was Saturday night but still early evening, and the bar was only about half full. The band had yet to set up.

"I went to see a locksmith today. Told him I had a STAR C-7 floor safe and I'd forgotten the combination and asked him if there was any way to open the safe, even if it meant destroying it."

"What did he say?" she asked.

"Liquid nitrogen will freeze the metal bolts that slide into place when the safe is closed. Once they're frozen, the metal fatigues, and with a few applications I should be able to snap the bolts like uncooked spaghetti."

"Sounds easy. Why don't crooks use it all the time?"

"Because most safes are wall mounted. When they try to apply the liquid nitrogen to the bolts on the safe, it just drips down the front. It's useless. But this one is a floor safe, so I can pour the nitrogen in the cracks and wait for it to freeze the metal."

"You going to give it a try?" she asked, finishing her beer and waving at the bartender for two more.

Gordon shifted on the red vinyl barstool. "I think so. I'll wait until tomorrow when I can use a flashlight and I can't be seen from the street. At night, the light might be visible."

"Well, you've already been through the place once with the realtor, so if anyone asks what you're doing, you can always tell them you're taking a second look."

He nodded. "It's not all that risky. Just the problem of getting into the safe."

A platter of chicken wings arrived and they dug in, Gordon going for the hot and Jennifer for the teriyaki. They finished the wings in a few minutes, had one more beer, then left the bar. Gordon waved down a taxi and they climbed into the backseat. They'd left her car and his rental on the street outside Jennifer's house.

"You sure you want to stay at the hotel?" she asked. "I've got a guest room."

He shook his head. "Maybe sometime, but not right now. I'm not trying to be rude, but I've got my reasons."

"What reasons?" she asked playfully.

"Not telling," he said. "Not yet, anyway."

"Okay, maybe later."

"Yeah, maybe later."

"I'll hold you to that," she said as the taxi pulled up in front of the Jefferson Hotel. A series of arched porticos cut from limestone and trimmed with brick highlighted the front of the century-old hotel. The grand staircase, constructed from Italian marble, was visible through the main doors. He gave her hand a squeeze and slipped out of the cab.

"Good night," he said.

"See you tomorrow."

Gordon watched the cab disappear into the traffic on Franklin, then headed into the hotel. In fact, there were two reasons he didn't want to stay at Jennifer Pearce's house. First, he was beginning to fall for her. And the last place he wanted to end up was in bed with her if the timing wasn't right. She was a beautiful woman, both physically and emotionally. And while she could be soft and tender at times, there was another side to the woman that he found equally impressive. She was highly intelligent and exceptionally focused. She had felt something was wrong when Kenga had died in St. Lucia and she had followed up on her suspicions. Flying across the country and approaching him at his mill must have taken incredible nerve. She was a strong woman with a clear sense of what she considered to be right and wrong, and she was a woman who acted on her convictions.

And she made him feel whole again. He didn't know how, but just being near her somehow eased the pain of the loss he had suffered. He had accepted the fact that Billy was dead, but the sadness that enveloped him was foreign. He'd never been a melancholy person, and the depression he felt in the weeks after his brother's death was new and unwelcome. But now it was lifting. And he saw Jennifer Pearce as the reason. She excited and intrigued him, and he wanted to know her better. But not until the time was right. It had to be when they were both ready.

There was another reason he had refused her offer. At nine o'clock, he was meeting the locksmith he'd visited that afternoon. The man had listened to Gordon's story, then agreed to supply the liquid nitrogen for five hundred dollars. Gordon checked his watch: eight forty-five. He walked through the Rotunda and up the elegant staircase, located an open chair in the Palm Court, and waited under the domed skylight. The stained glass, some of it original Tiffany, reflected the last rays of the day, then darkened as the sun set and the soft moon slowly rose, low on the horizon. At precisely nine o'clock, the locksmith, Brent Waldman, entered the bar, spied him, and headed over to his table.

He set a cylindrical black container about sixteen inches high on the table and reclined in the chair opposite Gordon. "I checked out your story," he said, ordering a beer when the waitress came by. "There was an explosion in a town house on Cooley Avenue back at the end of April, and the listing realtor recently showed the house to an out-of-town buyer matching your description."

"You did your homework," Gordon said, paying for the locksmith's beer when it arrived.

"In our business, we learn how to open doors and safes. We don't often impart that knowledge to thieves, Mr. Buchanan."

"So you're pretty sure I'm not a thief?"

"I didn't say that. You're taking liquid nitrogen to a deserted house and pouring it on a floor safe so you can open it and take things out that don't belong to you. That qualifies you as a thief. But I believe you're telling the truth about why you want whatever is in that safe. You see, I also checked with Arnie Boyle, the sheriff back home in Butte, to see if Billy Buchanan really did die a few months ago." He took a sip off his beer. "Sorry about your brother, Mr. Buchanan."

"Thanks," Gordon said. He looked at the container on the table. "That the stuff?"

"Yup. And a pair of heavy-duty rubber gloves as well. Don't touch the nitrogen without putting the gloves on first. It'll freeze your skin in seconds."

"Strong stuff."

"You wouldn't believe it. But it'll take a few applications to freeze the bolts to the point where you can snap them. Pour a bit on and give it a few minutes, then give it another shot. Just keep trying the handle on the lid and it'll eventually lift off. Careful when you put your hand in the safe, as the nitrogen may have leaked in and run down the inside of the metal. Keep the gloves on until you're sure there's no chance of touching any of the nitrogen."

"How do I dispose of the leftover?"

"I've only given you enough to eliminate the locking mechanism on the safe. Use it all. Leave the container in the safe when you're finished and cover it up. Chances are no one will ever notice it's there." Waldman finished his beer and stood up.

Gordon slipped his hand in his pocket and held out the five hundred dollars. "Payment for the nitrogen."

Waldman shook his head. "No, thanks. I told you, I don't like to help thieves. I just think what you're doing is probably the right thing. I don't want the money. Good luck." They shook hands, and the man left without looking back.

Gordon finished his beer and left the hotel with the black package. One of the doormen hailed a cab and he gave the driver a house number a couple down from Rousseau's on Cooley Avenue. It was dark now, the moon just a sliver over the James River. Gordon watched the city slip by, thinking about the quick history lesson his previous cabdriver, Bud, had given him. More Americans had died in and around Richmond during the Civil War than in all of the Vietnam War. Maybe more than World War II, he didn't know. But the grassy slopes leading to the James River were once slick with Union and Confederate blood. Soldiers getting up in the morning, knowing that they were being sent to their death that afternoon. God, what a way to die. March at the battlements and take a musket ball or a hot shard of shrapnel from an exploding cannonball. They entered Carytown and turned onto Cooley Avenue. Gordon paid the driver and watched him drive off.

The street was dark, save for the light from a couple of streetlamps. He walked to Rousseau's condo, stopped on the sidewalk for a minute, then moved quickly into the ruins. He waited until he was in the basement before turning on his flashlight, and even then shielded the beam with his free hand. He carefully picked his way across the piles of rubble and found the floor drain exactly as he had left it. The tight-fitting piece of wood came out a little easier this time, revealing the top of the safe. He slipped on the rubber gloves and opened the vial enclosed in the black case, then focused the flashlight into the hole and carefully poured the liquid nitrogen into the cracks between the lid and the body of the safe. He moved the vial around the lid as he poured, trying to get the liquid spread evenly around the entire diameter. He waited a few minutes, then repeated the procedure. Another few minutes and another application. There was a tiny bit of nitrogen left after he had made the third complete revolution, and he kept going until the last drops were out of the vial and on the safe. He screwed the lid on the vial and returned it to the black case. Tiny wisps of smoke exited the crack, and he sat back to wait.

He kept trying the handle, and after about fifteen minutes it moved a bit. He slipped on the rubber gloves, got a good grip on the handle, and gave it a steady pull. It resisted for a few seconds, then the bolts snapped and the lid came away in his hands. He set it aside and shone the flashlight in the hole. There was a solitary object in the safe, and he reached in and gently lifted it out. It was plastic, about three inches long by an inch wide, and shaped a bit like a cigar. On one side, the packaging read *Sony*, and on the other, *Micro Vault*. There was a split in the plastic at the midway point, and he gently pulled the two halves apart. When it came apart, one end was a protective plastic shield, covering some purple plastic and a metal end. He looked at the metal. It was a USB connector for a computer port. The object was a portable hard drive.

He slipped it into his pocket and replaced the lid on the safe after dumping the black case and the rubber gloves in the hole. He jammed the piece of wood in place and slid the drain cover into its slot. Then he picked his way back across the piles of junk and up the stairs. The street was totally deserted, the hour late. He walked a block or two until he hit Cary Street, where he found a cab waiting outside one of the bars. He got in the backseat and asked the driver to head for the Jefferson Hotel.

He retrieved the hard drive from his pocket and stared at it.

LETHAL DOSE

What was on the silicon chip inside this piece of plastic? Was it worth Albert Rousseau's life? Was it the evidence he needed to bring Veritas to justice? Right now, he had no answers.

Tomorrow. Tomorrow he would know.

39

The last of the reports were filtering into the Department of Homeland Security on Sunday morning when J. D. Rothery closed his door and addressed the representatives of the other federal agencies. He consulted the latest figures, updated at 0600, twenty minutes earlier.

"Good news and bad news, gentlemen," he said, setting the paper on his desk. "We have field reports back on twenty-five of the twenty-seven raids, and so far we're batting a thousand. Our teams have penetrated each lab and effectively shut them down. Casualties are minimal so far: three dead and seven wounded. The three dead are all British SAS forces. They were assigned the lab in Beirut and had completed their mission when the vehicle transporting them back to the beach was hit by an RPG." All men in the room knew what damage a rocket-propelled grenade could do to an unarmored car or SUV. "We're still waiting on reports from our teams in Tehran and Cairo."

"That sounds like the good news, J. D.," Tony Warner said. "What's the bad news?"

Rothery consulted the sheaf of papers on his desk. "We've

got sarin, ricin, cholera, Q fever, and anthrax. But so far we do not have a lab that was producing our virus."

"Jesus Christ," Craig Simms said. "I can't begin to tell you how this has hurt our operations, J. D. It's going to take the CIA years to regain these intelligence-gathering points." His face was deep crimson.

"We knew going in that the operation might not produce the results we wanted. This is not a total surprise. And keep in mind we just shut down two dozen labs that were producing chemical weapons. This is not a bad thing."

Simms was not easily placated. "The CIA operates under a microscope. Getting these covert teams and agents into place took years. And now the entire operation is shut down. In one day. And without the results we were looking for. If you ask me, this exercise was a total disaster."

Jim Allenby came to Rothery's defense. "The labs were on line and producing chemicals outlawed under international law. And these guys were ready to use them when the time came. Now the local authorities have the locations of all the labs and they'll shut them down for us. Plus we removed a lot of al-Qaeda operatives in one swoop. Even though we didn't find the source of the virus, this was not a waste of time, Craig."

"How many al-Qaeda guys did we kill?" Warner asked.

Rothery glanced at one of the columns on the top page. "Eighty-seven."

"Jim's right, Craig. That's a lot of bad guys out of the way. I don't see this as a total snafu."

"You didn't spend years putting the network in place," Simms shot back.

There was a knock on the door, and Rothery's personal assistant entered with two sheets of paper. She walked across the room, handed them to her boss, and left without a word. Rothery perused the printouts, his face darkening as he read the reports.

"The Israelis sent a Mossad team into Cairo. They gained entry and overpowered the enemy operatives inside the building, but they couldn't get out. Last report they radioed out was they were holding off up to one hundred bad guys. Satellite intel shows the building being overrun one hour and eight minutes ago. We've got to assume the entire team is dead."

"Shit," Allenby said. "This is not good."

"There's more," Rothery said grimly. "One of our teams, Delta Force, was dropped into Tehran. They shut down the lab, wired it with explosives, and blew it. But three of the six team members were killed on extraction. They managed to get their bodies on the chopper, so there's no direct proof we were responsible."

Silence engulfed the room. The Mossad team in Cairo would have been at least five men. That plus the three British commandos and now the three Delta Force casualties put the total number of dead at eleven. Plus the Egyptians would have no trouble identifying the Mossad team, and that meant they were about to be embroiled in an international incident. The Egyptians were not going to take kindly to Israeli commandos attacking targets in their capital city. What had appeared initially to be a reasonable success now had all the markings of disaster.

"Did either of the teams report back on what the labs were producing?" Tony Warner asked.

Rothery nodded his head slightly. "Shigella and tularemia. No virus."

"What a mess," Craig Simms said.

No one disagreed.

40

The valet handed Jennifer Pearce a tag and hustled her car out of the parking lane. She pocketed the number and cruised through the front door of the Jefferson Hotel. She skipped up the thirty-six steps of the grand staircase and spied Gordon Buchanan at one of the tables in Palm Court. He rose to greet her as she arrived.

"How was your night?" she asked. "I can't imagine anyone having a good sleep in a dump like this."

He grinned. "It's okay, but it's not your place. Nice scenery, but not very intimate." They sat, and she unhooked her laptop carrying case from her shoulder and let it drop on the seat bench beside her.

"Well, I'll take that as a compliment," she said, ordering a tea when the waitress came around. "So what's so important that I barely had time for a shower this morning?"

He looked sheepish. "I wasn't exactly truthful with you last night," he said. "I got some liquid nitrogen from that locksmith I called yesterday and went back to Rousseau's town house last night."

"You cracked the safe?" she asked, wide-eyed.

"Yeah. It wasn't that hard, actually. It just took a few hours. Patience was the key. Anyway, this is what I found in the safe." He retrieved the Sony Micro Vault from his pocket and handed it to her.

"We use these all the time to transfer data between BioTech Five and White Oak. It's like a portable hard drive." She pulled the two ends apart and checked the USB connection. "Do you know what's on it?"

"No. That's why I asked you to bring your laptop," he said, motioning to the case beside her. "I thought we could have a look together. If it's technical, I wouldn't know what I was looking at anyway."

"Sure," she said, unzipping the case and setting the laptop on the table. She powered it up and slipped the tiny solid-state storage unit into one of the USB ports. Windows recognized the new hardware and a screen popped up on her monitor, showing all the files Albert Rousseau had burned on the disc. There were seven in total, and Jennifer began opening them, looking carefully at the contents of each before going on to the next. She sipped her tea, at one point asking for a refill of hot water, and had just about finished the second cup when she closed the last file and sat back in her seat.

"Well, you've got the proof you need to go after Veritas," she said, allowing a small smile to creep over her face. "It's all there, Gordon."

"What? What does it say?"

"I'm not going to get technical, but the gist of what's on the disc is that Triaxcion does not react well with people who have A-positive blood. It inhibits the coagulants in the blood. You have the evidence you need. Any researcher with a master's or Ph.D. in pharmacology will be able to decipher what's on there in a court of law."

"Definitive proof," he said, his face a mixture of emotions. "So now I know for sure that the bastards killed Billy." He paused for a minute and contemplated his empty coffee cup. "I'm not sure how that makes me feel. On one side, I'm glad that I know for sure and I'm pleased to have something to take into a court of law. But on the other hand, I feel sick that this whole damn thing was preventable. There was no reason for Billy to die. If he hadn't been taking that medication, he would still be alive."

"So would Albert Rousseau and Kenga Bakcsi. These guys are murderers, Gordon, and you've got the proof. Just not enough to convict anyone in a court of law."

Gordon tensed slightly and threw her a worried look. "Put that way, I don't think I'll be sleeping too well for the next little while."

She thought about what he had said, then nodded. "I see what you mean. Being the only person with the information that could sink them could prove to be quite dangerous."

"Like you said, they're murderers. I'd feel better if I knew exactly who it was. Right now we're guessing it's the top brass at Veritas."

"I think it's a pretty good guess," Jennifer said. They were quiet for a minute, and watched as the waitress refilled Gordon's coffee and brought Jennifer fresh hot water for her tea. Finally, Jennifer said, "What are you going to do now?"

He shrugged. "Get this back to my lawyer in Butte. She'll know what to do with it."

"I could make a copy if you want. That way if that disc gets corrupted or destroyed, you haven't lost the data."

He was hesitant. "You mean on your computer?" he asked, and she nodded. "I don't know, Jennifer. If they found those files on your computer, they wouldn't think twice about killing you."

"How could they possibly find out the files are stored on my laptop? No one ever audits what is on my computer. And I could encode them so only the guys at Crypto-City could open the files."

"Crypto-City?"

"National Security Agency. NSA. That's what everyone calls their main complex at Fort Meade, midway between Baltimore and Washington. They specialize in cryptology. Don't worry about it. Bad choice of words. Anyway, I'll protect myself."

He still wasn't convinced. "Is there any other way to save the files?" he asked.

"Lots. We could buy a disk or another one of these things and copy the files over to it. That would give you a backup without having the data on my computer."

"I'd feel better if we did that, Jennifer. I don't want anything on your system that could link you to Triaxcion. Enough people have already died. I don't know what I'd do if something happened to you."

"I'll take that as a clue that you care about my well-being. Thank you." She was wearing an ear-to-ear grin. "But look around, Mr. Buchanan. Do you see any sinister types lurking about?"

Gordon scanned the room. A handful of tables were taken, most by businessmen having a late breakfast by themselves. Most were middle-aged white men dressed in business casual. One fellow, younger than most, wore golf clothes and was reading the sports section of the morning newspaper. Two tables were taken by couples, one elderly, the other young and with eyes for nothing but each other.

"It's the newlyweds," she said to Gordon as he finished looking about the room. "They're evil spies and they're going to report our meeting back to their leader."

He chuckled at the absurdity. "Okay, I'm just being a little paranoid. But I would be extremely upset if anything happened to you."

"I feel the same way about you," she responded, packing her laptop back in its protective case. "I suppose you'll be heading back to Montana soon."

"I'll see what flights United has available—I'd like to get this to my lawyer as quickly as possible."

"I understand."

They sat in an unusual awkward silence for a minute. Gordon asked their server for the bill, and when she returned he charged it to his room. He finished the last of his coffee, ignoring how cold it was, and pushed back his chair. She followed suit. They walked out together, their elbows touching despite the wide staircase.

One of the other morning diners placed his newspaper on the table next to his bacon and eggs and retrieved his cell phone from his pocket. He placed a call to another cell.

"They're leaving the hotel," he said, and hung up. He immediately dialed another number.

"Hello." The call connected to Bruce Andrews's private line.

"I'm just having breakfast at the Jefferson Hotel," the caller said. "And I think you'll be very interested in who I just saw."

"I'm sure I will be," Andrews said.

"Let me back up a bit. I had my people enter a search to watch for Gordon Buchanan's name to show up on an airline manifest. I coded it as a low priority so it wouldn't draw any attention. Yesterday, we were advised that Buchanan had flown to Richmond on Thursday, September eighth. I checked with the local hotels and found him registered at the Jefferson. And this morning, I was in the Palm Court when he met someone for breakfast."

"Who was it?" Andrews asked. He knew this man did not play games. This name was going to mean something to him.

"One of your research scientists. Jennifer Pearce."

There was a brief moment of dead air. Andrews said, "Are you sure it was Pearce?"

"Absolutely. I remember her face from the ad you ran in the newspaper when you hired her. That was only a few months ago. I'm positive it was Jennifer Pearce."

It had always been Andrews's policy to run a large ad in the local newspapers when he brought a new, high-profile researcher on board. It showed Wall Street, the competition, and the general public that Veritas was cutting edge. "What did they talk about?"

"No idea, but she had her laptop and they plugged in some sort of portable disk. She spent a few minutes looking at the contents, they had breakfast, and they left. I've got a tail on them."

"Excellent work," Andrews said. "Buchanan is becoming a major nuisance. He must be looking for evidence that Triaxcion was responsible for his brother's death. And who knows what he's got on that disk. We've got to do something about him."

"I think you should leave Buchanan alone. He has a direct tie to your company. I'd be looking at your researcher."

"Christ, how many employees can die before someone gets suspicious? I don't know. Touching her is risky."

"She has direct access to your database. Buchanan doesn't. No matter what we do to Buchanan, she'll still have access to whatever information she gave to him this morning."

"Okay, I'll think about it."

"We can take care of it," the voice said. He almost sounded anxious. Eager.

"No," Andrews said. "If I decide to go that way, I'll do it. I can actually kill two birds with one stone."

"Have it your way."

"Let me know what else they do today," Andrews said.

"I'll call you later."

Bruce Andrews replaced the phone in its cradle and stared at the green Virginia hills rolling off to the west. Clouds were brewing, dark clouds with the threat of rain. Through thermal convection they mutated from soft, white cumulus clouds into black waves that spilled across the sky threatening to dump cold rain and hail on the verdant countryside. Condensation happening on a massive scale, the moisture inside the clouds rising, then falling until hailstones larger than golf balls finally escaped from the blackness and pounded the crops and acreages that dotted the foothills. Unless the clouds were seeded. Then the hailstones failed to materialize and the precipitation fell as rain or sleet. No damage. Take care of the problem before it pounds you into the ground. That was the answer.

Jennifer Pearce had to die. She had crossed the line between asset and liability. But this time her death had to look like an accident. And no exploding stoves. Evan Ziegler was going to have to sell this one to the authorities. Another suspicious death could prove as fatal as leaving Jennifer Pearce alone with her fingers in the company mainframe. And this may be the opportunity he had been looking for with Evan as well. The man's future with the company was in jeopardy. In fact, the man's life was in jeopardy.

He checked the time and calculated the difference to mountain daylight time. It wasn't too early to call. He picked up the phone and dialed Evan Ziegler's number.

Unfortunately for Jennifer Pearce, she had made a fatal error.

41

"The test case was using a carrier," Jennifer explained to her staff, using the whiteboard in the meeting room. "She had the apolipoprotein E gene on her nineteenth chromosome. Her chances of contracting Alzheimer's were several times greater than a person without the genetic mutation. And in addition, she had presenilins present in her system, which trigger the gamma secretase enzyme. And that enzyme is responsible for splicing the amyloid precursor protein."

"But that still doesn't explain the massive destruction of neurons," one of her junior staff said.

"You're jumping ahead, Robert. It's the plaques and tangles that occur because of the amyloid precursor protein that cause the neurons to be destroyed." She stopped as the door opened and Bruce Andrews entered. He stood by the door and motioned for her to continue. "So our thrust is to block enzyme activity, not produce another acetylcholinesterase inhibitor." She set the marker down on the thin ledge at the bottom of the whiteboard and moved toward the back of the room. "Jeanette, please continue. I'll be back in a few minutes."

She reached the door and left the room, Andrews in tow. "What can I do for you, Bruce?" she asked.

He pointed back to the meeting room. "You should have finished. I like listening to brainstorming sessions. Takes me back to the days when I was a researcher, not a manager."

"Oh, managing seems to suit you just fine." She leaned against the wall to steady herself. "Seriously, what can I do for you? We're really busy chasing a new avenue. We've had some good success with one of our new molecules bonding, and I want to get this new idea over to White Oak so we can test it."

"I thought we might have lunch," Andrews said. "It's been a while since we talked."

Jennifer swallowed. "I'll check my Day-Timer. I may have an opening next week."

"I was thinking today," Andrews said. "No time like the present."

Jennifer read the tone of voice: casual but firm. This was not going away. "All right. Today is fine. I'll clear my calendar and meet you."

"Fine. I'll make reservations at the Lemaire. You know it?"

"I've seen the name somewhere, but I'm not sure where," she said.

"It's the formal dining room at the Jefferson Hotel. Do you know where the Jefferson is?"

Her mouth went dry. "Yes. I know where the Jefferson is."

"Twelve o'clock?"

She nodded and headed back into the meeting room. She motioned for Jeanette to stay at the whiteboard and sat near the back among her research staff. The words were coming at her, but they weren't sticking. The air in the room felt thick like porridge. Her breathing was shallow and fast, and her pulse was racing. What the hell was that all about? Why now of all times did Bruce Andrews want to have lunch with her? What did he know? What *could* he know?

She whispered something about having to make an important call to one of the staff members and slipped out the back door. The hallway was spinning, and she grasped at the wall to steady herself. A couple of workers in lab coats came rushing over to help, but she assured them she was okay and headed down the hall on shaky legs to her office. She needed to speak with Gordon. She reached her office, closed the door behind her, and grabbed at the phone. Her hand stopped inches from the phone and slowly retracted. Was there any way for Andrews to monitor her calls? She didn't know. Her cell phone was in her jacket pocket, and she pulled it out and turned it on. Gordon's number was in the phone's memory, and she found it and hit send. A few rings, then voice mail.

"Shit," she said, waiting as Gordon said his piece. When he was finished and the phone beeped, she said, "Gordon, it's me. Bruce Andrews has asked me to have lunch with him today, and I'm worried that he knows something. I don't know what to do. Call me when you get this message. Call me on my cell phone, not my office number."

She hung up and set the phone on her desk, running her hands through her hair and putting pressure on the sides of her head. How much of what she was feeling right now was unsubstantiated panic? Bruce Andrews was the CEO of Veritas, and she was on the verge of a breakthrough in her Alzheimer's research. It would make sense for the head of the company to spend an hour with the team leader to review their progress. That was his job, knowing where the different research groups were in their search for a new marketable drug. He was the one who went to the media and the investors and laid out the quarterly projections. Andrews had every reason to ask for an hour of her time. She felt herself begin to relax slightly.

Yet the timing was all wrong. It was two days since she and Gordon had sat in the Palm Court lounge at the Jefferson Hotel looking at scientific data that proved Triaxcion had been responsible for Billy's death. Two days—what were the chances? And Andrews had asked her to meet him at the upscale restaurant in the Jefferson. Again, what were the chances? Slim to none. She felt the panic begin to rise again. The clock on her desk read 11:20. Time to go. With shaking hands, she slipped her cell phone into her pocket and locked her office behind her. She felt like a Christian heading out to meet the lion.

Bruce Andrews watched Jennifer Pearce cross the restaurant with the maître d'. She looked composed, very businesslike. Her gait was normal, self-assured. She had changed since he saw her this morning, traded in the lab coat for a jacket that matched the pantsuit. She looked nice, he thought, for a dead woman.

What had ever possessed her to link up with Gordon Buchanan? The man was belly-button lint, a complete nobody from the wilds of Montana. He should have stuck to cutting down trees and left the business of prescription drugs to those who knew what they were doing. Look at the damage he had caused. Kenga Bakcsi had to be removed because Buchanan had dragged her into the Triaxcion mess. And now Jennifer Pearce. Andrews had had a man watching them who followed the pair to the airport. According to his contact, there had been quite a hug at the airport. Pearce and Buchanan, toe to toe, nose to nose, staring into each other's eyes like two puppy dogs in heat. Well, Gordon Buchanan was about to lose another person close to him.

"Hello, Jennifer," he said, rising from his chair as she arrived at the table. "Thanks for coming."

"It wasn't a problem, Bruce. Minor adjustment to my schedule."

They ordered drinks and lunch, talked about trivial things for a while, then Andrews steered the conversation to work at the office. He listened intently as she detailed the new direction her group was moving with respect to the new molecule she had discovered. He asked the right questions and she gave the right answers. They ate their main course and Jennifer declined desert. He asked for the check and set his napkin on his plate.

"That was excellent," he said. "Did you enjoy your food?"

"Very much. Thanks for the invite."

"It was time we got out together. A little one-on-one time. It's difficult to make time these days. I think we're all so busy that the little things get ignored."

She smiled. "That's true." His statement about little things triggered a sudden thought. "I noticed something at the office the other day. Something that didn't seem right."

"What was that?" he asked, sipping on his coffee.

"Some of our everyday expenses are being logged in under R&D. That would make them eligible for tax credits. I don't know if Accounting is actually claiming the credits, but if they are there could be some backlash. I know the forensic auditors are watching for stuff like that in the wake of the Enron scandal."

He nodded. "We've been monitoring that, Jennifer. Some of the accounting practices from years back are still in place, and we're trying to phase them out. It was common practice to shift some expenses into the R&D sector so the company could lever the maximum tax credits legally allowed. The remainder of unusable expense money is shifted back over from R&D once the limit is reached. It's entirely legal, but as you say, in the aftermath of Enron, it's better to be conservative."

He accepted the check from the waiter and slipped a Visa card in the leather folder without looking at the amount. "Veritas is a very important part of my life. Frezin and Marcon were instrumental in getting me to where I am, but they never had a part of my soul. Veritas does. I've given my entire being to make the company successful. And that's not something you give up easily."

"No, I suppose not," Jennifer agreed, wondering where this was going.

"Do you think it's important to stand up for what you think is right, Jennifer?"

"Yes, of course."

"I think so too." He leaned back in his chair, an easy smile on his face. "Veritas is the crown jewel in my working life. I can't imagine what my life would be like without it. I go home at night and life is good, but everything is intrinsically linked back to the office. I don't think I'd be happy, even living with wealth, if I didn't have Veritas. Do you know what I mean?"

She shrugged. "Not really. I like my job and I think it's important, but I've already lived through one failed marriage. I don't need another one."

"You're getting married?" he asked.

"No, I'm not. I just meant I'm not willing to sacrifice the rest of my life for the good of the company."

The smile was gone. "I am," he said. There was a cold edge to his voice.

She glanced at her watch. "I've got to get back. I'm due at White Oak in twenty minutes."

He pocketed the receipt for lunch and stood up. "You've been spending a bit of time at White Oak lately," he said.

"Half my research team is there," she replied, matter-of-factly. "I like to stay in touch with them."

"Right. Half your research team."

She gave him a questioning look. "You structured it that way, Bruce."

"Yes, I did. You're right. Sorry. Not thinking."

They walked out of the hotel into the September sunshine. A few popcorn clouds floated peacefully above the city, and the air was still. The valet brought her car around, and she tipped him generously. "Thanks again for lunch," she said, then pulled away, leaving Andrews waiting for his vehicle. She reached into her bag and turned on her cell phone. She set it on the seat beside her as she navigated through the afternoon traffic toward the distant lab. Ten minutes into the drive, her phone rang. She checked the caller ID and heaved a sigh. It was Gordon.

"Hi," she said cheerfully. "How are things in Montana?"

"Okay. I was in with my lawyer when you called. She was in Vancouver all day Monday. Today was the first chance I had to see her." Gordon paused for a second. "I've been trying you every ten minutes for the last hour. Everything okay?"

"I think so. I'm not sure. I just had lunch with Bruce Andrews. He kind of creeped me out."

"Why? What did he say?"

"Just stuff about Veritas being everything to him, that he couldn't imagine living without it. It was weird."

"I didn't know you had a lunch date set with him."

"I didn't. He showed up this morning and basically told me we were going to lunch."

"The timing is a little coincidental, don't you think? We get the goods on Triaxcion and the next thing you know he's asking you out to lunch. I don't like it."

"Neither do I. By the way, did you get the disk to your lawyer?"

"Yes. She's making copies and keeping one in the corporate safe. And she's bringing in some science expert to untangle the mess of numbers on the disk. It's Greek to both her and me."

"The evidence is there, Gordon. I'm positive of that."

"Okay," he said. "You going to be all right?"

"Honestly, Gordon, I don't know. This whole lunch thing has me pretty upset. I'm scared." She pulled into the parking lot at White Oak, found a spot, and killed the engine.

"I can head down to Richmond if you want."

"What about the mill? You should be there to run it."

He laughed. "I've got a great staff here, Jennifer. They can run this place without me. I'm highly expendable."

"If you don't mind, I'd feel better if you were here. Maybe just for a few days, until this feeling I have disappears."

"What feeling?" he asked.

"That I'm next on the list. That I'm going to die," she said quietly.

"I'm on my way to Richmond," he said. "Be at home tonight. I'll be there as quickly as possible."

She gripped the phone tightly. "Thanks, Gordon."

42

The four agency representatives were joined by Annette Jordan, a biologist from the Centers for Disease Control out of Atlanta, Georgia. An information dossier on the situation had been forwarded to Atlanta, and she was up to speed on the viral threat when she arrived for the Tuesday-afternoon meeting in Rothery's office at DHS. Rothery made the introductions and turned first to Jim Allenby.

"How's the situation in Boston?" he asked.

"Ugly," the FBI man said. "We moved one hundred and eighty-five agents into the Boston area within twelve hours of our last meeting. They've been swamped by the sheer number of people the infected victims were in contact with. They've implemented a limited quarantine, where the low-risk segment of the population is under self-monitored house arrest. The vast majority of people have been extremely cooperative. They're asking a lot of questions and we're being vague, but so far the lid is still on the can of worms."

"How many confirmed cases?" Rothery asked.

"Nine," Allenby responded. "And it looks like we've got the threat contained. This outbreak, at least."

"Nine people are either dead or going to die," Rothery said disgustedly. "Craig, any word since Saturday on the fate of the Mossad team in Cairo?"

"We got confirmation about 0900 this morning. There were six team members, all killed in action."

"Christ, the White House is going to be in a frenzy over that one," Rothery said. "What kind of spin can you put on Israeli troops attacking an Egyptian target at the request of the American CIA? It doesn't get much uglier." He turned to Tony Warner. "How are things going with the pharmaceutical companies?"

The NSA man glanced down at a sheet in front of him. "To date, we've got sixteen medium-to-large research companies onside. I've personally spoken with a number of their CEOs, and they all told me it'll take some time for them to assemble teams with the expertise and tools to work on our problem."

"How much time?" Rothery asked.

"Three to four days. I spoke to most of them yesterday or today, so they should be up to speed by Friday or Saturday. Miss Jordan is going to put together a package for each company."

"What's in the package, Annette?" Rothery asked.

"Everything that the autopsy specialists in Fort Detrick have on the virus will be included, as will the case files from Austin, San Diego, Miami, and Boston. The physical properties of the virus, its molecular structure, and everything we have on its external membrane will be in there as well. Given that amount of information, these private-sector scientists should be able to hit the ground with their feet moving."

"And you'll be working with us from now on to keep those lines of communication open?"

"Yes. I'm yours until this is over."

"Excellent," Rothery said. He rose from his chair and slowly paced the room. "Now comes the tough part. As you all know, I've called a press conference for this afternoon at three o'clock." He checked his watch. "That's in twenty minutes. I will speak first, but I want each of you directly behind me, on camera and ready to handle the questions that will inevitably come. This crisis cannot be contained any longer. The public must be told what is happening. Now, that said, we're going to temper things a bit. The word 'Ebola' is strictly off-limits. If a journalist uses the word, look at them like they've got two heads. Don't get sucked into a game of semantics with the press, because you'll lose. Even if you hold your own here, they'll twist things when they report them. Don't let them steer you toward any word that even resembles 'Ebola' or 'the plague.'

"Their first reaction will be to assume the worst, and they'll be looking at the sensationalistic aspect of the story. The first barrage of questions will be barbed and ugly. Sidestep these and the second round will be easier as they collect their thoughts and get back to asking more down-to-earth questions.

"Jim, you take the point on Boston. Craig, you'll answer anything that may come up about the recent raids, although I don't think anyone will have made that connection yet. Tony, you and Annette handle technical questions about the virus. Keep it to things like replication and transcription, words the general public won't be familiar with. Any questions?"

His team shook their heads.

"All right. Let's go."

Rothery led the way to the meeting room on the main floor. It had been arranged to handle eighty members of the press, with a slightly raised platform at one end of the room. As the team entered, they all noticed that every chair was taken and many journalists and camera operators were lined up down the sides of the room. A hush fell over the room as the group moved into position and J. D. Rothery took the microphone.

"Good afternoon, I'm J. D. Rothery, Under Secretary of the Department of Homeland Security. I head up the Science and Technology division of DHS. I have with me today a team of experts from the FBI, CIA, NSA, and the Centers for Disease Control who will be working with my agency in curtailing this situation. I'd like to introduce the team now."

The cameras were rolling and the microphones on as Rothery and his handpicked crew faced a terrified nation.

43

Creepy.

That was the only word Jennifer could think of to describe her lunch with Bruce Andrews. The whole thing had been really creepy. She tried to wipe the memory from her mental chalkboard, but it refused to leave. She gave her RX-8 a bit more gas, pushing the sports car well over the posted limit. Maybe a little adrenaline rush would cure her. She veered off Monument Avenue, leaving the parade of statues and the wide street behind her. She cut onto Strawberry Street and slowed a bit, the road now narrower and bordered by trendy brick town houses.

What had Bruce Andrews wanted? Certainly, she had given him nothing of any value—he couldn't possibly know about her and Gordon from anything she had said over the meal. But maybe he already knew what she and Gordon were up to before he had insisted she accompany him to the Jefferson. Why that hotel? No, something was up and she didn't feel safe. She was glad Gordon was flying in tonight.

She turned off Strawberry onto Main Street, going with the flow of the traffic. The streetlamps were just coming on and the first diners of the evening were beginning to fill the myriad of restaurants lining the revitalized strip. It was getting busy for a Tuesday. She liked this part of Richmond—hell, she liked Richmond. The only thing she didn't like was Bruce Andrews. Then something occurred to her that had not crossed her mind at lunch.

She had spent an hour across the table from a murderer.

A very real shiver shot up her spine and hit her brain stem. She shuddered from the impact. If what she and Gordon suspected was true, that the top brass at Veritas were killing people to keep their secrets intact, then that statement was an absolute truth. Her hands were shaking as she steered the Mazda off Main onto Plum Street. She found a parking spot almost in front of her unit and switched off the ignition.

God, she was a mess.

When she was a child, she had been miserable, but she had never feared for her life. Never. Not until now. She exited the car, locked it, and glanced up and down the street before slipping the key in the lock and opening her front door. She closed the door behind her and locked it.

Safe.

She let out a long, slow breath and turned to drop her purse on the chair next to the door. Something moved, fast, toward her. A figure. A man. His image registered for a split second, then he was on her, spinning her around and clamping his hand over her mouth. She sucked in air, tried to scream, but the hand was like a vise. And there was something else. Something she had smelled a thousand times before. But it wasn't a smell that should be in her house. What was it? She tried to kick and hit her assailant, but she had no power in her arms and legs. Everything was going black. What was that smell? She felt herself slipping away, then she knew.

Chloroform.

The room went black.

Why are the stars so clear?

That was the first thought Jennifer Pearce had when she

woke. Her second thought was *Why am I in my car? I was at home. What happened? How did I get here?* She tried to move, but her hands were fastened behind her back. Her feet were bound together as well. Her head started to clear from the chloroform and she began to piece the events back together. Entering her house, the man with his hand over her mouth, the familiar smell of chloroform. Then it hit her: She had been abducted and was now sitting in her car with her hands and feet bound. She looked about and saw some movement off to the side.

It was a man, white with a chalky complexion. He had brown hair, just over his ears, and as he came close she could see that his eyes were light blue, almost translucent. He looked surprised to see her staring at him.

"So you're awake," Evan Ziegler said. His voice was soft, nonthreatening.

"What are you doing?" she asked. "Why are we here and why am I tied up?"

He moved close to her and stared straight into her eyes. "Please don't take this personally. I have nothing against you as a person. It's a matter of survival, that's all."

"What are you talking about?" she asked, her senses returning to her. She now saw that she was in the woods, surrounded by mountains and her car perched on the edge of a drop-off. And she was sitting behind the steering wheel.

"My son's survival," he said. He was moving his hands about, but she couldn't see what he was doing. Then the odor of chloroform hit her. He was getting ready to drug her again.

"Wait," she said. "Before you put that cloth over my face, tell me what this is all about."

He stopped moving and looked at her. He glanced around then nodded. "Okay," he said, the smell of the chloroform slowly dissipating. "There's no rush." He leaned on the car door, close to her. "My son is in a wheelchair, and will be for the rest of his life if he doesn't get the technology your company is working on."

"Are you talking about Veritas Pharmaceutical?"

"Yes."

"What technology?" she asked. "What technology could Veritas possibly possess that would get your son out of a wheelchair?"

"Brain chips," he said. "Veritas is ready to begin Phase I trials on its brain chips."

"What?" Jennifer said. "Brain chips? Oh God, are you ever out in left field. Veritas isn't working on brain chips anymore. That department is being phased out."

His face turned mean. It took on color and his mouth twisted into a sneer. "You're just trying to save your ass," he said. "I know otherwise. My son will be included in the first set of Phase I trials. And they're scheduled to start two months from now."

Jennifer shook her head. "No, no, no, that's not right. Listen to me. I'm the head of the Alzheimer's research group at Veritas. Even I know what's going on, and I've got nothing to do with brain chip development. What I'm telling you is common knowledge." She shook her head a few times to clear the cobwebs. "I've seen it with my own eyes—they're dismantling the department." Desperation sounded in her voice. "In fact, I've got three new staff that came over to my team from brain chips." Her head was clearing a bit, and the words started coming easier. "When Duke University released their findings that fat cells can be transformed into stem cells which can then be used to regenerate damage on the spinal cord, the whole concept of brain chips went obsolete almost overnight." She saw the uncertainty in his eyes and said, "You have got to believe me. Veritas is not going to produce anything that will get your son out of his wheelchair."

"I think you're just telling me something to keep me from dumping your car over the edge of this cliff."

She shook her head. "If you kill me, you've killed an innocent person. And I won't be the first one, either."

"What do you mean?"

"Albert Rousseau. Kenga Bakcsi. Both Veritas employees. Both murdered. And both totally innocent."

"He told me they were going to derail the brain chip program," Evan Ziegler said, seething with anger.

"Kenga Bakcsi worked for me. She was in the Alzheimer's group. The only thing Kenga did wrong was to get information for someone. Information on Triaxcion."

"What's Triaxcion?"

"One of Veritas's big money-producing drugs. The last thing the company wants is for the FDA to recall a drug that's already approved and is generating them a ton of money. They'll do anything to keep the information under wraps. By the looks of it, that includes murdering innocent people."

"What about Albert Rousseau?" Ziegler asked.

"He had damning evidence that Triaxcion could cause people with A-positive blood to become hemophiliacs. And that was what happened to Gordon's brother. He was taking Triaxcion, and he bled to death when he cut himself."

"Who is Gordon?"

"He's the guy that Kenga was getting information for. But it was strictly on Triaxcion. There was no tie-in to the brain chip labs anywhere." She took a breath and said, "You're being lied to. You're killing innocent people."

The man backed off from the car and slowly walked to the edge of the embankment. He stared out at the night sky, cloudless with little moonlight. The stars seemed intense, bright against a stark black backdrop. Jennifer watched him, all the while wriggling her fingers around, trying to loosen the straps. Nothing was working. Whatever the man had used to tie her hands was not giving in the least. The same for her feet: They were lashed together tightly. She stopped struggling against her bonds as her captor returned to the car. His pace was impossibly slow, as though he was resigned to some unpalatable conclusion. He reached the car and gave her a hint of a smile.

"I'm sorry. I don't believe you."

The last thing she saw was his hand coming toward her face. And she smelled chloroform again.

44

Gordon paid up front for three days: pilot, copilot, and the Lear 31A. They departed Helena under a low cloud cover at eight minutes to six, MDT. Just before eight o'clock in Richmond. The Lear 31A was engineered to cruise at 533 mph at 45,000 feet, and the pilots had the plane up to cruising speed and altitude eighteen minutes after takeoff. Gordon dimmed the lights, stretched out on one of the seats, and pulled a blanket over himself. Sleep would be good.

But it never came. His mind was alive with what could be happening in Richmond. Jennifer having lunch with Bruce Andrews was not a good thing. Andrews must have been prodding her for information. She hadn't seen it like that, but maybe Andrews was that good and she had inadvertently given him what he needed. The man was dangerous, Gordon was convinced of that. Who else stood to gain from protecting Triaxcion? It was Andrews who zeroed in on Jennifer two days after they secured the data that would eventually give him the edge in court. And once his case was in the books, precedent would have been set. Litigation would be coming at Veritas from every conceivable angle. From the legitimate claims where a death was di-

Jeff Buick

rectly attributable to Triaxcion to a litany of ambulance chasers with sleazy clients looking for an easy buck.

Right now he represented a huge liability to Veritas, and therefore to Bruce Andrews.

But it wasn't his own personal safety that concerned him. It was Jennifer's. The memory of that moment in the airport came back to him, vivid and wonderful. Their lips were an inch apart, their bodies tight to each other. It was one of those defining moments when you knew things were right. When both man and woman wanted each other so much. He had been severely tempted to walk away from his flight, drive back to Jennifer's house, take her in his arms, and kiss her. But that would have been folly. The evidence he had so desperately sought was in his pocket. And until his lawyer had it in her possession, he was vulnerable. Logic had superseded passion. He had gotten on the plane and flown back to Montana. But now he was wondering if he had made the right decision.

Jennifer was scared. The lunch with Bruce Andrews had shaken her very being. For her to ask him to pack up and leave immediately for Richmond was totally out of character and showed how worried she really was about her safety. And she was probably right. Andrews was not someone to mess with. He had shown that by removing Rousseau and Bakcsi from the equation. He wished there were a quicker way to get from Butte to Richmond, but looking about the private jet, he knew he had taken the fastest route possible. He closed his eyes and finally drifted off.

He awoke with one of the pilots hovering over him. "We'll be landing in ten minutes, Mr. Buchanan," he said. "You should use the washroom if you have to, then get seated with your lap belt on."

"Thanks," Gordon said. He was groggy but waking up quickly. By the time the plane was on the ground, he was fully awake. He had both pilots' cell phone numbers and assured them he'd call at least three hours before he needed to fly. They required that time to get the plane ready and file a flight plan. The pilots headed for a nearby hotel and Gordon gave the cabdriver Jennifer's address. It was almost three in the morning, and although he wanted to phone her residence, he didn't want to wake her until he arrived. He sat in the backseat, staring blankly at the deserted city.

The cab pulled up to a dark house and he paid the tab, grabbed his overnight bag, and hustled up to the front door. He rang the doorbell, scanning both sides of the road for her vehicle. He couldn't see the Mazda RX-8 anywhere. He rang the bell again. Nothing. The house remained dark. He tried the door handle and it turned. A slight push and the door opened. His stomach was instantly in his throat, his adrenaline pumping through his body as he stepped gingerly into the foyer. He quietly closed the door behind him and stood unmoving in the darkness, waiting for his pupils to dilate. After a minute or two, he could see fairly well. He started through the main floor of the house, past the piano and the couches, and into the kitchen. The counters were clean and everything in order. He retreated back through the living room and up the stairs to the second level.

There were four doors off the upper hallway, all of them closed. He opened each door slowly, scanning the room intently before moving on to the next one. The last room he reached was the master bedroom. There was a slight creaking sound as he opened the door and he moved into Jennifer's bedroom. Her bed was still made, no signs of anyone having slept in it. He switched on the light and looked about. Everything was neat and orderly, just as she would have left it before heading for work in the morning. He retreated back to the main floor, switching on lights as he went, looking for clues as to what might have happened.

Nothing.

Gordon paced through the house time and time again, his eyes searching for even the slightest clue that would tell him what had happened to Jennifer. He left the house, walking quickly up and down the road and looking for her car. It wasn't there. He returned to the house, breathing a little easier as a logical idea came to him. Jennifer had probably stayed the night with a friend rather than come home. That would account for her car not being anywhere in sight. But other details still nagged at him. Why was the front door unlocked? Even if she had left the house open for when he arrived, surely she would have left a note somewhere in the house at least telling him that she was okay. Nothing was making sense.

Then the phone rang, shattering the ominous silence.

Gordon checked his watch. Three-thirty-five. Who the hell would be calling at this hour? Unless it was Jennifer calling to tell him where she was. He grabbed the phone and said hello.

"Who is this?" a man's voice asked. He sounded surprised.

"Never mind who *this* is, who's calling?" Gordon snapped back.

"I didn't expect to get a real person," Evan Ziegler said thoughtfully. "Thought I'd get voice mail."

"Well, you didn't. You got me. Now, what do you want?"

"Let me think." There was a pause. Ziegler said, "You must be Gordon."

That the man knew his name took Gordon by surprise. "Perhaps. Please tell me who you are and where Jennifer is."

"Yes, well, that's why I called. To leave a voice mail as to where you can find Jennifer."

Gordon's hand tightened on the phone, almost crushing it. He struggled to keep his breathing normal. "Where is she?"

"Well, she had a bit of an accident in her car. I don't think she's going to make it."

"You son of a bitch. Where is she?"

Ziegler's tone changed; a cold edge crept into his voice. "Careful what you say, Gordon, or you may never find her body."

Buchanan wanted to scream. "I'd like to know where she is," he said calmly, ready to explode.

"That's better. You should get a pen and a piece of paper, because unless you know this area really well it's going to be a little confusing."

Gordon found a pencil and grabbed a flyer with a picture of

a vacuum cleaner on one side. He flipped it over and said, "All right. Give me the directions."

"Write quickly. Miss a turn, you miss the crash site. Go west through Charlottesville and head up into the Shenandoah Mountains. At Waynesboro, you turn north. Go seven miles, then turn right onto the forestry road. It's a bit of a goat path, so don't miss it. If you hit Grottoes, you've gone too far. Once you're on the forestry road, go two miles, then veer right along the ridge. Watch for the gap in the trees and shrubs where a vehicle recently went over the edge. And be careful—the cliff is very steep and slippery."

Gordon finished writing the directions. "If she's dead, I'll hunt you down and kill you."

"Somehow I don't think so," Ziegler said, then ended the call.

Gordon was shaking so badly he could hardly dial a cab. He gave the dispatcher Jennifer's address, then called the Alamo booth at the Richmond airport. They were open twenty-four hours and he confirmed that they had cars available. He gave them his name and hung up. As he waited in the darkness for the cab, one thought kept running through his mind.

Was Jennifer Pearce alive or dead?

45

The night air was crisp and the sky clear as Gordon motored through Charlottesville and continued west into the Shenandoah Mountains. The road rose quickly, leaving the plains and small foothills behind. Pine, hickory, and oak bordered the road as it twisted along the east side of the ridge. He reached Waynesboro and made the turn, heading north on a secondary road that ran parallel to the massive ridge that defined the eastern edge of the Shenandoah Mountains. He reset the trip odometer on the Jeep and glanced at the dashboard clock. Five-eighteen. The sun was close to rising and the sky to the east began to lighten.

Gordon slowed as he approached the seven-mile mark. Even at twenty miles an hour, he was past the forestry road before it registered. He backed up and turned right, his hands starting to shake. He reset the trip odometer again and drove the narrow, rutted road at a reasonable speed. The last thing he needed right now was to slide off the road into a grove of trees or, even worse, over one of the many drop-offs that cut perilously close to the tire tracks. At two miles there was a fork in the road, with the main branch heading to the left. He took the right fork, now glad he had paid extra to rent the Jeep. He touched the four-wheel-drive control and felt the front transaxle kick in. The trees opened up on his left, allowing a spectacular view of the sun rising over the eastern seaboard and distant Richmond.

The caller had told him to watch for a gap in the trees where a vehicle had gone over, and as he drove he caught glimpses of the cliff he was paralleling. If Jennifer Pearce had gone over anywhere near here, she was most certainly dead. The drop was hundreds of feet to a base of rocks and large trees that would shred a fast-moving vehicle. He rounded a curve, and through the trees ahead he caught a glimpse of color. Blue. Jennifer's Mazda was blue. He pulled ahead, his heart racing. One more curve in the path and he could see it. The rear of Jennifer's car. He pulled up behind it and cut the engine. The silence was immediate. Slowly, he opened the driver's door and stepped out of the Jeep onto the rocky ground.

The car was perched precariously on the edge of the cliff. One good push and it would be over. He carefully picked his way through the surrounding shrubs and reached the driver's door. He took a deep breath and looked into the car.

Jennifer Pearce, her eyes wild with fear, stared back at him. At the sight of his familiar face, she broke into a huge smile and started to cry simultaneously. The tears rolled down her face. He reached in and gently brushed them away.

"Gordon," she said quietly. "Oh, thank God you're here."

"I'm here," he said, opening the door and reaching inside the car. It wobbled a bit, and he steadied it by pushing back against the frame. "Let's get you out of there," he said, surveying the situation. Her hands were bound with strips of leather, a thin piece of tanned hide between her wrists and the leather. The same with her feet. Her abductor had bound her in such a way that he could take the leather strips off and there would be no evidence she had ever been bound. The leather strips on her hands were pulled through the steering wheel, making it impossible for her to exit the car. Gordon untied her hands first, then her feet.

"Just slip out easy so you don't rock the car," he said, taking her by the hand.

She placed one foot on the ground and shifted her weight off the seat toward Gordon. Removing her body weight from the vehicle upset the delicate balance and the car started to move forward. Gordon yanked her out and they both went over backwards, he taking the brunt of the fall and she landing directly on top of him. There was a strange scraping sound and the Mazda disappeared over the edge. A few seconds of silence, then a distant crashing sound as the car hit the rocks hundreds of feet below.

Jennifer didn't move from where she was. She wrapped her arms around Gordon and burrowed her face into his chest, pulling him tight to her. He responded by closing his arms about her back and giving her a gentle squeeze. He could feel the warmth of her tears on his chest as they lay silently on the forest floor. Finally, she raised her head and brought her mouth to his. They kissed, softly at first, then with the pent-up desire that was simmering inside both of them. When they stopped, Jennifer lifted her head and stared into his eyes.

"How did you know I was here?" she asked.

"Whoever left you here called your house. He was going to leave a voice mail so the authorities could find you or your body. I was at your house when he called."

"Thank God," she said. "If you hadn't come to get me, there's no way I would have lived through this."

"We just got lucky," he said. "Very lucky."

"Yeah. Lucky."

"Did you know the guy who left you here?"

She shook her head. "No, I've never seen him before. But from some of the things he said, I'm pretty sure he was working for Bruce Andrews."

She told Gordon about how the man was killing to keep the brain chip program alive. How his son was in a wheelchair and that someone at Veritas had promised his kid a shot at a normal life. "It's all a lie, of course," she said. "The brain chip program is being dismantled. I've seen them physically taking the White Oak lab apart."

"This guy—he referred to the Veritas contact as 'he'?"

She thought about it for a moment. "Yes. He definitely called him 'he.' Not them. 'He.' "

"Andrews," Gordon said quietly. "The bastard."

"There's something else, Gordon. Some of the accounting practices at Veritas are questionable. They are shifting everyday expenses into the research-and-development sector, setting themselves up to receive unearned government tax incentives."

"Sounds like the Enron scandal."

"Oh, this is far enough removed from that to keep the forensic auditors at bay. For a time, at least. And I get the feeling that Andrews is banking on that—having enough time to fix whatever damage is being done."

"Well, it wouldn't surprise me if the snake had something up his sleeve."

"No, I suppose not," she said.

She let her neck muscles relax and gently set her cheek against his chest. She felt safe with him and, despite their predicament, glad to be exactly where she was. It had been many years since a man had stirred the feminine side in her. Many years since she had felt happy to be a woman. But Gordon was lighting some sort of long-dormant fuse inside her, and somewhere along that fuse was the true happiness that accompanies two people totally at ease with each other.

Gordon's cell phone rang, and he looked at the call display, then answered it. Jennifer could hear a muffled voice but couldn't make out what was being said. "Yes, I was employing him. Why?" He listened, then said, "I've never been to his office. He was a referral from a mutual friend." Again the other voice, then: "I've been in Montana, and I'm in Richmond right now." A moment of silence. "Yes, I can prove where I was at that time." The voice on the other end of the line spoke for a minute, and Gordon said okay a couple of times, then said, "Okay, thank you for calling." He closed the phone, a serious look on his face.

"Wes Connors, the private detective I hired, is dead."

"What happened?" Jennifer asked.

"He was shot in his office. The police have no idea who's re-

Jeff Buick

sponsible. They're just going through Wes's files and calling all his clients who currently have him on retainer. They're probably checking to see if he had any pissed-off clients, and to let his clients know he won't be sending out any more reports."

"You think Andrews had him killed?"

Gordon shrugged. "I don't know what else Wes was working on, but my guess would be that this is Andrews's doing. Wes Connors has been in the investigative business for years, and suddenly someone kills him. The timing is a little suspect. I thing Bruce Andrews is sending me a message."

"Nice message," Jennifer said.

"Yeah, from a real nice guy."

"What happens now?" she asked, resting her cheek back on his chest.

"Well, going home or to work is out of the question. If Andrews tried to kill you once, he's not going to back off now. We've got to stay out of sight, find some proof that Andrews ordered that guy to kill Kenga and Albert Rousseau. And you."

"How?" she asked.

He shrugged, and her head moved with his body. "There has to be some way to find that guy. Or something in the police files on Kenga and Albert that points toward either Andrews or the killer."

"I'm not so sure," Jennifer said. "Andrews is going to cover his tracks very well. He's not stupid."

She lifted off him and sat up. A small piece of paper that had been caught in the folds of her shirt fluttered to the ground. She reached over and picked it up. Her eyes scanned over what was written on the scrap, then she said, "Well, now I know how I survived."

"What do you mean?"

"I was arguing with the killer, trying to persuade him that Veritas was shutting down the brain chip program and that he was being used. I thought I was getting through to him, but the last thing I remember is him clamping the chloroform over my face and telling me, 'I'm sorry, I don't believe you.' I was sure he was

234

going to push the car over the cliff." She held up the paper so he could read what was written on it. "I guess he had a change of heart."

Gordon focused on the paper. *On second thought, I do believe you.*

"Well, that change of heart won't get him in Andrews's good books," Gordon said. He propped himself against a nearby tree and watched the sun hover over the landscape. Completely out of nowhere, he wished he had a camera with him, the view was so spectacular. Then the thought of where they would stay washed over him. "You know any tasteless hotels in Richmond?" he asked.

"Tasteless? Why tasteless?"

"I don't think using a credit card would be wise. Cash only. And you know what kind of place that gets you."

"No, not really, but I'll take your word for it." She twisted so she could see the view. "You know, when I was a kid I used to make things up. Like if I was walking to school and it was snowy, I'd be trying to get there before the polar bears caught me. If a song came on, I'd be Diana Ross, singing into my curling iron."

"Don't think that's too abnormal. I played a little Van Halen air guitar in my time."

She laughed. "No, more than that. I really tried to transfer myself to somewhere else—anyplace but where I was. I didn't have a happy childhood. Something changed when my little brother was born. I got downgraded to second fiddle. And after being the princess for so long, that's a pretty tough demotion. God, I really didn't want to be me."

He stared at her for a minute, then asked, "So what happened? Why is Jennifer Pearce so okay now?"

"I think she learned the world isn't perfect and that her parents didn't mean to hurt her. She learned to forgive. And she learned to appreciate the things that she *did* have in her life."

"She's a lucky woman."

She smiled, and for a moment the anxiety and fear were

gone, replaced with a feeling that life had brought her to where she should be. What the reason was or whether she would even live through this were unknowns. And instead of that scaring her, it excited and intrigued her. Having faced the very real possibility of dying and then having survived, she felt more alive than ever before. And just being close to Gordon gave her a sense of belonging that had eluded her for so long. He calmed her and at the same time made her feel that what she had done with her life was important. She liked that feeling. And she liked Gordon Buchanan.

In fact, she really liked Gordon Buchanan.

46

"Are you positive?" Bruce Andrews asked, reclining in his leather chair, the Richmond skyline visible out his office window. Clouds had crept in and intermittent rain threatened.

"Absolutely, Mr. Andrews," the technician said. "They definitely logged in under Dr. Pearce's ID."

"What time?" He finished the last of his coffee and set the mug on his desk.

"Two-thirteen P.M. About forty minutes ago."

"Where did she sign in from?"

"The main branch of the public library."

"And you said she accessed the accounting files for her department, the brain chip department, and the White Oak labs."

"Yes, sir. That and every open file the legal department has on Triaxcion. She was inside some personnel files as well: the files on Kenga Bakcsi and Albert Rousseau. That's how we saw that she was in the mainframe—she's not authorized to access those files."

"Then how did she get into them?" Andrews asked, perturbed.

"She bypassed the firewall somehow. We're not sure at this point, but it appears she knew the IP address and somehow came up with a port number. She would appear to be a very resourceful woman."

"Yes, very resourceful. Thanks—that's all for now. And please don't mention this to anyone. This is highly confidential."

The man nodded that he understood and left the office. Bruce Andrews picked up his private line and placed a call. "It would appear Jennifer Pearce is still with us," he said.

"What? I thought your guy had taken care of her," the voice said.

"I thought so too. It's Wednesday afternoon, so she's been running around for at least twelve hours getting into God only knows what."

"What do you want me to do?"

"She signed into the company mainframe from the main branch of the public library about an hour ago. Take a photo of her with you and ask around. Be discreet. Find out if it was really her using the computer. And if she's still with us, I'd like you to fly out to Denver tonight."

"I'd be glad to. Ziegler should have been gone a long time ago. I told you that son of a bitch would be trouble."

"Well, looks like you were right. Now you get to take care of it."

"Like I said, I'd be glad to. I'm off to the library."

"Thanks," Andrews said, and hung up. He thought about that for a minute and realized it wasn't often that he thanked people for doing things. But this time his colleague deserved it. It was he who had said bringing in Evan Ziegler was a bad idea. Retired navy SEALs were a different bunch, deadly and often tired of taking orders. And now he was relying on the man who'd said Ziegler was bad news to terminate him. Strange how things worked sometimes.

In retrospect, teaming up with his clandestine partner had been an excellent idea. Because of his position, the man had provided services most people wouldn't even dream existed. He was capable of opening doors—or shutting them, for that matter—when the timing was right. The organization he worked for had resources beyond imagination, and on a few occasions they had relied on those resources to keep things on track. And they were still on track.

"So close now," Andrews said to himself. "So close."

Andrews busied himself with damage control on the accounting problem. If Jennifer Pearce had noticed the deviations in standard accounting practices, moving operating expenses across to the research side of the ledger, then the forensic auditors wouldn't be far behind. And right now the last thing he needed was any attention drawn to the company. Time was a nebulous factor, an unknown. But one time frame he had to operate within was the expiry date on his options to purchase three million common shares of Veritas. And that date was looming in the near future. December 15 wasn't that far away, and time had a habit of sneaking by when you weren't looking. The phone attached to his private line rang and he picked up the receiver.

"It was definitely her," the man said. "The librarian positively identified Jennifer Pearce. And guess who was with her?"

Andrews's hand tightened on the phone. "Buchanan?"

"Yes. She ID'd him from a picture I pulled from the Montana DMV database. Not a great picture but she was sure."

"How did Buchanan get from Montana to Richmond without you knowing about it? I thought you were monitoring the airlines, watching for his name to appear on a manifest."

"We were and we are. I have no idea how he got to Virginia. The only plausible explanation is that he chartered a private jet."

"That's a bit of a stretch, don't you think?" Andrews said.

"Not really. The man is wealthy—the cost of hiring a Lear or a smaller Gulfstream would be well within his reach. It would give him anonymity and speed, either of which may have been important to him at the time."

"Check it out. Find out how he got here. But get to Denver first and take care of that problem. Things are starting to come unglued, and I want to tie up loose ends before everything unravels."

Jeff Buick

"Denver is not a problem. In fact, I'll quite enjoy it." The line clicked over to a dial tone.

Bruce Andrews sat back and smiled. Evan Ziegler had been a useful cog in the wheel for a while, but that usefulness was over. And since that was over, so was his life. Perhaps it was just morbid curiosity, but Andrews found himself wondering what method his associate would use to kill Ziegler. Certainly, a great deal of caution was necessary when dealing with someone as dangerous as Ziegler.

Killing the killer—what an excellent title for a book.

47

J. D. Rothery took the call on his cell phone as his driver turned onto Pennsylvania Avenue and approached the entrance to the White House. The caller was Tony Warner, and the NSA man had an update for him on the efforts of the big pharmaceutical companies in their quest to find an answer to the virus.

"Be quick, Tony," J. D. said. "I've got about two minutes, then I'm on the hot seat in the Oval Office. For some reason, the president wants to hear the latest directly from me."

"Okay, I'll be fast. The news is not entirely bad. Three of the companies we got packages out to have had some success identifying the nucleic acid genome inside the capsid. One of the three has already isolated the envelope."

"What's an envelope?" J. D. said, scratching notes as the car pulled up to the main security gate. "I'm not a viral specialist, but I've got to know what this terminology means when I pass this information along to the president."

"Some viruses are encapsulated with an envelope, which is a membrane of virus-encoded proteins, with either DNA or RNA genomes. Identifying these genomes is crucial to finding a drug that can penetrate the membrane."

"So how close is this company to finding a drug that might work against the virus?"

"No idea at this point, but the CEO is positive they're on the right track. He thinks this virus is beatable, not like Ebola."

"That's excellent news, Tony. Which company is it?"

"GlasoKlan. I've been speaking directly with Eric Stallworth, the head of North American operations, and he thinks this is doable."

The car passed through the security checkpoint and drove slowly along the winding drive toward the White House. "Call Stallworth and ask him to be near the phone in case the president wants to speak with him."

"Okay. Here's Stallworth's number at the office." Warner recited the number to the CEO's direct line, which bypassed the automated voice mail that answered incoming calls.

"You said there were three companies having success with the virus. Which are the other two?"

"Marcon and Beringer Ingels. Both are major players in the pharmaceutical business."

"I know who they are," Rothery snapped, immediately wishing he could have the comment back.

"Anything else?" Warner asked, his voice cool.

"No, just keep me in the loop with their progress."

"Good luck with the president."

"Thanks. Stay next to your phone in case I need to patch the president through. He may want to speak with you directly for an update from NSA."

"Okay," Tony said, his voice back to normal. The line went dead.

J. D. Rothery exited the car clutching his leather attaché case. He was ushered through security, joined by two serious-looking secret service agents, and whisked down the wide hallway toward the Oval Office. There was an urgency to their stride, and Rothery was pressed to keep up with them. He reached the outer door of the nation's most hallowed sanctuary and stood quietly as they got clearance to enter. One of the agents touched his earpiece, then turned to him and asked, "Are you ready?"

"Ready as I'll ever be," Rothery said. How could you ever be ready to face the president with the news that a lethal, contagious virus was being unleashed on the nation by an unknown enemy? The door opened, and he followed the agents into the room.

48

Thursday.

Two days since he had left Jennifer Pearce teetering over the edge of a cliff in the Shenandoah Mountains. Two days with no contact from Bruce Andrews. Two days of sitting on a powder keg with one burning question that had yet to be answered.

Was Veritas really terminating its brain chip program?

Evan Ziegler had no idea if what the woman had told him was true. And he had no way of finding out, save calling Bruce Andrews and asking him. And that was not going to happen. He had searched the Internet, using every keyword he could think of, to see if there had been any press releases about Veritas phasing out the program. Nothing. The only proof he had that Andrews was using him was the word of a woman facing certain death. And he knew that when a person was placed in such a predicament, integrity went out the window. Even the most honest person would lie if she thought it might save her life. He knew this from firsthand experience. Not knowing the answer to that question was killing him.

On top of that, Evan Ziegler's mind had been consumed with Jennifer Pearce's fate over the last 120 hours. She had been drugged and asleep when he left the scene, and still alive. But her car had been perched precariously on the lip of the drop-off. And the result of the car going over was not in question—she would die. A sudden gust of wind, an updraft surging along the cliff face, a small animal running across the hood of the car—all were insignificant events that could cause the vehicle to slide slowly into the valley. Jennifer Pearce could not possibly survive such a crash.

There had been no word from Richmond since Wednesday morning, and he took the silence as an indication that she had not survived. If Jennifer Pearce was alive and Bruce Andrews had found out, all hell would be breaking loose. Andrews would have called on the private line with questions. Questions that would be difficult, if not impossible, to answer. But that had not happened. And as time progressed, he had to assume there was only one possible scenario.

Jennifer Pearce was dead.

But the other factor that was weighing on his mind was the sudden appearance of Gordon, whoever the hell that was. Some guy who had talked Kenga Bakcsi into providing him with information on that Triaxcion drug. What had he been doing at Pearce's house early Sunday morning? Had he managed to find her before the car went over the cliff? And if so, why had he not heard from a pissed-off Bruce Andrews? Nothing was making sense.

And what had she said about both Albert Rousseau and Kenga Bakcsi being innocent victims? Had Bruce Andrews asked him to kill these people for other reasons? He'd been adamant that both Bakcsi and Rousseau were threats to the brain chip program. But Andrews could have been lying.

He glanced at the clock on his desk. Three-thirty. He shut down his computer and told his receptionist he was leaving early. She often closed the copier office when he was out on sales calls or enjoying a midweek round of golf. Traffic was light for a Thursday afternoon, but he figured that was probably because he was an hour ahead of the peak hours for commuters heading home. He pulled into his driveway and killed

245

the engine. His wife's van was parked on her side of the drive, the side that allowed her to load Ben's wheelchair in through the sliding doors. He pocketed his keys and entered the house, a slight gust of cool air exiting through the open door. It was strange, he thought, for his wife to have the air conditioner turned up that high. It wasn't that warm out today. He took a few steps into the house and stopped. Something was wrong. He had felt this before, many times. He felt the presence of death.

Ziegler moved quietly through the living room and down the hall to the master bedroom, where a fully loaded Glock 17 rested under some shirts in his drawer. The door was open and he slid into the room, every sense on high alert. He moved quickly to the bank of drawers and eased open the third one from the top. He slid his hand under the shirts and felt for the gun.

It was gone.

He turned and ran from the room, down the hall to Ben's room. He had no weapon save his skill at hand-to-hand combat, but he had to see that his son was okay. Ben's door was closed, and he opened it slowly, not knowing what he would find. As the door swung back, his son's wheelchair came into view. Ben was facing away from him, and all Evan could see was the back of his son's head. He glanced about, then crept quietly across the room. He reached the wheelchair and turned it slightly so he could see his son. And then, despite all his years dealing with violent death, he vomited.

Ben's neck was cut wide open from one side to the other; the knife had cut so deep that it exposed the boy's spinal cord. His shirt and pants were caked with blood, just starting to dry. His eyes were wide open and locked in a horrified stare, suggesting that his mind had known he was going to die but his body had been unable to defend against his attacker. Evan wiped the vomit from the edges of his mouth, his face contorted in rage. He turned back to the door, his stomach heaving again at the sight of his wife, nailed to the wall behind the door, her chest and stomach sliced open, her vital organs hanging from the cavities. In the doorway stood a man. He had a silenced gun aimed at Ziegler's head.

"Too bad about your family," the man said. "Your wife put up quite the fight, but your son just sat there. Never moved a muscle."

Evan rushed the man, his mind a blur of red. He felt the first bullet hit his chest but kept moving. The second slug tore into his neck and snapped his head back. He tried to push with his feet, but all momentum was gone. He crashed to the carpet, twitching as he bled to death. The man with the gun appeared above him, looking down as one would inspect a stepped-on bug that was still moving.

"Why didn't you kill her, Evan?" he asked. "What was it about Jennifer Pearce that was so different? All you had to do was kill her and we wouldn't have made this trip out to visit you and your family." He unscrewed the silencer from the gun and pocketed it. He slipped the gun into a shoulder holster and stood still, watching Evan die.

Evan's eyes slowly closed, his killer's face the last earthly image recorded in his memory. And he had a strange thought as he died. That he had seen that face on television recently.

49

They found a room at the Fairfield Inn on I-64 despite the problem with not wishing to use a credit card. It had a lot to do with Gordon offering five thousand dollars in cash as a deposit. The manager tucked it away in the safe and gave them a big smile every time they entered the lobby. What the hell, some people just didn't like credit cards.

Friday, September 16. Jennifer had missed Thursday without calling in to let them know she was okay. And now Friday. Her staff was going to be panicked at her disappearance. But what were her options? Call the office and let Bruce Andrews know she was alive so he could try and kill her again? Not a very smart idea. And with the information they'd garnered from their quick trip to the library Thursday afternoon, she and Gordon had amassed more evidence that pointed to Bruce Andrews as the guilty party.

The financial picture at Veritas was not what Andrews was painting. The company was in trouble. Millions of dollars in everyday expenses from almost every department with a research arm were being shifted over to R&D. The resulting tax credits totaled hundreds of millions of dollars. Even with the extra income the company was enjoying from the extended patents on metabolite-synthesizing drugs, the veil was slowly coming up on the fraud. Expenditures were through the roof. Despite the termination of the brain chip department, it still drew enormous amounts of the company's cash reserves, something that puzzled both Jennifer and Gordon.

And there was no way the CEO of the company did not know what was happening. It was at his directive that the departments were realigning their finances to divert the expenses to R&D. Andrews was the conductor, his team leaders the unwitting orchestra. With the exception of Jennifer Pearce, who, for her tenacity, was now in fear for her life.

"Is there anything in either Kenga's or Albert's files that could point to them having been murdered?" Jennifer asked. Gordon had spent a considerable amount of time going over the two personnel files they had printed out on the library LaserJet twenty-four hours earlier.

He sat back in the chair and rubbed his eyes. "Nothing. These files are a total dead end."

"That's not a big surprise," she said. "If there is any concrete proof that Andrews had them killed, it's probably tucked away in some secure file we'll never find."

"Probably," Gordon said. He flipped through a couple of pages on the small round table in the corner of the hotel room. "You know, the amount of money Veritas earns and spends is almost unfathomable. Income and expenses are all listed in the hundreds of millions of dollars. These figures are obscene."

She rolled over on the bed, onto her stomach. "It's big business. Huge, in fact. Hell, AstraZeneca pumped close to five hundred million into promoting Nexium. And that was just in its first year on the market. Once the market is established, the money keeps pouring in until the patent expires. And keep in mind that despite all the money they're putting into it, Nexium is a dog."

A puzzled expression crossed Gordon's face. "Why year after year? Don't the people taking these drugs ever get healthy?"

Jennifer laughed. "You're missing the big picture, Gordon,"

she said. "The major pharmaceutical companies aren't looking for a cure. Their objective is to come up with a pill that treats the symptoms. If they actually cured the disease, that would eliminate an entire segment of the market. It's sort of like Firestone bringing a tire to market that gets a million miles before the rubber on the treads wears out. Never going to happen."

"So you're not looking for a cure to anything, just a patch."

She nodded. "It's a little different with Alzheimer's because it's a disease that affects an aging population. Our client base has a high natural attrition rate, so if we come up with something that blocks the tangles and plaques in the brain that cause Alzheimer's, we will still have a huge clientele needing the drug. And that's despite many of our clients passing on from old age or diseases related to the aging process. Alzheimer's is one disease where finding a cure is still a win-win for the company. That's one of the reasons I chose to specialize in it."

"So you could look for a cure, not just a pill."

"Exactly." She grinned. "I guess I'm just a do-gooder at heart."

He rose and walked over to the bed and lay beside her. She cuddled into his side and they lay quietly for a few minutes. The television was on but muted. When the newscaster switched to a story covering the outbreak of the unknown virus, she hit the mute button so she could hear the report. The talking head was on location in Washington, D.C., and the outline of the White House was prominent in the backdrop.

"Yesterday afternoon the president met with J.D. Rothery, Under Secretary of the Department of Homeland Security and head of the special task force assigned to combat this terrorist threat. Since May, there have been reported incidents of the virus appearing in Austin, San Diego, Miami, and Boston. Numerous radical groups have purported to be in possession of the killer virus, but to date the task force has not confirmed any of the claims to be legitimate. But to say that the president is taking this seriously is an understatement. The task force is an amalgamation of many talents. The full resources of the FBI, the CIA, and the National Security Administration are at Under Secretary Rothery's full command.

"Last week's sweeping raids of targets across the globe is now thought to be directly related to the virus crisis. Unidentified sources have indicated that the raids, which occurred simultaneously on at least sixteen targets in five countries, were an attempt to find the source of the virus. No word on whether they were successful, but it has been reported that Mr. Rothery is enlisting the help of the private sector in isolating the virus and finding a drug to eradicate it. But one thing is certain: This threat is building into a crisis that could result in a devastating toll on human life if not brought under control quickly."

The reporter gave his byline and the broadcast returned to the studio. Jennifer touched the mute button again and the sound died instantly. "Now, that is scary," she said.

"What is it?" Gordon asked. "What kind of virus?"

"They're being very guarded about it, but from what I've seen and what I've heard, I think it's a hemorrhagic virus of some sort."

"What's that?" Gordon asked.

"Ebola or Marburg. Both very deadly viruses that liquefy internal body organs."

He twisted and pulled back from her a bit so he could look into her eyes. "I know what Ebola is. It's like the plague. Holy shit. How can you be so sure?"

"They've given up a few details that most people wouldn't be able to patch together. And the glimpses of the kids' bodies as they brought them out of the quarantine house in Boston. The symptoms were exactly what would show if Ebola was present. It all adds up to a hemorrhagic virus."

"Christ, that's serious."

She nodded. "Very serious. If some terrorist cell has Ebola in any quantity, we're in trouble. It's simple to introduce into a population, it spreads easily, and there's no known cure."

"There's no drug to combat it?"

She shook her head. "Nothing. The virus is protected by a

251

capsid, which also has a protective coating called an envelope. The envelope is composed of virus-encoded proteins, which we can't seem to crack. We just can't find a drug that can penetrate the virus and kill it. It's what we call a Biosafety Level Four virus, and only a handful of labs across the country are equipped to handle it. You need state-of-the-art HEPA filters, and exhaust and ventilation systems with backup systems upon backup systems. You're talking really nasty stuff."

"Well, let's hope they get these guys before they poison anyone else," Gordon said.

They lay on the bed for the next hour, talking, trying to bring some normalcy to their predicament. That they had been drawn together in difficult circumstances was a given. That they both cared for each other had only been confirmed by their passionate lovemaking the previous evening. And that they knew they were in dire circumstances was evident by the course their conversation took.

"We're positive Andrews is guilty of doctoring the books, covering up deficiencies in Triaxcion, and killing at least two people," Jennifer said. "But where can we take this without concrete proof? If we stick our heads above the horizon, we'll get them shot off. What do we do?"

"I don't know," Gordon said. "This is all new to me. I'm just a logger. What do I know about evil corporations killing their staff?"

"Turn up the volume," she said, cutting him off in midsentence and grabbing for the remote control. Gordon hit the button and the sound from the television reappeared. The picture was a double-ender with a split screen, a man in the studio on the left and a woman in front of a house on the right. The woman was talking into the microphone, with considerable police activity behind her. Pictures of a man, a woman, and a boy in his late teens were posted on the bottom of the screen.

". . . one of Denver's most heinous murders. An entire family is dead, but probably the most disturbing aspect is that Ben Ziegler, son of Evan and Louise Ziegler, was confined to a wheelchair and unable to defend himself. Police are at a total loss as to the motive. Evan Ziegler was the owner of a local photocopier supply company, and his wife remained at home to care for their quadriplegic son. Neighbors and coworkers have all described the family as wonderful people, involved in the community and regulars at the local Lutheran church."

The anchor broke in from the studio. "Amanda, I understand the level of violence involved in this crime is horrific."

"Yes, Adam, it is. The police will not let anyone inside the house, but I was shown the crime-scene photos and I'm not even going to attempt to describe them. I've never seen anything like it, not even in a bad movie."

"Thank you. That was Amanda Davis reporting from Denver. In other news—"

Jennifer motioned to Gordon to kill the sound. He did, and she got off the bed and walked over to the window. She stared down at the parking lot for a minute, then turned back to Gordon. The color had drained from her face and upper body, and she looked strangely white against her dark hair. She took a few deep breaths.

"The man on that newscast. The father. He was the one who left me dangling over the cliff in my car."

50

The ultimatum to the American government arrived in a small package enclosed in a plain brown wrapper. It was addressed to J. D. Rothery, Under Secretary of the Department of Homeland Security, L'Enfant Plaza, Washington, D.C. Standard security measures ensured that the package was X-rayed, opened, and the first ten seconds of the enclosed DVD viewed to make sure it was a functioning disk. When the security personnel saw the contents of the disk, the wrapper was immediately placed in a sterile plastic bag and the DVD tested for traces of biological agents. The moment it had a clear bill of health, it was rushed to Rothery's office.

The DHS chief had been contacted and was aware that the disk would be forwarded when it had cleared security; he had advised his colleagues at the FBI, CIA, and NSA that the disk would be in his DVD player the second it arrived. All three men were present. Also watching as the disk was slipped into the machine were Dr. Edward Henning and Annette Jordan. Rothery dimmed the lights and sat back to watch.

The scene on the television was a small concrete room painted gray. There were no distinguishing marks anywhere on the wall. Centered in the screen was a solitary figure wrapped in a floating robe typical of desert dwellers, with a mask concealing his facial features. His hands were enclosed in gloves and no portion of his skin was visible. When he spoke, it was in fluent English with a trace of an Arabic accent.

"I'm not going to bother spouting rhetoric about how the American government and the American people have interfered in global situations that were not their concern. That is a proven fact. That you have caused the death of many Arabs under the guise of branding all of us terrorists is also a fact. That you befriend the Israeli peoples while their armed forces launch missile raids against civilians in Gaza is merely another fact in a list that is much too long. You have repeatedly stuck your noses where they do not belong. You have caused us to raise our arms against you. You have been the harbinger of your own fate."

The masked figure shifted slightly, a small piece of paper visible in his left hand. "We are the Islamic Front for Justice, an organization that would prefer peaceful means to our ends, but we are also realists. The United States does not recognize such actions, only ones in which your people are threatened. So we must do what is necessary to gain your attention. We have in our possession a large quantity of a hemorrhagic virus that we are ready to release among your population. To date, we have infected four sites in four different ways, just to show you that we are capable of spreading this virus amongst your population if we wish. To prove it was us who inflicted these casualties, we wrote something inside the case of soda that infected the Boy Scouts in Boston." He consulted the piece of paper in his hand.

" 'A small mouse can cause great damage if let loose in the elephant's tent.' "

He closed his hand on the paper and continued. "This recording will be delivered to you on Friday, September sixteenth. You have one week to comply with our demands. At midnight on Friday, September twenty-third, we will begin an all-out assault on the American people. The extent of the damage will be far beyond what you can imagine. Our method of delivering the virus into your population is unstoppable. Once it is released, countless millions will die.

"The death of innocent American citizens is not our primary goal. We have demands which, if met, will cause us to cease this course of actions. Our demands are not unreasonable. First, you will deliver one billion five hundred million U.S. dollars to a location that I will advise you of later. Second, you will release a political prisoner. Just one. His name is Alisama al-Zawami. You are holding him in a secret location in Montreal, Canada. The world thinks al-Zawami is dead, but we know differently. You have kept him captive, without trial, for over two years. It is time for you to release him.

"These demands are not negotiable. If you choose not to deal with us in a civilized manner, we will have no alternative but to inflict incredible casualties on your population. We will be in contact with you again soon, Mr. Rothery."

The screen went black. J. D. Rothery walked across the room and switched on the lights. "How the hell does this guy know about al-Zawami?" he asked the room in general.

No one spoke for a few seconds. Tony Warner asked, "Who is this al-Zawami person?"

Rothery returned to his seat. He glanced at Jim Allenby and Craig Simms, but neither man spoke. "We captured Alisama al-Zawami about twenty-six months ago when we raided an al-Qaeda camp in Afghanistan. It was simply a stroke of incredibly good luck. It was a joint operation with the FBI and the CIA, so Jim and Craig are in the loop on this one. This guy is one of the silent al-Qaeda leaders—not well known, but very intelligent and focused. He isn't as militant as many other al-Qaeda leaders and has even suggested mediation to some problems rather than violence. We consider him to be a highly influential moderate in the al-Qaeda organization."

"Then why would this Islamic Front for Justice want him and only him released?" Warner asked.

"No idea," Rothery said.

"The guy on this DVD sounded more like a moderate than an

extremist," Jim Allenby said. "His tone was conciliatory, like he wanted to negotiate, not just release the virus."

"Perhaps," Rothery said. "I'll have some experts watch the footage and see if they can figure out who this guy is or where he came from. But the bottom line is we still don't negotiate with terrorists."

"But this time you're in a position where you can negotiate without anyone ever knowing," Craig Simms said thoughtfully.

"What do you mean?" Rothery asked.

"These guys have asked for one-point-five billion in cash. That can be done on the sly without causing a lot of ripples. And so far as releasing al-Zawami, no one knows we have him. We could do it quietly, and nobody outside a very small circle would ever know we had met their demands."

"*They* would know," Allenby shot back at the CIA chief. "And they would let every terrorist cell out there know they'd been successful. And that would just open the door to more of the same thing. I'm against giving these bastards the time of day, let alone over a billion dollars and one of their key personnel. Just think of what they could do with one-point-five billion. Christ, they could arm thousands of nutcases, buy state-of-the-art guided-missile systems to use against our fighter jets and airliners, and then, don't forget, they've still got the virus. Who's to say they don't just play this whole scenario out again in a year or two?"

"Jesus, Jim. They're threatening to unleash a plague on the country. Try to keep that in mind. The stakes here are extremely high. This isn't just black and white. It's very gray." Craig Simms's face was red as he glared at his FBI counterpart.

"Keep in mind you're not the only one with a family, Craig," Allenby said icily.

"Okay, enough," Rothery said. "We've got a problem, and now we've got a deadline. We know when they plan to release the virus and we know what their demands are. So right now, we're in a better position than we were an hour ago." He rose and paced about the room. "Straight off the top, this information remains inside this room. There will be no mention of the deadline to the press or to any member of your staff without top-level clearance. Is this clearly understood?" Everyone in the room nodded silently.

"Jim, this is going to fall mostly on yours and my shoulders, as the threat is inside our borders. Craig, we'll be looking for everything you can give us, despite the fact that the CIA is prohibited from using their powers domestically. Tony, get your rocket scientists at Crypto-City to calculate every conceivable method of releasing this virus on a mass scale. Every time you get another new scenario, forward it to Jim's office. Jim, you take the information from NSA and run with it. If they say that the virus could be introduced through contaminated cups at Starbucks, get to the factory that makes the cups and check it out. Nothing falls through the cracks.

"Tony, I want you to follow up with the pharmaceutical companies trying to decode this virus. Especially GlasoKlan. They were the ones who had identified the nucleic acid genome. Stay on top of every advance these research groups make. If we can come up with a method to fight this virus, we've got bargaining power with these guys." He stopped pacing for a moment and turned to Edward Henning. "Dr. Henning, what's your take on all this? How much danger are we in?"

Henning was thoughtful and took a few seconds to choose his words. When he spoke, it was in a clear and concise manner. "We are in very serious trouble, Mr. Under Secretary. If the terrorists are serious about releasing the virus in one week, their method of doing so is probably already in place. It may be too late, even for them, to stop it. And although they appeared quite composed and ready to bargain in good faith, I doubt that is the case. My feeling is that no matter what you do, they're going to release the virus."

The room was absolutely silent.

"In my opinion," Henning said quietly, "you have only one option. Find something to combat this virus."

"And if we can't?" Rothery said.

"Then be prepared for the terrorists to unleash the virus. And be prepared for it to be a lethal dose."

51

Jennifer finished the last of her twenty-five laps in the pool and toweled off. The sun was hot for mid-September and the mercury was static at eighty-nine. Logically, September should be hot; technically, it was still summer until the twenty-first. She wrapped the towel around her waist, walked barefoot back through the lobby, and took the elevator to the fourth floor. Gordon let her in when she knocked.

She dressed and dried her hair, put on a few touches of makeup, and joined Gordon at the small table next to the bed. He was splitting his time between the computer, which was tied in to the Internet, and the television, which was locked on CNN. It was the top of the hour and a serious-looking man in his thirties was giving an update on the biological terrorist threat. Jennifer stood next to Gordon and watched the broadcast with her hand on his shoulder.

"There are conflicting reports as to whether the government task force, headed by J. D. Rothery of the Department of Homeland Security, has actually received demands from a group calling themselves the Islamic Front for Justice. Rothery and his counterparts from the FBI, CIA, and NSA are all denying there has been any communication. But CNN has information that appears to be authentic that indicates Rothery's task force was issued an ultimatum yesterday. The ultimatum contains two as yet unknown demands with a deadline of September twenty-third. If that is true, the government has six days to avert what could become al-Qaeda's deadliest strike against Americans on their own soil. When asked about the ultimatum, Rothery's reply was terse."

Rothery appeared on the screen walking into L'Enfant Plaza. The small printing in the corner read, "Saturday, September 17, 11 A.M.," two hours earlier. Rothery did not stop moving as the reporter asked him about the demands but shot back a barbed reply. "I don't know where you guys are getting your information, but you're going to panic a lot of people for no reason." The camera caught his back as he entered the building and then the screen flashed back to the reporter.

"This is Jason Langen reporting from Washington, D.C."

Gordon set his hand on Jennifer's and they interlocked fingers. "This is getting serious," he said. "That Rothery guy looks pretty stressed."

"He's in the hot seat, all right. I wouldn't want to be him right now."

Gordon turned slightly to face her. "I've been surfing through some of the files on Enron and I've got an idea."

"What's that?" she asked, sitting on his knee.

"The securities commission are the big dogs here. They're the ones who can bite. If we give them what we've got on Veritas, it'll turn the heat on Andrews. He'll be too busy trying to patch things up before the commission begins a formal investigation to worry about us. And once the securities auditors get their noses into the books, Andrews is in serious trouble."

She nodded. "That's an excellent idea. Too bad today is Saturday. We'll have to wait until Monday to call them."

"You think it might cause him some grief?" Gordon asked.

"Absolutely. I can't believe I didn't think of that. Turning the securities commission loose on him is brilliant. Once we've got him on the defensive, we can get whatever information we have on the murders to the police. He's not as likely to try to kill us once we've pointed a very public finger at him. He'd be the prime suspect if we disappeared."

"Okay, that gives us Albert, Kenga, and Wes Connors, who were all murdered. A competent homicide investigator could probably tie each of those murders back to Andrews."

"And add to that we know the murder of that family in Denver is somehow tied to Bruce Andrews. He probably killed that man because he let me live." She felt a shudder up her spine at the thought. She lived and he died. No mercy in Bruce Andrews's books. "God, his whole family is dead."

"He brought that on himself," Gordon said. "If he wasn't involved with Andrews, it would never have happened. He might have been the person who killed Kenga Bakcsi and Albert Rousseau. You'll probably never know how deeply involved he was."

"You're right. Okay, Monday it is. We put a call in to the securities commission and give them everything we've got on Bruce Andrews and Veritas."

Gordon smiled at her enthusiasm. It was good to hear a positive tone in her voice again. "Monday, then," he said.

52

Keith Thompson arrived at J. D. Rothery's office early Sunday morning with a thick file under his arm. His normal cheerful disposition was muted, his face showing more age lines than his thirty-three years should. His Scandinavian heritage showed through in his blond hair and blue eyes, and he wore baggy black pants and a T-shirt, his usual attire for the office. That he had a one-on-one meeting with one of the most influential men in the.Department of Homeland Security meant little to him. What was in his file was all that was on his mind.

Thompson was an expert on cultures and linguistics, a product of the Cognitive and Linguistic Sciences program at Brown University in Providence, Rhode Island. He was widely acknowledged as the school's leading expert on Arabic studies, including nuances in the Arabic language that give clues to the person's origin. He officially worked for the Central Intelligence Agency but was often on loan to the other intelligence-gathering agencies that spent their time trying to keep America a safe place to live. Today he was on loan to DHS.

Rothery glanced up from his desk as Thompson entered. They had met before on a few occasions, and the science and technology chief greeted the linguistics expert with a casual handshake. "Nice haircut," Rothery said. On their previous meetings, Thompson's hair had been shoulder length.

"Kids kept pulling it," he said, sitting in one of the wingback chairs facing Rothery's desk. "And it hurt."

Rothery managed a hint of a smile. "What have you got for me?" he asked.

Thompson shook his head. "This is the weirdest tape I've ever been asked to dissect," he said, withdrawing two copies of a six-page report he had prepared for Rothery. He kept one and handed the other across the desk. "Straight off the top, I have no idea what kind of accent this guy is speaking with. In fact, my guess is that English is his first language."

"What?" Rothery said, looking up from the typed pages. "What are you saying?"

"People of Arabic descent who grow up with their mother tongue have certain intonations and inflections to their speech, just as people who grow up speaking English or French have. This fellow has an Arabic accent, but his speech patterns are that of an English-speaking person who has learned Arabic as a second language, then spent time in that culture, allowing an accent to creep into his speech."

"English was his first language?" Rothery asked. "What the hell does that mean?"

"There are a lot of second- and third-generation Arabs who were born in the United States and raised to speak English, then who learned Arabic later in life. I would suspect our guy is one of those. And by his choice of words, he's an educated man—my guess is a prominent American University."

"He's an American?"

Thompson shrugged. "I can't say for certain what his citizenship is, but my feeling is that he was raised in America. In fact, I'd say he was from the eastern region of the country and schooled at Harvard or some school of similar stature."

Rothery leaned forward, the veins on his forehead throbbing. "Tell me how you know this, Keith."

"The first clue is the word 'rhetoric.' I've never heard an Arab

Jeff Buick

use that particular word. They don't consider their words or their message to be simply rhetoric; they consider them to be the law according to Mohammed. The second word that's totally out of context is 'guise.' That you have caused the death of many Arabs under the guise of branding all of us terrorists is also a fact.'" Thompson read the line from the script. "To the radical Arabs, the Americans are not acting under any sort of guise. They perceive that we act under our own set of rules, with complete disregard for anyone else. We answer only to ourselves, not to the peoples of the world or to God."

Rothery interjected a thought. "But to an Arab sympathizer who was raised in America, that person would see the American involvement in tracking down Arab terrorists as subversive at times. Do what we can to get the bastards, and if a few innocent Arabs are thrown in the mixture, who cares."

"Exactly. Our guy has a definite North American slant to his thinking. Then he uses a triad."

"A what?"

"A triad. That's when you say the same phrase, or portion of a phrase, three times for impact." Again, Thompson consulted the text from the speech. "'You have repeatedly stuck your noses where they do not belong. You have caused us to raise our arms against you. You have been the harbinger of your own fate.'" He looked up from the page. "I've heard Arabs use the same words to hammer home a point, but never with such precision. This guy uses the triad as a polished public speaker would.

"Then he goes on to say that they would prefer a peaceful solution to the issue. Since when does a terrorist cell prepare a major strike against the United States, then tell us they don't want to hurt us? It makes no sense. And there's more. He uses the word 'hemorrhagic' when describing the virus. Most radicals would simply say they are going to unleash a plague on us. 'Plague' is a much more powerful word. And then there's the strangest part of the whole speech."

"What's that?" Rothery asked.

Thompson read from the transcript. " 'First, you will deliver one billion five hundred million U.S. dollars to a location that I will advise you of later.' " He looked up at Rothery.

"So . . ." Rothery said.

"He refers to himself as 'I,' not 'we.' I have never, and I stress never, heard that before. These terrorists are groups of like-minded radicals brought together to achieve a common goal. They don't refer to themselves as 'I.' Never."

"So what have we got on our hands, Keith?"

Thompson sat the file on the table next to the chair. "You've got an American of questionable Arab descent who doesn't want to kill millions of Americans, but who will if you don't meet his demands. He's ready to do it, of that I'm sure. But capitulate to his two conditions and I think this guy will back off."

"You keep referring to him as 'this guy.' You think it's just one person?"

"God, no. He's got a network of some sort in place, but I don't think it's a cohesive terrorist cell in the sense that we're used to. In this case, he's in charge and the rest of the members of the cell are subservient."

"How do we catch him?"

"That's tough. He's going to be completely invisible. He grew up in America, he's well educated, and he can probably blend in to almost any setting. He has resources at his command and is well organized. Personally, given the time frames he's got you under, I don't think you *can* find him. I think he's got you. And he's given you the opportunity to meet his demands without the American public ever finding out you acquiesced."

"So he's smart."

"Extremely."

Rothery steepled his fingers and gave Keith Thompson a long, hard look. Finally, he said, "Okay, Keith, thanks for the quick work. You've done an excellent job." He stood up and offered his hand.

"Good luck, sir," Thompson said as he left.

Rothery walked to his window and looked out over the na-

Jeff Buick

tion's capital. The Sunday-morning traffic on Seventh Street was light. People sleeping in, going to church, spending time with their families. Normal things to do on a Sunday. But what would next Sunday bring? And the Sunday after that? If the virus was released in six days, by next Sunday morning, innocent people would be infected. And by the following Sunday, they would be dead. And countless more people would be infected.

Somewhere out there was a single person with enough hatred to put this scenario in motion. And that person was American. And invisible. Christ, this whole thing was spiraling out of control. And as things stood right now, he had almost nothing to work with.

Jim Allenby had initiated a cohesive effort within the FBI and had freed up agents for the sole purpose of working the virus crisis. The new information from Keith Thompson would be a boon to Allenby's task force. At least they now knew that the man they were searching for was an American of Arab descent. And one with resources. The list would be long and the hunt arduous, but now they had a target.

Craig Simms was still livid over his organization's losing the clandestine intel the labs had been providing. But the CIA had taken its kicks and survived in the past, and they would do so again. Simms was monitoring all international communications between known terrorist organizations, listening for something that might point them to the source of the virus. Now, with Thompson's take on the DVD footage, Simms would have to realign his agents.

And Tony Warner and his staff over at the National Security Agency were suddenly of great importance. The scientists at Crypto-City were without peer when it came to deciphering codes and sorting data. Given the profile, they could search the nation's data banks for possible suspects and forward that information to Jim Allenby at the Bureau.

As Rothery reached for the phone to call together the key personnel in his task force, he had one thought. Maybe, just maybe, things weren't as bleak as they seemed.

It was a big maybe.

266

53

They met at a roadside turnoff six miles from the entrance to Bruce Andrews's estate. It was getting on toward late afternoon on Sunday, and traffic on the secondary road was slightly higher than usual, many motorists heading back into Richmond after a weekend in the country. Trucks and cars whizzed by, unaware of who was meeting at the rest stop or why. Had they known, most would have taken more than just a passing interest in the conversation.

"How did Buchanan get to Richmond?" Bruce Andrews asked the other man as they walked slowly through the deserted parking lot.

"As I suspected, he chartered a plane, a Lear 31A. He paid up front for three days but called as the deadline was approaching and paid for another week. Obviously, he wants air transportation nearby and ready in case he needs it."

"Where did the call to extend the charter on the plane come from?"

"Somewhere in Richmond. They're not sure."

"What about call display? The charter company doesn't subscribe to it?" Andrews asked.

"Yes, they do. But Buchanan called from a pay phone. Somewhere in northwest Richmond. He probably traveled a ways from wherever he's staying just to use the phone. For a rank amateur, this guy is no dummy."

A cloud drifted across the sun's path and the ground darkened with its arrival. The intense heat diminished and a cool breeze accompanied the respite. Both men were dressed in khakis and short-sleeved shirts, and the shade felt good. Another car pulled into the rest area and stopped a hundred feet farther along the parking lot. Well out of earshot. Three kids piled out of the car and made a beeline for the grassy expanse bordering the parking lot. The parents walked slowly to one of the seven anchored picnic tables and sat down, the father lighting a cigarette and watching the kids as they played.

"Everything else okay?" Andrews asked.

"Busy but fine. We're exactly where we want to be."

"Good. Do you have time to take care of Buchanan if he sticks his head up?"

"I'll have to. Who else have you got? Ziegler is out of commission."

A perturbed look crossed Andrews's face. "That was stupid. You didn't have to slaughter them. You could have killed them and dumped their bodies in some remote mountain gorge. The local bears and wolves would have picked the bones over long before hikers would have found them. That was really dumb."

Andrews's associate didn't look amused at being chastised. "You take care of things on your end, I'll take care of things on mine. And if I want to have a little fun while I work, well, so be it."

"Fun is gutting that woman and slicing the kid's throat right to the bone? Jesus, you are one sick son of a bitch."

"Keep that in mind," he said.

Andrews ignored the remark. He sat on one of the wooden posts that delineated the parking lot from the surrounding grassy area. The father finished his cigarette and returned to the car, the three kids in tow. A puff of exhaust accompanied the ignition's turning over; a quick flash of the brake lights and the car pulled back into the traffic. The area was deserted again. The cloud passed and the sun returned, its rays hot and unwelcome. "I want them dead," he said.

"Who? Buchanan and Pearce?"

"Yes."

"I'm busy, Bruce. I have to be careful right now."

"That's fine. Just find them and kill them. But this time, don't have quite as much fun as you did in Denver. Just find them, kill them, and dump their bodies somewhere remote or anchor them down and sink them under water. Nothing too difficult. Not for someone with your resources."

"All right. I'll find them and shut them up. But right now they're second on the priority list."

"Of course. Priorities are important right now," Andrews said. He walked to his car, got in, and adjusted the air-conditioning. The man was irreplaceable. He could never hope to achieve his goals without his help. But to that end, his partner was being paid well. Very well. And that often elicited the highest degree of loyalty. Right now, loyalty was crucial.

He pulled out of the rest stop and headed home. Sunday night. Tomorrow was going to be a very busy day. And a very profitable one.

54

Gordon chose anonymity over speed, and they left the Lear sitting in mothballs at Byrd Field and drove north to Washington first thing Monday morning. By nine o'clock, they were sitting in the reception area of the headquarters of the U.S. Securities and Exchange Commission. After fifteen minutes, a well-dressed, trim woman in her early fifties approached them. Her hair was graying and age lines were beginning to take their toll on her features, but her eyes were lively and she moved with alacrity.

"Are you Gordon Buchanan and Jennifer Pearce?" she asked in a pleasant voice.

"Yes," Gordon replied, rising from the leather couch.

"I'm Elizabeth Ripley," she said, shaking both their hands. "You asked to see someone about an alleged accounting fraud by a publicly traded company?"

"Yes."

"Fine, let's go to my office." She led the way through a series of richly appointed offices and boardrooms until they reached a midsized office with her name on the door. They entered, and she closed the door behind them before sitting down. "What is the nature of your complaint?"

They had decided Jennifer would speak, as she was best versed in the method and extent of the fraud. "I work for Veritas Pharmaceutical . . ."

Ten minutes later, the SEC investigator looked up from the notes she had taken while Jennifer talked. "These are very serious allegations, Ms. Pearce," she said. "If true, the accounting differences would total into the hundreds of millions of dollars."

"I know," Jennifer said. "We're both very aware of how serious this is." She paused for a moment. "Now that you have the information, how do you proceed?"

Ripley laid her reading glasses on her desk and reclined in her chair. "It's complicated, Ms. Pearce. We're a small organization by government standards—we manage to get by with just over three thousand staff in eighteen regional offices. So our resources are spread a little thin. That said, when we get a complaint of this caliber—and by that I mean from someone working at the company with access to its financial records—we take it very seriously. And we're not toothless. We bring up to five hundred civil actions against corporations or individuals every year."

"Civil actions?" Jennifer asked. "Not criminal?"

She shook her head. "No, we don't have criminal enforcement authority. But we manage the investigation: interview witnesses, conduct forensic audits, review brokerage records, and carefully check trading practices. Once we have something to run with, we bring in the appropriate criminal authorities. If the criminal activity has crossed state boundaries, the FBI is often given jurisdiction. Sometimes it's the local police, if the crime was committed in a city where the police have a department capable of handling the investigation. And we work very closely with Congress, all the stock exchange houses and especially the state securities regulators. Not much gets by us once we're on it, Ms. Pearce."

"What sort of time frames are we looking at, Ms. Ripley?" Jennifer asked.

She glanced at her notes. "I'd like a couple of days to review the year-end financials Veritas has filed over the past few years. And I'll need to confirm with the appropriate departments inside the government that Veritas has been utilizing the tax-credit program in the manner you've suggested they are. I would say the earliest we could meet again would be in about a week's time. And that is placing it in the highest priority."

"So this is not a quick process," Gordon said.

"Not in the least. We've got to be sure, Mr. Buchanan. And whatever we find in the next couple of weeks will have to then go through the Office of the Chief Accountant. They're the ones who order and perform the necessary audits."

"Damn it," Jennifer said under her breath.

Elizabeth Ripley looked concerned. "What's wrong, Ms. Pearce? Why is time so important a factor for you?"

Jennifer glanced over at Gordon and he gave her a slight nod. She looked back to the securities investigator. "Everything we've told you so far this morning is entirely accurate and can be backed up with a forensic audit. But there's more." She hesitated, knowing the next few sentences were going to sound crazy. "With very good reason, we suspect one or more of the top executives at Veritas is responsible for at least two murders."

Elizabeth Ripley did not laugh. The lines around her mouth drew tight and she sat forward in her chair. "What makes you think that, Ms. Pearce?"

The immediate and serious reaction from the SEC woman was not what Jennifer had envisioned. She swallowed and continued. "One of my research assistants, Kenga Bakcsi, was murdered while on holiday in the Caribbean. She had been supplying Mr. Buchanan with information on one of our drugs. Another employee, Albert Rousseau, was killed when his gas stove exploded. He had proof in a floor safe in his condominium that one of Veritas's drugs was dangerous. And late last Tuesday, I was abducted from my house in Richmond, driven into the Shenandoah Mountains, and left teetering over a cliff. If Gordon hadn't rescued me, I would also be dead. And the man who left me there was the one whose family was murdered in Denver a few days ago. It was on all the news stations."

"I saw it," Ripley said. She toyed with her pen for a moment. "Who do you think is responsible? And I realize you're only speculating at this time."

"We have good reason to think the company's CEO, Bruce Andrews, is the man behind all this."

Gordon cleared his throat. "You seem to be taking this a little more seriously than we thought you might."

The intensity in Elizabeth Ripley's eyes was almost frightening. "I've been doing this for a few years, and you are not the first people to sit across that desk fearful for your lives. Individuals who are willing to commit fraud on a large scale are often willing to protect their indiscretions." She leaned back in her chair and glanced out the window at the D.C. skyline. "A few years ago, I had a young woman, perhaps thirty, come in my office and offer information about a fraud inside her company. She told me that the man who was responsible was acting in a threatening manner. I told her I would do everything I could and sent her home. She showed up in the Potomac River eight days later. She had three children. So you see, when people come to me of their own free will with tips of insider trading or accounting fraud, I take them seriously. When they tell me they fear for their lives, I take them extremely seriously."

"Thank you for that," Jennifer said.

"I'm going to fast-track this file," Ripley said. "I'll schedule a meeting with the chief accountant for this afternoon. We'll subpoena financial records from the government department that handles the tax credits and have the information on our desks within forty-eight hours. We'll know in four days—by Friday, next Monday at the latest—whether we can proceed against Veritas. That's the best I can do."

"That's good enough," Jennifer said. "Thank you."

Elizabeth Ripley walked them to the reception area, wished them the best, and shook their hands. She disappeared back into the labyrinth of offices before the elevator arrived. They rode the sixteen floors in silence. Once on the street, they picked up the rental car from the parking lot and headed back toward Richmond. The meeting had gone well—extremely well, in fact—but lingering in both their minds was one burning question.

Could they survive until the securities commission removed Bruce Andrews from power?

55

"What have you got?" J. D. Rothery asked eagerly.

"We're pretty sure we've located the lab," Craig Simms said. He unrolled a large map onto the table. Jim Allenby, Tony Warner, and Rothery crowded around the table in the Under Secretary's office. It was just after twelve noon on Monday, September 19. The map Simms had spread out depicted Orlando, Florida.

"The building in question is a warehouse, zoned for industrial painting, located here, on Dowden Road in south Orlando." He stabbed at the map, then overlaid another plat, this one showing the industrial district of Taft in greater detail. "The warehouse is one bay in a series of six, all connected together. They share the same gas lines, water lines, and sewer network. Ventilation systems are independent, and this one has quite the setup from what we can see." He dropped another sheet of paper atop the township plat. It showed the same building, but the picture had been taken with a heat-sensitive camera. The end bay on the east side was glowing in five concentrated areas. "These five hot spots are HEPA filters. All are fully functional and capable of filtering the air to less than one one-

275

thousandth of a micron. Total overkill for what the business would require."

"You said it's zoned for industrial painting? Don't those businesses need good ventilation?" Rothery asked.

"Good ventilation, yes. HEPA filters, no. These filters run about two hundred grand each, and they're mostly used for work in clean environments, like manufacturing plants for silicon chips and medical research."

"A million dollars in filtration systems on a single industrial bay," Jim Allenby said. "It definitely seems like overkill."

Simms nodded. "The building owner is this man, Ismail Zehaden." He produced a handful of black-and-white photos of a fifty-something man of Arabic descent with gaunt cheeks and a long, slender nose. His hair, cut about halfway over his ears, was thick and dark, with touches of gray. The eyes were steely and penetrating. "He's been in the United States for thirty-nine of his fifty-one years. Spent his first twelve years in Bandar-e 'Abbās, a port city in Iran across the Strait of Hormuz from Oman. His father worked in the oil industry in Qatar and Oman as a well-site geologist. They emigrated to the United States in 1966. Lived in Houston for ten years, where the father worked for Exxon as a geologist in the production and exploitation division. By the looks of things, the family appeared quite normal while they were in Houston.

"Ismail, who now goes by Sam, was the middle of three boys. He was accepted to and graduated from MIT, with a degree in electrical engineering. In 1992, he moved to Orlando and started a high-tech company that manufactured guidance systems for surface-to-air missiles. The company name is Istal Technology, probably named after his father, whose name was also Istal. Most of his office and lab space is on Sand Lake Road, adjacent to Martin Marietta's research facilities."

"Do they sell to Martin Marietta?" Rothery asked.

"Yes. That's Istal's main client."

"Then it makes sense for them to have office and lab space next to Martin Marietta. But why in Taft? And why an industrial bay zoned for painting?"

"We suspect it's a cover for the ventilation systems, J. D.," Simms said. "Nobody says boo when a company that sprays anything toxic puts adequate ventilation in place. That just makes them a good corporate citizen."

"All right, we know who Sam Zehaden is, but why is he intent on killing millions of people in the country he's called home for almost forty years?"

"There was an incident about eleven years ago that seemed to change him. Three of his uncles and one aunt were in the wrong place at the wrong time. They were in a restaurant in Shirāz, a moderate-size city in central Iran, when the place was blown to bits by a smart bomb."

"What?" Rothery said. "What the hell happened?"

"The rear of the restaurant was being used as a meeting place for an al-Qaeda faction. The Israelis had good intel that there was to be a high-level meeting on that day at that time, and they hit the building with one perfectly placed bomb. Totally destroyed the restaurant, killing six staff, twelve diners, and an unknown number of terrorists. But it would appear the damage was done. Sam Zehaden blamed the United States, his own country, for sanctioning the Israeli attack."

"Is there any proof he turned?" Allenby asked.

"He began traveling to Iran on a regular basis. He was seen in the vicinity of known al-Qaeda members and started sending money back to Iran. Prior to his relatives' deaths, he had been quite visible in the community, supporting the local children's hospital and numerous other charities, but after the incident he dropped out of sight. Went off the radar."

"That's all good stuff, but why do you think the lab is in that building?" Rothery asked.

"We had a call from a citizen about the HEPA filters. She's a nurse in a local hospital and knows what constitutes necessary filtration. She figures that in its current state, that particular bay is at about a BioLevel Four status. That and the timing. The filtration systems were moved in the last week in August. My biological experts have calculated the amount of time needed to produce a quantity of virus that could constitute a major threat at about three weeks. Today is September nineteenth, J. D. The timing is perfect."

"How reliable is your source?" Rothery asked.

"First class," Simms said. "We can't identify her at this time. That was part of the deal. She's scared shitless that if Zehaden is indeed al-Qaeda, someone will come looking for her after the fact. We guaranteed her anonymity, but it didn't help. She wants her name kept out of it."

"One more question, Craig," Rothery said. "How does the CIA know so much about Sam Zehaden? He lives inside our borders, a place your powers as an agency do not extend to."

"We picked up on this guy when he started to visit Iran on a regular basis. It was prudent to follow up on his activities, even if that meant keeping a file open on him while he was at home."

Rothery nodded. He turned to Jim Allenby. "What do you think, Jim? This is going to be your operation. You think it warrants action?"

Allenby was silent, weighing the facts. Finally, he said, "The upside definitely outweighs the downside. If we miss, we haven't really lost anything. We're just doing our job. But if we get lucky, we're saviors. If this warehouse is the lab, we've ended an extremely serious crisis before the terrorists could strike. Not only will that bolster the confidence of the average American, it will send a firm message to other terrorist cells. I think we should move on it, J. D."

"Okay," Rothery said. "Do you want to coordinate it, Jim?"

"Sure, but I'll want some SWAT backup as well. I'll contact the Orlando PD and set it up. I'll have everything in place for early tomorrow morning."

"Tony, you okay with this?" Rothery asked the NSA man, who to this juncture had been quiet.

"I think it looks good."

Rothery leaned back from the table with the maps and crossed his arms on his chest. "All right, gentlemen. You've got the green light. Let's shut this operation down. And let's keep our fingers crossed that this is it."

56

Things just kept getting better.

At two o'clock on Monday, September 19, less than two hours after the viral task force had met, J. D. Rothery received a call from Tony Warner at the National Security Agency. The news was beyond belief. "One of the pharmaceutical giants has discovered a drug that inhibits the virus from attaching to host cells. And while searching for the inhibitors, they uncovered a drug that appears to inhibit viral genome replication," Warner said.

"What the hell does that mean?" Rothery asked Warner.

Tony Warner was so excited that he couldn't keep his voice from quivering as he spoke. "They've decoded the virus, J. D. They have a drug that targets the synthesis of viral polymerases. Even once the virus is in the body, this drug can immediately stop its progress. They've got the cure."

"How sure are you of this?" J. D. asked, his breath coming quicker now. *Jesus, tell me they're positive they've nailed this thing.*

"Ninety-nine-point-nine percent, J.D. The CEO and his leading researcher are ready to fly up to D.C. and meet with you. Initial tests are absolutely definitive. Their drug stopped the virus from encoding. And without genome replication, the virus is dead in the water."

"Fantastic," Rothery said, wiping his brow, surprised at the wetness on his hand. "Get them up here now."

"Yeah, boss."

"By the way, Tony, who did it? Which company?"

"Veritas Pharmaceutical. The guy you'll be meeting with is Bruce Andrews—he's the CEO. His lead researcher on this is Dr. Chiang Wai."

"Tony, you are the man."

"I'm the man, J. D.," Warner said, and hung up.

Rothery stood on wobbly legs and walked to the window. Was this really happening? Were they cutting the threat off at the knees? If Jim Allenby and the SWAT team were successful in locating and shutting down the lab in Orlando and Veritas had the cure to the disease, they were out of the woods. What had appeared to be the mother of all terrorist threats was about to fizzle out. He leaned against the windowsill as he felt his knees buckle. God almighty, the American people had lived through enough of this crap, and they didn't need any more. And maybe that's who was behind the sudden surge of luck. Maybe there was a God and He *was* watching. Maybe He was sick of the horror these radicals inflicted on innocent people and He decided that enough was enough. Perhaps the answers had come from a higher place than the White House or the Pentagon this time. Maybe they had come from Him.

Andrews and Wai arrived at ten minutes to seven in the evening and were ushered directly into the Under Secretary's office. Craig Simms and Tony Warner were present. Jim Allenby was in Orlando, coordinating the raid set for seven o'clock the next morning. Allenby had insisted on having the proper containment equipment on hand when the raid went down, and that equipment took time to assemble. The three remaining members of the Viral Task Force, as the press had dubbed them, were waiting for Andrews and Wai, and all three rose and hook hands when the researchers arrived. They retook their seats and Rothery directed his first question to Bruce Andrews.

"How sure are you that you've got this thing beat?" he asked.

"We were at about ninety-five percent last night, Mr. Under Secretary," Andrews replied. "But today we're at a hundred percent. We are positive we have a drug that will stop the virus once it's in the body." Andrews accepted the coffee that was being distributed and continued. "Would you like me to explain? My English is probably a bit better than Dr. Wai's."

"Please," Rothery said.

"When we were given the sample of the virus, we immediately attacked the problem by looking at the viral inhibitor. We got lucky. Really lucky. We used a computer model based on the virus and cross-correlated that to the fusion-peptide exposed when the gp41 protein binds and its cellular receptors mutate. It took a few hundred thousand models to get the one we wanted, but where we got lucky was that we started out on the right track. And with the supercomputers we have at Veritas, the modeling was done in one one-millionth of the time it would have taken by conventional methods."

"What made you decide to take the approach you did?" Rothery asked.

"We've had an antiviral drug sitting on the sidelines for about thirteen months now, waiting for FDA approval. We thought the base structure of that drug may have some bearing here, and we were right. Essentially, the drug we have to combat the virus is almost exactly the same as the drug we had ready for FDA approval. We needed to test it, of course, and that we've done. We are positive we have the drug to stop this virus."

"Would your drug work on Ebola as well?" Rothery asked. "I understand this virus is quite similar to Ebola."

"Similar in some aspects and very different in others. They are both hemorrhagic viruses, but their cellular structure is not at all the same. This drug cannot stop Ebola."

"Well, what's important right now is that we've got a cure for the disease once it's been contracted." Rothery turned to the

Jeff Buick

researcher who had accompanied Bruce Andrews to the meeting. "Do you concur, Dr. Wai? Do we have a cure?"

"Yes," Dr. Wai said. "That's what we have."

"Excellent. Then let's get our teams working together to get the drug out of the labs and into the hands of emergency rooms and public and private clinics across the country. How long will it take you to move into a production stage, Mr. Andrews?"

Andrews scratched his chin thoughtfully. "We've got a hurdle to cross before we can get to that point, Mr. Rothery."

Rothery's smile immediately disappeared. "What hurdle?" he asked. His voice was anxious.

"It's nothing that will hold us up, but it's something that must be done. Veritas cannot bring a drug to market without FDA approval. We will not allow even one pill outside our labs until the FDA stamps their approval on our technology."

"Why hasn't that happened already?" Rothery asked.

"We're stuck in the NDA stage. That's the New Drug Application. We submitted our application complete with all our clinical trials about a year ago. We've been held up by red tape ever since."

"Why?" Rothery asked. "Is there something wrong with the drug?"

Andrews shook his head. "Nothing that would make it stand out among all the other drugs on the market these days. There are side effects, but every drug has some sort of downside. Zancor is no different."

"Zancor?"

"That's the trade name for this drug. When it hits the shelves, that's what retail customers will ask for, like Viagra or Accutane."

"What can we do to get FDA approval?" Rothery asked.

Andrews shrugged. "I don't know. We've been dealing with one of their lead investigators, Barry Flath, since we first filed for an NDA. He's the guy you should talk to."

"I'll call him," Tony Warner said. "I've met Barry a few times at professional functions. He's not a bad guy." He turned to Rothery. "I'll get him to contact you if he's got any problems with issuing an approval on short notice. These are extenuating circumstances. He'll come around."

"Get him to come around quickly, Tony," Rothery said. "We need that drug."

57

By six-twelve, the sun was peeking over the eastern regions of Orlando. Streetlamps on timers switched off and traffic lights reverted back from in-ground sensors to timed operations. City crews pulled out of the lots and the first morning flights readied for departure at Orlando International. All in all, it was just another normal Tuesday morning in the city that was host to Walt Disney World. Everywhere except on a quiet stretch of Dowden Road.

Sixty-four law-enforcement officers, forty-one from the Orlando PD and twenty-three FBI agents, were in position and waiting for the word from Jim Allenby, who was directly across the street on the second floor of a similar industrial warehouse. At six-seventeen, Allenby had the two-way radio in his hand and was preparing to give the order when a Cadillac Escalade pulled into the parking lot and parked directly in front of the access door to the bay. A solitary figure was in the car. The backup lights flashed as the driver shifted the SUV into park, and a second later the door opened. Ismail Zehaden exited the vehicle.

"Everyone hold your positions," Allenby said. "Our guy just showed up. Let's wait for him to get inside."

Zehaden glanced about, walked to the main door, fumbled with his keys, opened the door, and entered the warehouse. A light went on in the front office and Allenby watched as Zehaden moved through the open space to the door that led to the rear of the bay. He opened the door and disappeared from view.

"All units go," Allenby said. "And be advised we have one hostile in the rear of the building."

Seven vehicles appeared in the next few seconds. Dark Bureau cars filled with FBI agents, marked Orlando police cars, and a SWAT van careened into position outside the front of the building and men poured from the vehicles, moving quickly into the target bay. Allenby's radio squawked and a voice came across the air informing him that the second team was moving into the rear of the building. He left his listening post and scrambled down the stairs. As he ran across the street, the reports came over the walkie-talkie. The building was secure, Ismail Zehaden in custody. He raced through the front door, crossed the office space, and entered the rear of the building.

Against the far side of the industrial bay was a series of five glass-enclosed tables, each one covered with radically differing types of glassware and three Acculab scales. A number of polarizing microscopes lined one table and two Eberbach shakers and a Turner spectrophotometer were among the highly technical electronic equipment. A HEPA filter was attached to each of the five glass structures. Adjacent to the five enclosed labs was a series of unprotected tables, some piled with black containers about one cubic foot each. Standing alone and in front of one of the tables was Ismail Zehaden. At least thirty guns were trained on the man.

"Ismail Zehaden?" Allenby asked as he walked into the open area between the SWAT troops and FBI agents and the terrorist.

"Yes, I am Ismail Zehaden," the man said. "What is going on here?"

Jeff Buick

"Good question," Allenby said. "What's with all the equipment?"

Zehaden glanced over his shoulder at the lab, then back to Allenby. "I have no idea. I've never seen this stuff before."

"Do you own this warehouse?" Allenby asked.

"Yes."

"Then who else would have set up this operation?"

The man's response was angry. "I don't know. I have nothing to do with any of this. And I want your men to stop pointing their guns at me immediately."

"What you want is quite unimportant right now," Allenby said. "Step away from the table."

"What is all this stuff?" Zehaden said. "I demand to know what the hell is going on."

"Step away from the table," Allenby said. "Now."

"I'm not moving until someone tells me what this is all about." Zehaden turned and looked over the containers piled on the table behind him. "Where did all this equipment come from?"

"Mr. Zehaden, it's imperative you move away from that table and put your hands over your head immediately."

Zehaden reached over and made a motion to pick up one of the containers. Allenby yelled for him to stop, but the man was intent on grabbing the closest box.

"It could contain the virus," Allenby yelled. "Don't let him pick it up."

There was only one option open to the SWAT team. No one could get to Zehaden before he reached the containers. At least ten SWAT team members opened fire simultaneously, each with a single killing shot. Zehaden took every bullet in the chest, his body jerking spasmodically as the slugs tore through his flesh and ripped into his heart and lungs. The shots came from different angles, pushing his body one way then the other, the impacts canceling each other. The net result was a corpse, still standing where a live person had stood two seconds before. The gunfire, which sounded almost like a single shot, diminished and the echoes inside the warehouse died out. For another second or two, Zehaden remained upright, then gravity went to work and he collapsed in a bloody heap a couple of feet from the table with the containers.

Allenby was the first agent to reach the body. He stared down at the Arab with disgust and gave the corpse a nudge with the toe of his shoe. There was no movement. Blood was spreading out on the concrete, and he moved back so the thick brown liquid didn't soil his shoes.

"Secure the area," he said to the leader of the SWAT team. He turned to his second in command. "Get the experts in here and let's find out if we've got the right place. I want to know if the virus is here, and if it is, in what quantity."

"Yes, sir," the agent said.

Allenby let his eyes run over the glass-enclosed lab. The operation was definitely high-tech. The tables were polished steel, with solid tubular legs and one stainless-steel chair in each enclosure. The equipment was clean and well organized, with rows upon rows of tubes and beakers, culture dishes, and state-of-the-art centrifuges. Including the HEPA filters, millions of dollars in hardware.

Millions of dollars spent with one goal in mind. To kill innocent people.

Jim Allenby turned his back on the scene and walked out. His people could clean up. He would wait for the experts to determine whether they had the right lab, then he would make a phone call. And right now, one man sat next to his phone in L'Enfant Plaza, wondering when that call would come, and when it did, what would be the news.

58

He was expecting the call, but when it came, he hesitated before picking up the phone. The next few seconds were crucial. The country was embroiled in severe crisis, fighting a horrific disease with a new wonder drug, but would they still be wondering where the production facilities were or would they know? That was the question this call would answer. Slowly, he closed his hand on the phone and lifted it to his ear.

"Rothery," he said. At least to him, his voice sounded weak.

"We got it," Jim Allenby said. "We got the lab, J. D."

Rothery let out a long breath. "Are you sure, Jim?" he asked.

"Positive. The CDC guys are all over it. They've identified traces of the virus and have confirmed that the setup is correct for viral production. They've quarantined the building and will be dismantling the operation and moving it to the U.S. Army Medical Research Institute of Infectious Diseases at Fort Detrick. They'll put it in storage and keep it for evidence. Not that we'll be pressing charges against Ismail Zehaden."

"Why not?" Rothery asked.

"Zehaden showed up just as we were getting ready to go in.

He made a move for a container we thought may contain the virus. The SWAT team took him out."

"He's dead?"

"Very. Took at least ten bullets to the chest."

"Okay, it shouldn't be hard to sell that to the general public. This guy is ready to dump a ton of lethal virus on us, and when we catch him in the lab we shoot him. Pretty cut-and-dried."

"Yeah," Allenby said. "But we do have one small problem, J. D."

Rothery stiffened. Jim Allenby didn't play stupid games. Something was wrong. "What is it, Jim?"

"There's no stockpile of virus in the lab. Whatever was manufactured here has been moved."

"Christ Almighty," Rothery said. "So whatever plan Zehaden had in mind could potentially still play out. He's sure to have other members inside his cell that are responsible for getting the virus out into the community."

"I would think so."

"Jim, get every man and woman you have on this. Find out what's been going on around the warehouse in the last couple of weeks. Have there been delivery trucks, unmarked half-tons, or vans pulling in or out? Was there more human activity than normal? Were they working odd hours? Whatever. Find out if anyone noticed anything. We need to find out where that virus went."

"Yes, sir," Allenby said. "I've got a full contingent of agents with me. We're already on it."

"Thanks, Jim," Rothery said, hanging up the phone. He hit the intercom button and his receptionist came on the speaker-phone. "Get me Barry Flath at the Food and Drug Administration." He was getting impatient waiting for Tony Warner to get back to him with the results of his conversation with the FDA employee. Less than two minutes later, the phone buzzed.

"Barry Flath on line two, sir."

"Barry," Rothery said. "How are you this morning?"

"Well, thank you," Flath said. "How can I help you, Mr. Rothery?"

"How are things going on approving Zancor?"

"I have a problem with that, Mr. Rothery. I've already discussed this with Tony Warner."

"What problem?" Rothery asked. The ice in his voice could have frozen the fiber-optic cable that connected the two men.

"Well, there are side effects to the drug that concern me. I'm not going to get technical with you, sir, but they can be quite serious at times."

"Bruce Andrews at Veritas has indicated that many of the drugs the FDA has approved have serious side effects. Is that true?"

"Well, yes, I suppose. But we measure things by evaluating the benefits of the drug as they relate to the downside. Zancor is, in my opinion, not worthy of FDA approval. The benefits don't outweigh the corresponding side effects."

"Listen to me very closely, Barry. Unless Zancor kills people outright, the benefits now far outweigh whatever the side effects are. This drug is necessary to stop the spread of a hemorrhagic virus that could be released in two days. I want the approval, Barry, and I want it today."

"This is highly irregular, Mr. Rothery," Flath said. "I'm not used to being threatened."

"Well, Barry, get used to it. If you don't approve Zancor and people start to die because the cure is tied up in red tape, I'll make sure the entire world knows it was you who refused to okay the drug that could have stopped the virus in its tracks. You will be the most hated man in America, and a hero to al-Qaeda."

"These threats are not necessary, Mr. Rothery."

"Then what is?"

"I'm just concerned that once I approve this drug, it will become a household name and some people will suffer. I'm not kidding when I say there is a real downside to this medication. And if this hits the shelves, it will be widely used."

"So just pull the approval down the road. You guys recall drugs all the time."

"Recalls are not that simple, Mr. Rothery. "We need definitive proof that a drug is dangerous. And with the side effects that Zancor causes, that may be hard to prove."

"Jesus, Barry, you're all over the map. First you say it's dangerous, now you tell me you won't be able to prove it's dangerous."

"If you have the time, I can explain it to you, but it's complicated. Zancor is an antiviral medicine, and patients only take the meds when they're sick or have an infection. It's like Cipro, the Bayer Pharmaceuticals antibacterial drug that was so effective against the anthrax scare of 2003. Three hundred million people have taken Cipro, but none of those users have taken the drug long-term. So does Cipro have a downside? We don't think so, but without a test group who are on the meds for a long time, it's difficult to say. And that's the problem we'll run into with Zancor, except we know it has some ugly side effects."

"I appreciate the explanation, Mr. Flath, but I'm running out of time. I have a press conference set for just after nine o'clock this morning. That's in about ten minutes. I need an answer right now."

There was dead air on the phone for at least thirty seconds. Finally, Barry Flath said, "All right, Mr. Rothery, you've got your approval. I'll have the paperwork completed and sent over to Veritas by noon today."

"Thank you, Barry. And could you please send a copy of that approval to my office as well?"

"Yes, sir." The line died a quick death.

Rothery punched the intercom button again. "Are the guys from Veritas here?" he asked.

"Yes, Mr. Rothery."

"I'll be right out. Call down and let the press know we're on our way."

"Yes, sir."

Rothery tidied up his desk, which entailed pushing one piece of paper to the side. He stared at the polished wood, then around the office. He had worked so hard for so long to achieve this position. And now he had proved to the nation that when the forest was on fire, he was the guy to douse it. He had put together a cohesive team that had checked their egos at the door and brought the resources of their respective agencies to the table. Through interagency cooperation on the highest level, they had found the source of the virus and had stimulated the private sector to find a cure. Christ, he couldn't have orchestrated a better outcome if he had tried. He checked his watch. Nine o'clock. Time to face the press.

He met Bruce Andrews and Dr. Chiang Wai in the reception area and the three of them proceeded down to the press-release room. Andrews just nodded that he understood when informed that FDA approval was immediately forthcoming on the new drug.

"That's good news, Mr. Under Secretary," Andrews said. "We'll begin production without delay."

"Excellent. Coordinate the release of the drugs through Tony Warner over at NSA. They've got a great network in place. Let's make use of it. You can bill his agency for the cost of the drugs, and I'll have him forward that to the appropriate department afterward."

"Yes, sir," Andrews said. They reached the elevator, and as they waited for it to arrive on their floor, Andrews asked, "What are we going to say at the press conference?"

Rothery smiled. "You and Dr. Wai are going to tell the nation that you've beat this thing. You've discovered a cure, and that the threat from the virus is almost nonexistent. You may want to mention what some of the early symptoms are, in case the terrorists manage to release the virus. That way anyone who is infected can get to the nearest medical center quickly."

"I understand," Andrews said.

The elevator doors opened and the three men moved inside. The doors closed and the elevator headed down to the main floor to where the press waited. An entire nation waited for the elevator. They waited by their television sets to hear what J. D. Rothery had to say. And today, the American people had some good news coming their way.

59

The news conference was a highly anticipated event. Rothery had readied the media and the American people for news of some substance. The cat was long since out of the bag, and it was common knowledge that an unknown terrorist cell, with suspected ties to al-Qaeda, had a deadly virus they were threatening to unleash on the United States.

Gordon and Jennifer were seated in the restaurant at the Fairfield Inn watching CNN, and when the Under Secretary of the Department of Homeland Defense strode into the press room and took the podium, the restaurant manager turned up the volume. A hush fell over the diners as Rothery shuffled a couple of papers about.

"What do you think he's going to say?" Gordon asked Jennifer, stirring some cream into his coffee.

She shrugged. "They're dealing with a hemorrhagic virus, Gordon. I'd be surprised if they've made any headway."

"We have some good news to report this morning," Rothery said, looking up from his notes into the camera. "This morning at 0630 hours, a task force consisting of FBI agents and Orlando Police Department SWAT teams raided an industrial bay near the Orlando International Airport. Inside the building was a fully functional laboratory, designed to produce the hemorrhagic virus that has been threatening our country. The building, identified as a target due to the large number of highly sophisticated HEPA filters that were found on-site, is owned by an American citizen, Ismail Zehaden, who showed up at the lab just as the raid was about to begin. Mr. Zehaden was captured inside the building, and when he tried to grab a container that police suspected may contain the virus, he was shot and killed.

"The lab and the surrounding buildings are under a strict quarantine at this time, and members of the Centers for Disease Control are assessing the situation. We are quite sure of one thing at this time. We have shut down the production facilities for the virus." Rothery shifted his papers, then continued. "But that does not mean that this threat is not still very real. It is. There remains the possibility that the terrorists have moved some of the virus from the lab and may be prepared to use it against us. We cannot ignore this threat. It is very real.

"To that end, I have additional good news." He turned and motioned to someone off camera. "Our task force enlisted not only the resources of the various government agencies with research-and-development capabilities, but also those companies in the private sector with similar resources. Many of the major pharmaceutical companies agreed to help and created research teams specifically geared to finding a drug that would combat the virus. One of these companies was successful."

The camera widened a bit and the two men who had been just off to Rothery's left moved onto the podium and came into view: Bruce Andrews and a slender man of Chinese descent dressed in a three-piece suit.

"Well, I'll be damned," Jennifer said, her hand, holding a teacup, stopping in midair. "Look who it is."

"I'm joined this morning by the CEO of Veritas Pharmaceutical, Bruce Andrews, and one of his research scientists, Dr. Chiang Wai. Veritas Pharmaceutical has discovered a drug that can penetrate the virus and kill it. I'm going to leave the technical details to the scientists to explain, but the bottom line is this: These men and their team at Veritas have in a very short period of time and under incredible pressure created a drug capable of stopping the virus even after the victim has been infected. They have created a drug that will save lives, countless lives."

He moved aside and Bruce Andrews stepped up to the microphone. He waited for the clapping to stop, then said, "I'm not the technical expert here, but my English is a little better than Dr. Wai's, so I'll try to explain the best I can. Initially, we had to concentrate on one of three distinct methods of attacking the virus: inhibiting viral attachment and entry, stopping the virus from uncoating or inhibiting the viral genome replication. We chose to use the genome replication method . . ."

"No way," Jennifer said, shaking her head. "Absolutely no way."

Gordon looked away from the television set, where Andrews was now using layman's terms to explain the process they had used to defeat the virus. "What do you mean, no way?" he asked.

"There is no way on earth that they found a method of inhibiting the genome replication of a hemorrhagic virus in one week. Not one chance in a million."

"What are you saying?" Gordon asked.

"I'm not sure," she said, setting her teacup on the table and listening to the rest of Andrews's monologue. When he had finished, she took a couple sips of tea. "You have problems in Montana with beetles killing the Ponderosa pines, don't you?"

"Sure. Pine beetles. It's a huge problem."

"Okay, then, here's an analogy. Pine beetles attack your forest, threatening to destroy three million acres of healthy pines. The forestry service panics, calls every company that produces pesticides, and asks them to concentrate on developing a spray that will kill the beetle and not harm the trees. They've got one week to find the answer. And guess what? One of the companies comes through. They have the answer to a problem that has eluded every research team at every pesticide company for years. The pine beetle problem is solved overnight. What are the chances?"

"Zero," Gordon said, nodding. "Good analogy."

"There's no way in hell Andrews came up with that drug in that short a time period. No way." She stopped and stared at the television as Dr. Chiang Wai spoke in halting English. "I know that man," she said. "But from where?"

"That's probably not unusual," Gordon said. "You and he work at the same company."

"It's a huge company, Gordon. And I've only seen him once or twice." She racked her brain, trying to dredge up the memory. It wouldn't come. "Damn it, I can't remember."

"Not a big deal," Gordon said. "So what does all this mean, these totally unrealistic time frames?"

"I would say that Veritas already had the drug. In fact, that makes perfect sense. Andrews wouldn't release the drug to the market without FDA approval, and that takes time. It takes years. Which means Veritas had a drug in the pipeline, already in for NDA."

"What's NDA?" Gordon asked.

"New Drug Application. It's the big hurdle with the FDA. They demand positive Phase III trials and make you jump through a number of very difficult hoops before they issue their approval on an NDA."

"So you're saying Veritas already had this drug in its arsenal. 'All dressed up and nowhere to go' sort of thing."

"Yeah," Jennifer said slowly. Then she snapped her fingers and said, "I know where I saw that researcher. He was at the White Oak facility back in late August when I got called out to check over some erroneous results in the lab. It was at the entrance to the brain chip lab. He was arguing with one of the moving men." The color drained from her face and she stared at Gordon, her mouth open.

"What's wrong?" he asked.

She tried to speak, but nothing came. She picked up a glass of water and drank almost half of it. "Gordon, when I was in the lab the night I saw Dr. Wai—or whatever his name is—there was a moving crew there."

"Right. You said Wai was arguing with one of them."

"I didn't hear what he was saying, but I did see what they were moving."

"What?" Gordon asked.

"High-efficiency HEPA filters."

Gordon leaned back in his chair. "Like the ones they found this morning at the lab in Orlando?"

She nodded. "Probably. I can't say for sure. But I can certainly tell you that something isn't adding up here. Andrews has a drug ready for NDA approval that is capable of killing a virus that appears at just the right moment. And the task force locates the lab in the nick of time. How? How did they find the lab? It could have been anywhere on the planet, and they've only got a few days to sort through hundreds of thousands of tips from every person who thought they saw something unusual. Yet they key in on the right one and find the lab. What are the chances?"

"Pretty slim," Gordon agreed.

"And then we've got extremely high-end HEPA filtration systems being moved out of White Oak while the clandestine lab was uncovered due to someone noticing high-efficiency HEPA filters in some obscure warehouse in Orlando. Christ, this is something out of a James Bond movie."

"What are you suggesting?" Gordon asked, leaning forward.

Jennifer shook her head. "I don't know what I'm suggesting, Gordon. Just that something is all wrong here. Things are too perfect." She leaned forward and cupped her head in her hands, staring at the table. "I've got to think, put this all together."

Gordon watched her as she sat unmoving, her eyes closed and her fingers gently rubbing her temples. *What is going through that mind?* he wondered. She was a brilliant woman in more than just the sciences, and he felt almost privileged at times to have become a part of her life. She was intimate in bed, very giving. And to him, that was not out of context. Her very being was dedicated not to Jennifer Pearce but to the betterment of the world she touched. And that touch was far-reaching. Her work in pharmaceuticals was an extension of her desire to make the planet a more livable place. He liked that side of her character.

The television was still focused on the virus scare, and with Jennifer deep in thought he reverted his attention back to the screen. A reporter was standing on the doorstep of an elegant home, interviewing a hysterical woman. The small printing at the bottom of the screen indicated that the woman was Ismail Zehaden's widow. She was being supported by two other women as she alternated between sobbing and yelling.

"My husband was no terrorist," she said. "He was a good American. A businessman who had done very well. He disliked some of the American foreign policy, but that was his right."

"But the lab was discovered in a building your husband owns," said the reporter, an attractive redhead in her late twenties.

"Ismail bought that warehouse as a storage facility. He was getting quotes from contractors on renovating it so he could move some of the raw materials he needed for his factory to another site. That warehouse was empty. It has been empty since he bought it."

The reporter ignored any line of questioning that may have come from that statement and pressed ahead. "Your husband made frequent trips back to the Mideast," she said. "Can you explain what those trips were for?"

"He had many friends and some family back in Iran. There are no laws saying my husband cannot visit his family and friends," she snapped, obviously irritated with the direction the interview was going.

"Unless those friends are al-Qaeda," the reporter said, sticking the microphone back in the widow's face.

"You heartless bitch," she said as she turned and retreated into the house. She slammed the door and the camera focused on the reporter.

"Ismail Zehaden's widow, not denying that her husband was traveling back to Iran to connect with other al-Qaeda factions . . ."

Gordon shook his head and looked back to Jennifer. She was sitting upright, also watching the television. "Not a very good reporter," he said.

"No, she treated that woman despicably. I hope the network

gets sued." She took a sip of cold tea and said, "I think the answer is at White Oak, Gordon. We have to get inside the lab where I saw Dr. Wai. We need to know what was in there."

Gordon looked puzzled. "I thought you said it was the brain chip department. And that they were dismantling that part of the company. That would explain why the HEPA filters were being moved."

"Perhaps," she said. "But I have other suspicions. I want to get inside White Oak."

"When?" he asked.

"Tonight."

60

The first thing Bruce Andrews saw when he returned to his BioTech Five office after the press conference with J. D. Rothery was the Tuesday *Richmond Times-Dispatch*. After one look at the local headlines, he slammed the newspaper down on his desk and swore under his breath. How could this have happened? The front page of the second section featured a picture of Jennifer Pearce's Mazda RX-8, wrapped around a large hickory and smashed almost beyond recognition. The caption under the picture read, "Where is she?"

The article, two columns in length, raised more questions than it answered. It reported that the car belonging to the Ph.D. graduate pharmaceutical researcher had been found in the Shenandoah Mountains early Monday morning by hikers walking a seldom-used trail. The car was suspended above the path in the tree, but how long it had been there was unknown, as the trail was a demanding one and only seasoned hikers attempted it. Forensics experts from the state police had searched the car but had found nothing. No traces of blood. No traces of the woman. Nothing. It was a mystery.

And the media loves a mystery, especially when the person

involved was a doctorate-level researcher in the pharmaceutical industry. A picture of Jennifer Pearce accompanied the article. One paragraph was dedicated to a brief history of her working life, including her current status at Veritas. And there was no chance that the reporters were going to miss the connection. Monday morning, a Veritas researcher's car shows up at the bottom of a cliff and the next day the company announces it has a drug to combat the virus. This was the last thing he needed right now. Goddamn Evan Ziegler all to hell. Why didn't he just kill her and dump her body? Now he had to deal with the aftermath.

Andrews checked his watch. Almost one o'clock. The news conference and the flight back from D.C. had taken the entire morning. He glanced down at the pile of correspondence and mail piled on the corner of his desk. He shuffled through it until he reached the fax from Barry Flath at the Food and Drug Administration. NDA approval came through quickly when you had J. D. Rothery at the Department of Homeland Security in your corner. He read through the document, a hint of a smile on his face. The paper was standard twenty-pound bond, but that one sheet was worth over two billion dollars to the company. He set it on his desk and stared at it for a minute or two before diving into the stack of mail. Even being the CEO had its mundane tasks.

The manager at the Fairfield Inn ripped out one article, then set the newspaper on the concierge desk and took the elevator to the fourth floor. He knocked lightly on the hotel room door and waited. A few moments later, the door opened and Jennifer Pearce looked out.

"Can I help you?" she asked. She recognized him as the hotel manager.

"I'm Donald Sarka, with the hotel. Could I speak with you, Dr. Pearce?" he asked.

The sound of the man using her name stunned her for a few seconds, then she backed off from the door and let him in. The door closed behind him. He handed her the article he had torn from the newspaper. "Have you read the paper today?" he asked her.

She stared at her picture. It was a good one, the same picture the paper had run for the announcement that she was moving to Veritas. There was no denying it was she. "Well, I guess you know the answer to that question," she said, reading the headline.

"I don't want to pry, Dr. Pearce, but I've already stretched one of our rules by allowing you and your friend to pay for your room in cash, without a credit card authorization. And now this. I like my job, Dr. Pearce, and I don't want to get fired for knowingly harboring someone the police are looking for. I think it would be fair if you told me what was going on."

Jennifer motioned to the small couch against the wall. The manager sat on the cushions, and Jennifer swung one of the chairs from the table and sat facing him. "It's kind of a long story, and I'd rather give you the short version, if that's okay."

"Short version would be fine, Dr. Pearce."

"Veritas Pharmaceutical is a dangerous place to work, Mr. Sarka. Two employees, one who was on my team, are dead. And I suspect both those people were killed. Right now, because of some knowledge that I have, I'm concerned for my own safety."

The look on Donald Sarka's face was almost amusing. He went a strange off-white color and almost choked when he tried to talk. "I'm used to teenagers running up and down the halls, Dr. Pearce, not companies killing their employees. This is a little out of my league."

"We'll move immediately," she said. "You're not the only person who will have seen us here. The police will be stopping by at some point, I'm sure."

The sound of a card being inserted in the slot caused both Jennifer and Sarka to look at the door. It opened and Gordon Buchanan entered. He focused on the hotel manager as he moved toward them. Then he held up a copy of the newspaper and asked, "Is this why you're here?"

Sarka nodded. "I wanted to know what was going on," he said. "Dr. Pearce has given me a quick explanation."

Jennifer added, "I told Mr. Sarka we would be leaving right away."

"I think that's a good idea," Gordon said. "It'll just take a few minutes for us to pack."

Sarka rose from the couch. "I'll work out your bill and bring the leftover cash back up to the room," he said. "It shouldn't take me more than five minutes."

"That would be appreciated," Jennifer said. "And thanks for asking us what was going on rather than just calling the police."

"Not a problem," he said. "I'll be right back." He let himself out, the door closing quietly behind him.

Gordon dug into the bag he was carrying. He pulled out a blond wig. "It's real hair, for whatever that's worth. I picked it up at the mall after I saw the article in the paper."

"I've always wanted to be a blonde," she said, pulling the wig over her real hair. "What do you think?"

He surveyed the new look and shook his head. "Not as good as the original, but still pretty darn nice."

She walked over to the mirror and adjusted it so none of her natural hair showed. "Where do we go from here?" she asked.

"Not sure. We'll see if you look different enough with the wig and sunglasses for us to go out in public. A lot of people around Richmond will have seen your picture. If no one recognizes you, we can have dinner before we head for White Oak."

"You're sure you're up to checking out the technology park?" she asked. "It could get dangerous."

He came up behind her and slipped his arms around her waist, breathing lightly on the back of her neck. Her body relaxed into his and they were quiet for a minute. "You know, ever since we met, just being near you has been dangerous," he said.

"I think it may be the other way around," she said.

"Well, whichever way it is, I'm sure tonight will be no different."

61

"She's in Richmond, at the Fairfield Inn, just off I-64," the man said. "We had two sightings and a confirmation. It's definitely her. I just flew in from Washington and I'm on my way over there right now. That guy from Montana, Gordon Buchanan, is with her."

Bruce Andrews couldn't help the urge to smile. "Be careful," he said. "You're a public figure right now. We don't need any more press on this."

"I've got two guys with me, Johnny and Ivan. I'll stay in the backseat, out of sight."

"Let me know when you're finished."

"No problem." The man snapped the cell phone shut and replaced it in the leather holder on his hip. He glanced at his watch. Four-fifteen. Traffic was just beginning to pick up for the afternoon rush hour. The sun was intense today and the sidewalks in Shockoe Bottom were crowded, a few pedestrians taking their time crossing the road against the DON'T WALK sign. He wanted to jump from the car and kick their asses out of the crosswalk. Picking up Ivan had meant a trip through the crowded streets close to Main Street Station and Shockoe Slip, out he felt the extra time was worth it. He only had two men in Richmond he trusted, and right now he couldn't be seen abducting Jennifer Pearce from a local hotel. Especially since the police were looking for her, or her body. Way too many questions if he was seen. Even just being in Richmond was risky.

The driver, Johnny Altwater, finally broke free of the traffic snarls and entered the on-ramp for I-64. Rush hour had yet to jam the freeway, and although traffic was heavy it was moving at the speed limit. They took the closest off-ramp to the Fairfield Inn and slowed to the posted speed. The Fairfield Inn grew in size as they approached it, and Altwater glided the car into the parking lot with the slow, sure motions of a skillful driver. He pulled up just short of the front door. He and Ivan checked the pictures of Jennifer and Gordon, took the safeties off their pistols, and double-checked the room number.

"Don't kill them here unless you absolutely have to," the man in the backseat said. "Just get them back to the car and we'll take them to where we're going to dump them."

Ivan nodded. "Radio check," he said into his mouthpiece as he turned from the car toward the hotel.

"You're live," the man responded. He watched the two men disappear into the hotel. Putting his own network in place had taken a great deal of time and money, but now it was paying off. He had men he could trust in numerous cities, Richmond included. Most of them affiliated themselves with his little operation more for the thrill of being able to operate outside the usual laws than for the money. But when they did get paid, they got paid well. And that didn't hurt.

Killing innocent people was a tough sell sometimes and he had to outright lie to his men, spinning yarns about how the person or people they were tracking were clandestine terrorists or something other than simply a threat to his other concerns. He didn't mind the lies, but they were dangerous. The men he was lying to all carried guns. And they were all trained to use them. Well, no one got rich in this business without crossing the boundaries and taking some risks.

He watched a couple exit the front doors and walk to a

parked SUV. The man strongly resembled Gordon Buchanan but the woman was blond. She was about the right height and body structure but the hair was all wrong. He concentrated on her face, the lines of her cheekbones, her forehead, and her lips and chin. He mentally stripped away the hair and the picture fell into place. He touched his two-way and spoke quietly.

"Johnny, Ivan, get down here. They're outside the front doors."

He watched as the Jeep backed up and pulled up to the curb at the street. A steady stream of vehicles was passing by and Buchanan had to wait until it was safe to make a left turn. Just as the traffic cleared, the two men came running out the front door of the hotel. They were in the car and into traffic in seconds, Pearce and Buchanan's SUV within sight. They settled in a few cars back. When the time was right, Jennifer Pearce and Gordon Buchanan would disappear.

But this time it would be for good.

"Where do you want to eat?" Gordon asked as he cut through Court End, a collection of older estate homes on massive lots, and headed for the city center.

"I don't care," she said. "Why are we heading into an area with lots of people? Shouldn't we go somewhere less crowded?"

"I remember reading once that if you want to blend in, the best place to do it is in a crowd. It's when you're someplace with hardly anyone around that other people will really look at you. They notice things that they wouldn't if you were just another face in the crowd."

"Okay, Monsieur Poirot. Whatever you say."

"There were a bunch of decent restaurants on Cary Street. Want to check it out?"

"Sure," she said, adjusting her wig slightly. She lowered the sun visor and opened the mirror. "I think I like being blond. I'm going to dye my hair when things get back to normal."

"That'll be nice," Gordon said. "Platinum blondes always look so classy with an inch or two of dark roots."

He angled off Canal Street at the Richmond Ballet and headed south under the Expressway until he reached Byrd Street. The traffic was lighter here and they made decent time, passing the old Tredegar Iron Works, the supplier of many Confederate cannons during the war. At Meadow Street, Gordon turned north again and popped out on Cary Street, just at the start of the strip of trendy shops and restaurants.

"I'm impressed," Jennifer said. "You didn't tell me you know how to get around Richmond."

"I'm learning. That cabbie I had before I met you for dinner at Amici was great. Getting around Richmond isn't too bad, but the traffic sure is."

"That's the same everywhere," she said as he pulled the SUV up in front of Limani Mediterranean Grill. "This looks nice," she said of the restaurant. A menu was posted on a wooden pulpit. She strained to see it. "They've got lots of different kinds of fish—arctic char, swordfish, red snapper. Some Greek food if you don't want fish. Want to try it?"

"Sure," Gordon said, slipping off his seat belt. He stopped halfway through the motion, his eyes glued to the side mirror. After a few seconds, he said, "Put your seat belt back on, Jennifer." The tone of his voice was deadly serious, and she snapped the buckle back into place. He waited for about thirty seconds, then pulled out again into traffic again. He slid in behind a dark blue Crown Victoria and set his pace to match the preceding car. The back window was tinted, but with the sun ahead of them in the west, they could see the outline of three people inside the vehicle. For no apparent reason, the car slowed in the middle of a block and Gordon matched the speed and stayed planted behind it.

"What's going on, Gordon?" Jennifer asked, fear creeping into her voice.

"I think these guys were following us. Two of them were watching us while the driver looked for a parking spot. They wanted to stay behind us, but there were no spots." The car sped up a bit and he matched their pace again. "Check the

307

map and find me the next north-south street that goes under the I-95."

Jennifer unfolded the map, checked a street sign as they drove, and found their location. She looked ahead on Cary Street for the next north-south through street. "Robinson," she said. "It's right after Davis and two after Stafford."

"Okay, we just passed Stafford, so this should be Davis," he said as they cruised through the intersection. He checked the street sign and nodded. "Hold on," he said.

"What are you going to do?"

"See if these guys ahead of us really were following us," he said, waiting until he was halfway across Robinson before cranking the steering wheel hard left and stomping on the gas. The Jeep cut through a narrow gap in the traffic, and Gordon floored it once he was safely around the corner. The shrill sounds of honking horns told them what the other drivers thought of his abrupt and unexpected move. The lights at Park-wood Avenue were green, and he whipped through the inter-section at almost double the posted speed. He slowed once they passed the next two side streets and entered the under-pass. He glanced in his rearview mirror, then pushed the pedal to the floor again. The Jeep's engine roared and the SUV leaped ahead. A block and a half ahead was a dead end—the begin-ning of Maymont Park.

"What are you doing?" she yelled above the motor noise.

"They're behind us. And this time they're not just following us, they're gaining," he said, fighting the steering wheel as he slammed on the brakes and sent the vehicle up on two wheels at the T intersection. He raced down Lake View Avenue, the his-toric park on their left, trees and cars flashing by as Gordon again increased his speed to dangerous levels. He risked a quick look in the mirror. The Crown Vic was gaining on them. He gave the Jeep more gas, the speedometer now climbing to over eighty miles an hour. People, houses, cars, trees were all just a blur now. They reached the far western end of Lake View and Gordon wove through the traffic, sideswiping one newer-model Subaru and almost losing control, a line of mature trees dangerously close on the left side. He regained control of the Jeep and wove through the maze of cars and vans southbound on Blanton. Directly behind them was the Crown Vic.

Blanton forked at Park Drive and Rugby Road, and Gordon chose Rugby to the left and bordering the west side of William Byrd Park. The lesser-used road was almost deserted, and he put the pedal to the floor. The Jeep's speedometer crested 105 miles an hour as he took it into the long sweeping left turn just south of the World War I memorial. As they came abreast with Dogwood Dell, he hammered on the brakes, locking up all four tires and sending a plume of smoke into the air. The Crown Vic, which had been ready to pull alongside, went flying by, fishtailing as the driver also slammed on his brakes. Both Gordon and Jennifer saw an arm come out of the backseat, and a split second later the windshield disintegrated as a bullet hit it at a critical angle and shattered the glass. The imploding glass showered both of them, and Jennifer screamed as Gordon cranked hard on the steering wheel and the vehicle slid sideways down the road on two wheels. For a few seconds, the Jeep teetered between rolling and coming back down on four wheels. Gordon eased off on the brakes and the Jeep crashed down onto all fours. A tenth of a second later, the SUV hit the curb and went airborne. Eighty feet later, it smashed down on the grass in Dogwood Dell, the rear bumper catching on a log and ripping off. The Jeep fishtailed across the grass, then Gordon hit the gas and straightened it out. He got some open grass in front of him and turned to look for his pursuers. Unable to navigate the dell without four-wheel drive, the Crown Vic was heading south on Pump House Drive, aiming to circumnavigate the park and catch them at the north end.

Gordon headed directly for Blanton and melted back into the city traffic. He drove north on Sheppard Street until Cary, parked the Jeep in the first parking lot he saw, and jumped out. Jennifer was ten feet behind him when they reached Cary Street. Gordon saw a cab about halfway down the block and waved. The driver swung out into traffic and pulled in beside them.

"Where to, buddy?" he asked as they merged into the steady stream of cars.

"Just drive, please," Gordon said, breathing heavily. He dug in his pocket and handed the man a wad of twenties. "South Richmond, on the other side of the river. I'll tell you where in a few minutes."

The driver flipped through the wad of bills and grinned. "Take your time, my friend. You just bought my services for the entire night."

Gordon turned to Jennifer. "You okay?" he asked.

"Yes, but no thanks to your driving. You're a maniac."

"Better than getting shot," he said.

"Those guys were serious," she said, starting to shake. She slid in beside him and he slipped his arm around her, pulling her close. It felt good. "Jesus, they actually shot at us."

He nodded. "And the car," Gordon said. "Crown Vic with tinted windows and a bored-out engine."

"What's that got to do with anything?" she asked.

He pulled away a touch so he could look in her eyes. "It's a government car, Jennifer. Whoever those guys were, they work for one of our government agencies."

62

"This is not a difficult request," Bruce Andrews said. "I simply want you to kill Gordon Buchanan and Jennifer Pearce."

"I know what you want," the voice snapped back. "Buchanan spotted us and we couldn't catch him."

"I don't know where or when you'll get another chance," Andrews said. "But if you do, don't miss. These two people are turning out to be quite the liability."

"They will not escape again," the man assured him.

"I hope not," Andrews said, hanging up the phone. He was at home in his study, his private retreat from the world he had created. The phone line was private, the number known only by a precious few whom he considered either privileged or necessary. It seldom rang, and when it did, the ensuing conversations were always interesting, to say the least. But this one was not what he wanted to hear. Gordon Buchanan was proving to be a formidable opponent. He was wealthy and knew how to use his money to his advantage. He chartered planes, keeping his movements from city to city off the radar. He paid cash rather than using credit cards and knew when to keep his head down.

And Jennifer Pearce—now, there was a major mistake. He couldn't count the times he had wished that he had never hired her. The Alzheimer's group was far enough removed from Albert Rousseau and Triaxcion that she should never have been a factor in any of this. Yet Gordon Buchanan had got his talons into Kenga Bakcsi and that had drawn Jennifer Pearce into the fray. And she was proving to be as tenacious as Buchanan. Together, they posed the most cohesive threat to his plan—a plan that to date had unfolded almost perfectly.

Zancor was finally through the New Drug Application and was now FDA approved. The economic difference to the company was in the range of two billion dollars. And a few hundred million of that would come quickly as he geared up the production facilities and provided a few million doses of Zancor to Tony Warner at NSA. Things were perfect, with one exception.

Buchanan and Pearce.

One obstacle with one solution.

Keith Thompson reloaded the last series of tests and watched the results play across the screen. There was no doubt in his mind. He picked up the phone and dialed a number at the Department of Homeland Security. He fully expected J. D. Rothery's voice mail and was surprised when the man answered the phone.

"You're working late tonight, Keith," Rothery said. "It's after eight o'clock."

"Oh, just a typical Tuesday," the linguistics expert said. "Great news conference this morning, by the way. I think everyone is going to sleep a little better tonight."

"Thanks, Keith," Rothery said. "What can I do for you? I'm sure you have a reason for calling."

"Yes, I do. The DVD that you received from the terrorist. I ran some additional tests on it and I've come up with something. A few years ago, I developed a program that samples idiosyncrasies in speech patterns. It looks for certain inflections common to specific dialogues and languages. In this case, our guy is Arabic, so I input every known dialect into the program and ran it through the supercomputers over at NSA. It took a while to come up with the final results, but they are conclusive."

"What did you learn?" Rothery asked.

"The guy on the tape is not Arabic. Never has been, never will be. The accent is entirely fake. This guy is an English-speaking person, probably from the eastern United States. It's difficult to establish exactly where he's from because of the fake Arab accent, but if I had to guess, I'd say somewhere near Boston. And one other thing that is without question is that Is-mail Zehaden is not the man on the tape."

"You're sure," Rothery said quietly.

"I'm positive."

"Who have you told?" Rothery asked.

"No one, Mr. Rothery. You're the first one to know."

"Keep it that way for now, Keith. We've got enough on our plate without this going public. I'll deal with it."

"Yes, sir."

Keith Thompson hung up and looked back at the computer screen. The series of jagged lines cutting across the monitor were as definitive as a fingerprint. They just needed a voice sample from the same person and they could match the two. Then they would have their man.

He shut off his computer, locked the office and left for the night. He felt good about his work on the DVD, but something wasn't quite right. He couldn't put his finger on it, but something was bothering him. And when he reached his car and turned the key in the ignition, the strangest thing happened. He saw a split-second image of his car exploding into a giant fireball.

He sat in the parking lot, his body shaking as his car idled, and one thought kept running through his mind: *Do I know too much?*

63

White Oak Technology Park was very different at night. In the muted moonlight, the silver buildings appeared dark gray, and aside from the streetlamps lighting the long winding road leading to the structure housing the Veritas labs, the grounds were dark. An occasional light glimmered out through the thick glass, but most of the labs were deserted, the staff at home for the evening. Gordon and Jennifer's cabdriver pulled up to the front entrance of the Veritas building. He slipped the transmission into park and swiveled about to face them.

"Okay, let's make sure I've got this straight. You want me to park near the south end of the building. There's an exit about fifty or sixty feet from the corner. There are no markings over the door, just a small staircase with black railings. I'm supposed to shut off my car, stay in the shadows, and wait. When I see you come out, I'm to come racing up and get out of here as fast as I can."

"Yeah, that's about it," Gordon said.

"And this is all legal?" the driver said. "Right."

"Do you have today's newspaper?" Jennifer asked. "The *Times-Dispatch*."

314

"Of course. We cabbies would be bored without newspapers," he said, dredging up the daily from under his seat. He handed it to her.

Jennifer pulled out the second section and then slipped off her wig. He stared at the paper, then at her. "Somebody in the company tried to kill me," she said. "And we need to get in one of the Veritas labs. Tonight."

"Oh, this just gets better all the time. Now you're a missing research scientist on the run from an evil person intent on killing her." He turned to Gordon. "And who are you?"

"Just a friend."

He was silent for a minute, scratched his head, and said, "Ah, what the hell. It beats waiting on Cary Street for a couple of drunks looking for an after-hours club. Anyway, I think I believe you. It's too crazy a story for someone to make up."

"Thanks," Jennifer said, slipping her Veritas ID from her pocket and holding it up. He gave it a quick look. "Holy shit, you're not kidding. You *are* her."

"Remember," Gordon said as they exited the cab. "The south end of the building. And be ready. We shouldn't be more than twenty minutes, tops."

They walked up the wide sidewalk and opened the outer door. She looked at Gordon as she held her card above the reader. "This is it. Once I swipe this card, we're going to be visible."

"Let's do it," he said, giving her a grim smile and checking the time on his watch. "You figure twenty minutes?"

"I think that's about what it will take for Andrews to get someone out here from the city. Could be a little more or less." She ran the card through the reader and the light next to the inner door switched from red to green. They entered the building. The security guard stared at her as she approached the desk.

"Dr. Pearce," he said. "I thought—"

She smiled and gave him a small wave. "Total misunderstanding," she said. "My car slid off the road in the rain. I managed to jump out, but it took me quite a while to walk back to the nearest house." It was a lame story, but he bought it.

315

"Could you sign in, please?"

"I'll need a guest pass as well," she said, scratching her signature on the night sheet.

The guard dug out a visitor's badge and pushed another sheet of paper across the desk. "Name and address of your visitor, please." She filled in the blanks, and he gave it a perfunctory check, then said, "Thanks, Dr. Pearce. Glad you're okay."

"I'm fine, thank you." They walked to the doors that accessed Veritas's half of the building and she swiped her card again. The light blinked green and they entered the short section of hallway before the steel security doors. "This is the big one," she said as they approached the door. "All these doors are at different levels of security. If they've downgraded me at all, I won't be able to open it." She held her breath and pulled the card through the slot. The light went green and Gordon pulled the door open.

"So far, so good," he said, checking his watch. "Just over four minutes."

"Let's move," she said, walking quickly down the long hall. Blue doors flashed by on both sides as they hustled down the never-ending hall. They reached the first fork and turned right. Jennifer stopped at the second door on the left. "This is the lab where I saw Dr. Wai arguing with the moving man." She held her card above the reader. "Keep your fingers crossed," she said. She swiped the card down in a decisive motion and the light immediately went green.

"Wow," Gordon said. "Being with you makes it easy to get into places."

"I'm one of the team leaders," she said. "There are only eleven of us in the company, and we all have top-level clearance. I've yet to find a door I can't open."

They moved into the lab and switched on the lights. "I'm surprised Andrews didn't terminate your security clearance when you went missing."

She was moving quickly to one of the many tables loaded with equipment. "No, I didn't think he would cancel my card.

That would almost be an admission that he knew I was dead. Which, of course, he thought I was." She reached the first lab table and said, "You keep an eye on the time and I'm going to see if I can figure out what they were doing in here."

"Okay," Gordon said, looking at his watch. "Seven minutes and ten seconds."

"Good. This is going just fine," she said, concentrating on the equipment.

His pager went off thirty-two seconds after Jennifer Pearce first swiped her card. He glanced at the message, then left the restaurant, his cell phone already dialing out. Johnny Altwater answered on the second ring. "The White Oak facility. She's in the building."

"We're on the east edge of the city," Altwater responded. "We can be there in fifteen minutes, give or take."

"I'll be ten minutes behind you," he said. "For Christ's sake, don't miss her this time. Do what you have to. I don't care if we have to carry a dead body out of the lab, just don't let her get away."

"Okay, I hear you."

His car was almost a block from the restaurant, and he walked as quickly as he could without attracting attention. Bruce Andrews was worried. Exactly how much Jennifer Pearce knew was an unknown, but to Andrews, she was a very real threat. And Gordon Buchanan, the country hick from Montana, was proving to be no slouch. Together they were opening doors that Andrews preferred remained closed. And when someone threatened Bruce Andrews, they were threatening the goose that laid the golden egg. And that golden egg was so close now. Everything had gone exactly as Andrews had predicted. Everything except the unexpected appearance of Jennifer Pearce. But she had made one too many mistakes, and this time they had her trapped.

He reached the car and sped away from the curb, headed for White Oak Technology Park.

64

The equipment contained in a lab tells a story. To the trained eye, it reveals what the lab is being used for and can also tell what the lab was used for in the past. Since the removal of the HEPA filters, the function of the space may have changed, but its current use didn't interest her. Its previous function was what Jennifer was interested in. She ignored most of the equipment on the tables, concentrating on the clean room near the back.

The clean room was set aside from the rest of the lab, delineated by floor-to-ceiling sheets of glass joined together with strips of inflexible rubber. Empty exhaust vents were the only evidence that HEPA filtration systems had once been in use. Jennifer looked at the Olympus microscopes, noting that most were the IX2 series, motorized inverted models. Serious machines. A couple of explosion-proof freezers sat against the back wall, still plugged in. She opened one and glanced in. Almost empty, save for a few small boxes, and very cold. She closed the lid and moved on. An entire set of shelves was dedicated to chemical and reagent storage, and she made mental notes of which chemicals were present. There were a couple of

Burrell shakers and a Jenway spectrophotometer amid a scattering of calipers and micrometers. A high-pressure PVS rheometer used for viscosity measurements sat in a back corner. She spent some time going over it carefully and collected a small sample from one of the relief valves. She quickly prepared a slide and switched on one of the microscopes. She adjusted the slide, chose her magnification, and focused on the sample. Satisfied with the results, she shut down the microscope and slipped the slide in with the remainder of the sample from the rheometer.

Two computers sat on one of the desks, and she quickly powered them up and took a look at the contents. One computer defaulted to English, the other to Chinese. She ran her fingers around the second computer's casing, then dropped to her knees and looked under the desk. There was a small package taped to the underside of the desk, and she tucked it into her inside pocket. She took one last glance and returned to the regular lab outside the clean room.

Gordon was looking at his watch when she emerged from the glass enclosure. He pointed at his wrist. "Eighteen minutes," he said. "We've got to get out of here."

"It's okay, I've got what I need," she replied. In her left hand was a small vial inside a clear protective plastic case. She held it up. "You're not going to believe what's in here."

He started for the door and she fell in behind him, slipping the vial into her pocket. "I have no idea." Gordon reached the door and looked out into the hallway. It was clear. "What's in the vial?"

"The virus."

Gordon stopped in his tracks. "What?" he said. "What do you mean, the virus?"

"The hemorrhagic virus that was terrorizing the country. We just found the real lab where the virus was developed."

"Jesus Christ," Gordon said, starting down the hallway at a fast pace. "Are we infected?"

"No, the virus I found is dead, but I can still see the molecular structure." She fell in beside him, her legs moving fast to keep up with his long strides. "Andrews created the virus in this lab. Or at least he had Dr. Wai create it. And my guess is that he never planned on releasing it. He just killed a few people and threatened to dump it on the population to create a crisis." They reached the fork in the hall and took a left. "Once the government was convinced they had a terrorist ready to kill millions of people, he suddenly holds up an antiviral drug that's been languishing in nowhere land waiting for FDA approval and says, 'Hey look what I've got. The cure.' And everyone buys it. Andrews is the hero, and he gets his drug through the FDA."

"That's it?" Gordon asked. "That's what this has been all about? Getting a new drug through the regulators?"

"That's my guess."

"Why? Why kill all those people? Why create something this dangerous? Where's the upside?"

"Money, Gordon. A lot of money. If I had to guess, I'd say in excess of two billion dollars a year in sales, maybe three. A new antiviral drug, even with side effects that would keep the FDA from approving it, is a gold mine. But they're hard to get approved, because they all have some rather disturbing side effects. And with a viral drug, you don't take it all the time, so the effects take years to show up. But the damage is being done. And since the FDA had this new drug stalled, it must be pretty bad."

"Holy shit," Gordon said. They had reached the steel security doors, and he reached for the button on the wall to open them. Then he froze. Looking directly at him through the small glass window was the driver of the Crown Vic. Gordon had only caught a fleeting glimpse of the man when the car went flying by the Jeep, but he was sure it was the same person. "Jennifer, let's go," he yelled, grabbing her arm and pulling her back the way they had just come. A clicking sound behind them indicated that someone had tripped the automatic locking system and the doors were opening. Just as they reached the fork in the hallway, they heard a strange muffled sound and a bullet chewed into the wall inches from Jennifer's head. She screamed as they rounded the corner, moving at a full run.

"They're shooting at us," she managed to gasp as they ran.

"The hall's too long," Gordon said. "They'll be at the fork before we reach the end. Quick, open one of these doors."

They stopped abruptly in front of one of the blue doors and she swiped her card through the reader. The light blinked red. "Shit," she said, turning her card over and swiping it again, this time with the magnetic stripe on the right side. The light turned green and she opened the door. A second bullet hit the metal doorjamb and sparks flew. They piled through the door and pushed it shut behind them. They heard running footsteps coming toward them and it sounded like there was more than one pursuer. Jennifer flipped on the light, they took a quick look around, and she snapped the light off.

They were in a small lab, perhaps one-quarter the size of the lab Andrews had used to create the virus. Two long lab benches, anchored securely to the floor, ran perpendicular to the wall that housed the door they had just entered through. They were covered with equipment and sophisticated-looking machines. There was a secondary exit at the far end of the lab and Jennifer headed for it, groping her way in the dark and trying to remember where the lab benches were from the brief glimpse she'd had when the light was on. Gordon moved to one of the benches and ran his hand along until he found a sharp metal spike used for stirring liquids. Then he returned to the door and rammed it into the light switch. Outside, he could hear the men on the phone calling back to the security desk with the lab number.

"Move, Jennifer," Gordon said quietly as he came up behind her. "They're talking to the security guard. They're probably asking him to open the door remotely for them."

The door clicked and it opened, throwing a beam of light from the hallway into the lab. Gordon and Jennifer were on the far side of one of the long tables and out of the light. The man entering the lab tried the light switch, but the metal spike had destroyed it. He cursed and moved slowly into the semidarkness, searching for Gordon and Jennifer.

"You can't get away," he said quietly. His voice carried through the empty room. "Just come out and we'll talk. We need to talk with you."

Jeff Buick

"Bullshit," Gordon whispered to Jennifer. "Andrews's guys. They need to kill us."

He could barely see her shape in the darkness, but he could tell she was nodding. "The rear exit," she whispered back. "Let's get out of here."

They crawled along the floor, staying below the level of the lab benches. Jennifer's hand bumped into a stool, and it wobbled for a second until Gordon caught it and stopped it from toppling over. They remained motionless for a minute, then continued. Behind them they could hear the sounds of unsure feet shuffling across the tiles. Jennifer reached the exit and asked quietly, "Are you ready?"

"Ready."

She gripped the handle firmly and pulled. An alarm instantly sounded and the emergency lighting system kicked in. Jennifer was already through the door, and Gordon dived after her. He had a fleeting glimpse of a man with a pistol aimed at him, then that strange sound and a searing pain in his right leg. His momentum carried him through the doorway, and Jennifer slammed the metal door behind him.

"Damn it," he said, grabbing at his leg. His hands came away bloodied. He pulled his pant leg up and looked at the wound. There was a small hole in the calf muscle where the bullet had entered. He felt on the other side of his leg and found another hole. "It went through," he said, struggling to his feet. "Just a flesh wound. Now get out of here. Head for the exit at the south end of the building and I'll be there in a minute."

"I'm not leaving without you," she said.

He grabbed her by the shoulders. "This isn't a movie. And it sure as hell isn't time to get heroic. Get back to the cab. I'll be there in a couple of minutes."

She opened her mouth, then shut it. He was serious. She set off down the secondary hallway at a brisk run. She glanced back at a corner in the hall and saw Gordon kicking in a door with his good leg. Then she was alone, running for her life down the dimly lit corridor.

Gordon smashed in the wooden door marked MAINTENANCE.

322

Inside was standard fare for cleaning an industrial building. He pulled a mop off its hanger and swung it hard against the wall. The mop broke off, leaving just a splintered handle. He grabbed a bottle of ammonia and unscrewed the lid. A second later, the door crashed open and a man entered, a silenced pistol in his outstretched hand. Gordon stabbed at the man's hand with the sharp end of the mop handle, the splintered wood driving into his attacker's wrist. The gun flew from his hand and he howled in pain, the shattered handle shoved clear through his arm. He looked up at Gordon with disbelief in his eyes and saw a liquid coming at him. The ammonia hit his exposed eyes and he dropped to the floor, screaming and clawing at his face. Gordon gave him one well-placed kick in the head and he went silent, unconscious.

The alarm from opening the back door had ceased; that worked for Gordon, as he needed the quiet. He knew from the footsteps in the hall that there was more than one person after them. He took deep slow breaths, his ears in tune with every noise. Nothing for a few seconds, then a slight scraping sound just outside the door. The second attacker was right there, just on the other side of the wall. Gordon put his foot on the first man's arm and pulled the mop handle out. Then he moved back a couple of feet and rammed the sharp end of the handle into the wall. It punctured the drywall on both sides of the studs as if it didn't even exist, then hit something solid. Gordon heard a strange sound, something he'd never heard in his life. It was like air escaping an enclosed space, except that it was accompanied by the strangest gurgling sound. He waited a minute until the sound had diminished to almost nothing, then ventured a quick peek around the corner. The sight brought bile to his throat.

The second attacker was impaled by the broken handle, like a pig on a barbecue spit. Blood poured from his mouth and he made feeble efforts to dislodge himself. It was useless—he was dying. Gordon looked at the man, into his eyes, and felt sick. The stare was vacant, almost as though his spirit had already left his body and the physical part of his being had yet to expire. He had just severely maimed one man and killed another. He took one last look and ran down the hall, toward Jennifer and the cab.

The driver was exactly where they had asked him to wait. Jennifer was already sitting in the backseat, and she broke into a smile when he came running out the fire door. He sprinted to the cab and jumped in.

"Get us out of here without anyone else seeing us and there's an extra thousand in it for you," he said as he collapsed into the seat.

"That would be a good thing," the driver shot back. "I'm sure that if anyone sees me leaving and gets my plate number, I'm going to be in some serious shit. Another thousand bucks is just a little more incentive to do something that was already on my mind." He steered the car back into the parking lot, switched off his headlights, and took the back roads until he reached the main access to the I-64. He turned his headlights back on once he was on the ramp to the freeway. He accelerated up to the posted speed limit and blended in with the night traffic.

"You okay?" Jennifer asked Gordon.

"Sort of," he said, thinking of the look in the dying man's eyes. "I'll be all right. How about you?"

"Scared," she said. "Scared shitless."

"Well, at least we've got proof of what Andrews was up to."

"And this," she said, pulling out of her pocket the small package that she had stripped off the underside of the lab table. She opened it and showed him. It was a CD with Chinese markings on the top. "It's a trick lots of researchers use. We hide disks near our computers with confidential information on them. That way, if someone hacks into your computer or steals it, they don't get your latest research. It seems Dr. Wai thinks the same as I do. This was hidden under the desk."

"What do you think is on it?" Gordon asked.

"I'm not sure. Probably something to do with the work he was doing for Andrews in the lab. It could be another nail in Andrews's coffin."

"Then let's get somewhere with a computer and find out what's on it."

"Slight problem," she said, pointing to the writing. "You speak Mandarin or Cantonese?"

He was quiet for a minute. "No, but I'm getting hungry. How about Chinese?"

She took a good look at his leg. "After we get something to bandage that and get you some painkillers."

"It's a flesh wound," Gordon said, putting some pressure on it and wincing. He saw the look on her face and grimaced. "Okay, first the leg, then dinner."

65

The cabdriver, whose name was Eric, found an ATM on the southeast outskirts of Richmond and Gordon withdrew three thousand dollars. He counted out fifty twenties and handed them across the front seat. Eric slipped them into his pocket with a nod of his head and a grin.

"They already know where we are, so this is probably a good time to stock up on cash," he said to Jennifer.

He had the cabbie stop in front of a pharmacy, and Jennifer ran in and stocked up on extra-strength Tylenol and some compresses and white tape. She carefully bandaged his leg in the backseat of the cab and he took two of the pills. She had a close look at his wound while applying the gauze. Gordon was right—the damage was mostly superficial. The bullet had gone right through and the muscle was damaged, but the bones were intact. When they were finished, Gordon asked Eric, "You know where we could get some authentic Chinese food?"

"Hey, I live on Chinese. I know the best places. You care which part of the city we end up in?"

"Get us away from the ATM I just used," Gordon said. "Other than that, I don't care."

"What happened to the guys chasing us?" she asked.

"You don't want to know."

They lapsed into silence and watched the darkened city flash by. Everything so normal: cars stopping for red lights, couples out walking their dogs. But for them things were far from normal. They both knew that this fight had become a fight for their life. And Bruce Andrews was not going to stop. Somehow they had to take him down. But the question that was running through both their minds as Eric pulled up in front of a restaurant was *How? How can we convince someone in a position of power that Andrews is corrupt?* They had the SEC on his tail with the accounting irregularities and they now had samples of the virus taken from the White Oak lab, but whom did they go to with the evidence? It was a million-dollar question.

Eric told them he preferred to sit in his car and ordered some takeout while they were in the restaurant. They sat in a booth tucked away in a corner, and when the server came around with Chinese tea, Gordon asked her, "Is there anyone here who speaks and reads Mandarin?"

She gave him a strange look. "This is a Chinese restaurant. We all speak Mandarin, and a couple of the cooks speak Cantonese."

"Okay, is there anyone on your staff with a technical background? Medical, sciences, that sort of thing?"

"Sure, that would be Kelly, one of our waiters. He's in his third year at university, majoring in biology. Want me to send him over?"

"Yes, please."

A few minutes later, a young Chinese man approached with a puzzled look on his face. "You were asking for someone who speaks Mandarin and knows something about biology?" he asked.

Jennifer slipped the CD from her pocket and held it up. "We need to know what's on this disk. We'll pay you to translate it."

"I'm working right now," he said. "I can do it tomorrow."

Gordon pulled out the remainder of the cash from the ATM withdrawal. "Three hundred dollars says you plug that into your

Jeff Buick

computer and do it now." He set the money on the table and placed a saltshaker on it.

Starving university students love cash. Kelly smiled and said, "Give me a minute. My computer's in the back." He returned a minute later with a Sony laptop and set it up on the table adjacent to Gordon and Jennifer's. He took the disk and slipped it into the CD drive.

"This goes nowhere but between us and you," Gordon cautioned him.

"For three hundred bucks, I don't have a problem with that. I'll even get them to throw a few extra shrimp in your chop suey," he said, a huge grin pasted across his face. Fifteen minutes later, he joined them at their table. He wasn't smiling. "Do you know what's on here?" he asked.

"We have our suspicions," Jennifer said, setting down her chopsticks. "What did you find?"

Kelly ran his hand through his hair and shook his head. "This is really serious stuff. Really serious." He looked upset and his hands were shaking.

"We suspect that there are research notes on that disk for a hemorrhagic virus," Jennifer said. "A lethal virus that was developed by a Chinese research scientist for a local pharmaceutical company. Is that fairly close?"

Kelly swallowed, his hands shaking so badly he set the disk on the table. "Yes. That's what is on the disk. How did you know that?"

"It's a long story. But you can trust me when I say we're the good guys here. We're trying to nail the people who created this bug."

"Is there anything else on the disk?" Gordon asked.

"Just a footnote at the end." He dug into his shirt pocket and pulled out a napkin with some writing on it. "I jotted down the translation." He handed it to Jennifer, who was closest to him.

" 'He has someone of great influence and power working with him. I am convinced it is one of the four.' " She read it one more time and asked Kelly, "The reference to 'one of the four'—does that mean anything in Chinese?"

Kelly, who had stopped shaking, thought for a minute, then

328

said, "No. There's nothing in Chinese culture that emphasizes anything about 'the four.' I don't think it's on the disk simply because the author was Chinese."

"Okay, thanks," Gordon said, retrieving the disk from the table and handing the money to the young man. As an afterthought, he said, "Here," and handed him another two hundred dollars. "Don't say anything about this. Okay?"

Kelly looked scared. "Absolutely no way am I saying one word about this. I read the newspapers and watch television. I know what this is all about and I don't want to be involved."

"Thanks, again," Gordon said. The waiter disappeared into the kitchen and Gordon turned to Jennifer. "Well, what now? What do you think Dr. Wai was saying with that little quip?"

Jennifer was slow to answer. When she did, it was with carefully chosen words. "I think the 'he' and 'him' in the message refer to Bruce Andrews. Certainly, it was Andrews who had Dr. Wai develop the virus so they could get Zancor through FDA approval. But who is 'of great influence and power'?"

"I'm still in some sort of a state of disbelief that this whole thing was about getting a drug approved. I can't believe people would kill just to get an FDA approval."

"It's all about money, Gordon," Jennifer said. "You have no idea what goes on behind the scenes with the pharmaceutical companies and the regulatory boards. Veritas and the other Big Pharma have enormous influence in D.C. and in Congress. But there are times when drugs get stalled in the NDA and someone digs in their heels. When that happens, the company can either accept the hundred- or two-hundred-million-dollar loss for the R&D that went into the drug's development and move ahead, or they can resort to slimeball tactics to try to get it through. Sometimes they'll dig up dirt on the FDA employee who's keeping the approval from going through. In some instances, they've been known to physically threaten people. And you heard what Elizabeth Ripley over at the SEC said about that young woman with three children."

"So they're willing to kill in order to get their drugs to market. Christ, what a bunch."

Jeff Buick

"Don't paint them all with the same brush, Gordon. Marcon, for one, would never push a drug beyond Phase II trials if it was dangerous."

Kelly returned with their bill. He set it on the table and said, "Sorry about coming unglued there, but what you guys had me look at is pretty scary."

"It's okay," Jennifer said, taking the bill and digging into her pocket.

In his other hand was a newspaper. He held it up, folded in half so the second section was visible. "This is you, isn't it?"

She glanced at the picture accompanying the story about her car being found at the bottom of the cliff. "Yes, that's me."

"Take care," he said, setting the paper on the table and accepting the money for the bill. It was over by twenty dollars, and he handed her the tip back. "You've already given me enough money tonight. Thanks, but no thanks."

She pocketed the twenty and pushed her plate away. It hit the newspaper and the top section flipped back, revealing the front page. "I'm finished," she said. "Totally stuffed." She set her chopsticks on the table and stopped. She stared at the newspaper, the front page of the first section now visible. "Gordon," she whispered. "Tell me I'm crazy."

"What?" he said. "What are you talking about?"

"Look at the picture," she said.

On the front page of the late edition of the *Richmond Times-Dispatch* was a picture of six men, all dressed in suits and standing side by side. The two on the far right were Bruce Andrews and Dr. Chiang Wai. The remainder of the six were the representatives of the four agencies that had formed the task force to combat the threat of the virus.

"Take away Andrews and Wai, and what are you left with?" she asked quietly.

"The guys from the CIA, FBI, NSA—and Rothery, from the Department of Homeland Security. Why?"

"Four men," she said.

Gordon stared at the picture. He grabbed the translation Kelly had left with them. " 'He has someone of great influence and power working with him. I am convinced it is one of the four,'" he said. He read the names from the caption under the picture. "Craig Simms, Deputy Director of the CIA, Jim Appleby, Special Agent in Charge with the FBI, and Tony Warner with National Security Agency. And, of course, J. D. Rothery, DHS and head of the task force. All household names these days."

"One of the four," Jennifer said.

"Christ," Gordon said. "This just keeps getting better."

66

Two cars sat in front of the White Oak Technology Building that housed the Veritas labs. Inside the front foyer, a man spoke quietly to the security guard while another man cleaned up the mess outside the maintenance room. The body was loaded into the trunk of one of the cars and the injured man was taken to a nearby clinic, where his eyes were flushed, the bones in his wrist set, and his skin stitched.

"You understand what will happen if any word of what happened here tonight leaves this building," the man said.

The security guard could barely swallow. "Yes, sir, I understand fully."

"So I can trust that you'll keep this between us?"

"Absolutely."

"Then I think we have an agreement and I can be leaving now. Take care, Robert," the man said. He walked back to the second car and drove out onto Technology Boulevard. What the hell was going on? He had sent two experienced agents in to take care of a female research scientist and a country hick, and he had just collected one dead body and one seriously injured agent. How well the injured man would ever see again was in question. Not that he really cared, just that things like this generated questions and he didn't need questions right now. He checked his watch and swore under his breath. He needed to get back to D.C. before he was missed. He entered the traffic on I-64, then cut off at the turn to the airport.

Christ, Andrews was going to blow a fuse when he found out they had missed Pearce and Buchanan yet again. But what could he do, short of sending in an entire SWAT team? He dialed Andrews's private number as he approached the airport.

He was not looking forward to this conversation.

67

They drove north of Richmond until they found a small motel in Hanover that would take a cash deposit. They thanked Eric for the ride and settled into the small room. It was completely tasteless, with a flowered bedspread, flowered wallpaper, and flowered curtains. And nothing matched. It was like living in a poorly designed greenhouse. Jennifer took one look at the bed and lay down on top of the covers with her clothes on.

"Well, I guess that explains why the car chasing us through Richmond was government issue. Must have been friends of our good guy turned bad."

"Gordon, we're talking about four of the most influential men in the country when it comes to law enforcement and espionage. All four of these men are heavy hitters. And the agencies they work for are huge and have unlimited resources. How the hell are we supposed to smoke out the one working with Andrews?"

"If we could get in the room with all four of them, maybe we could get the traitor to make a mistake and give himself away."

She shook her head. "Getting in the room with all four of them at the same time is next to impossible. And even if we do manage to get in that room, we can't rely on him cracking. We're not dealing with an amateur here. These men are all professionals, and any one of them could twist any proof we have in a totally different direction."

Gordon stared at the picture in the newspaper. "So one of these men knew all along that the virus threat was completely bogus. What a prick. Whoever it is deserves to go down real hard."

"What have we got?" Jennifer asked rhetorically. "Andrews owns a ton of stock and options in Veritas. He has to exercise those options by mid-December, and from what has just happened, Veritas stock is set to go through the roof. So his three million common shares and his options will make him close to a billionaire. That goes to motive but doesn't prove anything. He manipulated the company books by moving regular expenditures into the tax-credit column. But trying to pin that directly on him could be difficult. He's probably insulated himself from the actual fraud by setting up some poor suckers as scapegoats. Elizabeth Ripley at the SEC is working on that, but I'm not sure I'd hold my breath there.

"We're pretty sure he ordered the deaths of Kenga Bakcsi and Albert Rousseau, but we're without definitive proof. He tried to kill me. And he probably had that family in Denver killed as well. Again, we have no trail leading directly back to him. We need to nail his accomplice. We need to have whoever it is that worked with Andrews on this scheme implicate him. He's too well insulated otherwise."

Gordon looked up from the paper. "We trust these men to keep us safe, Jennifer. We sleep well at night because men and women inside these agencies risk their lives to protect us. And when one of these men in a position of great power abuses that privilege, he has to be brought down."

"Wow," Jennifer said, grinning. "A speech. Very good."

He grinned and fell on the bed beside her. "Sorry, I was getting preachy. But I feel strongly that abuse of power should be dealt with in the harshest possible manner."

"I do too," she said. "We just need a way in."

Gordon flipped on the television and surfed through the channels until he found a Washington feed with late news. The big story for the day was still the early-morning news conference with the leaders of the antivirus task force, and Bruce Andrews and Dr. Chiang Wai. They watched the telecast again, both of them looking closely at each man now that they knew one of them was dirty. But which one? There were no clues. No sideways glances or uneasy posturing. All four men played the part of savior perfectly. Their agencies had cooperated fully and effectively to bring this threat under control. And they had found a cure for a deadly virus as well. Heroes.

All but one.

Gordon was half listening to the sound when something struck him. He sat up and concentrated on what the newscaster was saying. It was a recap of how the threat had initially been delivered to them and how the team had pooled its resources to find the lab. After the anchor was finished, Gordon said, "I've got an idea. We need to use one resource we already have and we need to secure one more. If we do, I think we can get inside the same room with those men and maybe figure out who it is."

"I'm listening," she said, rolling over to face him.

68

The last of the four, Tony Warner, arrived at just after five o'clock on Wednesday afternoon, apologizing for being late but blaming it on traffic coming in from Crypto-City. He accepted a coffee from Rothery's executive assistant and thanked her. He stirred in some sugar and a touch of cream and glanced about the office. Allenby, Simms, and Rothery were all sitting in easy chairs with coffee or drinks.

"What's going on, J. D.?" he asked. "What's with the sudden meeting? We did the big press conference yesterday morning."

Rothery shrugged. "I received a call from the Securities and Exchange Commission this morning. They were adamant we meet this afternoon. She insisted that the entire task force be here. I don't know what it's about."

"The SEC?" Warner asked. "What the hell do they want with us?"

"That's been the big question since we arrived," Jim Allenby said.

"Anybody cheat on last year's prospectus?" Simms asked wryly.

All heads turned as the door opened and a mid-fifties woman entered. She wore a blue pantsuit and carried an ex-

337

pensive leather briefcase. She set the briefcase on a table in the center of the room and approached each man individually, introducing herself as Elizabeth Ripley and thanking them for coming. When she had finished the introductions, she reached into her briefcase and pulled out a file. She sat in the last open easy chair and addressed the room.

"Gentlemen, we've got a bit of a quandary over at the SEC. We are concerned about the effect this crisis might have on the market. Not just New York, but also Tokyo, Toronto, and some of the European stock exchanges. We suspect the terrorists may have hedged against the possibility of failure by purchasing short-term options on some of the larger pharmaceutical companies. I'd like to hear from each one of you as the representative for your various agencies as to if there has been any discussion about possible market manipulation. If there has, I'd like you to describe the actions you've taken to ensure that the markets will remain solvent. Mr. Rothery, perhaps we could start with you."

Rothery sounded a little confused as he spoke. "Well, I'm not sure this line of thinking has ever reared its head at DHS. We are concerned about the safety of the markets from a physical sense, but we didn't touch on market stability as it related directly to this particular crisis."

"Thank you. Mr. Allenby?"

"The FBI is a law-enforcement agency, Ms. Ripley. I can't recall ever worrying about the boys on Wall Street. I think they do quite fine without us looking over their shoulders."

There was a chuckle at his response, but Ripley continued on unfazed. "Mr. Simms. Did the CIA see fit to give this issue any thought?"

"I can't say we did, Ms. Ripley. Our main area of concern was and still is gathering intelligence from around the world that may affect American interests. We have no dealings inside the continental United States, nor do we monitor the international markets on a daily basis. We watch for general trends, but in this particular case, we didn't look for anything out of the ordinary."

"Mr. Warner?"

"Well, yes, we did watch for any one person or organization buying large chunks of stocks that we felt might be affected by the crisis. That's standard policy. We look closely at situations by inputting data into our computers and analyzing the output. But we didn't notice anything that we considered out of the ordinary."

"Thank you," Elizabeth Ripley said. A moment later, her cell phone rang and she said, "I'm sorry, gentlemen, but this is one call I must take." She answered, said "okay" twice, and hung up. She looked over at the door to Rothery's office and said, "I'm going to turn over the meeting to someone else."

The door opened and Jennifer Pearce entered, followed by Gordon Buchanan and Keith Thompson. Thompson was carrying a large and apparently heavy black case. Gordon remained by the door while Jennifer and Keith walked directly to the table where Elizabeth Ripley had left her briefcase. Keith set his case on the carpet and retrieved a recording device from Elizabeth Ripley's briefcase.

"What's going on here, Keith? And who the hell are you?" Rothery asked Jennifer. She didn't answer, and Rothery turned to Elizabeth Ripley. "This meeting isn't about the SEC, is it?"

"No, it's not, Mr. Rothery," Ripley said. "After I heard what these people had to say, I agreed to set up the meeting for them. I think you'll find this is not a waste of your time."

"This had better be pretty damn good," Rothery snapped. "What are *you* doing here, Keith?"

"I was asked along to run a little test, Mr. Rothery. At the request of the SEC. Sorry." He busied himself with opening his case and setting up a strange-looking two-sided television screen and a computer. He hooked the recording device from Ripley's briefcase into a USB port and powered up the system. "Ready to roll," he said to Jennifer.

"My name is Jennifer Pearce. I'm a research scientist in the Alzheimer's division of Veritas Pharmaceutical. I work for Bruce Andrews, the same man who just discovered the drug to combat the virus. But there's a bit of a twist to this whole thing that three of you four gentlemen have missed. And that twist is that there was never a crisis. We were never in any jeopardy."

Rothery's tone was icy as he responded, reaching for the phone on the table beside him. "This is preposterous," he said. "I want you out of here immediately."

"Elizabeth Ripley was correct, Mr. Rothery. This is not a waste of time. If you allow me just a minute, three of you gentlemen are going to find what I have to say very interesting."

"That's the second time you've referred to three of us, Ms. Pearce," Jim Allenby said. "What are you implying?"

"Let me tell you a story," she said. "Bruce Andrews over at Veritas develops a drug that he considers to be the next big thing. This baby is going to generate his company billions of dollars in sales. He's so sure of its success that he manipulates the company books in order to assure himself the capital he needs to send the drug through Phase II and Phase III trials. Ms. Ripley has looked into the illegal use of tax credits by Veritas, and she assures me that there will be civil actions arising from her investigation.

"But this goes so much deeper than just stock manipulation. Bruce Andrews had two Veritas employees killed and he wiped out a family in Denver. He tried to kill me three times, but obviously he missed. And here's the part you guys are going to love.

"Bruce Andrews actually developed the virus threatening our country. It makes coming up with a cure so much easier when you're the one creating the problem. Andrews or one of his associates distributed the virus to random locations across the country at carefully selected intervals to let the tension build. Finally, when your task force decided to ask the private sector for help in finding a cure, he was ready. Andrews bided his time, waiting for the fuse to burn down a bit, then handed the cure to Rothery with one condition. Get the drug through the New Drug Application stage and get FDA approval. And that, gentlemen, is what it was all about. Getting a potentially dangerous drug on the market."

LETHAL DOSE

"Why?" Warner asked.

"Money. Billions of dollars that without Zancor getting FDA approval would be flushed down the drain. And with the tax-credit accounting scandal ready to hit without the money being replaced, and with his stock options coming due in December, time was of the essence for Bruce Andrews. He needed Zancor on the market. What better way than to create a false crisis? Just the first round of invoices from the government to protect the population against a threat that was never going to materialize was worth hundreds of millions of dollars. If everything goes according to plan, Mr. Bruce Andrews is a billionaire.

"But he needed help. No one person can sit at the helm of a huge pharmaceutical company, murder people, create dangerous viruses, and manipulate the company stock all by himself. And he *had* help. Someone in a very influential position. Someone in this room."

Four pairs of eyes stared at her and she stared back, allowing her gaze to rest on each man's eyes for a few moments before switching to the next. Nothing. Whichever man it was had the poker face of the millennium. She turned to Keith Thompson.

"I remembered reading about Keith's work on the case in one of the local newspapers. I called him and asked him for a favor. He agreed to help." She waved her hand at the split-screen television. "Keith's brought some high-tech equipment with him today, and I'll let him explain it to you."

Keith Thompson took over. "The recording device in Ms. Ripley's purse has a sample of each of you speaking tonight, in response to her question." He turned on the screen. The right side remained dark, but the left side showed an image of the masked terrorist threatening the country. Keith let it run for a sentence then stopped it. *The death of innocent American citizens is not our primary goal.* He pointed at a series of wiggly lines that appeared on the right screen. "This is the voiceprint of the terrorist. He hit another switch and J. D. Rothery's voice came over the speaker. *Well, I'm not sure that this line of think-*

341

ing has ever reared its head at DHS. A second wiggly line appeared just above the first.

"This line is Mr. Rothery's voice," Keith said, moving a cordless mouse and drawing the two lines together. Once they were overlaid on each other, he moved the cursor to the right, dragging the second line across the first. After about five seconds, he said, "No match. Mr. Rothery is not the man in the video."

"Damn right I'm not," Rothery said.

Our main area of concern was, and still is, gathering intelligence from around the world that may affect American interests. It was Simms's voice. Keith moved the two wiggles on top of each other and tried to cross-correlate them. No luck.

"Mr. Simms is not our man," Keith said, loading another voice. *We look closely at situations by inputting data into our computers and analyzing the output.* "That was Mr. Warner," Keith said, working the mouse. Nothing. All eyes focused on Jim Allenby.

The FBI is a law-enforcement agency, Ms. Ripley. Keith moved the final line across to the other screen and pulled it to the right. The two series of sine waves lined up perfectly, and once the match was made, the program froze the image on the screen. Keith didn't say a word. No one did; they just stared at the screen and at Jim Allenby. Before anyone in the room could move, Allenby slipped a handgun out from his shoulder holster.

"Jesus, Jim. Why?" Rothery asked. "We've worked together for twenty years. What the hell have you done?"

"Why, J. D.? I'll tell you why. Money. I finally decided to take care of myself. Something the government never considered important. I've been working my ass off for over a quarter of a century, and I've got shit to show for it. Two failed marriages, three screwed-up kids because their dad was never home, and my health is starting to go down the tubes. And you couldn't even dream what Bruce Andrews was offering me. You couldn't even dream the amount."

"Money, Jim? Money? That's a pretty lame reason."

"Twenty million dollars, J. D. Twenty million. That buys a lot of nice things for my retirement years. And it's not just the money. The Bureau doesn't give a shit about us anymore. Nothing's the same as it was when I first got in. Used to be the Bureau was run by law-enforcement guys. Cops. Now it's all controlled by the fucking bean counters. And don't put your toe over the line or it'll get shot off. I'm sick of it. Sick of it."

"You killed innocent people, Jim. You betrayed your country. You killed Boy Scouts, for God's sake."

"I was careful where and how I introduced the virus. Austin and San Diego went exactly as I planned. I didn't know the Scout troop would pick up that case of Pepsi in Boston. That was just bad luck."

"You sick, twisted asshole," Rothery said, leaping from his chair. He moved toward Allenby, his hand outstretched. "Give me the gun, Jim."

Allenby trained the Colt 1911 on the Under Secretary. "You come one inch closer and I'll kill you." Rothery stopped but didn't move back. "You know, this whole thing was working until you two got involved," he said, looking at Gordon and Jennifer. "Now look what's happened. Everything's totally screwed up."

"So where does it end?" Craig Simms asked, leaning forward in his chair. "You're in the middle of a secure building. You won't get out the front door unless it's with an escort or in a body bag. This is no way to end things, Jim."

"To hell with you it's not. I've lived my entire life with a gun under my arm or my pillow. Live by the sword, die by the sword. But first, I'd like to pay someone back for all their help." He jerked the gun around, trained it on Jennifer Pearce, and pulled the trigger.

"No," Gordon screamed, and threw himself in the line of fire. Too late. The bullet hit Jennifer in the chest and the impact sent her crashing back into an end table. The table took out her legs and she went over on the back of her head on the floor. She lay unmoving, a pool of blood spreading under her on the carpet.

"You bastard," Gordon yelled, and lunged for Allenby. A quick movement with the gun and a second bullet hit its target.

This time it was Allenby lifting the gun to his head and firing. The bullet entered his temple as a small piece of red-hot metal and exited the other side of his head in fragments, taking a six-inch chunk of skull with it. Gray matter spattered across the room and Allenby dropped to the carpet.

Gordon froze for a second, then looked at Jennifer. Simms and Rothery were already working on her, trying to stop the bleeding, and Elizabeth Ripley was on the phone, demanding an ambulance immediately. He stood in the center of the room surrounded by death. Then something washed over him and he felt a hate that he had never experienced. A loathing so horrible that only one action could cure it. He grabbed the Colt from the floor and ran into the hall. There was nothing he could do to help Jennifer that the men inside that room couldn't do twice as well. And he had seen the bullet hit. She was fatally shot, he was sure.

Tears welled in his eyes as the elevator arrived and he pushed his way in. He tucked the .45 pistol into his waistband and pulled his shirt over the handle. He had one thing left to do. And nothing was going to stand in his way.

69

"Where's Buchanan?" Simms asked, looking about the room as paramedics rushed Jennifer Pearce from the room on a stretcher, one of them calling ahead to George Washington University Hospital and clearing an emergency OR.

"He went running out right after Allenby shot himself," a shaken Keith Thompson said. He was sitting in one of the chairs, aghast that he had just seen a person die. It was a first for him, and he didn't like it.

"Christ, he's heading for Richmond," Rothery said. "He's going after Bruce Andrews."

"You want to get some men out to Andrews's house?" Simms asked.

Rothery thought about it for a minute. "The less commotion we cause right now, the better. We've got a containable situation at this point. Allenby killed himself and Dr. Pearce took an accidental bullet. We can put a decent spin on it. But if we start involving our resources in Richmond in this, it's out of our hands. Let's keep a lid on it. Christ, if the general public finds out one of the task force leaders was involved in creating the crisis, the shit's going to hit the fan like you won't believe."

"What about Buchanan?" Simms asked. "He's out there and he knows what's going on."

"We'll worry about Buchanan when we catch him. We might be able to convince him that keeping this thing quiet is in the best interest of the country. If we can't, we'll have to deal with it."

"And Dr. Pearce?" Simms asked.

Rothery shook his head. "She won't make the hospital. Probably dead already. It's Buchanan we have to work on."

"What if he beats us to Bruce Andrews?"

Rothery shook his head again. "Not a chance. I'll call down to the airport and get the Gulfstream ready. By the time he drives down or catches a commercial flight, we'll be at Andrews's house."

"Maybe it's best that we just give the press exactly what happened in here," Simms said. "That would be the easiest way of dealing with this mess."

Rothery was thoughtful. Then he said, "I'm not sure, Craig. Maybe we'll have to. But for right now let's see if we can contain it. Okay?"

"Not a problem." Instinctively, they both knew that the lid was going to come off, but it was first nature in their business to try to minimize the damage.

Rothery stood in the middle of the room and stared at Allenby's body. Then he turned to Tony Warner and Craig Simms and asked, "Where is Jim's gun?"

70

Twenty-seven minutes after storming out of L'Enfant Plaza, Gordon boarded the Lear 31A at Reagan International. He and Jennifer had decided that leaving the plane on the ground and driving up to D.C. for the second time was being overcautious, so they had flown up in the jet. He had used the cabbies' cell phone to call ahead and have the pilots file a flight plan for Richmond. When he pulled up to the private terminal, the Lear was already fueled and waiting.

Access to the private section of Washington's terminal is much easier than the main commercial area, and Gordon moved quickly out to the plane, the Colt 1911 still tucked in his belt. He boarded the private jet and they were rolling down the runway inside three minutes.

"Third in line for takeoff, Mr. Buchanan," the pilot's voice came over the intercom.

Gordon cursed the delay. Every moment counted. He knew the three remaining men in Rothery's office would be scrambling to get down to Richmond. It was a race. They wanted Bruce Andrews for prosecution. He wanted Andrews dead.

The plane was equipped with a phone, and he busied him-

347

self calling about for the location of Bruce Andrews's house. When he called, he identified himself as J. D. Rothery, which wasn't a hard sell as most of the country had just seen Andrews and Rothery on television together. One of the staff at Veritas, thinking he was speaking with the Under Secretary of the Department of Homeland Security, dug into the files and found the CEO's home address.

"It's a rural address in Chesterfield county," the man said. "He had a barbecue out there a year ago and he supplied all the employees with directions. First, you take the 360 south out of Richmond until you cross the Appomattox, about twenty miles outside the city boundaries. Turn south on the 153 until you reach Scott's Fork. Then take a left and drive back to the river. Mr. Andrews's estate is the third driveway on the left."

"Thank you," Gordon said. He hung up the phone and stared out the window. It was still light and would be for another hour or two. Enough time to find the estate, but it would likely be dark as he approached the house. Probably a good thing. He reached down and pulled the handgun out of his belt. He had fired a lot of rifles and was a decent shot, but he had never fired a handgun in his life. He looked over the gun, found the safety, and snapped it on. Then he set the gun on the leather seat next to him and closed his eyes.

Jennifer Pearce. The image of her body jerking back with the impact of the bullet replayed through his mind. So much blood. Rothery and Simms trying desperately to stem the flow. All hell breaking loose. Jim Allenby lying on the floor with his head blown apart. Keith Thompson staring at the scene in horror. Elizabeth Ripley standing quietly in a corner, watching with scared eyes. What a mess.

He let his eyes open and felt the tears spill out. Christ, why were all the people he cared about dying? First Billy, now Jennifer. He felt the plane begin to descend and he tucked the gun back in his belt. He could think about that later. Right now, Bruce Andrews was foremost on his mind.

He rented a car at the booth that serviced the private section of the airport and checked the map for the best route across

the southern tip of Richmond to Highway 360. It was a bit con-
voluted, but half an hour later he pulled onto the 360 just north
of Swift Creek Reservoir and double-checked the directions.
He crossed the Appomattox, took the turns the man had dic-
tated to him, and finally pulled onto a paved lane running parallel to the river, perhaps half a mile to the north. In the waning
daylight, he counted until he reached the third driveway. Bruce
Andrews's estate.

The front gate was impenetrable without calling up to the
house and getting someone to open it—that or crashing
through it with a vehicle. Neither option appealed to him. He
continued driving down the road, looking for an opening to
the river. Most of the frontage along the river was taken by other
large estates, but about a quarter mile to the east he found an
open lot with access directly to the river. He parked the car and
set off at a quick jog. The ground was mostly clear, with groves
of trees punctuating the rolling grasslands. He kept to the edges
of the trees as much as possible until he reached the river. As
he doubled back to the west, the first two estates were not
fenced flush to the water, and he simply ran along the gently
sloping riverbank toward Andrews's estate.

The acreage next to Andrews was fenced right to the river,
and he had to cling onto the edge of the fencing while hanging
over the water in order to broach it. He made it without falling
in the water, then ran quickly across the grassy expanse to the
next property boundary. Usually, fenced yards meant dogs, and
the last thing he needed right now was to have to shoot a guard
dog. He reached the perimeter of Andrews's estate and repeated the procedure of skirting the fence by hanging over the
water. He was in.

The house was set on a knoll to the south and, with the ad-
vent of the approaching night, lights were coming on in the
house. He moved quickly along the fence, hugging the small
groves of trees wherever possible. He was within a hundred
feet of the house and could see the dogs in their enclosure.
They were standing at the wire mesh fence, staring at him. Excellent guard dogs: trained not to bark, just to attack. Lucky for

him, Andrews had chosen to kennel the dogs. He ran the last hundred feet to the house and tried the basement door. It was locked. He set the gun down and took off his shirt. He wrapped it around his fist and gave the glass a good punch. The glass shattered, but didn't make much noise as the broken shards fell on carpet. He reached inside and unlocked the deadbolt, then quietly let himself in. He set the gun on the pool table and slipped his shirt on as he looked about.

The lower level was shrouded in darkness, but he could see it was mostly used as a games room. The pool table, a regulation six-by-twelve, was the centerpiece, with a shuffleboard against one wall, a dartboard on another, and a twenty-foot walk-up bar covering the far wall. He moved slowly through the open room, watching the corners of the room for security sensors. His eyes, adjusting now to the low light levels, picked up the sensors, but they were turned off. First the dogs in their pen and now the security system turned off. Bruce Andrews was a little lax on his security tonight.

Gordon started up the staircase to the main floor. It was curved, carpeted, and open to the main level. The light increased as he rounded the corner and the well-lit main floor came into view. His grip on the rosewood handle of the Colt 1911 tightened. He stopped two stairs from the top and fumbled with the gun, trying to find the safety. He switched off the upswept grip safety and continued on, now moving into the wide hall leading from the front entrance to the great room in the rear of the house. Soft music played over the sound system, and he could hear a television somewhere in the back of the house. He moved quietly along the hall into the great room. The ceilings were at least eighteen feet and the entire back of the room was a bank of windows, looking out over the grass that ran down to the river. The room was unoccupied. He skirted the great room, keeping close to one of the interior walls. The sound from the television was louder now, and when he reached a narrower hallway, he could see the flicker from the television reflected on the hall walls. He tiptoed across the hall, took a deep breath, and leapt into the television room, the Colt outstretched in front of him.

His brain processed the scene in a split second. A leather love seat flanked by two leather chairs, a coffee table, two glass-top end tables, and an entire wall taken up by a built-in entertainment center with a sixty-inch plasma television. But no sign of Bruce Andrews. As he turned to leave the room, there was a voice from directly behind him.

"Don't move an inch or I'll kill you."

Gordon froze, the pistol still pointing into the media room. He heard a slight rustling behind him and then a whooshing sound, and everything went black. When he opened his eyes again, he was lying on his back in the center of the great room. His head was throbbing and his eyesight was blurred. He started to lift his head and got a boot in the stomach for his trouble. He doubled over into a fetal position and caught sight of his attacker for the first time.

Bruce Andrews was standing over him, a gun in his hand and a sneer on his face. "You dumb country hick," he said, aiming another boot for the midsection. The kick connected with Gordon's solar plexus and winded him. Gordon struggled for breath as Andrews hovered over him. Then the man backed off a bit and leaned against one of the couches. "Everything was going just fine until you and that dumb bitch had to stick your goddamn noses into something that was none of your business. You have no idea the damage you've done."

"You killed my brother, you sick piece of shit," Gordon managed to wheeze.

"Are you talking about Triaxcion?" Andrews said. "A doctor prescribed that medicine and your brother willingly took it. He died because he was vain and wanted nice thick hair. Don't blame me for your brother's death." He leaned forward. "But you can blame me for Jennifer Pearce's."

Gordon managed to struggle up on one elbow and glower at Andrews as he tried to catch his breath. Unbridled hate burned in his eyes. "How do you know about Jennifer?"

"It's all over the television, you dumbass. Do you really think you can have a shoot-out in the office of the Under Secretary of the DHS and not have it end up on prime-time television? How do you think I knew you were on your way? I penned the dogs and turned off the security system because I wanted to kill you myself. There would be no justice in letting the dogs rip you apart." He moved a little closer, the gun pointed at Gordon's head. "You ever been shot, forest boy?"

"Once," Gordon said. "By one of Allenby's thugs. Didn't do much damage, did it?"

The sound of the gun firing was almost deafening in the confines of the room. The instant the sound hit his ears, he felt a searing pain in his left shoulder. He grabbed at the area where the bullet had hit and his hand came away covered with blood. "Jesus Christ," he said. "You bastard."

"*I'm* the bastard?" Andrews yelled back at him. "I had a perfect life, you asshole. And you took it all away. You ruined the perfect plan. Zancor would have generated billions of dollars for Veritas, my shares and options would have gone through the roof, and life would have continued with no one the wiser. But you two stumbling idiots screwed everything up."

"We aren't responsible for your fall from grace," Gordon snarled back. "You knowingly marketed a defective drug and killed innocent people who stood in your way. You threatened and terrified the entire country with a deadly disease just to get your latest drug on the market. Nobody brought this on you but you."

Andrews leaned over and picked up an object from one of the end tables. It was the Colt 1911 pistol Gordon had brought with him from Washington. Andrews checked the clip, then snapped it back in place and set his pistol on the table where the Colt had been.

"Is this Jim Allenby's gun?" he asked. "Jim always preferred a Colt 1911 with the rosewood grip. It looks like his."

Gordon didn't say a word, just stared at him.

"Well, I think it's fitting that Jim's gun is the one that kills you. I think he would like that." He stretched his arm out straight and pulled the trigger. Nothing happened. He aimed and pulled the trigger again. "What the . . ."

Gordon was on his feet and lunging at Andrews just as the man pulled the trigger for the second time. Andrews dropped the Colt and grabbed for his pistol. Too late. Gordon hit him in the midsection with his right shoulder, driving Andrews back and toppling him over. Andrews swung at Gordon, but he ducked and countered with a fast right. The fist caught Andrews half on his nose and half on his cheek. Blood instantly poured from the broken nose, and Gordon swung a roundhouse left at the prone man's head. It landed but was totally ineffective, all power in the arm sapped by the bullet wound. He got two more quick shots in with his right before Andrews managed a counter and caught Gordon in the side of the head.

The blow stunned him for a second and Andrews used the opportunity to push Gordon off and leap back to his feet. For a big man, he moved with surprising alacrity. He barreled down on Gordon, aiming to drive him into the floor. Gordon rolled at the last possible split second and Andrews slammed into the hardwood. Gordon spun around on his back on the hardwood and used the momentum of the spin to drive his foot into the side of Andrews's face. He heard the jawbone break, and Andrews bellowed with pain. Gordon spun again, this time kicking out at the end table Andrews had set the pistol on. His leg caught the table and knocked it over. The gun came crashing down on the floor, and Gordon grabbed it.

He slipped his finger into the trigger guard and jumped on Andrews, ramming the barrel of the gun into the side of the man's head. The room took on an eerie silence as Gordon cocked the gun. Neither man moved for a few seconds, save to breathe.

"Until yesterday, I'd never killed a man," Gordon hissed. "I didn't like it, but somehow I don't think killing you is going to bother me." His finger tightened on the trigger.

"Don't do it, Gordon."

Buchanan looked up, the business end of the gun still pressed firmly against Andrews's head. Standing in the doorway was J.D. Rothery. Immediately behind him were Craig Simms and a couple of faceless agents. They moved slowly into the room, their guns trained on Gordon.

"Don't kill him, Gordon. It's not worth it."

"Oh, I think it is," Gordon said, the gun unmoving in his hand.

"You pull that trigger and you'll be charged with murder," Rothery said. "You'll spend the rest of your life in prison. And for what? Killing him is giving him the easy way out."

"How do you figure that?" Gordon asked. He and Andrews's eyes were locked, neither man flinching.

"Bruce Andrews is finished. You know it and I know it. He's going to jail for manipulating his company's stocks, terrorism, and murder. He'll never see freedom again in his life. Not from the second we take him out of this house. He's ruined, Gordon. There's no reason to kill him."

"He was responsible for my brother's death and now Jennifer's. Letting this prick live is wrong. He deserves this bullet."

"Gordon, wait for one minute. Just one minute. Let me check with the hospital in Washington to see if Jennifer is alive or dead." He nodded to one of the men behind him, who was immediately on the phone. "What have you got to lose, Gordon? If she died, we're still faced with the same problem we have now. But if she's alive, that changes things."

Gordon didn't take his eyes off Andrews. "You've got one minute," he said. The gun trembled slightly in his hand, and he shifted slightly to take the pressure off his injured arm. The motion almost caused the gun to fire.

"Thirty seconds," Gordon said, perspiration dripping from his brow. "Fifteen."

"I've got the hospital on the line," the agent said, handing the phone to Rothery.

Rothery introduced himself to the person on the other end of the line and made sure they understood the urgency in finding out Jennifer Pearce's condition. He waited, making an occasional motion with his hand for Gordon to hold on. A voice came on the line, and he responded by saying "okay" a couple of times. Then he said, "I'm going to put someone on the line, and I want you to tell them exactly what you just told me." He set the cell phone on the hardwood floor and gave it a good push. It slid over to Gordon. He managed to pick it up with his wounded arm.

"Go ahead," he said.

"This is Dr. Anne Archer at the George Washington University Hospital. Jennifer Pearce was admitted to the Level-One trauma center with a bullet wound about two hours ago. She underwent emergency surgery, and although she is still in extremely serious condition, we do expect her to live."

"Thank you, Doctor," Gordon said, the tears spilling freely. He dropped the phone and loosened his grip on the trigger. He looked up at Rothery. "Thanks," he said, lifting the gun from Andrews's head. He stared at Andrews and said, "I always thought there was nothing on earth more useless than burnt timber, but I was wrong." His words were filled with loathing. "You are."

He stood up and staggered to the couch and sat down, his head spinning. The two agents rushed to grab Andrews and handcuff him, and Rothery took the pistol from Gordon. Simms picked up the Colt from the floor.

"The beavertail safety is still on this one," he said to Rothery.

"What?" Gordon said. He felt unconsciousness slipping over him. The last thing he heard before blacking out was Craig Simms saying something about the Colt 1911 having a double safety: an ambidextrous thumb safety, which was off, and a beavertail, which allowed the gun to fire only if the shooter applied sufficient pressure. Unless Andrews knew about the beavertail safety, he wouldn't have squeezed the handle with enough pressure to cause the gun to fire. Lucky Andrews wasn't a gun lover.

Then blackness consumed him.

71

"Hi, you," Jennifer said weakly. She had been unable to see visitors for almost seventy-two hours, and when they had finally given the go-ahead, Gordon Buchanan was first in line, walking with a slight limp and his left arm in a sling. "What happened to your arm?"

"Nothing too serious. I'm okay." Gordon smiled and held up some flowers. Roses and lilies. "You look great."

"How can I help but look good with these tubes up my nose and four or five IVs in my arms?" The sentence tired her and she took a few deep breaths to recover.

"Dr. Archer says you're doing really well. She said if the bullet had hit a fraction of an inch to the left, you'd have died in Rothery's office."

"Well, thanks to Jim Allenby for being a rotten shot."

"Yeah, thanks for that."

"Did she tell you how long I have to stay in here? The food sucks."

"Just until you're well enough to travel. Then you can go home, providing you have someone to come in and take care of you."

She managed a slight nod. "What's going to happen to Bruce Andrews?"

"He's been charged with numerous securities violations and complicity in Kenga and Albert's murders. But the most serious charge is treason. They're going to nail him to the wall on the virus thing. That really got in someone's craw in D.C., and they're after him with a vengeance."

"So he's toast," she said lightly.

"Yeah." He grinned at her stab at humor. "He's toast."

"When are you going back to Montana?" she asked.

"Thought I'd wait until you were able to go home. I'd hate to leave you alone in this big hospital."

"And what am I going to do at home all alone, Mr. Buchanan? I hardly know a soul in Richmond."

Gordon looked down at the sheets that covered her and said, "You could always come back to Montana. You're welcome at my house."

"Really?" she said.

"Yeah, really," he answered, leaning over and kissing her on the forehead.

"For how long?" she asked.

He cocked his head slightly and smiled. "I'm kind of cheap. I was thinking of buying you a one-way ticket."

She smiled, her eyes closing as sleep overtook her. "That would be fine," she said, drifting off.

MAX McCOY
HINTERLAND

Andy Kelsey is a reporter who may have just stumbled on the story of a lifetime. He's infiltrated a white separatist group in the Ozarks, an underground organization ready to fight and die—and kill—for their extreme beliefs. The deeper Kelsey gets in the group, the more he's trusted, and the bigger his story becomes. Until he realizes the shocking extent of their scheme...

The separatists have finalized plans for a spectacular cataclysm that they hope will bring about Armageddon. What terrifies Kelsey is that they have the weapon and the means to achieve their mad goal. Will he be able to fight them from the inside without being discovered? Or has he gotten in too deep to ever get out?
